THE ORDER DUET

STILETTO SINS & LIPSTICK LIES

KRIS BUTLER

The Order Duet
Stiletto Sins & Lipstick Lies
Plus Bonus Content
By: Kris Butler

First Edition: Oct 2023
Published by: Incognito Scribe Productions LLC
Kris Butler

Proofreading: © 2022 by Owlsome Author Services
Formatting: © 2022 Incognito Scribe Productions LLC
Cover Design: © 2023 The Pretty Little Design Co

❀ Created with Vellum

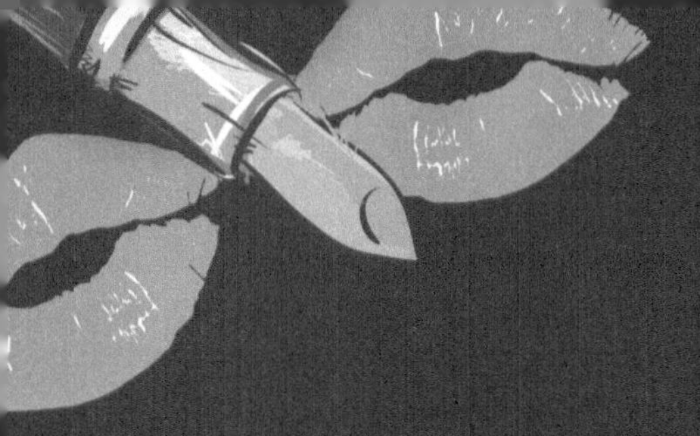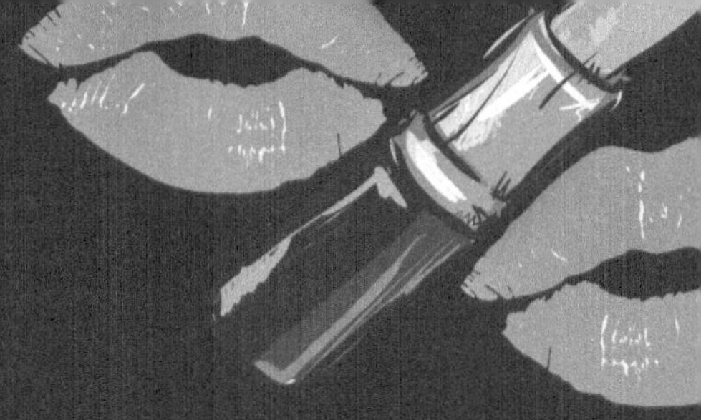

THE ORDER DUET

Stiletto Sins & Lipstick Lies

KRIS BUTLER

Contents

LIPSTICK LIES

EXTENDED EPILOGUE

Blurb

Secrets. Hidden Pasts. Mistakes.

I was tired of pretending I had it all together. I was ready to do whatever it took to redeem myself.

I just hadn't expected them to be part of the equation.

It was time for Finley Reyes to save the day.

These shoes, they were more than just sinful, they were deadly.

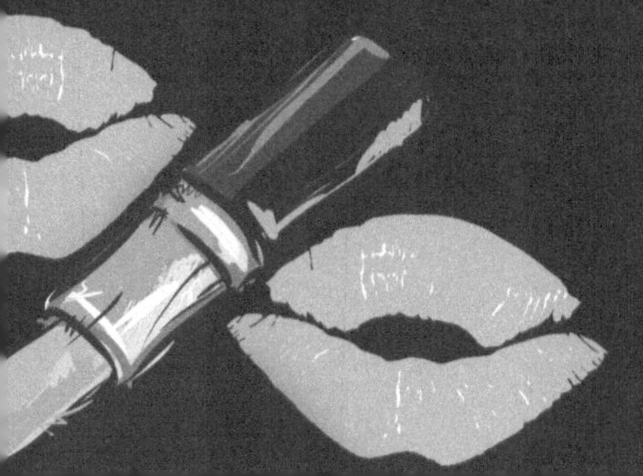

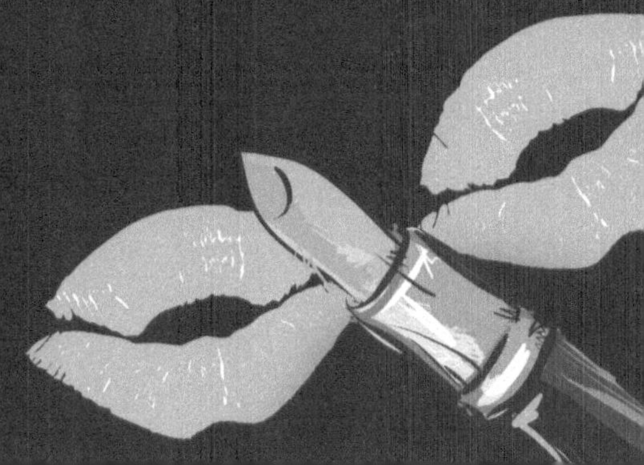

Foreword

This is a spin-off of The Council Series, but it isn't necessary to read first. Some characters will crossover, enriching the experience, but aren't required to know in order to enjoy the story.

This book contains light MM and can be skipped if desired (marked by the author).

This book has sexual scenes meant for adults. It is a why choose romance, so no choosing here. The steamy scenes are steamy, and this book uses the F-word on occasion, though, Fin has her own way of cussing.

Below is a list of content. While brief, they could be sensitive issues, so please make sure to take care of yourself. I strive to do the characters and the issues justice.

CONTENT

- Suicidal thoughts
- Self-harm
- Stalking

- Torture
- Violent situations and themes
- Active shooter situation
- 'God, Jesus, Hell, Damn' used casually or in a sexual context

WHAT TO EXPECT:

- Multiple POV
- Spy games
- Hacking
- Riddles
- Underground secret organization
- Good vs Evil
- Forced Proximity
- Threesomes and Moresomes
- DVP
- Anal
- Light praise
- Light bondage
- Pierced peen
- Sweet guys
- Cocky guys
- Possessive, no jealousy
- No cheating
- HEA
- Found Family

Sometimes it takes a while to find your voice. Never stop trying, no matter how many walls you have to knock down, or times you fall. Your voice matters.

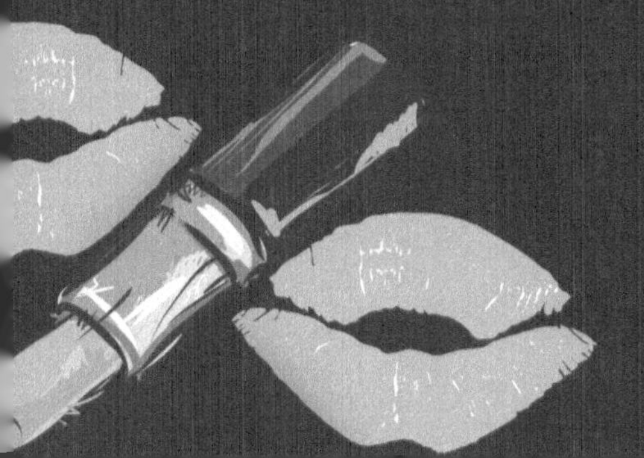

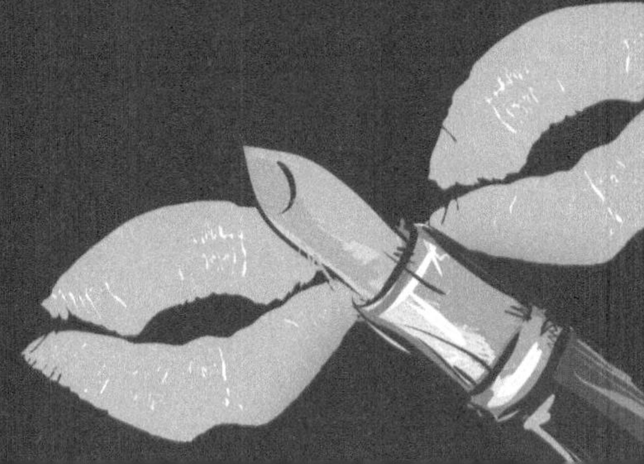

Stiletto Sins

THE ORDER DUET BOOK ONE

Prologue

FINLEY

FINLEY, AGE 17

If you'd asked me two years ago if I'd be handcuffed against a squad car, I would've first asked if you realized you were talking to me, the school nerd, and second, told you there wasn't any dimension where I, Miss Perfect, would be arrested.

Funny how trauma can change the whole trajectory of your life.

I might still be a nerd, but I was far from perfect—current circumstances solidified that fact.

"Do they really need to be so tight?" I huffed, pulling at them.

"You're lucky it was me, Finley. I know you think this is all fun and games, but kids get shot all the time for doing the stupid shit you do," Officer Friendly sighed, heavy disappointment in his voice as he read me my rights.

And yes, that was his real name. I often wondered if he went into the profession just because of how it would sound, making him the perpetually good cop?

I'd known him for most of my life, his daughter being part of the same skating club as my brother and… Well, yeah, I didn't hang out at the skating club much anymore, and Officer Friendly liked to remind me of who I'd been back then. I think he was just tired of arresting me and having to see my parents be even more disappointed in me.

Me too, Officer Friendly, me too.

And yet, here I was, making another reckless decision in order to fill the ever-increasing void in my life. Though, shoplifting, changing grades, making fake IDs, and driving without a license were all minor compared to this.

In the past, I'd always been let off with a warning and a call to my parents to pick me up at the station. But not tonight.

Fudge, I'd messed up. Big time.

Sighing, I banged my head against the window, cursing Blackhawk under my breath. He was supposed to be here, but he and our other teammate, Obsidian, had never shown. I was beginning to think I'd been setup. Shuffling in my red stilettos, I cursed my outfit of choice for the evening.

Double fudge, I was a gullible idiot. I *had* been setup. It was official. Finley Reyes was a loser. Blackhawk hadn't been interested. Just another guy to make me look like an idiot.

"I need to search you; spread your legs," the female officer said dryly.

Rolling my eyes, I sighed and did as she asked, spreading my legs. I tried not to think about the fact that this cop was getting further than any boy had before. Just another reminder of how much of a loser I was.

"Clean," she reported before opening the door. "Duck your head."

I had two seconds to process what she said before my head was pushed forward to get into the car. Climbing in, I tried not to flash the cops as I awkwardly flailed around with my hands behind me. Sitting sideways against the seat, I tried to figure a way out of this mess. When nothing came to mind, I dropped my head and noticed my red dress had risen up, reminding me how stupid I was. I looked more like a hooker than a spy.

Who wore a red cocktail dress with matching stilettos to steal something?

Me, that was who.

The girl who thought it might be her first actual date, but instead, apparently was a setup to take the fall. Not that I was entirely innocent, I'd gone into this mission knowing what I was doing. It was my last test before I was inducted into, The MidKnight Guild, the dark web club I'd stumbled upon a year ago.

Though, since I'd gotten caught, I probably hadn't passed. I'd just add it to the list of things I'd lost tonight.

My freedom—I was sure to be grounded until I was thirty by my parents after this stunt.

My friends—if you couldn't hack the initiation, you didn't belong.

My first crush—it was a pretty clear sign of rejection when the boy you liked let you get arrested.

I couldn't deny it any longer. I was an absolute mess, and now everyone would know it, too. It was hard to pretend you were okay, hiding behind white lies to everyone you knew, when your guilt would be splashed across the front page of tomorrow's paper.

I'd like to say I had my reasons, my best friend had disappeared, and no one seemed to care. But at this point, I'd done it for myself. Something about the rush of the job, cracking into a system you weren't supposed to be in, and taking what you wanted filled my veins with more emotion than I'd felt in years. And I craved it like an addict.

Sariah might've been the reason I started, but I kept going because I liked how it made me feel—alive. I just never meant for anyone to get hurt, myself included. It was dumb to think that no one would. I could see that now.

Obsidian and Blackhawk had been my blind spots. They made me feel like I belonged, and I hadn't felt that in years. If only it all hadn't gone so wrong. There was too much damage now, too many sins on my hands to just brush it all off.

No, I needed to make a stand, and that started with taking him down. No one made a fool of me and got to pretend like it hadn't happened. Blackhawk would rue the day he made me his enemy. We'd see who was laughing when it was all said and done.

Fire filled my veins, a scorching sense of righteousness accompanied by a need to mete out my own justice.

But as Officer Friendly listed all the charges they could bring against me, a sickening feeling developed in my stomach and I wondered who I even was anymore. I hadn't meant for any of this to happen. Where *had* it all gone so wrong?

As the lights flashed against the dark night on the drive toward the police station, through my fingerprints being taken, and my mug shot, I tuned out all the thoughts and feelings and focused on one thing, and one thing only—revenge.

It would have to do for now.

PRESENT DAY, FINLEY, AGE 22

Asa's fingers pumped inside me, filling me with pleasure, and I knew that we wouldn't stop this time. My hand gripped his cock, and I dragged my hand down, feeling how hard he was. Peering into his eyes, I saw the need reflected there, and I nodded, glad that we seemed to be on the same page. He reached over with his free hand, grabbing a condom, and I watched as he tore it open, sliding it on. It truly was a marvel to behold, and I was sad it might be the only time I got to see it.

Part of me hated what I was doing, but the other part of me, the one that had come to rule more often than not recently, relished in the dark ecstasy of our actions. It felt right that the first time we made love would be the day I was planning to leave.

"You sure? You're ready?" he asked, stopping at my entrance as he stared down at me.

"I'm ready. I want this." I pulled his face down, kissing him as I wrapped my legs around him. Asa braced his arms above me, stopping himself from entering me.

"I want to see your face," he said, pulling back, looking me deep in the eyes. Sucking in a breath, I nodded, staring back at him.

Slowly, oh, so slowly, he began to push in. Asa watched my every reaction, ready to stop this if it was too much. But I knew there was no way I was letting him stop.

It might seem weird that my boyfriend of almost eight months and I were just now having sex, but it wasn't from a lack of trying. At first, he'd wanted to hold off, making sure we really knew one another, and then there had been the kidnapping. But once we'd crossed every base multiple times, I was going insane.

The first time we tried was a disaster. Quickly followed by the second, third, and fourth. I wondered if I'd permanently scarred my boyfriend when he hadn't tried again for almost two months.

But here we were, attempt number I didn't even remember, and I knew without a shadow of a doubt that it would work. It had to because I was out of time.

"You okay?" he asked, and I nodded, smoothing my hands over his hair.

"Yeah, I'm great. Don't stop."

Asa nodded, pushing in a little further, and I used my feet to push on his amazing buns of steel, propelling him even deeper into me. Once he was seated, we both let out a sigh of relief.

Peering down into my eyes, he brushed his thumb across my cheek. "Ready?" He smiled, a giddy excitement taking over. There wouldn't be any disruptions, family emergencies, illnesses, or broken beds to stop us this time. No, this morning, we would cross that line in our relationship, and then I would break his heart.

Bit morbid there, self.

Closing my eyes, I couldn't think about what I was doing this evening; I just wanted to focus on this moment between us now. It was selfish of me, but if Asa didn't forgive me, I wanted to have one experience of sex with him. As he began to pull out and push back in, I wondered if I just liked to punish myself.

Because losing this would be akin to torture.

"Fudge, you feel good," I heaved, my breath coming out in a moan that even I was impressed by. Asa smiled his million-dollar smile, and butterflies erupted, my core tingling with need.

"I could say the same, but you sound so much cuter saying it."

Sticking out my tongue, I soon forgot my annoyance at him as he rolled back into me, his pelvic bone rubbing right against my clit. Arching my back, I pressed my boobs into him, the sensitive peaks brushing against his hard pecs. Moaning, my head fell back as I enjoyed the sensations.

"Yes, fuck, Finley, you feel more amazing than I even imagined. I knew this would be everything."

My perfect boyfriend leaned back, lifting my hips as he upped his pace, thrusting in and out of me quicker. I stared up at his perfect physique, getting wet at how hot he was. Blond hair, green eyes, and tanned muscles from hockey were all on display as he lost himself in me.

Picking me up by my ass, he brought our chests back together, kissing me with an intensity I hadn't felt from him yet. I never knew if Asa held himself back at times from politeness, fear, or worry. Either way, I was glad his wild side seemed to have taken over, allowing him to plunder me like the dick-loving-slut I was.

"More, more," I chanted, wanting him to fill me up as much as possible. His fingers tightened on my hips, and I wrapped my legs tighter, the muscles in my thighs screaming as I clung to him. Weaving my fingers through his hair, I pulled as he brought me to my peak, my orgasm crashing over me. My muscles clenched, and I squeezed him as they began to pulse, screaming out my release.

"Yes!" I wheezed, my voice gone from the loud moan that had just released.

Asa grunted, slamming into me one more time as he slumped down on the bed, his cock twitching in me. We lay there for a while, our breathing returning to normal, before he rolled over and disposed of his condom. He turned back, and I grabbed his hand, needing to say something before losing my nerve.

"I love you, Asa."

He stopped, peering down at me, love shining in his eyes. "I love you, Fin." He dropped down, his lips catching mine as he gave me a kiss. When he pulled back, I had tears in my eyes, and he looked at me with concern.

"What is it, Fin? Do you regret it?"

Shaking my head, I grabbed his cheeks, wanting to touch him as much as possible. "No, no, that's not it. I'm just so happy."

"Then why do you look like you're saying the opposite?" he asked.

Sucking in a breath, I held it, trying to slow my heart. "I'm good. So, good. I promise. I just wanted you to know how I felt. You must remember this moment. That everything here was real. Promise me?"

"Why does it feel like you're trying to prepare me for something?" he asked, ignoring my question.

"I'm not. I just want to remember the good times."

"Well, there are many more to come, babe. Let's get dressed before my sister comes and tries to ruin our fun." Asa laughed, walking to the shower.

I watched his butt as he walked away, hoping that he would still think that when I did what I needed to do. Regardless, it was a risk I had to take.

THE WEIGHT OF MY DECISION SAT HEAVILY ON MY SHOULDERS, LEAVING a bad taste in my mouth. Was I really going to do this? Could I? It felt so wrong to leave, but the more I thought about it, the more I realized I needed to. Picking up the pen, I wrote the hardest letter of my life.

Dear Asa,

Selfishly, I want you not to hate me, but since I already hate myself for what I'm doing, it's unlikely you won't.

I have to go.

I have to right a wrong I made years ago and put that part of my past to bed. I thought I was over it, but if this past year has shown me anything, it's that trauma and bad decisions have a way of catching up to you.

The night I was taken reminded me of how reckless I can be and how I rely on the goodness of others to get me out of trouble. I can't be that girl anymore. I won't be that girl.

I want to feel strong when I look in the mirror, but all I see is a frightened girl who can't figure out what she wants.

Everything in my life is going well, and on paper, it's perfect. You're the best boyfriend a girl could ever have. My parents are finally listening to me and being honest. My brother is happy and skating again. My best friend is back and living her life free of the men who tried to control her. And yet, inside, I feel like I don't belong with any of you.

I'm not good, Asa.

There are so many things in my past that I regret, so many decisions I made in the pursuit of the truth, that now fill me with dread. One day, if you can forgive me, I'll tell you about them, I promise. I'm done hiding, and that starts with facing them and, well, *him*.

I hope you know I love you, Asa. And I pray that this will clear my head of all the misguided and confusing thoughts that seem to live up there. I want a life with you. I know I can be happy if I get rid of the darkness surrounding me. I need to purge my sins once and for all, which points back to the man who was the first to darken me.

I wish I could say how long it will be and when I'll be back. But the truth is, I can't. I don't know the answer to that. I just know that I need to do this now and to do that, I have to go off the grid.

I promise you this isn't about Milo or Cohen. I don't know what I feel for them, but that's something we can talk about when I get back if you want. I know I don't deserve any allowances made on my behalf for doing this, so if you forgive me and your decision is to not talk about them, then I'll accept it. I just wanted you to know this wasn't about them, and I'll stop ignoring the conversation we need to have around it. I promise.

I'm sorry to do this after the amazing morning we shared as well. Again, I was being selfish and knowing I wanted to experience it once with you in case I never got to again. I hope you understand. I'm afraid no one else will, and Sawyer and my brother will try to come after me.

Please, I need to do this on my own. I promise to be safe, and I'll get back in contact when I can.

If this is the last time I get to speak with you, I just want you to know that you were the best thing to ever happen to me. I love you, Asa, and I hope to see you again.

Love, Fin

Wiping my tears, I laid down the pen and folded the paper into three, sliding it into the envelope. It was odd how such a heartbreaking letter could fit on a single sheet of paper. My whole world was about to shatter because of a few paragraphs.

A sound in the hallway had me hurrying in my task, and I slipped the letter into my journal, picked up my phone, and pretended to be scrolling social media just as someone entered my room.

"Fin, come on, it's time for dinner, and then we have to sing to Rhett. If we take too long, he'll escape, and we'll never be able to force him to sit with the party hat ever again," my best friend said, giving me a look.

Schooling my face, I nodded, pasting a smile on it. "Sure, one sec. I just need to send a text. I don't want Rhett to go all grumpy butt on us," I teased, hoping the mention of her sourpuss boyfriend would distract her.

"You're not wrong. You're okay, though, right? You've been distant, and I miss you." She walked into the room, giving me a concerned look.

"I'm great, promise." Standing, I took a few steps toward her as I pulled up my conversation with Milo, my last chance to back out at my fingertips.

ME: Everything is set.
Milo: I'll be there in an hour.
ME: See you then.

"Okay, let's go." I hooked my arm in hers, dragging her along so she wouldn't start to investigate more. Sawyer couldn't help it, she was a good best friend, but I didn't need her looking into anything too deeply if I wanted this to work.

And I *needed* this to work.

Two

FINLEY

Everyone laughed and celebrated as Rhett blew out his candles. The big grump had a smile on his face despite wearing a paper hat, and I knew I'd never seen him happier than here at his Granny's house that he'd inherited. The house was magnificent, and the ocean was literally right outside the back door. It was paradise.

So why did I feel like crying? It only reminded me how happy I should've been but wasn't. All I could think about was how miserable I was, cementing my decision to leave. It was now or never. I couldn't keep living a half-life where I pretended to be "perfect Fin" any longer.

Asa placed his arm around me, knocking me out of my thoughts as he drew me close, and I forced a smile. He was what real happiness looked like. I only wished I could feel as happy as he did. He'd been the absolute best after I'd been kidnapped by the Council. He'd been caring, patient, and understanding of my mood swings. I knew my silence was hard on him, yet he'd given me time to figure it out at my pace. The worst part was I wished he hadn't been so nice about it because then I wouldn't feel as guilty for pushing him away.

But I'd fallen in love with him for a reason, and now I was punishing him for his eternal sunshine. It wasn't fair, and I knew it. He deserved better from me. Except now, I was going to ask him not to hate me for leaving.

It might sound irrational, but I couldn't get past the trauma. I hated that I flinched every time someone knocked on the door or came in with a "you'll never believe this?" I hated that I constantly thought about boys I shouldn't. The guilt had built to an oppressive weight, and I was suffocating. Every day, I walked along a perpetual ledge, constantly re-balancing as I waited for the other shoe to drop, knowing it was just around the corner. Because it was always around the corner.

Funny how shoes were what had gotten me into this mess in the first place.

Asa handed me a plate, and I pasted on a smile. I looked around at our friends and family gathered, trying to soak in their happiness like a leech.

My best friend, Asa's twin sister, was surrounded by her seven boyfriends, one of which was my brother, Henry. They stared back at her with love in their eyes, and despite everything they'd gone through last fall with the Council, they were all stronger than ever. If anything, it had brought them all closer.

I couldn't say the same for myself. I'd been kidnapped, drugged, and put up for auction by the Council due to my own stupid mistakes. Sleep evaded me, and nightmares of the past and present played on an unrelenting loop, adding to my constant state of awareness. My secrets were catching up with me, and I couldn't hold them off any longer.

How Asa was still with me, I didn't know. How anyone had put up with my sour moods and distance only proved how much better they all were than me. They'd all rallied, but I was failing miserably. Once again.

The simple truth was, I didn't belong.

Not with the things I'd done. Not with my past. I hated that the sins of my youth were now destroying my future. It turned out that burying things wasn't a healthy way to cope. Shoving some cake into my mouth, I knew what I needed to do. It only confirmed that my decision was right.

I couldn't stay.

This trip had been the last push I needed to convince myself things had to change. In order to live the life I wanted, to feel happy… I had to make right the damage I created when I was seventeen.

I had to face *him*.

The only thing standing in my way was me, and it was time I faced the mistakes of my past instead of running.

Except now, I had to run.

I needed to distance myself from the people I loved—especially Asa. He was too good, too pure, and I couldn't taint him with the sins of a misguided youth. No, this couldn't come back on him. I didn't think we'd survive it, and losing him that way would crush me.

It was better for me to go now. This way, I could control the fall-out, and perhaps once I was done, once I'd completed my mission, we could start again. Better. Stronger.

It was the only sliver of hope I'd allow myself to hang on to.

"Want to go with everyone to the beach? I think some sea turtles were laying their eggs?" Asa asked, bringing me back to the present.

I looked down, realizing I'd eaten all my cake and hadn't even noticed. Turning into him, I kissed his cheek as I tried to hide the falling tear.

"I've got a headache. I'll call it a night, but you should go."

Asa observed me, trying to gauge my feelings. He'd done that a lot in the past six months. "I can stay with you."

He took my hand, squeezing it. The comfort he was providing

was too much, and I knew I was about to cave. Shaking my head, I cupped his cheek, taking in his face for one last time. I wanted to remember this look of love he had in case he never held it again.

"No, it's okay. I promise I'm fine. Go, have fun and make sure none of them get into trouble. I don't think anyone can deal with seeing Sawyer naked again." I chuckled, trying to distract him from my goodbye.

Asa grimaced, recalling how we'd been greeted yesterday morning before responding. "Are you sure? I don't mind staying back."

"Positive. I know how much you were hoping to see the turtles. Go. I promise, I'm good." He hesitated and I could see him wavering. Buckling down, I spread my most perfect Fin smile across my face. Asa melted, giving in.

"Okay. I'll check on you in a bit then."

"I love you, Asa," I said, holding the tears from my voice.

He kissed my cheek. "I love you, Fin."

It was everything I needed to hear and what I would hold on to over the next few months. He walked off, joining the group, and I waved, trying to keep in my emotions, not wanting them to see what I was feeling. I needed this time to make my escape.

Once they were all gone, my body relaxed for a second before the adrenaline of what was to come surged through me. My heart began to race as I walked up the stairs to my room. This was it. I was really doing it.

Stepping into the space, I could smell Asa's cologne mixed with my perfume, and I took a breath, needing to store the memory. Wiping the tears that fell unashamedly now, I pulled the letter I'd written earlier out of my journal, and placed it on his pillow. Tears dropped onto it as I tried to wipe them away. It was cowardly to leave this way, but I wouldn't have the courage to do it any other way. I just prayed he'd forgive me.

Changing quickly, I grabbed the bag I'd packed with the essentials and a couple of outfits and tiptoed down the stairs to the front door in case anyone had returned. Tears trailed down my face quicker as I left everything and everyone I knew behind. I opened the thick front door and walked through with determination, promising myself it was worth it.

Dressed in black leather pants, a black top, and black boots, I blended into the night as I crept down the driveway. I might be running away, but I could still do it in style. No one would ever accuse me of being boring at least.

I spotted the car idling for me at the end of the road. A warm sensation filled my body at Milo coming through, but I shoved it away with everything else I refused to look at where he was concerned.

I knew leaving this way would hurt; it was a punch to the gut, but I'd run out of options. If I didn't do this, if I didn't go now, I'd always be watching over my shoulder, waiting for him, never truly growing. Regret would rule my life, and I didn't want to live that way anymore.

I would never be happy—not until he'd been dealt with.

Shoving my bag into the tiny trunk of the expensive sports car, I opened the door, sliding in.

Milo smiled over at me, his eyes twinkling in the lights of the interior. "You get out, okay?"

"Yeah. No one saw me. Thanks," I paused, swallowing, "for doing this for me."

"You know I'm here for you, Finley, whatever you need. Besides, it's kind of my thing to be the one to save you."

Smiling, I tried to ignore the confused butterflies erupting at his words. It didn't matter, though. They were there, swirling around with everything else I felt guilty about. I was tired of feeling guilty. Buckling up, I settled in for the drive and pulled out the list I'd made.

1. Find him
2. Take him down

3. Make him pay

At one time, Blackhawk had been my salvation until he became my damnation. It was time I became my own saving grace.

My sins were dark, my spirit broken, but I was no longer weak. It was time I remembered who I'd been. It was time I returned to Oblivion.

And this time, my stilettos wouldn't just be sinful. No, this time, they would be deadly.

MOST OF THE RIDE WAS QUIET AS I PONDERED OVER MY CHOICES. WHILE I knew I needed to do it, I couldn't deny the pit in my stomach that I was making the wrong choice. I was risking everything and hoping the people in my life loved me enough to forgive me after it was all said and done.

"You hungry?" Milo asked, and I turned, blushing. I'd kind of forgotten he was there. Not that I thought the car was driving itself, but I'd zoned out so far that I felt alone in time and space.

"No, I ate before..." I didn't need to say anything else. He nodded, keeping his eyes on the road.

"You know, we haven't talked much about what this is all about, just that you needed to escape for a while where no one could find you. Are you in trouble?"

"No." I shook my head, watching the trees fly by through the car window. "I'm trying to rectify a mistake."

"Is it going to be dangerous?" he asked, his voice sounding odd, so I faced him.

"It could be. Why?"

I watched as his hands gripped the wheel harder, his jaw flexing a little, and I couldn't figure out why he was so upset about this.

"You seem, I don't know, more upset than I thought you'd be."

He laughed in a way that let me know he didn't find it funny. "Oh? Is that so?" Milo shook his head, making me even more unsure of what was going on with him. I kept watching, hoping if I stared at him long enough, he'd cave and give in to the pressure.

A few minutes went by, and he sighed, glancing over at me. He put on his blinker, the sound filling the space as he turned down another dark street.

"It's nothing. Forget I said anything."

I frowned, my brow creasing in concern. "I feel like I just failed a test I didn't know I was taking."

He chuckled again, this one sounding a little more like himself, the carefree guy I'd met in one of the darker moments of my life.

"You don't even see how amazing you are, Fin. That's all. I worry about you. I... *care* about you. More than I should since you have a boyfriend, but the simple fact is, I do. But that's not your problem."

"I..." I swallowed, not sure how to respond. "Thank you, Milo. I couldn't have done any of this without you. I'm just not in the place to really make any big decisions. I need to do this before I can even think about what my life will look like after."

"You keep saying that, but I wonder if it's more an excuse than a real reason."

I shook my head, the rebuttal quick on my tongue to argue, but it died when I looked at his face, at the pain I seemed to be causing him. Regardless of the reason, I knew I had to focus on the future, which meant fixing the past.

"It's all I can offer you," I finally said, turning back in my seat and sliding down into it. I laid my head back against the plush leather and closed my eyes, pretending I was going to sleep. It was shitty of me and cowardly, but after the emotional toll of leaving, I was spent, and it was all I had left.

Besides, I was great at ignoring things until they blew up in my face.

Three

FINLEY

A FEW HOURS LATER, WE PULLED UP TO A HOTEL, AND I SAT UP, stretching, going along with my fake sleep ruse. Milo chuckled at me, and I knew he hadn't bought it but was at least indulging me in my delusion.

"Sit tight. I'll go get the room. I know you want to stay off cameras."

Nodding, I smiled my thanks, reaching across to squeeze his hand. "Thank you, Milo. I know I've been a crappy friend, but I appreciate everything you've done for me."

His lip curled up on one side, and he squeezed my hand. It hurt my heart a little to see him so unsure of things, especially when I was the cause.

Sighing, I sat back and pulled out a burner phone to check in on the situation back at the house. I knew I had only a small opportunity before they got Cohen or someone else techy on the job, and then I would lose my window, but for now, I would be selfish and peer into their world to see the mayhem I had caused. A part of me felt I deserved to witness the pain I'd inflicted on them.

Clicking on the camera icon, I cloaked my location and then

selected the main room. I'd been busy hacking into the security system yesterday while everyone was swimming in the pool. The camera pulled up easily, and I found the room filled with a few people talking.

I hesitated, debating if I wanted to hear what they were saying or not. I might not like what I heard, and it wouldn't be something I could un-hear from my friends once it was out there. But again, I was a glutton for punishment and felt I deserved whatever vitriol they wanted to throw at me.

"How far do you think she's made it?" Sawyer asked, pacing back and forth.

"Maybe we should just let her do what she needs to?" Mateo offered.

"It could be dangerous. She's doing her usual 'I can fix it on my own' thing, and that never ends well," my brother said, sighing into his hands as he rubbed his face. "Why now?"

I'd been avoiding looking at Asa, but when he spoke up, I could no longer ignore the forlorn expression he wore or the dejected way his body melded into the sofa.

"Because whatever it is, it's more important than us," he said, throwing the letter I'd written onto the table and standing up. "I'm sorry Sis, but I can't stay here. I'm going to stop by a few places I like to surf and spend some time on my own. You won't be mad if I miss the rest of the vacation?"

My best friend stood, walking over to Asa, and wrapped her arms around her twin. Despite the fact they'd only known about each other for less than a year, they had already developed a tight bond.

"I'll miss you, but I understand. Let me know when you make it somewhere, and make sure to keep me updated. I don't want you to run off and do anything foolish because you're heartbroken."

He kissed her head, a tear falling down my face at the misery I was causing. This wasn't helping, but I couldn't find it in myself to turn it off now that I was watching.

Rhett stormed into the room, a phone in his hand. "I got a hold of your father, baby. Samson will have Cohen look into some possible leads and brief us back in Utah. We'll find her, and then I'll wring her neck for skipping out on us like this."

He pulled his tiny girlfriend into his arms, and I realized I'd had enough; plus, I didn't really need to see any mushy stuff between one of my good friends and my bestie. There were some lines I wanted to keep. I was already scarred enough from walking in on a naked scene between her and my brother that I could've lived my whole life without.

Closing out the app, I laid my head back, debating with myself again. "They'll be okay. They'll forgive you. You had to do this. It's okay to pick yourself every once and a while."

"Talking to yourself?" Milo asked, and I jumped, not realizing the door had opened.

"Oh, did you hear that?" My face flushed, and I unhooked my seatbelt to get out of the door he held open for me. He smirked, not answering, which was an answer in and of itself. He handed me my bag, and I pulled out a hoodie, pulling it over my head to hide my face, and we walked into the back entrance together, his frame blocking mine.

"I'll get a few hours of sleep before hitting the road. The car I got for you will be dropped off in the morning, and I told the guy to drop it and the other items you asked for at the front desk and for them to slide the envelope under the door. You should have minimal contact here, helping to hide your presence as long as you need. I even have the room for a week if you change your mind."

His hand was on the lower part of my back as we walked, and I tried not to focus on how nice his heat felt. "Thank you, Milo. Once again, I don't know how I'll ever repay you."

Milo dropped his hand, using the key card to open the door and pushing it open into a luxurious room. "In my life, friendship is something I value more than anything. But," he paused, biting his lip as he debated, "maybe we could go to dinner sometime?"

He adjusted his glasses as I watched him, and I fought with myself. I knew how I wanted to answer, but I was back to whether I deserved it or not. Someone as reprehensible as me shouldn't deserve such a nice guy like Milo to like her.

"I'm not sure I'm worth that much, but if it's what you want, then I will."

"You make yourself sound like the world's worst criminal, Fin." He rolled his eyes, moving further into the room. "Don't forget who my family is."

I nodded, setting my bag on the bed closest to the door. While I knew what he meant, considering his family was part of a secret organization bent on taking over the world, it wasn't the same. At least, not in my eyes. I'd chosen to do the things I'd done; he just had the unfortunate luck to be born into the Council.

The Council was made up of seven families that used the Olympics and the young athletes training for them as their mules to import and export everything from drugs, weapons, and stolen artifacts, while also holding the market in every major industry. Despite the Council being taken down last winter, he still had connections. Milo's family had been on the automotive side of things, which helped me out when I needed a car my family couldn't trace.

While Milo was a Bellamy, he wasn't part of their misdeeds, making him innocent, in my opinion. He'd even saved me from being auctioned off in one of their human trafficking rings. It was the first night we met and the night I realized I liked him as more than a friend. There was just that pesky detail about my boyfriend. And while my bestie Sawyer had found a way to have seven men adore her, I didn't feel I was that lucky, or perhaps, worthy enough to be greedy.

Though, even as I thought that, I knew Sawyer wasn't being greedy. She loved her men, and they loved her. It was just how it was.

But yet, the logic didn't seem to fit me. I was too selfish, too undeserving, and too reckless to have more than I was allowed.

"Do you need the restroom?" I asked, fidgeting on the spot. Everything felt too much at the moment with us in this room alone.

"No, I'm just going to sleep."

Biting my lip, I felt like I was letting him down and that I should say something, but for once, words were failing me.

"Okay, well, um, thanks again." I picked up my bag and walked into the bathroom, leaning against the door as it closed. I didn't really need anything in here, but it felt like the safest space for the time being. Stripping off all my clothes, I took a long shower, hoping it would provide enough time for him to fall asleep and allow me to continue to avoid the conversation I needed to have.

"Yeah, because that keeps working out for you," I berated, hissing at myself under the water.

Sucking it up, I got out, brushed my hair and teeth, and applied the world's most generous amount of lotion one could ever use.

"You're just stalling. And talking to yourself. You're losing it, Fin."

Rolling my eyes, I threw everything into my bag and braced myself. When I stepped out into the room, one lamp was on, cascading the room into shadows. Quietly, I tiptoed over to the bed and crawled under the covers, lying on the pillow.

It took a while, but eventually, I quieted my mind enough that I could fall asleep. It felt like only a few seconds later when a hand brushed the hair out of my face as a body hovered over me. I knew it was Milo. He was the only person I knew who smelled like rainfall and a campfire. His scent surrounded me, and I fought everything in me not to open my eyes and give in to the yearning I knew I'd find staring at me.

As I kept my breathing even, he bent down and kissed my forehead softly. "Be safe, darling." His fingers trailed over my cheek, and I urged my body not to give in to the shudder it wanted to do.

When the door clicked shut a few seconds later, I braved it and opened my eyes, finding the room empty, the sun starting to rise.

The absolute silence weighed on me, and once again, I wondered if I was doing the right thing. An overwhelming sense of fear, dread, and loneliness filled me, and I replayed the last few seconds with Milo in my head. I could no longer stop the tears from falling. The night everything changed no longer wished to be buried and it rose up, reminding me how stupid I was.

THAT NIGHT

Oblivion: Do we all know our parts?
Blackhawk: Yes, little hacker, we've been over it a few times. We're good. We got this, babe.

Whenever he called me that, my pulse raced, and I wished I could hear him saying it. Tonight would be the first time we met in person, and I was excited about putting a face to the name, to the boy I'd been crushing on for a year.

Obsidian: After tonight, we'll be full members of MKG. Assuming we don't fuck up. I know I won't, so it's on you two.
Oblivion: Don't get your panties in a knot, Sid. We got this. I can hack circles around this system, and you know there hasn't been a lock I haven't been able to get through. We've been building up to this for a year. Trust your team.
Blackhawk: The only one who wears panties is you, Oblivion. Just to be sure, we should show each other.
Obsidian: Stop being a perv. You're right. We're the best.
Oblivion: Sure, you go first.
Obsidian: Don't let him devalue you. You're too good for

that, Oblivion. He's just a pretty boy who happens to be good at coding.

Blackhawk: Ah, thanks for the compliment, Sid. I wish I could say the same for your face.

Obsidian: Bite me.

Blackhawk: Oh, fiesty. Now, go and review your program. It's important.

Obsidian: You're not the boss. If anyone is, it's me. I'm the oldest and have the most experience. You just want to flirt.

Blackhawk: Whatever you need to believe.

Oblivion: You two are cattier than the girls at school.

Obsidian: You should let me show them not to mess with geeks. I'd make them wish they never met you.

Oblivion: Maybe next week. I just want to focus on the mission.

Blackhawk: And they say romance is dead. Now, who's flirty?

Obsidian: Whatever. I gotta go. See you both in a few hours.

Obsidian signed off.

Blackhawk started a private chat.

Blackhawk: Ah, I hurt his feelings.

Oblivion: Yeah, I think you did. It's so unfair you two know each other. I feel like the third wheel. Especially since Mongoose.

Blackhawk: Yeah, well, we won't talk about Mongoose. But you could never be the third wheel, little hacker.

Oblivion: Are you, you know, being flirty?

Blackhawk: Do you not know when a guy is hitting on you, little hacker?

Oblivion: Not really. Remember, I've never had a guy flirt with me? Most of them ignore me.

Blackhawk: I forget most of the time you're still in high school. Which reminds me… when do you turn 18 again?
Oblivion: In a few months. Why?
Blackhawk: No reason, jailbait.
Oblivion: You're only, what four years older than me? You act like it's a decade.
Blackhawk: Um, sure. Let's leave it at that.
Oblivion: You're infuriating.
Blackhawk: Are you nervous about our final mission? The other things were easier.
Oblivion: Maybe for you, but remember, I haven't been doing this as long. I only started a few years ago. It's all been hard for me.
Blackhawk: You're crazy talented for only doing it a few years, babe. Have you found any new information about your friend? Did my contact work out?
Oblivion: He's looking, but I'm starting to wonder if I'm crazy. I just can't accept that she's dead. I'd know it.
Blackhawk: She must be pretty special. I've never had a friend like that.
Oblivion: Not even Obsidian?
Blackhawk: We're roommates and only because we didn't know anyone else, not because we genuinely like each other.
Oblivion: I'm not sure if he'd say the same thing, but, well, you're my friend.
Blackhawk: God, I do love your innocence. Okay, I'll be your friend. I'll try not to corrupt you too much.
Oblivion: Too late for that.
Blackhawk: Look at you, being all flirty. I'm looking forward to meeting you tonight, little hacker. I'll see you soon.
Oblivion: See you soon.

Shutting the laptop, I set it aside as I kicked my legs up on the bed in happiness. The immediate need to tell Sariah arose, squelching a little of my joy. I wish I could tell her these things. I wish she was still here. I needed to find her. Henry was becoming a shell of the person he was. He hadn't been able to find another pairs skater, so he'd started speed skating. He'd become so withdrawn, though, I worried I would lose my brother, too.

I didn't know if I'd survive that. I couldn't lose him and Sariah. It was why tonight was so important. If I made it into the MKG, I'd have better connections and resources to dig deeper and find the information on where she went. It all hinged on tonight going well.

Not only would I finally belong somewhere and be able to uncover the secret of Sariah's disappearance—I refused to say death—I would finally get to meet the first boy I'd managed to semi-flirt with.

Deciding to go for it, I pulled out the ruby red dress and matching heels. When the stilettos arrived, I knew they were from him. We'd all talked about our weaknesses, and I'd said mine were shoes. A few days later, the most gorgeous pair of red stilettos arrived.

Coincidence? No, I didn't believe in coincidences.

The note had just said, *"I can't wait to see you in them,"* letting me know even more that tonight was the night I should wear them—the night we'd meet and our futures would change forever.

Once I was dressed, I climbed out my window, holding the shoes in my hand as I climbed over the overhang and slipped to the ground. Placing them on, I quickly made my way to Sullivan Street behind my house, where I'd told the car to meet me. The sedan waited at the curb, and I quickly hurried over, sliding in.

It wasn't until later, when I was being handcuffed, that the implications of the night had set in. I was dumb, naive, and now a juvenile delinquent. Go me.

PRESENT DAY

The burner phone pinged, drawing me back to the present. Sucking back my tears, I dried my eyes and climbed out of bed. Crying wouldn't do any good. I couldn't let myself go down that hole again. I had to focus on the mission. The memory had reminded me just how important it was.

When I pulled out my phone and signed into the app the notification had come from, it made my last thoughts even more detrimental.

Blackhawk: Oblivion, babe, where have you been? I've missed you.

Four

FINLEY

I STARED AT THE MESSAGE LIKE IT WAS ALIVE AND HE WAS ABOUT TO jump off the tiny screen and strangle me where I sat. A million emotions coursed through me at the thought as fear took hold. I thought I was ready, that the moment I stepped away from everything else and faced this, it would all come to a head, and I'd know what to do.

But as I stared at the message, sweat building on my upper lip, I realized I had absolutely no freaking clue what I was doing.

Outside of my 'get revenge' list, it seemed I was poorly equipped to actually do anything else. Which in the grand scheme of things didn't surprise me. It was my fatal flaw, after all. This time it seemed, I'd been the recipient of my own assumptions.

Not begrudging my brother his talent because I knew he had his own battles to fight, but growing up in his shadow had been hard. Henry was the one who seemed to flawlessly get everything right the first time. When he and Sariah started to win competitions, the spotlight around them became even brighter.

As theirs increased, it felt like all the light around me was sucked away into a vacuum, and I was left with a mere glimmer. I didn't like feeling envious of my best friend and brother, so I found ways to share in their light, persuading others I had something worth looking at.

That was the start of my downfall.

I faked so many things, I convinced even myself I could do them, forgetting half the time I was only pretending.

But when I got a taste of that limelight, I couldn't let it go, wanting it more and more like an addict. Once people thought you were perfect, it was hard to be anything other than that.

But it was exhausting constantly pretending, and when Sariah went missing, I no longer had their light to steal.

It was a sad realization that you missed your best friend because she made you brighter.

Standing, I walked over to the window, peeking behind the curtains to stare out into the parking lot. The sun was starting to rise, the day beginning, and I felt none of it. A sinking weight settled on me, and I struggled to stand as it pressed into me. Bit by bit, it would break me down, crushing me until I was nothing but a pile of rubble.

Squeezing my eyes shut, I pressed my fists into them, begging the pressure to lessen. All the thoughts swirled, folding into themselves, and I was on the verge of losing it.

"Shit, shit, shit."

I hadn't felt this out of control since… *No! Don't go there.*

The memory I worked so hard to control came roaring back now that I was alone, filling all my crevices with the darkness, sucking out all the joy, and finding any space to root itself as I fell back into a flashback of how I ended up on the path that would lead to my greatest sin.

FINLEY, 16

Slamming the door, I stomped over to my desk, breathing heavily as I panted in and out.

"I hate you!" I yelled.

Dropping into the chair, the tears fell before my butt even hit the seat. Pulling my legs up, I wrapped my arms around them, leaning my head against my knees as I sobbed, rocking slightly.

No one understood. No one seemed to care. I was so alone in this house. I missed my friend.

The thoughts repeated as I continued to sit there, stewing in my feelings, wondering if I would ever find happiness again. Maybe it was time to just say fuck it all and do everyone a favor? If I was gone, they wouldn't have to worry or deal with me anymore.

Sliding open the top drawer, I placed one knee on the ground, staring into the dark space. It resembled my mind so much that it felt both familiar and disarming. I was so tired of feeling this way. I could just take care of it.

Pulling out the bottle of pills I'd stolen, I spun them around, the contents clicking against one another as I twirled them. I'd done it slowly, taking a pill here and there from my mother, grandparents, and even friends' houses I visited.

It was like an odd fixation I had now to open people's medicine cabinets and see what they left out for everyone to see. I didn't even know what some of them were, but I had to assume that this much of anything wouldn't be good for a person to ingest.

Blue pills, yellow ones, red ones, and even some white tablets filled the old container. Some days, I'd pull it out, twirling it around like this, and the knowledge I had a way out was enough to calm me.

Other times, I'd dump them out onto my desk, sorting them by color and counting, taking myself a little bit closer to the edge before I tossed them back in, the anxiety gone, and my breathing returned to regular.

Today, it felt like nothing short of going through with it would help.

Twisting the cap, I poured them into my hand, feeling their weight as I jostled them around. It always shocked me how something so insignificant as these small things could create such chaos in one's body. The sweet oblivion they would provide, the quietness of my thoughts for once, felt worth any chaos I might endure.

Grabbing the water bottle out of my bookbag, I stared down at the colorful handful. This was it. It was now or never. Lifting my hand closer, I watched them move in slow motion like I was witnessing it outside of myself. As I reached my mouth, I opened it, ready to dump them all in and finally say goodbye to all this self-hatred, turmoil, and disgust I felt inside.

My hand froze, and I stared, and stared, and stared.

A ping from my computer jolted me, and I tensed, almost falling out of my chair. My hand closed over the pills, only a few escaping. Quickly, I dumped the ones I had clasped between my palm into the bottle and jumped down to collect the few that had fallen. It felt vital to have them all. If I was missing even one, I wouldn't be able to go through with it.

I tried to ignore that by placing parameters on my own suicide, that might mean I wasn't actually ready to take that step. But it felt too much like failing at something else to say it out loud.

The computer pinged again as I reached under my desk, reaching for one blue pill that had bounced all the way to the back. Grunting, I pressed against the wood, straining to reach it. The particle board cut into my arm, scraping it, but I pushed on. I ignored how much effort I was putting into keeping the thing I was banking on killing me like it was my lifeline.

Finally, my fingers clasped around the pill, and I drew it back, my heart returning to normal as I placed it into the bottle. *There, everything was right again.* Screwing on the cap, I tucked it safely back into my drawer. I needed it close to remind myself it was there. It had become a weird safety blanket.

The ping sounded a third time, and I turned to my computer, opening the message that kept going off. It was a person I'd met on a random site responding to my request. Adrenaline began to rush through me at what this could mean.

User584: I think I found what you were looking for. I'll send you the invite. The password is l3mon_fizz!e.
User827: Sweet! You're the absolute best.

I tapped my fingers on my desk as I anxiously waited for the message to come through. I'd been teaching myself coding for the past year and had taken a few classes at the local college. It had been the one thing my parents had let me do, thinking it would help to distract me. I didn't tell them it was to help me find more information on Sariah. They could believe what they wanted.

The link popped up, and I hovered the mouse over it, a last-second urge to stop myself clawing at my mind. Glancing over at the picture frame on my desk, I took in the picture of the three of us, so young, carefree, and happy. When I looked at my brother now, he was a shell of himself. I couldn't stop until I had real answers.

Straightening my spine, I looked back at the monitor and clicked on the link, determination coursing through me.

The screen began to pixelate and went black, and I gulped, hoping I hadn't just been played until a command popped up.

C:/what is your code name?

The blinking cursor mocked me as it waited for me to enter my name. A hacker name, I needed a hacker name. Hmm, what could I be?

Fashionista? Too girly.

Little sister? Too dumb.

Dark Cloud? Too morbid.

For some reason, I pulled open the drawer, staring at the bottle of pills that had become the answer to my problems, hoping I'd find something within it. Though, the only solution they truly offered me was oblivion and a release from my dark-ness. The realization slammed into me, and I knew what my hacker name would be. It was really the only thing that made sense.

C:/Oblivion.
C:/Welcome to the dark web, Oblivion. Password?
C:/l3mon_fizz!e
C:/ Access granted. You've been entered into the pool for admittance to The MidKnight Guild. You'll be given a series of tasks to perform with fellow initiates. Fail to perform them, and you don't belong. Your success is in your hands. Do you accept?
C:/ Yes. I accept.
C:/Welcome to the games. We'll be in touch.

The screen returned to normal, and I exhaled, realizing I'd been holding my breath through the exchange. I was in!

Happiness and excitement, a foreign feeling, whirled to life in me, and I sat back, smiling. The drawer stood open, almost mocking me, reminding me what I'd been ready to do ten minutes earlier. Slamming it shut, I wasn't prepared to let it go yet, but I didn't need to necessarily be reminded of my weakness either.

Walking to my bed, I pulled another picture frame of my best friend and me off the nightstand, and I held it to my chest as I lay in bed.

"I'll find you, Sariah. I promise."

IN THE END, I DID FIND HER, BUT NOT BECAUSE OF THE DARK WEB. No, that had only led to my destruction.

I stayed in the hotel room for a few days, licking my imaginary wounds. I was embarrassed to admit it took me that long to pull myself out of my funk, shower, and have a stern talking with myself. If I kept letting myself fall back into the past, I wouldn't be able to correct my future; I'd only be ruining it more.

"Time to suck it up, girl. Message him back and tell him how you really feel."

Taking a deep breath, I pulled out my most prized possession after my sewing machine—my custom-built laptop. Smoothing my hands over the surface, I touched the stickers I'd placed on it adoringly, reminding myself of what I'd intended when I'd settled on each of them. The one that caught my eye today was, "Nevertheless, she persisted." With one final push, I opened the lid and powered it on.

I used to get a jolt of adrenaline each time I sat in front of this screen, the thrill of a new adventure awaiting me on the other side. After the fallout with Blackhawk and Obsidian, it all felt too broken and contaminated. It took me a while to find I could use my skills for good, and my white hacking site was born.

"Though, how well did that turn out last time?" my sins whispered to me, reminding me how well I'd assisted someone who ended up being human trafficked anyway despite my 'help.'

Pushing that reminder to the far recesses of my mind, I knew I couldn't open that can of worms just yet. There were so many things attached to it, and I wasn't ready. I didn't know if I ever would be. It was much better to focus on the thing I could right now and strangle this demon instead of letting them all breed. Yeah, sound advice.

Signing into the app I hadn't frequented in years, I clicked on the message that had sent me spiraling.

Blackhawk: Oblivion, babe, where have you been? I've missed you.

There he was. It felt surreal that he was right there. My nightmare had been at my fingertips all along. Tapping my nails on the keyboard, I debated how to respond. I honestly thought he'd put up more of a fight. I hadn't expected to find him this soon. Now that I had, what did I say?

Hey, asshole, thanks for ruining my life. Now, please meet me at the 7-Eleven so I can kick you in the nuts?

No, I didn't think that would work. Plus, I wanted to destroy him more than just leaving him unable to bear children. An idea formed, and I knew what I needed to do—exactly what they'd done to me.

Lure him into a false sense of security. Make him think we were friends and then crush his spirit. All the while, in the background, I'd destroy everything he loved and cherished. Nothing would be safe.

Unless he had a dog, then I'd just steal it and make him think it ran away. Yes, this was the way to go about it.

Feeling invigorated with my new plan, I cracked my knuckles and rested my fingers on the familiar keys. The power that lay beneath my fingertips was what always amazed me, pushing me to press them. If people only knew the real power they had to destroy others. Scratch that. I didn't need to go full rebellion, just revenge. And maybe some redemption for the other things.

Okay, now that I had my mindset, I typed in a response. Time to play a little game, asshole.

Oblivion: That's rich coming from you. I'm surprised your balls haven't shriveled up inside you from how much of a coward you are.

I hit send before I could take it back and realized I'd gone a little harsh, but it was fine, totally fine.

Crap! Crap! Crap! How did I unsend something? Fudge, why did I let myself think I could do this?

While I was having a mini panic attack, I missed the fact that he sent back a message. So when the ping sounded, I jumped, hitting a bunch of random keys. Furiously hitting delete, I forced my eyes up to read his reply.

Blackhawk: How I've missed your wit, little hacker. It's been lonely on here these past four years. But I must ask, why do you think I'm a coward?

I didn't even have to think anymore as I typed out my response. If he was here to chat, it was time to find out some information. The problem with finding Blackhawk all those years ago was that I didn't know much about his real identity outside of his hacker name and random facts we shared. I needed more than his favorite pizza this time if I was going to destroy him.

Oblivion: You're even more of one if you have to ask.
Oblivion: What have you been getting yourself into? It has been a while, hasn't it?

Okay, good, that was good. Ease him in nice and slow there. I waited, but nothing came, and eventually, I got bored, so I clicked on the next screen, my mouse hovering over the confirm button.

Did I want to violate my friends' privacy more? It wasn't so much I wanted to violate them, but the need to know how they were doing was thumping at my brain, desperate to know. At this point, the pain reminded me I was still vital, important to them. It was selfish to use their suffering to validate my own need to feel important, but it was what it was, and I couldn't stop myself now.

Besides, I was too much of a chicken to actually look at the one person I wanted to know the most about—Asa. Instead, I would vicariously feed off the others like a parasite, hoping to glean some knowledge to whet my curiosity.

Pushing the button, I didn't find anyone in the living room or the boardroom, so I clicked on the kitchen, hoping I'd find someone. I'd only put them in a few areas, not wanting to accidentally stumble across something I didn't want to see. Not that these areas were completely safe, so I shut my eyes, listening first before I peeked out.

When I only heard voices talking, I was glad to find they were clothed. Sawyer and my brother sat on the stools at the island, talking with Samson, Sawyer's dad.

"How could she just disappear with no trail?" Sawyer asked, hurt laced in her voice. "There's really nothing?"

"As of now, no. She covered her tracks well enough that we haven't been able to pick up any leads on what direction she was headed. We see her walk down the driveway, but once she's at a certain distance, it's like she just vanished. We've checked all the traffic cams and hotels within 100 miles and are still coming up short. We have to sit tight and wait for her to make a move."

"I think we should just let her be," my brother said, finally looking up. He had dark circles under his eyes, and I hated how much I seemed to be stressing him out.

"How can you say that?" Sawyer asked, gasping.

"Fin has been struggling for a while. She apparently needs to do this. Until then, she's not going to let herself be found. Not by us, at least. If we keep searching for her, we're only going to push her further underground, and then she might never return. At least this way, she has the chance to do what she needs without worrying we're going to send in the calvary."

"No. I disagree," Sawyer said, shaking her head. "I can't let her go off on her own. She's my best friend. I need to know she's safe."

My brother picked up her hand, smoothing his thumb over the top. "I know, Smalls. But you didn't see her after you were gone. She went to some dark places, did some things she regrets. I don't know everything that happened, but I do know I don't want my sister to feel she has to push everyone away forever. So, I'll give her some time to figure things out. I promise, I'm not letting her just ride off and fight her battles alone. I refuse to lose my sister, but for now, we let her. We need to focus on training and our competition. She wouldn't want us to lose focus. So, she's got a month, and then I'll go and kick her butt."

Sawyer nodded, tears running down her face, and my brother pulled her into his arms. When he looked up to where I placed the camera, I jumped, feeling like he'd caught me. But he couldn't know? Could he?

Either way, I quickly exited, shoving my computer off my lap like that made a difference. At least I'd learned I had a couple of weeks to make some plays before they came for me. It was more than I thought I'd get. The urge to not let them down filled me, and I jumped off the bed, putting the few items I had spread out around the room back into my bag. I picked up my trash and straightened the bed a little.

Grabbing my computer to put it in my bag, I opened it up to check one last thing and found that Blackhawk had responded.

Blackhawk: Oh, this and that. Just keeping things in order. You know how it is.
Blackhawk: Hey, listen, I actually have a job I could use your help on. Interested?

Seemed my luck was finally turning. Before I slipped the laptop back into the case, I replied, feeling a piece of the puzzle click into place. Slinging my bag over my shoulder, I dumped out the envelope that had been shoved under the door, picking up the car keys and putting them in my pocket. A fake ID and prepaid debit card laid on the bed, warming my heart at Milo's thoughtfulness. He truly was so much more than his lineage.

Pocketing them as well, I crumpled the envelope and tossed it into the trash before glancing around, taking in my surroundings once last time. This was it. The moment I stepped out of this room, I was no longer Finley Amelia Reyes but Oblivion. I couldn't stop until I took Blackhawk down, and only then could I return to being the woman I wanted to be.

> **Oblivion:** Depends. Will you be there? I'm heading to a new location, so I'll be off the grid for a day. Send me the details, and I'll look them over. XOXO

Five

ASA

THE WAVES CRASHED AGAINST THE SHORE, not bringing me the sense of calm they typically did. I'd been sitting in the sand, staring out into the ocean, trying to figure out what to do. In the past, I'd come out here when I had a hard decision to make, and the sounds of the waves as I surfed soothed me, bringing what I needed to do to the surface, casting all the other junk away.

But today was the same as yesterday, which was the same as the days before. It had been one week since I'd found Fin's letter and had my heart ripped out of my chest. One week since we'd joined our bodies together, consummating our love for one another in a way we hadn't before. One week since I'd felt like I no longer had a direction to go in. One week since my world had stopped.

What I hated the most was how I hadn't realized how much I loved her until it happened. We'd exchanged "I love you" before, but for some reason, I hadn't known what that truly felt like until it was gone. A gaping hole sat in my chest now, and I didn't know how to fill it so I could be whole again without her.

Giving up on the ocean being a mind whisperer, I fell back onto the sand, staring up at the darkening sky. When my phone buzzed in my pocket, I pulled it out, hoping it would be her. Sighing at the screen, I answered it as I stared off.

"Hey, Mom."

"How you doing, hun?"

I let out a long breath, rubbing my eyes. "Not so great. The ocean hasn't brought me the same clarity as usual. I don't know how to wait for her to finish whatever she wants to do. I feel like if I don't go after her, then I'll lose her forever. But that would be going against her wishes, and I don't want to do that."

"Asa, honey, I love you so much, and you've become a great man. In your efforts to be the complete opposite of Orson, though, you might have taken the perfect thing a little too far, and I'm saying that as your mother who loves you dearly. It's okay to break a rule, to go after what you want, to say hell with it all, and be selfish for once in your life."

"I...." I swallowed, feeling slightly shocked by my mother.

"I know. It's not what you expect me to say, but honey, take it from someone who didn't go after her heart and settled. Time goes by too quickly. In many ways, Samson thought he could do one job and return to me, but it ended up being more complex than he could've ever imagined. At that point, he felt committed to staying the course. Don't let that happen to Fin. I know how you feel about her and how she feels about you. Go. After. Her."

"It's that simple?"

"Yes. Fin is brilliant, but she's also stubborn. She probably thinks she's doing you a favor by shielding you, but all she's doing is keeping herself from experiencing joy. You just have to show her you're more tenacious and can get your hands dirty." She paused, taking a breath, and I knew she was gearing up to tell me something I might not want to hear. "I think Cohen could help you."

"Oh, um, I dunno."

It wasn't that I didn't want his help. There was just this weird tension since the whole incident when Fin had been kidnapped by the Council that made it awkward. But maybe that was just on me?

He was working with Samson now, so that had to mean he was good.

"What does Sam—, I mean Dad, think?"

"Honey, no one is forcing you to call him Dad. We both know you didn't grow up knowing he was your father, and the man who claimed to be wasn't worthy of the title. He and Sawyer had a previous relationship, so it was easier for her. It took her a while to call me mom, and I didn't rush her. It will be better when it's natural for you and him. So, don't feel guilty about it at all."

Sighing, I rubbed my face, spreading sand over my forehead. I'd forgotten I'd been playing with it as I sat staring out into the ocean for answers.

"Yeah, I know."

Standing up, I dusted off my pants and shook the sand from my clothes. Usually, the sand didn't bother me because the surfing was worth it. When all I did was sit in it, I found it a bit of a nuisance.

"As for Samson, he thinks Cohen is probably already looking into it more despite Henry saying to stop. He thinks Cohen has a bit of a crush on Fin. Is that why you hesitate to reach out? Are you feeling unsure of your role in her life?"

It might be weird to talk about your love life with your mom for some people, but it wasn't for me. My mom and I were super close, only having each other growing up, and I shared practically everything with her.

"I don't know what it is. When I met him, it was after she'd been taken. He came in cocky, and I didn't know how to take him. Since then, I know they've worked on a few things, but she was always cautious in choosing her words and didn't say much about it. I kept waiting for her to bring it up. Even Sawyer said something to me, but Fin never did, so I guess I shoved it aside, figuring I didn't have to look at that piece too closely if she wasn't going to."

I started to head back to the beach house I was staying in; the sun almost set at this point. My stomach growled, reminding me I was hungry as well and I would need to figure something out to eat.

"I don't know what it feels like to love more than one person romantically at a time, but I know your sister does, and she makes it work. If you're struggling, talk to one of the guys. Ollie and Ty would know how you're feeling. I'm not saying you'll find yourself in a similar situation, but if you're worried about it, I think you'll feel better if you have all the information. You were always one who liked to be prepared as a child."

Climbing the stairs that led to the back of the property, I thought about what she said and how right she was. I didn't do well with uncertainty. Even if this wasn't the direction my life went in, maybe I needed to figure out if I could be okay with it first, and there was no time like the present to do that. Fin was hiding, giving me the perfect time to figure out my own mind and heart.

"You're absolutely right, Mom. Thanks. I'll give Cohen a call and see if he has any leads. It's a good place to start."

"I'm so glad I could help. I've been worried about you. Let me know if you need anything else. I love you, Son."

"Love you too, Mom."

I ended the call, sliding it back into my pocket as I walked over to the water pump. Turning it on, I rinsed my feet and shins free of sand. I snagged a towel off the rail that had been lying in the sun, and I dried my feet as I hopped into the back door.

Walking into the kitchen, I debated if I wanted to fix something or order in tonight before I dug my head out of my ass and called the one person I should've called from the start.

"I ordered some Chinese food," a voice said as I turned on the overhead light.

"Jesus Christ!" I shouted, jumping back at the sound. When I realized I wasn't about to be attacked, I stopped, holding the doorway as my heart returned to normal.

"Why am I not surprised you're here?" I said, bending at the waist as I peered at him.

"Have you been thinking about me, pretty boy?" he teased.

He slid off the barstool he'd been perched on and walked toward me. As he neared, I took in his tall frame, disheveled dark blond hair, and the wrinkles on his clothes. Cohen could tease all he wanted, deny he felt more for Fin than just a friend, but the facts were staring at me in the face. I could either be brave and face them like my mom suggested or keep my head buried in the sand, potentially losing her forever.

Since I was finding I had a strong dislike for sand, I think it was time to face this obstacle head-on and discover where that left me.

"I was actually going to call you. We need to talk." I righted myself, placing my hands on my hips as I stared him down. He wasn't a skinny nerd like you'd think a tech genius would be, but my years of hockey had him beat on the muscle side.

"Oh?" He stopped his forward approach, and leaned back against the counter, crossing his arms. "You know, when I broke into your house, I thought it would be harder to get you to listen to me." He smiled like he'd already won. "Go on, what do you have to say?"

"I want to help you find Fin, and I think we should talk about your feelings for my girlfriend."

He stared at me, his eyes searching for something. He wasn't teasing or making light of the situation for once, showing me he could be serious when needed.

"Now, I'm really glad I ordered Chinese food. This will be a better conversation over some noodles and rice."

Relaxing, I walked to the fridge and pulled out two beers, handing him one. "So, where do we start?"

Cohen smiled, and I realized I didn't hate the guy. In fact, he was pretty easy to get along with when he wasn't incessantly flirting with me. The doorbell rang just as my stomach growled again, and I was thankful it was one less decision I'd have to make tonight.

As he paid the delivery person and placed copious amounts of food on the table, I sat down, feeling more clear than I had all week. It seemed the ocean had helped to at least bring me to the place I needed to be to face what I'd been hiding from.

"I have an idea of where she is and how we can intercept her," Cohen said, scooping out some food.

"You have my attention."

He handed me a carton, and I began to eat, listening to his plan. When he finished, I nodded, wiping my mouth.

"I'm in. Now, how do you feel about Fin?"

Six

FINLEY

Two weeks had passed and I had nothing to show for my time away except a mild addiction to vending machine mini donuts. Blackhawk had been quiet the past week, and I wondered if he'd somehow caught wind of my thoughts and knew what I was up to. Not that I was up to much of anything other than becoming a slob.

Looking around my new hotel room, I realized how disgusting I'd become. Wrappers littered the floor, soda bottles tumbled out of the trash can, and the few outfits I had were strewn about.

"Jeez, I've turned into Henry," I mumbled. Since I only had myself for company, I'd gotten used to talking aloud so I wouldn't feel so alone. I avoided thinking how sad that was.

Heaving myself off the bed, I sniffed my shirt, the stench making my nose curl up. I smelled worse than my brother's gym bag.

Okay, first things first, I needed to clean up. I couldn't think in this pigsty. No wonder I hadn't made any progress. I'd fallen into a rabbit hole and forgotten to check for light every now and then. Shoving all the wrappers into a new trash bag, I sat it and the one with bottles outside my door. Opening the curtains, I squinted as the sun filtered into the room, shining some light into the dark space. Tiny dust particles floated around, making it even more obvious I needed to get out of this room. I was becoming one with the dust.

Grabbing all of my clothes, I shoved them into a laundry bag. I'd have to figure something out there. I hadn't thought the limited amount of outfits through when I'd packed. I was tired of wearing the same three things. Even off the grid, I still wanted my fashion, it seemed.

"You can take the girl out of fashion school, but you can't take fashion out of the girl," I chided, laughing at myself.

Okay. I was losing it. Perhaps a stroll to get food would be wise. Nodding my head, I made my way to the bathroom, determined to make myself clean.

Thirty minutes later, I smelled better and felt like a human again. Placing a blonde wig on my head, I pulled out some makeup and applied eyeliner and lipstick. Stepping away from the mirror, I found a new version of myself staring back.

"Time to be a badass," I whispered.

Grabbing my bag of dirty clothes, I'd head to the front desk to see if they had any laundry services. I wasn't expecting much, but it never hurt to ask. The elevator was quiet as it descended, and I quickly made it to the bottom floor. The nice thing about this hotel was how empty it seemed to be. Probably not for them, but it worked well for me wanting to stay hidden.

"Good afternoon, ma'am. How can we help you today?" the lady at the desk asked. God, I loved the south and their hospitality.

"Um, yes, I wondered if you had laundry services or knew a nearby place?"

"There's a laundromat around the corner open 24-7. Would you like me to draw you a map?" she asked.

"Sure, that'd be helpful." I'd been hoping they had one on-site so I wouldn't have to sit with them. But it was better than dirty clothes. I'd have to grab some more in the meantime.

Taking the paper, I stepped out of the hotel, shielding my eyes from the sun. I looked left and right and decided to go right first. A few food places were open already, and people went to and fro. I spotted the laundromat and peeked in, checking out the establishment.

Continuing on my walk, I found a little boutique a few feet further down that snagged my interest. Stepping into it, I was able to find a few things to add to my wardrobe and help me not run out of clothes as quickly. Feeling energized by the new threads, I decided to grab some food and eat there, hoping the social interaction would be good for me. I'd never been one to be a hermit, so going two weeks without interacting with more than the housekeeper was starting to get to me.

A bar a block over caught my eye, so I stepped in, blinking as my eyes adjusted to the darker environment. The place wasn't busy since it was late afternoon, so I made my way to the bar and placed my bags on an empty stool. It felt easier to sit at the bar since I was alone. I looked out into the space, people watching as I waited for the bartender to walk over.

"What can I get you, doll?"

"I'd like the cheeseburger. Hold the onion with a side of onion rings. And the largest Diet Coke you have."

He stopped, raising his eyebrows. "Hold the onion, but onion rings?"

"Yep." I nodded, not feeling I needed to explain myself. He laughed, shaking his head.

"They taste different," a rich voice said as they sat on a barstool over from me.

I turned toward the sound, finding myself ensnared in deep chocolate eyes. They reminded me of chocolate brownies with a layer of caramel mixed in. I tried to catch the gold strands, but they seemed to move with the light. That was when I realized I'd been staring at this guy, moving my head to see his eyes better.

Placing my head on my hand, I pretended to have been looking for a spot to put my elbow. "Exactly. He gets it," I said, turning back to the bartender to find he was no longer there. "Hmph."

Patting the counter, I tried to ignore the chuckle I could hear next to me. I did not need to turn and acknowledge him. Nope. I did not need to. With a strength I didn't know I possessed, I managed to keep my gaze focused straight ahead for a solid minute.

When I finally gave in to the urge to turn, I let out a breath, realizing I'd been holding it simultaneously. It sputtered over my lips, making the guy laugh.

"Easy there."

His voice sounded like he was perpetually laughing at you, keeping a secret only he knew. I could tell he was the type of guy that would ruin me, and for once, I was glad I wasn't on the market. Well, I hoped I wasn't.

The knowledge that Asa was out there made my mood drop, and I turned back to the front, this time having no difficulty keeping my gaze there.

"Sorry if I offended you," the guy said a few minutes later, a hint of remorse in his voice I wasn't expecting.

"No, I just remembered someone I miss."

"Ah. Far from home?"

"Yes, but don't think you can kidnap me, and no one would notice. Because they would. In fact, I have to check in every 30 minutes, so, yeah." I crossed my arms, lifting my chin. *Try to steal me now, potential kidnapper.*

He chuckled, holding his hands up in a placating gesture. "No plans to kidnap you here. But that's good to know about the check-in. That's smart."

When he acknowledged my thinking, it did something to me. A fluttery feeling beneath my breastplate began to emerge, and I found my cheeks heating. Ah, sugar sticks, I was blushing. I didn't need to be blushing over a random guy.

Clearing my throat, I pulled out my phone to pretend it was

time to check-in. It seemed to work as he didn't interrupt me again. My food came out a few minutes later, and I dug in, realizing how starved I was. Those vending machine donuts only went so far.

"I'm impressed," the guy said when I'd cleared my plate, only a burned onion ring left behind.

Shrugging, I decided it was better to not engage with this guy to save myself from embarrassment. I waved the bartender over once I was done, ready to put some distance between the too handsome stranger with the deep voice and magic eyes and me.

"Can I grab my check?"

"Sure thing. Do you need anything else?"

"Nope. I'm going to run to the little girls' room, but I'll be back."

He tapped the bar as I slid off, walking down the little hallway with my bags. If I was going to sit and wait for things to be clean, I'd better wash them all. Slipping on the new things, I tossed the tags into the trash and turned in the mirror, checking them out. I'd gone with a simple blue jean skirt that had some rips in it and a navy-blue sleeveless polka-dotted shirt that had a cute bow in the front. It paired well with my Chucks. I looked cute. Not that I was trying to impress anyone. Nope.

Grabbing everything, I walked out and relaxed when I saw the guy was no longer at the bar. I sighed, even if I was a little disappointed he was gone. Looking for the receipt, I realized there wasn't anything in my spot either.

Motioning for the bartender, I waved him over. He looked at me oddly, probably realizing I'd changed.

"Can I help you, ma'am?"

"Um yeah, I thought you were getting my check for me?"

"Oh, the guy you were with paid for them both. He said he'd wait for you outside." The bartender looked at me funny like I was the one imagining things.

"What?" I asked, even though I'd heard him clearly. He started to explain again when I waved him off, turning to walk out.

Shielding my eyes from the brightness of the sun, I looked in both directions, but didn't see anyone.

Why on earth would he pay for my meal? I couldn't let the thought go, and I thought about it all through the next few hours as I sat at the laundromat waiting for my clothes to dry.

Just who was that guy?

A FEW DAYS LATER, I FINALLY HAD A RESPONSE BACK FROM Blackhawk, and now indecision and regret sat heavy in my belly. I needed to make sure that I didn't lose myself in the hunt this time. That I didn't let my need to be right or prove I was smarter make me lose everything I had waiting back in Utah for me. I refused to think they wouldn't be there. So for now, I was happy in denial mode, believing everything would work out if I could just show Blackhawk he wasn't as good as he thought he was.

Blackhawk: So, that job? You interested?
Oblivion: Yep. Where have you been?
Blackhawk: I had something come up. It's not important.
Oblivion: Because that's not cryptic.
Blackhawk: Are you wanting to play our game, little hacker? A trade for a trade?

Thoughts of nights spent trading secrets rushed me, and I tried to blink them back, but they filled my mind with teenage angst and longing. Blackhawk was too charming. He had been from the start.

FINLEY, AGE 16

C:/Enter your name

C:/Oblivion

C:/Welcome Oblivion. You will be assigned to a team.

An email popped up with a web address. Clicking on it, I was directed to a closed server on the dark web. My fingers itched to type as I waited for others to populate the chat. Adrenaline pumped through me that I'd made it this far.

I didn't want to seem too eager, so I sat back as they started to chat, observing their interaction so I could know how to play it.

Mongoose: Hi. Is this our team?

Blackhawk: Hi Goose? Can I call you Goose? Yes, looks like it's the four of us.

Obsidian: Really? Why must you always be in the same chats as me?

Blackhawk: Because my awesomeness makes up for your boringness.

Obsidian: That doesn't make sense. You're the worst.

Obsidian: See, you scared the other member away.

Blackhawk: Nah, that was your lameness.

Blackhawk: Hi. Don't be scared. He's mostly harmless.

Oblivion: I'm not scared. I'm just observing you guys like animals in a zoo.

Blackhawk: Oh, what animals are we?

Obsidian: Great, you're both dumb. Can we get to business and leave the animal talk for another time? Preferably when I'm not there.

Oblivion: Sure, sour puss. You'd definitely be a baboon, by the way.

Blackhawk: Okay, Oblivion. You're cool. I like your wit.

Obsidian: Our first task is to infiltrate a business and create a dummy account without being detected. I'll handle logistics. Hawk, you got security? What're your skill sets Oblivion and Mongoose?

Panic rushed through me. They seemed so much more professional than me. I could tell this wasn't their first time. I needed to sound like I was competent.

Oblivion: Um, hacking.

Crap that did not sound smart! That didn't even sound confident.

Obsidian: Fine, play it cool. I'll give you a job, and you'll just have to deal with it.

Phew, that somehow worked.

Obsidian signed off.

Private message from Blackhawk.

Blackhawk: Okay, so realness here. You have no idea what he was asking do you?
Oblivion: Was it that obvious? This is my first time joining something like this.
Blackhawk: Sid assumes everyone is a smartass, so you're good on that front, and Mongoose just seems along for the ride. What's your hacking skill?
Oblivion: Why should I tell you? What's in it for you?
Blackhawk: Fine, how about a trade. A secret for a secret? We don't know one another, so what's the harm in sharing?

I thought about it and realized he was right. He didn't know me, so I could be honest with him without it costing too much.

Oblivion: Okay. I'm interested. But you owe me two since you already know one thing about me—that I'm clueless.

Blackhawk: Budding extortionist. I like it. Fine. One secret to even us out. I'm scared of the dark and have to sleep with a night light.

Oblivion: Wow. I'm speechless.

Blackhawk: I know. It's a shocker for most people.

Oblivion: I'm rolling my eyes so hard I hope you can feel them.

Blackhawk: Okay, spill. Why are you here if it's your first club initiation?

Oblivion: I'm not sure what my hacking skill area is. I taught myself and took a few classes. I'm here because I want to find out information about a friend.

Blackhawk: What things have you done well? What did you use as your entrance piece?

Oblivion: I created a way for teenagers to mask their location so their parents don't know where they are. Is that a thing?

Blackhawk: Yes, that's pretty badass. It sounds like Bait and Switch then. Just say that if someone asks.

Oblivion: Thank you. Your turn.

Blackhawk: I was hoping you'd forget that part. Fine.

Blackhawk: Hacking is the only thing that I'm good at. There I said it.

Oblivion: How is that possible? Shouldn't you be good at math and other things, then?

Blackhawk: You'd think that, but no. Nothing else sticks but hacking. I can do it in my sleep.

Oblivion: Wow, that's kind of sad.

Blackhawk: Geez, thanks. Well, I gotta go. Time to turn on the night light. Be good, kid.

Oblivion: I'm not a kid!

Blackhawk: Sure.

Blackhawk signed off.

PRESENT DAY

From that point forward, a trade was established, and we shared secrets back and forth like mono. Him bringing it up again was like a stab to my heart that I wasn't ready for.

> **Oblivion**: No trade. What's the job?
> **Blackhawk**: You're no fun anymore. Fine. I need one of your specialties. A Trojan horse.
> **Oblivion**: Done. Send me the specs.
> **Blackhawk**: Ah, no chatting?
> **Oblivion**: I have nothing to say to you. I need the job. That's it. I'll send you my banking information too. I want to be paid half upfront.
> **Blackhawk**: Fine. I'll send it over. You're not as fun anymore.

Oblivion signed off.

My heart hammered, and I was sure it was about to beat out of my chest. I hadn't gained as much information as I wanted, but it was a start. The worst part was that I hadn't expected jumping back into this role would be so difficult. Especially when memories kept flooding me. I needed to find him soon and end this before I forgot why I was tracking him in the first place.

Seven

FINLEY

The alarm started to blare, and I cursed as I twisted the lock pick to the right. It had been easy to break into my room when I'd practiced, but this office building was causing more problems than I'd anticipated. I took a deep breath and twisted the pick again, finally hearing the satisfying click as the door unlocked. Wiping my brow, I skirted into the room and raced to the alarm panel.

"Guys, you there?" I asked, tapping the phone app Blackhawk had developed for us to use to chat while in the field. It disguised our voices and location but allowed us to have real-time access to one another.

"Yeah, that was close," Obsidian said. Even though his voice was masked, I could still hear the reprimand he wanted to give me. I'd come to feel Obsidian didn't respect me, but I didn't take it personally. He didn't respect anyone, from what I could gather. "If you get caught, you're on your own."

"Gee, thanks," I huffed, rolling my eyes.

"You know we wouldn't do that," Blackhawk said. The only reason I knew it was him was the familiar kindness in his voice. Our games of trading secrets had become a regular thing, and I was beginning to understand the mysterious hacker on a real level, unlike the other two.

71

"Mongoose, you ready with the alarm key?" I asked, popping the panel off.

"Yeah, it's, um, 85923."

Typing in the code, I held my breath as I waited to see if it worked. I only had another minute before the police would be dispatched.

Error flashed up on the screen, and my nerves racketed up. I was beginning to regret volunteering to be the one to go out into the field. It had felt like a good option at the time to make myself valuable to the team. I wouldn't admit it because I was too nervous to say I didn't know how to do the other things. Nope. Obsidian didn't need another reason to hate me.

"Um, that didn't work. Do you have another one?" I asked, some of the anxiety creeping up my voice, making it high-pitched to the point I wasn't sure the app could mask it.

"Hold on, Oblivion. I got you," Blackhawk soothed, calming me by his mere presence.

"That's another strike, Mongoose," Obsidian yelled. "One more, and you're off the team."

"I… I'm sorry. It should work. He must've updated it or something."

"Can you save the bickering for later and give me the fucking code already! I'm this close to being arrested, and I'm too pretty for prison," I shouted, stopping their argument.

"Type in 85932," Blackhawk said. Trusting him, I typed it in, holding my breath. I looked around for the closest exit. Thankfully, this one worked.

"See, I just had the last numbers inverted," Mongoose argued. Obsidian and he started to go back and forth, and I couldn't take their distraction anymore, so I muted the channel, focusing on my task.

Scanning the room, I looked for the thing I'd come for. When smoke began to fill the space, I coughed, not understanding. Turning, I was met with a purple elephant and a polka-dotted bear chasing me down the hallway as I searched for a window. Sounds of shouting followed me as I jumped.

Sitting up, I gasped for breath, the nightmare having felt too real. My skin felt clammy, and my neck was sweaty. The AC kicked on, rattling to life, and I jumped, the sound scaring me but bringing me more into the present. Goosebumps rose up on my skin, and I rubbed my arms.

"You're here. You're not there. It's in the past." I rocked back and forth as I said the statement repeatedly, trying to rebury a night from my past I'd rather forget.

Once I'd calmed down, I looked over at the nightstand, reading the clock. *4:00 am.* No time like the present to get started on revenge. The nightmare was a good reminder of what was at stake. Climbing out of bed, I took a quick shower to clean off the remnants of the dream. Sitting down at my computer, I got to work. I could sleep when I was back with my friends and family.

A FEW DAYS LATER, I'D BEEN ABLE TO TRACE THE LINK THAT Blackhawk had sent me, but it led to a dummy IP address. I knew he was better than that to lead me straight to him, but I hoped he'd be lax enough not to go through the effort of cloaking his location.

"Guess I'll have to trust that he's not sending me into a trap," I mumbled, getting dressed. Sliding on the leather pants I'd left the house in, I paired them with one of the new tops I'd gotten, my black heels, and a black jacket. I looked like a real Femme Fatale, helping me lean into the part I was playing.

Throwing some essentials into my messenger bag, I picked up the few things in the room, working harder to keep it clean. I reminded myself how much nicer it would feel to come back to a clean room afterward. Checking my watch again, I adjusted my glasses and headed out. No time like the present.

Sitting outside a dry cleaners a few hours later, I began to wonder if I'd encoded the coordinates wrong. The bus bench had grown warm throughout the day, but it was beginning to become colder with the sun setting. Sitting on metal in the cold was not really my forte, and these pants did nothing to hold in the warmth. When another ten minutes went by, and there was still no activity from the dry cleaners, I decided to move into the cozy coffee shop on the corner. I'd have a more angled view of this place, but I didn't think it would matter all that much. I was pretty certain I'd been had. I was just too stubborn to admit it.

Slinging my bag onto my shoulder, I ducked my head from the cameras, adjusting the pink wig I was sporting today. I kept changing my looks, hoping it would buy me some time before the others found me.

Entering the coffee shop, the few guests ignored me, all too busy on their own computers, as I made my way to the counter. Quickly, I ordered a cookie and lemonade, deciding the last thing I needed right now was caffeine. I was jittery enough on my own. The tapping foot as I waited was a clear indicator.

The waitress eyed me but didn't say anything as she handed me my order. She probably thought I was a junkie. Oh well.

Taking my goodies, I scouted out a place near the front window that was semi-private, allowing me to have my back to the wall so no one could see my screen. I needed to use the free Wi-Fi and didn't need nosey people peeking over my shoulder trying to guess what I was doing.

As I settled, no one had even glanced over at me, so maybe I was among my people and wouldn't need to worry. I checked on the dry cleaners but still found it dark and empty.

I was to look for a man with a cowboy hat. Once I made contact with him, then he'd give me something. Blackhawk hadn't said what, just that I would know when I saw it.

It had taken me a few days to get to this sleepy town of South Carolina. I didn't know if it was where Blackhawk was or just where his contact was going to be. It was strange traveling this much on my own. I was so used to always being part of a pair with Henry, or Sawyer, and then Asa. Being here as just Fin felt odd, but

I didn't hate it as much as I'd expected. I was learning new things about myself, which was the good part.

Checking one more time for the mysterious man, I signed into a secure server to see if I could do any more leg work on just who Blackhawk was. I realized that finding him physically was much harder than I'd anticipated. While I'd tracked him down online, it meant nothing if I couldn't see him face to face to exact my revenge.

Though, I had to admit my plan on what I was going to do when that step came was just as shoddy. I really had jumped into this with both feet, not even looking to see where I was landing. Which was both good and bad.

Good, because typically, I was so anal about things it made everyone around me bonkers.

Bad, because the longer this took me, the more time I missed away from my boyfriend and friends.

It was time to let some of my "Finleyness" out to roam. I needed to be more prepared, so when I got to the end of this revenge list, I knew how it ended.

Before my big scandal, the one I tried to not think about anymore, I'd been working on a program to find Sariah. I just needed to tweak it and add the information I knew about Blackhawk, and then maybe I'd have better luck finding him.

Signing in to the program was easy, and I found my fingers typing in the familiar code as the prompts came up. Every now and then, I'd peek up to make sure the contact wasn't there, but I still had no sign of the man. I passed the security measures with one last prompt, and I found myself in the program.

The familiar page stared at me, and emotions I hadn't felt in years began to permeate my being. I'd been such a lost and confused teenager, and staring at the screen, I remembered how desperate I'd been to feel something, anything other than the emptiness inside me.

It had been a hopeless recklessness that led me to my choices, and I briefly wondered if I was repeating the same pattern of mistakes as I had back then.

I didn't dwell on that for too long, shoving everything back into the depths of my mind where it belonged. I could dive into those thoughts later when I had the time, but now I needed to focus. Glancing up one more time, I almost missed the man I'd been waiting all day to see.

I'd been expecting to see nothing, so I had to look twice to catch the black cowboy hat as it moved away from the door and around the alley.

"Fudge!" I hissed, jumping up and slinging my bag over my shoulder as I grabbed my computer in one hand. I knocked into a few chairs, startling the other customers, but I couldn't focus on it, needing to get outside before I lost the contact. While I'd been happy with my corner for privacy earlier, I cursed it now as I tried to make my way around bags and legs to get to the door.

The humid air hit me as I made it outside, and I dashed across the street as fast as possible, once again cursing my selected footwear. "Why do I keep insisting on wearing heels?" I muttered as I careened around the corner, catching sight of the man as he ducked into a door.

I clicked and clacked down the alley toward the door as fast as I could. Lurching forward, I grabbed the handle a millisecond before it closed. I stood with it in my grasp for a second, amazed it had worked. Realizing I was losing time, I pulled it back and slid in, stopping as my eyes began to adjust to the darkness. It looked like the back of a bar or club, the kegs and boxes of beer along one side cluing me in. I began to make my way down the hall, watching for random boxes as I went.

Movement further down the hallway caught my eye, and I stepped around cases and bottles as I tried to catch up to him again. I didn't know if I should make myself known and call out to him or just follow at a distance. I needed to get more information from Blackhawk next time.

"Next time?" I admonished myself, realizing how quickly I'd seemed to have lost the plot. I was here to stop him, not join his club of illegal activities.

Music and voices grew louder the further down the hall I went, so I wasn't surprised when I turned and found myself in a dive bar. The only problem, the bar was full of men with cowboy hats.

I stood there, mouth open, trying to find the one I'd been chasing. "What? How? Huh?"

"You okay there, darling?" a southern drawl asked. Turning, I found a woman dressed in short shorts and a flannel shirt tied at her waist.

"Um, I was meeting someone, and they came in here, but now I can't find them. Is there something going on?"

"It's Friday night," she said, like that explained it.

"Right. Tourist," I said, pointing. She laughed a little and then pointed at a sign that read "Friday Night Square Dancing."

"If you're staying, you better pair up quick before all the good ones are taken. You don't want to get stuck with handsy Steve." She pointed to a man who looked like he barely had any teeth and smiled over at us.

Doing a full-body shudder, I thanked the woman and made my way to the bar. Maybe if I sat there, I'd be able to find the one guy in a cowboy hat I was supposed to meet. Sounded plausible.

Shoving my laptop back into my bag, I zipped it and squeezed between two couples at the end. The only open stool was sticky, and I hoped it was only from spilled drinks. Perching on it carefully, I looked out into the crowd, surveying all the men with black hats.

After twenty minutes, I realized the futility of trying to find one person in a bar full of people who all looked alike. It was impossible. Especially when I didn't even know his name or what he looked like. Sighing, I slumped off the stool, ignoring the squelching sound, and walked toward the door. I was only a few feet away when a waitress collided with me, spilling her tray of drinks all over me.

"Son of a biscuit!"

"I'm so sorry, hun. Here, let me help you." She started to pat me dry with the cocktail napkins, but it was of no use. I was covered from head to toe in the sticky substance.

"Don't bother." Dropping my head, I sulked out of the bar as everyone watched me. I felt humiliated, but at least I had the good fortune that no one knew me. The biggest inconvenience was the fact that this was my last set of clean clothes. Looked like another long night at the laundromat. Sighing, I trudged along. Each step was crucifying as I made a sticky sound when my feet lifted from the pavement. I was so consumed with my situation I didn't see the man outside the bar leaning against the wall until I practically ran into him.

"Ma'am," he said, startling me. His voice sounded familiar, but I couldn't make out any features with most of his face in the shadow, hidden below his cowboy hat.

"Sorry, sir. I wasn't paying attention."

"I believe I'm to give you this." He held out an envelope, placing it in my hand. "Good day."

He was gone before I could call out to him, my body frozen to the spot at my luck. Had he seen me inside? How did he know who I was but not the other way around?

Opening my bag, I realized too late that the contents of it were now sodden and bright red. I was too upset to check my computer; the device's fate was pretty much guaranteed to be ruined.

Trudging back to the hotel, I tried to come up with possible outcomes and solutions. But I had to face the facts. I was woefully unprepared, and the only thing I had succeeded at was being covered in a sticky mess. Not even the fun kind.

Maybe it was time to call it quits. I'd been wrong. I wasn't cut out for this. It was just another area of my life that I failed at.

I'd gotten so good at pretending I had it all together, I'd almost convinced myself the same, but the reality was, I had no idea what I was doing or where to go from here. It was time to throw in the towel and face the facts.

Finley Reyes was a loser. I'd known it at seventeen, and it was still true, six years later.

Eight

FINLEY

Tears streamed down my face as I stared at the destroyed mess of my baby. There was no bag of rice big enough to save it from the liquid damage that tray of drinks had caused. It was toast, ruined.

And I'd never felt more lost in my life.

In a weird way, my computer had become my safety blanket, my emotional support. It had been there for me when everything felt too chaotic and out of reach, providing me with a way to try to find some answers or even some hope. That was why I'd joined the MidKnight Guild, to begin with. It was a place for me to connect with others who didn't know me as the little sister, or the screwup, and hopefully uncover the lies we'd been told about Sariah.

And it had been a safe haven for a while. Obsidian and Black-hawk had become my friends.

FINLEY, AGE 16

Obsidian: Has anyone heard from Mongoose? He missed another check-in.

Oblivion: No, I haven't. Did he ever send over the files from the mark he was working on?

Blackhawk: Yeah, I got them. He said he had some things to take care of in his personal life, but would be back on for the next task.

Obsidian: I wish someone would've told me. I'm team leader.

Blackhawk: Only because no one else wanted it. Don't get too high on yourself or I'll sic Oblivion on you.

Blackhawk: Speaking of, I can't believe you changed the name of the mean girl so that every teacher called her "Anita Hoare" on the first day of school roll call. That's hilarious and hardcore.

Oblivion: Been looking at my application again? Anyone ever tell you that you have some stalker tendencies?

Blackhawk: All the time. Don't ignore the compliment, little hacker.

Oblivion: That was a pretty great one. By the end of the day, her face was so red that I almost felt bad for her.

Obsidian: What about when you programmed the teacher's phone to make a moaning sound every time he got a message, Hawk? He never could figure out how to make it stop. Now, that was hilarious.

Blackhawk: That's because I disabled all of his settings. He was an asshole. Always trying to look down girls' tops and let the popular kids get away with whatever they wanted. It wasn't right. Especially when that one guy superglued your seat to your butt. He needed to be taught a lesson.

Oblivion: Wait? Do you guys know each other in real life? I just thought it was from other hacker clubs.

Obsidian: We've known each other for years, actually. We were placed in the same foster home for a while and then ended up at a group home around the same time.

Blackhawk: Yep, and now Sid is my roommate.

Oblivion: So, you're both in college? Or high school?

Obsidian: Getting a little too personal, Oblivion. We can share what we wish, but asking directly is frowned upon.

Blackhawk: Oblivion is cool, Sid. We can trust him. Yes, we're in college.

Oblivion: Well, if we're sharing information, then you should know I'm not a him, I'm a her.

Blackhawk: Really? That explains a lot, actually, but also badass, Oblivion.

Obsidian: Oh great, now Hawk will be obsessed with you. Before he starts mooning over the hacker chick, is everyone prepared for the next task?

Oblivion: Yep. I'm ready.

Blackhawk: I'm not mooning. Geez.

Blackhawk: But yes, your royal pain in my ass, I'm ready.

Obsidian: Good. We can't mess up another task. I'll see you all tomorrow at 22:30. Mongoose better be there or he's off the team.

Obsidian signed off.

Private message from Blackhawk.

Blackhawk: How do you feel about the task? You prepared? Do you need any help? I know things went a little haywire last time.

Oblivion: I'm good. That wasn't because of me. Why are you so invested?

Blackhawk: Something about you makes me want you to succeed. That's all, little hacker.

Oblivion: So, it's not because I have tits, and now you think I can't hack it?

Blackhawk: Oh, it's definitely because you have tits. But not in the way you're thinking.

Blackhawk: Sid can be an ass, but he wasn't lying. I already thought you were cool when I thought you were a guy. So, now, it's blowing my mind.

Oblivion: Um, not sure what to say now.

Blackhawk: Did I make it awkward? Sorry, I have a terrible habit of doing that.

Oblivion: No, it's just… guys don't really talk to me. So, I'm not sure how to take this. I feel like I'm about to walk into a bad '90s teen movie, and I'm some kind of bet.

Blackhawk: Well, kids at school are all schmucks. Everyone is trying to impress each other so that they don't take time to notice the actual cool people.

Oblivion: Speaking from experience?

Blackhawk: Maybe. I wasn't a jock, and being a foster kid made it more difficult to blend in. Remember, I'm horrible at school, and I have my whole bad-boy attitude going on for me, but I'm a nerd at heart. Shh, don't tell anyone.

Oblivion: You're secret's out now. I'm going to blackmail you so hard.

Blackhawk: Badass, Oblivion. Not that it would matter. College is a different game. I'm still not cool, but I found my people.

Oblivion: Hacker people?

Blackhawk: Some, like Sid, but just others who are intelligent and crafty.

Oblivion: You sound like you're building a nerdy gang.

Blackhawk: Maybe I am. Want to be part of it?

Oblivion: Sure, I'm your girl if you need someone to make you costumes.

Blackhawk: You're so much more than that, little hacker.

Oblivion: If you say so. Everything feels so bleak right now. The only light is this.

Blackhawk: Have you had any luck with your friend?

Oblivion: No. I'm beginning to wonder if maybe she is dead.

Blackhawk: I've heard of another hacker who might be able to help. Do you want his info?

Oblivion: Really? That would be awesome. Thank you.

Blackhawk: No problem. Just don't forget who your favorite hacker friend is.

Oblivion: Definitely, Obsidian.

Blackhawk: Oh, you hit me in my core. You know, I'm much prettier and smell better. I don't think the guy showers. You definitely don't want to be around that.

Oblivion: Mmm, BO, my favorite boy smell.

Blackhawk: Hey, little hacker, boys your age are dumb. Just saying.

Oblivion: Still convinced I'm a kid?

Blackhawk: No, but I know you're still younger than me.

Oblivion: Good thing we're just friends then. That's allowed, right?

Blackhawk: Sure thing, little hacker.

Blackhawk: I'll send you Chaos info. I've never talked to him, but I hear things, and he's good. Some brainiac already through school.

Oblivion: Thank you.

Blackhawk signed off.

PRESENT DAY

Staring at the screen, I blinked the memory away, not needing to add the loss and deception of my first real friends to the mix. Looking at my computer, it was almost sinister how it looked the same on the outside, but nothing remained the same on the inside. Kind of eerie how I was the same. Trying for the billionth time, I hit the on button, but nothing happened.

"Screw it," I sighed, closing the lid.

Pulling out my burner phone, I texted Blackhawk that I had an unfortunate computer malfunction, but I had the envelope and to let me know what he wanted me to do with it. I tossed the phone down as I laid back on the bed, and debated the same thing I did every night.

Was I making a mistake? It felt like it at this point. I had nothing to show for my efforts.

Maybe I had pushed all the blame onto him? These earlier memories of our friendship were clouding my judgment, making it difficult to remember the hurt and pain at the end. This was the problem with pushing your emotions down. You almost forgot the part that hurt.

Picking up my phone, I rolled over to my stomach and opened the cloud storage app I had. My thumb hovered over the photos icon and I clicked it, deciding a little pain might do me good.

Pictures of Asa and me, Sawyer and the BOSH crew, our time at TAS filled my screen as I flicked through them. When the album was done, it automatically opened the next one and I froze as screenshots filled the screen. My mental shields were down, my security blanket gone, allowing the flashback to take over before I could stop it.

FINLEY, AGE 16

Obsidian: Check the news.
Oblivion: Why? What's going on?
Obsidian: Just do it. I'll wait.

Rolling my eyes, I minimized the chat and clicked a new tab on the browser. My fingers hesitated as I tried to figure out what news source I should look up. Deciding to do a broad search, I typed in the local station and opened them in one tab, and one of the national news channels in another. Opening them both, I didn't have to scroll down far to find what I assumed he was talking about.

A building was on fire, and it was surrounded by emergency vehicles. Clicking on the video, I watched as the crews rushed to put it out to no avail. When a part of the structure fell, two people rushed out, a body slung over the arm of one of them. The reporter began talking and I only paid attention to parts of it as I searched the video for whatever clue Obsidian was referring to. He liked to send me tests to see if I could figure it out, so I had to assume this was one of those instances.

"... a teen body found... believed to be a club initiation... broken into... files stolen."

When the reporter said something about files, I zeroed in on her, giving her all of my focus. That was when I saw it, the tagline under her name.

Possible arson at the Magnolia House. An abandoned homeless shelter.

Bile rose up, and I pushed back my chair as I raced toward the bathroom. I managed to make it to the toilet as I heaved up my lunch and most of yesterday's contents as well.

"No, no, no, no, no," I cried, rocking back and forth. This couldn't be happening.

"Fin?" Henry yelled, stepping into my room. Quickly, I wiped my eyes and flushed the toilet, ridding it of my shame.

"Just a minute," I shouted, splashing some water on my face. It was time to be the perfect sister, not a possible homicidal hacker.

PRESENT DAY

Shaking my head, I cleared away the heavy fog of grief, shame, and regret that seemed to be my only companions these days. Wiping my eyes, I dropped the phone on the bed and rested my head on my arms. I hadn't thought about that night in years. I never did get to talk with Obsidian about it, and I supposed now I never would.

I laid on my arms for a while, lost in thoughts of what-ifs when the bed started to vibrate. I briefly wondered if I'd stumbled into one of those weird hotels and had a malfunctioning vibrating bed until I remembered I'd thrown down the burner. Moving my hand around, I searched for the device until I felt the hard shape in my hand. Pulling it to my face, I read the message across the screen.

Blackhawk: Open the envelope.

Sitting up, I reached over to the table I'd laid it on and dragged it to me. Ripping off the top, I peered inside, trying to figure out what it was. Sliding the paper and key out, I stared at the sheet, blinking, wondering if I had imagined things.

Want to play a game? Tag, you're it.

Blackhawk: Even with drinks spilled on you, you looked pretty, little hacker.
Oblivion: You were watching me? We're not going to get far in this job if you can't trust me.
Blackhawk: Confession time. I didn't have a job. I just wanted to meet you since you bailed on me all those years ago. I've been waiting for the opportunity for you to return. I've made the ultimate cat and mouse game for us.
Oblivion: Me? Bailed? I don't want to play your stupid game!
Blackhawk: That's too bad. If you change your mind, I'll be at the location for a while. If you can figure out the clue, you'll catch me first. If not, I'll leave you another.
Blackhawk: I've missed you. I'm glad you're back so we can play our games again. You'll want the prize at the end of this one.
Blackhawk: Game on, little hacker.

Rage coursed through me, and the earlier melancholy evaporated as a new emotion emerged.

Vengeance.

All the times I'd been made a fool of, all the situations at school where kids laughed at me, and all the little hoops I'd jumped through, it was never enough to prove my worth to any of them. I was tired of being the fool.

Fine. If he wanted to play a game, then we'd play.

Only this time, I wasn't a teenager with a crush. No, this time, I was a woman on a mission, and he just reminded me why.

Blackhawk acted like my friend, but he was a trickster, turning my whole world upside down for his own amusement. This time, I'd be the one laughing.

But first, I needed to make a phone call, or I wouldn't get anywhere.

My hand hovered over the keypad, but eventually, I made myself dial the number. As the phone rang, nerves skated up my arms, and I sucked in a breath as I waited for them to answer.

"Hello? Fin, is that you?"

"Hey. It's me. I, um, I need your help."

Nine

FINLEY

MILO CAME THROUGH AGAIN, SENDING ME TO A STORE TO PICK UP A computer he ordered for me. I was going to owe him a few dinners at this rate. I told him I'd pay him back once I could use my bank account since I only had a limited amount of cash and the debit card he gave me. My budget hadn't included buying a new computer, but he told me not to worry about it. I didn't feel right taking something else from him, so I would either mail him the money, donate it in his name, or send him something of equal value. It felt like the right thing to do.

That and I didn't like owing people.

Taking the shiny computer out of the box felt close to an aphrodisiac. It was sleek, and I couldn't help but smile that he'd gone for the rose gold. I sat petting it for a few seconds, okay, a few minutes before I finally opened the screen and turned it on.

The speed it booted up was amazing, and I realized I might've needed a new one longer than I'd realized. Thankfully, I was neurotic about saving everything to three different cloud servers, so it didn't take long to log in and regain all my files. I didn't know if I would've been able to deal if I'd lost all the years of hacker programs I'd developed or had gleaned from others.

Actually, no, I definitely wouldn't have been able to deal. I would've curled into a ball and sobbed and then called my brother to come and rescue me.

At least this way, I was still trying to fight the fight and regain my sense of self. *As long as you avoid thinking about that place,* my subconscious whispered. And ignore.

My email box blinked at me, begging me to click on it, but I found a new email from Asa each time I gave in to checking it. I was too worried to see if they were "I hate you" emails or "I love you" ones to read them.

Yeah, chickenshit needed to be my middle name after loser.

Focusing on the code Blackhawk had left me, I plugged it into a program and then pulled up the one I'd been working on before the whole "chase a cowboy" incident had left me in a sticky disaster.

Staring at the information needed, I realized I didn't have much to go on. I didn't know his real name. I knew he lived in the south at the time of initiation and was attending a state college with Obsidian. But I didn't know what he majored in or even if he had graduated. I didn't even know his eye or hair color. I would need to change the parameters to use this to find him.

Reaching into a new bag, I pulled out a pen and notebook. I'd had to replace them too, but fortunately, they were within my budget, and something I eagerly would shop for. Stationary was my jam.

Tapping the purple pen on the notebook, I tried to think of all the things I knew about Blackhawk.

College.
Foster care.
Roommates with Obsidian.
Scared of the dark.

Once bought me red stilettos.

~~Was funny and kind.~~ Nope, scratch that. He was annoying and an asshole.

Mid-twenties.

Not good at math.

Really good at staying hidden.

Part of a few hacker clubs.

Worked for some organization.

It was more than I'd had, but it wasn't a lot of identifying information. Based on how he'd covered himself at the bar with his cowboy hat, I couldn't even tell what his facial features were. Okay, so he was tall and had muscles. That was obvious. And his voice…

The realization hit me like a ton of bricks, and I knew why it had sounded familiar earlier. He'd been the guy at the bar, the one with the eyes I'd gotten lost in.

Nope, back that train up. I would not think the man who let me get arrested and ghosted me after had nice eyes. Big scoop of double nope.

So, what? He'd been following me for days? He knew who I was and how to locate me easily. Which meant his skills had improved, and I would be wasting my time trying to find a bread crumb if he didn't want me to.

But it also meant I had more information to enter into my database, and it might just be the thing that he didn't take into consideration.

Typing in dark hair, 6ft tall, brown eyes, light stubble, sharp jaw, well-built with muscles, and a deep voice into the search criteria, I realized I had just described every teenage heartthrob I had a crush on.

But surely, not all good-looking guys in their mid-twenties would have hacking skills. There had to be some criteria to filter out all the obvious people. I just had to keep digging.

Feeling slightly better and ignoring the mild attraction I had to the asshole, I switched over to the other program running through his code. When it beeped, I grinned, excited to have a location. Hopefully, he'd still be there four hours later, and I could end this tonight. But with the time it took for me to wallow and then go and get a new computer, my time might be up.

At least this time, I was prepared, and I'd be taking every precaution as I hunted his ass down.

He thought I was the mouse, but I'd show him he would be the one to fall into my trap in the end.

WALKING UP TO THE STOREFRONT, I DEBATED IF I SHOULD HAVE JUST waited until morning. It was close to midnight now, and everything within a mile radius was closed, making the street eerily dark. The bookstore in front of me looked like an odd place for him to be, but I was confident in my program to have figured out his clue.

Cloak-N-Dagger Books looked like a regular bookstore, but after some hacking into their system and a thorough search on the dark web, I'd found they were actually a secret hangout for a club. I wasn't sure which club yet as that was all hush, hush. But the fact that it was more than meets the eye had me believing this was the right place. It was just like Blackhawk to pick something like this. He liked his puzzles, after all.

Walking down the alley, I looked for the brick with the X on it. It had been painted with black light paint, so I used the app on my phone to scan over all the bricks. I wasn't sure if they would make it a real big X or if it would be tiny, and I didn't want to miss it if it was.

Finding it halfway down, I pulled it out, where a key card slot was now revealed. Taking the card that Blackhawk had given me, I slid it in, holding my breath that it would work. I nearly jumped with joy when it beeped green a few seconds later. The door hissed open, and I tugged at it, amazed at how it pulled away from the other bricks. They'd done an excellent job of making it appear as part of the wall.

Stepping into the dark corridor, I suddenly felt dread hit me that maybe I should've told someone where I was. Just another reckless decision I kept making for the books. Huh, that was funny, considering I was in a bookstore.

Strolling through the store, I shook off my dark thoughts as my whole body came alive with energy at the realization I was closer than I'd ever been to finding him. This could be it, the night I had my vengeance and got to return to my family. Maybe it was that giddy deliriousness that had me not watching my steps.

As soon as I stepped over the threshold into the store, a loud sound erupted, something popping over my head seconds before I was covered in a liquid. A squeal left me as I sputtered. I stood, frozen, not sure what had just happened.

"Tsk, Tsk, little hacker. You're gonna have to up your game if you want to catch me. Better luck next time, babe," a recording said, playing through the speakers.

I blinked, wiping the wetness from my eyes. "What is it with people dumping shit on me today?" I screamed, my frustration coming out at last. Thank God I'd left my computer at the hotel this time. If I had destroyed two in one day, I would call it quits. Computer endangerment and all that.

Lights began to flicker in a pattern, annoying me even more. When I realized it was morse code, I ran over to the counter, grabbing the first thing I could find that I could write on. Which happened to be a roll of register paper, but it would work. Grabbing the pen, I started to write the dots and dashes down. It began to repeat after about a minute, so I stopped, staring at it. I guess this was my next clue.

I smiled, feeling alive in a whole new way. This was what we'd excelled at together. Back before, he betrayed me and broke my heart.

FINLEY, AGE 17

> **Blackhawk**: Okay, little hacker, if you were deserted on an island, who and what would you take with you?
> **Oblivion**: I'd obviously take that nature survivalist guy and a big machete. No one would mess with me with Beer and a big knife.
> **Blackhawk**: Ah, babe, you're so cute. You don't even realize it.
> **Blackhawk**: Also, wise choice, but he might take offense if you call him Beer.
> **Oblivion**: What? Why? Isn't that his name?
> **Blackhawk**: No, little hacker. I'll wait.

My cheeks flamed, but I couldn't deny how happy I was either. Blackhawk made me feel seen in a way I never had before. Googling, I quickly realized my mistake.

> **Oblivion**: Well, I think it would be a joke between us because we'd be such good chums. Bear wouldn't mind at all.
> **Blackhawk**: I could see that. You're probably right.
> **Blackhawk**: You ready for a new puzzle? I've been working on it.
> **Oblivion**: Oh, yes, give me! But first… I have a truth for a truth for you.
> **Blackhawk**: Hit me with it. I live for these.
> **Oblivion**: I feel sad for you if that's true.
> **Oblivion**: Okay, my truth is that I sometimes hate that my brother gets to act broody, and my parents accept it, but if I

show any emotion that isn't pleasant, I'm called out. I don't begrudge my brother, he lost someone too, but I hate that he's allowed to actually grieve it while I'm told to smile.

Blackhawk: That's understandable that you would feel that way, little hacker. I don't know the whole story, but I know how close to this person you were. It's not fair that you can't grieve however you see fit.

Oblivion: Thank you, that means a lot knowing I'm not crazy.

Blackhawk: Okay, I'll give you a truth somewhat similar. I kind of had the opposite thing. Everyone told me to feel sad when my mom died, but I didn't. She was abusive and consistently high. I was relieved. That's horrible of me, but it was how I felt.

Oblivion: So basically, people need to keep their feelings to themselves and quit telling us how to feel?

Blackhawk: Yep. That sounds about right.

Oblivion: Thanks for the laugh. Now, send me the puzzle. I'm eager to crack this one to prove to you my superiority.

Blackhawk: Good luck, babe.

Blackhawk: And anytime, little hacker. I'm here. Always.

PRESENT DAY

Stopping at the staff bathroom, I used some paper towels to get as much of what I was now sure was glow-in-the-dark paint off me. The part of me that wanted to stay and snoop around and find the secret underground club struggled to leave, but I knew I needed to get back to my computer and solve this next clue before I lost him again.

Trudging back to the hotel, I kept replaying all the times Blackhawk had been kind to me, a true friend. It was why it hurt the worst when he betrayed me. Obsidian had always been stern, and

Mongoose, well, he didn't last long. In the end, it was Blackhawk who meant something to me and then he'd betrayed me.

I needed to confront him and find out why. I just wasn't sure if I was ready for the answer.

Stepping into the hotel room, the light flicked on, and I barely stopped myself from squealing for the second time tonight.

"I wondered when you would show up."

Ten

COHEN

Most people probably had several moments they wished they could redo in their lives. Me, I only had one. That might sound arrogant, but I strove to lead a life of no regrets. And for the most part, I'd been successful, living my life to the fullest. If I wanted to kiss a boy, I did. If I wanted to kiss a girl, I did. If I wanted to fly to New York, I did.

Too much of my childhood had been limited, so I'd vowed to live a life of abundance when I could. And it had worked out, until her. The only mishap had been Finley Reyes—the girl with the magnetic eyes.

When I met her that first summer, I was enamored with her, but she was seventeen, so I put her firmly in the "do not think about" category. I hung out at her house a lot that summer and got to know her and Henry. Fin hadn't been around as much due to her community service obligations that summer, making it easier to ignore my attraction.

It took me longer than I'd like to admit to figure out she was Oblivion. Mostly because I had a massive crush on Oblivion and didn't want to reconcile that she was the seventeen-year-old daughter of my boss.

So when I discovered that the unattainable girl who made me curious was the same as the online hacker I'd befriended, I froze, not knowing what to do. So, I did what I did best and ignored the parts of my life that I didn't want to acknowledge.

I pretended it didn't matter. She hadn't met me, and I continued on with my flirting.

The moment her eyes landed on mine last year in that conference room, I felt the unmistakable regret I'd worked so hard to avoid. She pierced me with her hypnotizing eyes, a look of pure betrayal staring back at me, and it felt like someone had reached in and ripped my heart out.

I'd never felt so ashamed of myself, and I'd done a lot of shady things. But that look made me regret not coming clean with her sooner. Maybe then I could've had a chance with her instead of the scraps I'd been relegated to devour.

Despite her cold shoulder, I couldn't seem to leave, and I found any excuse I could to stay in Utah. First, it had been to help the Agency take down the Council. Then was the job offer from Samson to work with him at Alpha Security Solutions. I took a hiatus from my post, so I could be near a girl who didn't even like to be in the same room as me.

So when she disappeared, I knew it was time to quit staying in the shadows, hoping she'd recognize me and forgive my transgression. Sawyer had sat me down at one point and told me that the fastest way into Finley's heart was to be honest, but I couldn't even seem to be honest with myself.

Facing her departure, I knew it was time. Time to correct the one regret I had in my life.

So, I used all my resources, and I tracked her down and went to Asa, knowing I needed to figure out a way to make it work. If Fin wouldn't give me a chance, at least I could bring them back together. I owed her that. Asa was a good guy and someone she deserved. He'd surprised me when he asked my feelings about his girlfriend, and for a second, I'd hoped before remembering the crushing reality of my life. I didn't get the girl.

"What do you mean?" I asked, shuffling my feet. "I care for her. She's a good friend."

"Listen, I know I haven't been the most open, avoiding the fact that my girlfriend seems to collect men like they're lost puppies. I can't say I know what she feels, but she's worked hard at ignoring you, and the other guy we don't mention, too hard for it just to be friendship."

"Milo?" I asked, raising my brow, purposefully ignoring the part about me.

"Yeah, but since you're here, let's talk about you."

Sighing, I nodded, dropping my arms. "I met Fin when she was seventeen, both online and in person. I didn't know they were the same girl for a while. I had a crush on her, it's hard not to. But that's not in the cards for us. I'm here to make sure she's safe and to help you get her back. She deserves to be happy."

Asa watched me for a while before walking over. He dumped his empty plates into the sink and turned to look at me. "I didn't know how I'd feel thinking about my girlfriend with someone else, but I can't deny that it's nice having you here. You're a good guy despite your outward appearance. I won't stand in the way if Fin decides she wants to give you a chance. I've experienced life with and without her now, and I much prefer the one with her. Even if that means sharing her, I'm cool with that. We can figure something out together."

"Yeah, well, let's just focus on finding her first."

I knew the reality of this and told myself the plan was to let her go, to let them be together. But when she walked into that hotel room looking like a drowned rat, I couldn't seem to catch my breath.

I was only kidding myself if I thought I could let her go without a fight again. Asa had said he wanted to figure something out, so maybe I should take him up on that conversation for once.

"I wondered when you would show up."

Sitting forward, I rubbed my sweaty palms on the knees of my jeans. I looked her over, assessing for any sign of injury. It didn't appear she was hurt, just covered in some substance and she'd never looked cuter. I pushed aside the urge to go to her and wrap her in my arms. I hadn't earned that privilege yet.

"You didn't make it easy."

She snorted, reaching into a bag to pull out some clothes and sniffed them. She cursed, holding up a pair of stretchy pants and a tank top, and I assumed they were dirty. She sighed, sitting on the edge of the bed, looking at me.

"I've had a shitty night, and I haven't had time to do laundry, and now I'm out of clothes. So, can we possibly move this interrogation to the laundromat, or even better, wait until morning?"

I was tempted to let her have the time, but I knew if I did, she'd somehow manage to escape me, and it would be another month before I found her.

"No can do, sweetheart. I'll do you one better. Go take a shower, and I'll have something for you." She eyed me, her gaze calculating as she tried to figure out my angle.

"I'm too tired to care. Fine. Don't touch anything."

I snorted, like that would stop me. I'd already gone through all of her things anyway. Nothing for me to find now. I didn't even regret placing a tracker on her laptop while I waited. It would be interesting to see how long she took to find it.

She grabbed the few things she had and went into the bathroom. As soon as the door was shut, I pulled out my phone, needing to send a few messages.

ME: She's here and in need of some clothes. You got it or want me to send out for something?
ASA: I'll take care of it. Does she know I'm here?
ME: Not yet. How far out are you?
ASA: I'm in the lobby. I'll go grab some things and be right up.
ME: She's in the shower now
ASA: Okay, thanks, Cohen.

I sent the other two I needed to send with that out of the way.

ME: Located the target. In possession. Will update you on progress.
Samson: Good job. I'll update the others.

ME: Contact made.
Superior: Good. Be discreet.

I snorted at that. I didn't think we had the same definitions of the word, but I'd be as discreet as possible. The water shut off, and I put my phone away, wondering if she was one of those girls who would take an hour after she got out or be out here in five minutes. With Finley, I never could tell. She was high maintenance without always being high maintenance, leaving me confused about what to expect from her most of the time.

A knock at the door had me standing, so I walked over and peeked out, finding Asa standing with a shopping bag. Letting him in, I took the bag and knocked on the bathroom door while he slipped behind me so she wouldn't see him yet.

"Fin. I got your clothes."

The door opened a crack, and her hand reached out. I placed the bag into her grip, and she pulled it back, closing the door. I went back to the chair I'd been sitting in and sat back down, nodding to Asa as he stood by the wall. He looked nervous, and I didn't blame him. She'd been somewhat receptive to me so far, but I wasn't sure how she would react to him.

When the door opened a few seconds later, she stepped out in new clothes and a towel on her head. She narrowed her eyes at me, her arms crossed.

"I don't know if I should be impressed you knew my sizes or weirded out. I'm beginning to think you're some kind of stalker, Chaos."

"It's Cohen. I only go by that online. You know how it is." I shrugged, wanting her to see me as a person outside of my hacker identity. It was the first time I'd wanted that, and it felt important.

"As for the clothes, I didn't get them. He did." I nodded to the corner Asa stood in. At my motion, her head swiveled, the towel swinging with the movement. I heard her gasp, and her body moved a step before she stopped herself.

"Asa," she said, her voice soft and unsure.

Apparently, it was all he needed, and he took the rest of the steps between them, pulling her into his arms. I should've given them a moment, but I was greedy, and I sucked up their reunion like an emotional parasite, pretending it was for me.

Finley clung to him in a way no one had ever touched me, and I envied their relationship. If I was more selfless, I'd let her go and let them have their love story. But I wasn't. I'd been kidding myself earlier.

I was greedy and lived my life taking what I wanted, and I knew now this was something I couldn't walk away from. I never pictured myself as part of a poly relationship, but if it got me a chance with the girl of my dreams, then I'd try it. Besides, I wasn't one for convention anyway, bucking tradition with everything else I did in my life.

I cleared my throat when the emotions became too much, and Asa looked up, meeting my eyes. His gaze held something I didn't want to think about, his assessment of me too on point for my liking.

"Fin, I know you wanted to do this independently, but I couldn't just stand by. I tried, I really did, but I was miserable. So, I'm being selfish and asking you to let me stay. Let us help," he pleaded as she clung to him.

Her shoulders sagged as she turned, taking a step away from his embrace. She looked between the two of us, and I could already see the rejection on her face. I'd gotten used to that look from her. So, I stepped in, hoping I could use my powers for good.

"I know who you're trying to find, and you won't. Not without my help."

Her retort died on her lips as she huffed, crossing her arms. I lifted an eyebrow, waiting her out. She knew it was true, even if she didn't want to acknowledge it. I leaned forward, my elbows on my knees as I watched her, not breaking eye contact.

"Give us a chance, Fin," Asa begged, reaching out to touch her. She didn't shake him off, and I knew she was close to submitting.

"How about we broker a trade?" I asked, sitting back and placing my leg over my knee. I knew how Fin operated by this point in our friendship. She didn't like to be a burden and would be more likely to give in if it was a trade.

"What kind of trade?"

The corner of my mouth tilted up, and I moved my hand to cover it. "Well, it would do me a huge favor to have your boyfriend off my back about finding you, first off. He's been such a chatty fellow, so I could really use the quiet time to get some actual work done." Asa snorted, but let me continue.

"That doesn't seem like much of a trade, to be honest. No offense, honey," she said, blushing up at Asa.

"Okay, fine." I blew out a breath, debating how much to reveal. They told me to be discreet, but I was learning that didn't really work with Fin. "Let us help, and I'll give you access to my computer for one hour. Anything you can find program-wise, you can copy. That's it. My final offer."

Her eyes went huge, and she licked her lips. Accessing another hacker's system with free rein was the ultimate gift. I was taking a gamble she wouldn't find anything too incriminating about what I did in my spare time. It felt worth it to win the chance to do this with her. No matter the cost.

"Deal." She stuck her hand out, and I stood, taking it. I pulled her closer, rubbing my thumb over the backside of her hand.

"You can't get rid of me now, sweetheart."

I could've sworn I saw her gulp, her eyes dilating at the message, but it flicked away so quickly, that I couldn't be sure.

"So, what have you learned so far?" I asked as she sat on the bed, Asa next to her. I leaned against the dresser, cutting the distance between us. This was my last chance to win over Finley Reyes, and I would make sure she couldn't ignore me.

Eleven

FINLEY

Cohen peered at me with such an unrelenting gaze I didn't know how to handle it. Over the past few months, he'd constantly been there, waiting for me to say something. But I never did. The fear of wanting too much, of being scared to take more than I was given, held me back.

That and I didn't know how to trust him.

While he hadn't betrayed me in the way that Blackhawk had, it still stung to know he'd known who I was and hadn't told me. Years of friendship, and he kept that from me. It made me feel like he was keeping something else hidden.

And that hit too close to home for me to examine. Better to push him aside, so I didn't have to look at my own flaws.

Asa's hand picked up mine, and I gave up the fight of trying to push him away. Asa always had a knack for making me putty in his hands. He was too good, but I was too weak at the moment after weeks of no contact to deny myself any longer.

That small amount of contact gave me the strength to answer Cohen's stare.

"Not as much as I'd like. I found Blackhawk and he reached out, saying he had a job for me. He sent me to this town."

"Blackhawk?" Asa asked, pulling my attention.

"When I was first looking for your sister, I taught myself to code and took a few classes. I needed information that I couldn't get from legal sources, so I asked around and discovered a club, The MidKnight Guild. Being part of MKG would've granted me access to databases, programs, and keys to almost anything. In order to be part of it, you have to prove your skills. They match you up with other hackers, and as a team, you're given tasks. They varied in skill and difficulty. There were four of us at first, but by the end, it was just Obsidian and Blackhawk. I thought we were friends..." I shook my head, fighting back the tears that wanted to fall.

"I'd met Blackhawk through another club, and he sent me Oblivion's information. I was, um," Cohen cleared his throat, the first sign of remorse I'd ever seen from him as he spoke. "I'd just gotten a summer internship with Fin's dad. I didn't know she was Oblivion until afterward when I heard the news of her arrest. I didn't want to believe that the badass hacker chick was the seventeen-year-old daughter of my boss."

He paused, stepping forward and squatting so he was at eye level. Cohen picked up my free hand, his thumb rubbing across it in a way that felt too natural.

"I'm sorry I never told you afterward that I knew you. That wasn't cool of me. At first, I didn't want to blur lines. But after a while, it felt too late to say anything. The dread weighed on me that you wouldn't hear me out if you ever found out. I'd just be the weirdo who kept this huge secret from you. I'm sorry for that. It wasn't fair. And I hope you know that it's the one thing in my life I regret. Your friendship meant something to me, and I should've been brave enough to tell you the truth."

I searched his eyes, realizing how blue they were this close. They always seemed so stormy far away, but not at this moment; they were as clear as a sunny day.

"You're forgiven, and honestly, I wasn't too upset when I found out. That night was a lot to deal with, so it was easier to pretend it was because of you. I've been cowardly not saying anything either when we've worked together, so I'm sorry."

He smiled, and I couldn't deny how it made my insides flip. Even when I thought he was just my dad's dorky intern, he always had. I was just too lost in my own world to notice back then.

"Just to clear the air," Asa started, clearing his throat.

Looking at him, I was worried I'd see the disgust on his face after I stared into another guy's eyes, but I didn't. Asa proved to me again how good he was and how much I didn't deserve him. He looked at me with nothing but love and understanding.

"Cohen and I talked a lot these past weeks, and I've gotten to know him. Whatever you two feel for each other or don't feel for each other, that's for you to decide. Don't let me stand in the way of that."

"Wait!" I shouted, grabbing his hand firmly as fear started to engulf me. "Are you saying you're walking away?" Tears I'd been holding back for weeks came to the surface, and I felt like I was on a precipice as I waited for him to answer. Asa screwed up his nose, and I couldn't take it any longer as words began to flow out of my mouth.

"Asa, no, please don't do this. I'm sorry. I thought I had to leave, that we were strong enough. I don't want to lose you. I can't. I love you." I threw my arms around his neck as I sobbed, deciding I'd find a way to hold him hostage or something until he loved me again.

"Fin," he soothed, "Fin, no, it's not that. Shh, don't cry." He rocked me back and forth, his hand rubbing up my back. The towel I had wrapped around my head had gone askew from the movement, and my wet hair began to fall out of it. I couldn't make out words as he tried to comfort me, too consumed by my own fear.

I felt the towel be moved off my head, releasing a lot of pressure. It took a while for me to realize that someone was combing it out as well, the gentle strokes soothing me even more. When I finally was able to stop my tears, I could hear what Asa was saying.

"I love you, Finley. I'm not walking away. I'm just saying you don't have to just choose me. I don't want to live my life without you. You're my everything. I've been so lost without you these past few weeks. I promise I'm not leaving. I just want to be with you. Always."

I sat back, wiping my face, looking at him. His green eyes sparkled, and I realized it was because of the tears he'd shed as well. I cupped his face, kissing his lips briefly. I hadn't let myself do that earlier, too afraid of the answer. But now, it felt like the most natural thing, and I knew we both needed it.

When I leaned back, I felt another body behind me. I tensed for a second but then relaxed, knowing it was Cohen and he'd been the one to brush my hair. Leaning my head against him, I tilted it up and found him peering down at me.

"Thank you, that felt nice."

"Anytime, sweetheart. Especially if I get to be part of the activity that makes you wet, to begin with." He winked at me, and I froze, not sure how to take the flirting. When I heard Asa chuckle, it released the tension in me, and I let out my own giggle.

"I will have to get used to you flirting with me, aren't I?"

"It's my love language." He grinned, and I had a feeling I'd come to crave those smiles if I let myself.

Sitting up, I turned so I could look at both of them. "I'm not sure where my heart is right now. I've denied it for so long; I think it's default is to hide away from me. I know that there are times I feel like my insides might explode when I'm around you, but it's hard for me to reconcile that. I've never been the girl that guys wanted. I was the nerdy, weird girl in school and then once I got in trouble, only the guys who thought that meant I was easy were interested. Before Asa, I'd only had sex twice, and it hadn't been pleasant. I'm scared that if I let myself want more, that it will be taken away from me."

Asa squeezed my hand, kissing it. "I'm not going anywhere, and maybe you just need to let yourself be open to the idea instead of putting pressure on yourself to know now."

"I'm not expecting you to just start making out with me, you know. There needs to be foreplay," Cohen said, chuckling before his face turned serious. "For now, I'm just making my intentions known so that there's no miscommunication. Maybe we should get back to why we're here and leave the matters of the heart for another day?"

"Right, yes, perfect." I nodded my head a little too aggressively, my hair swinging back and forth as the wet strands hit my cheeks.

"So you were telling us about Blackhawk," Asa prompted, giving me my out.

"Yes, I thought we were friends. But on the last mission, I was set up and arrested. It wasn't my first time. I'd gotten into a few other things over the year but always let off. This… it was more serious. I was charged, and after a night in juvy, I was given 300 hours of community service. It left a bitter taste in my mouth, especially when I got my computer back and found I'd been kicked off the server and ghosted by my two supposed friends."

I took a breath, the anger and rage coursing through me again.

"So, you're what, after revenge? And why just Blackhawk and not Obsidian?" Asa asked.

"Because Blackhawk and I had a relationship outside of our team. Obsidian wasn't part of that. He was a bit of a control freak, but he was sweet overall. No, it was Blackhawk. He was the one who told me to meet him, and then he never showed, but the police did."

"How much of a relationship?" Asa asked.

I sighed, blowing out a breath. "He was the first guy I thought I loved. I was only seventeen, and he fought his attraction to me, but eventually, things between us became more. He sent me gifts and was the one person I felt saw me during that time. It was a dark period of my life, and he saved me in many ways. His betrayal hurt, but I also realized how far down the dark side I'd gone. He'd set me up to take the fall, and the things I did, I hate myself for them. Until I deal with him, I don't feel like I deserve a future. He stole some of my innocence, and I will never get it back. But maybe I can stop him from hurting others. I don't really know why it's so important, but after I was taken, it was like, all I could think about was the first reckless mistake I made, and how maybe if I corrected it, then I'd be okay, I'd have a chance at a future without feeling so broken."

Tears threatened to come again, and I realized how much I'd just spilled to them. More than I'd admitted to even myself. Purging it from my chest felt good, though, and it helped remind me of my purpose.

"You think revenge is the best course?" Cohen asked.

"It's the only way I think I can get that part of me that was broken that night, by making him pay."

"Okay, I'll help. It's not going to be easy."

"Thank you. I appreciate it." I turned to Asa, needing to know his response. "You?"

He bit his lip, looking me over. "If this is what you need, I'll help however I can."

I kissed his cheek, squeezing his hand. "I love you, Asa."

He softened, kissing my temple as he pulled me into his arms. I looked over at Cohen as he watched us. I didn't know what I expected to see, but it wasn't lust. Swallowing, I dropped my eyes, not ready to examine that yet.

"Once I got here, Blackhawk sent me to do surveillance on a building and then wait for his contact in a cowboy hat. It turned out, it was him, but I didn't know that until I got back to the hotel room and opened the envelope. In the process of searching for him, I was doused with a tray of drinks, and it ruined my computer. I had to call Milo to get a new one."

"Milo? Is he here?" Asa asked.

I shook my head. "No, he's just been helping me."

"The one person we didn't think to ask," Cohen said, smiling. "You're smart, Finley Reyes. So, what happened after that?"

Getting up, I grabbed the paper and handed it to Cohen. "Apparently, there wasn't a job, but another puzzle to find him. By the time I got to the location, I was too late and was doused in paint. Though," I said, snapping my fingers and pulling out the piece of register tape from my pocket. "There was a message in morse code. We just need to decode it."

Cohen's eyes lit up, reaching for it, but stopped himself. "May I?"

Nodding, he took it, and an excited look came across his face as he went back to the table and pulled out his laptop.

I sat back on the bed, taking Asa's hand. "I am glad you're here. I'm sorry for running away. I thought it was the best option at the time."

"I know, Fin. I'm here now." He kissed me, pulling me into a hug. "You have to be the one to tell Sawyer, though."

Cringing, I knew he was right as a laugh bubbled out of me. "Fine."

Twelve

FINLEY

"YES, YES, I PROMISE." SIGHING, I HUNG UP THE PHONE AND STAYED against the wall for a moment. I'd stepped out into the hallway for some privacy since I knew Sawyer would yell, and she had, but then there had been a lot of tears and talking through things that had been needed.

It was sad to say that it had taken me this long to realize I was stubborn and didn't like to let people help me. Shocker, I know.

Feeling lighter now that I wasn't hiding from everyone, I inserted the keycard and stepped back into the room. Asa and Cohen were bent over his computer as they worked on the morse code riddle at the table. It had taken Cohen no time to crack it; apparently, he was fluent in morse code. But the message hadn't made sense.

I can crawl, I can fly, I have hands but no legs or wings either. What am I? Have you forgotten?

Asa looked up when the door clicked, meeting my eyes. It felt nicer having him here, not doing this alone. I needed to remember that for the future and stop running off by myself.

"How'd she take it?" he asked, coming closer.

"There was a lot of yelling and then crying, but I feel better. I promised her I'd stay with you and wouldn't try to leave you guys once you fell asleep."

"Shit, I hadn't even thought of that." His face whitened, and I felt even worse for the pain I'd caused him.

"Yeah, well, I wouldn't say I hadn't thought about it, and Sawyer knew me well enough to call me out on it. But, I realized how lonely I was and out of my depth. I need you guys for my own sanity. I'd started talking to myself for the company, which isn't a fun place to be." I cringed, my cheeks blushing.

"Oh, to be a fly on the wall for those conversations." Asa chuckled, making me feel better. He always had a knack for doing that.

"You guys make any progress?" I asked, a yawn following it.

"A little bit, but it can wait until morning. Come on, let's get some rest."

It was on the tip of my tongue to argue, but I could see the dark circles under his eyes. Asa and Cohen had said how they'd followed my trail together for a while, but at the last stop, they split up, not knowing which direction was the right one. When Cohen found me, Asa turned around and met him here. They'd both been up for almost twenty hours at this point.

"Okay, that sounds great."

"Cohen, you going to keep working?" I asked, leading Asa to the bed. There was only one in the room since it had just been me. He peered up, looking at us. It took him a second to realize I had asked something.

"Oh yeah, I'll catch some sleep in a bit. Don't worry about me." He yawned, and I saw the dark circles under his eyes too.

"Nope," I decided, dropping Asa's hand to walk over to the table. I shut the laptop and grabbed his hand. He didn't make it easy as I tried to pull his big frame up from the chair. "You could help, turd."

"Turd? Ah, you do like me," he teased.

Rolling my eyes, I kept pulling, and he finally gave in and

stood. Asa had already crawled into the bed on one side, and I realized what it meant. Me between them. Okay, girl, you could do this. It wasn't a big deal.

Swallowing, I turned off the main light and crawled into the bed, letting Asa wrap his arms around me. Cohen hesitated for a second, looking at us.

"Come on, turd. You need sleep. We can be adults and share a bed."

He nodded, debating something. Eventually, he kicked off his shoes and began to unbutton his jeans.

"Um, what are you doing?" I screeched, covering my eyes. I could feel Asa's chest rumbling behind me.

"It's fine, Fin. He's just taking off his jeans. They're not the most comfortable thing to sleep in."

"Oh, yeah," I said, realizing how I'd jumped to conclusions too fast. My cheeks flamed, and when I dropped my hand, I found Cohen smirking at me. He slipped under the covers and turned off the lamp on the table. It was quiet as we all settled, our own thoughts running through our heads.

As the breathing evened out, I fell asleep quickly, for the first time in a while, if I was honest. I didn't have to be on guard now. I had people with me who would help take watch. It was nice, and I fell into a deep sleep and didn't wake again until morning.

WHISPERING WOKE ME THE FOLLOWING DAY, AND WHEN I STRETCHED, I noticed that the bed was empty. Something about that had me pouting as I opened my eyes. When I looked around for the guys, they were grinning at me.

"What?" I asked, wiping my face for any drool.

"You're cute when you sleep," Cohen said, looking at me in a way I wasn't used to.

"Here," Asa said, picking up a bag and cup off the table. I eagerly sat up, pushing the covers down when I saw what it was.

"Ah, you do love me," I beamed as Asa handed me the cup of coffee.

"I do." He smiled lovingly, making me realize how dumb I was. "But Cohen was the one to get the food and coffee."

"Oh," I said, my fingers around the coffee as I inhaled it. "Thanks, Cohen." I looked up at him from under my eyelashes and found him blushing. It was such an odd look on his usually cocky face that I did a double-take. "Are you blushing?" I teased.

He scoffed, waving me off as he focused on the computer. "Nope. I don't even know what that is."

Laughing, I took the chocolate croissant that Asa held out and immediately shoved it into my mouth. A moan escaped me as the chocolate and flaky pastry melted in my mouth. "That's so good."

When I finished licking my fingers, I looked up to find both guys watching me with hungry looks. I was used to seeing it from Asa, but it still surprised me to find it reflected back in Cohen's eyes.

"Sorry. I was hungry."

"Never apologize for enjoying something, sweetheart," Cohen said, his voice a little soft. "I, um, I think I figured out the clue."

My eyes went wide, and I scooted off the bed so I could look at the screen. Cohen didn't move when I approached, my body brushing against his arm as I leaned closer to inspect what he had. Turning my head, I found him watching me.

"Am I in the way?" I asked. I think I heard Asa snort behind me, but I didn't dare look away from Cohen.

"Nope. In fact, you have a seat right here." Before I could protest, he pulled me down into his lap, locking me in with his arms around my waist. Resting his head on my shoulder, I heard him sigh.

"So, I realized that he was using a quote from a book—*Forgotten Time*."

"Huh, that kind of makes sense." Memories of us discussing it began to emerge, and I shut them down, not wanting to fall into the past when I was with them.

"Based on that, I think his next location will be the theme park."

"It's real?" I asked, not realizing it had been about an actual place.

"I don't know if it's the one from the book, but there is one named Raven Time. I think he'll be at the funhouse."

"How do you know that?" I asked, turning my head, forgetting I was sitting on his lap, bringing our faces dangerously close.

He swallowed, his eyes bouncing back and forth from my lips to my eyes. "Because after the quote was the following. 'The fun begins on Tuesday at 7:00 pm.' So, my guess is he's telling you when and where. You just had to figure out the where first."

"You're brilliant, you know?" I smiled, happiness fluttering through me. I never would've solved that in time.

Cohen's cheeks did that thing he denied and reddened, causing me to smirk. I liked how I was affecting him.

"How long does it take to get there from here?" Asa asked.

I grabbed the phone and put it on the map, and he hovered over my other shoulder as it calculated. "Looks like about eight hours," I sighed.

"Looks like we're going on a road trip then," Asa beamed down at me. I grinned back, not hating the idea with him along.

"You make everything better. I was stupid to think I could do this without you," I admitted. Reaching up, I pulled his face down to mine, kissing him.

"If you're going to be handing out kisses, my lips are right here," Cohen said into my ear, his lips brushing against my neck in the process. Tiny tingles shot through me and goosebumps appeared on my arms at the slight touch. I sucked in a breath, and I could've sworn I heard him growl in my ear as he shifted beneath me.

"Shit, I have no clothes," I said, remembering I needed to do laundry as I tried to distract myself from rubbing my butt into the hard length I felt growing beneath me.

"We can buy you some things for now and do it once we're there," Asa offered.

"Or you just go naked," Cohen stated, no longer trying to hide how aroused he was from me sitting on his lap.

Swallowing, I tried to focus on the computer screen. "Clothes, yeah, good idea."

Cohen chuckled darkly behind me, the air fanning against my neck, doing nothing to help with my current state.

"Do you need to take a shower?" Asa asked, a hint of amusement in his voice. "I can go grab you some more things if you do."

"Shower, um, no, not really. I'm good for now. I guess we can pack up then and head out. Do you guys have a car? I hopped between a rental and the bus."

"Yeah, I have a car," Cohen said, not releasing me. I kept tapping his arm, hoping he'd get the message. My self-control to not rub my butt into his cock was lessening the longer I sat there.

"Perfect. It's settled then."

He still didn't let me go, and I looked up to find Asa, smirking. "I'll be back in a few minutes then. Don't kill each other."

With that, my boyfriend left me practically panting on another guy's lap as he strolled out like he didn't care. Rude.

"Um, can I get up, please?" I asked, deciding to try going for the direct approach.

"Nope," he said, doubling down and pulling me closer. "I kind of like having you here where you can't get away."

"Okay, cool, but I can't live here."

"Why not?" he asked, and I could hear the smile in his voice.

"Well, as nice as it is, I need to pee and do other things at times. And it would get awfully sweaty after a while, I bet."

"I'm hoping it gets sweaty, sweetheart. That means it's good."

Gulping, I nodded, trying to find words. "Well, okay, good, um, but still."

He laughed, his breath cascading over my neck again. "Fine. I'll let you up. This is my new favorite thing, though. I should've told you who I was years ago. Be prepared for more of this. Once I latch on, I don't really let go."

The barest of kisses was placed under my ear. His lips were warm, only giving the slightest pressure, but it was enough to send a ping straight to my core, making it throb as my toes curled under.

"I honestly don't think I would've been ready for you back then," I admitted, standing up once his arms released me.

When I stood to turn, his hand reached out, taking mine. "I'm glad we have now."

It was the simplest phrase, but it resonated with me. "Me too, Cohen."

I found myself smiling as I stepped out from between his legs and began to pack up the few meager belongings I had scattered around the room. Asa was back in a few, and I changed in the bathroom. I realized they'd also changed clothes, small bags sitting next to mine when I returned. It felt odd to be leaving with them, but I liked it more than having to sneak out on my own.

"Alright, let's hit the road."

FINLEY, AGE 17

Blackhawk: You kind of remind me of the heroine from the book, Forgotten Time. Have you ever read it?
Oblivion: Are you joking with me right now?
Blackhawk: No. I read. I'm kind of offended you think I can't read.
Oblivion: No, that's not it. Sorry. It's just… that's one of my favorite books. I've read it a million times probably. It's kind of surreal that a guy is telling me I remind them of Raven. She's kind of a badass.
Blackhawk: So are you, little hacker.

Oblivion: It doesn't feel that way in real life.

Blackhawk: You'll find your friend. I believe in you. Did you message Chaos?

Oblivion: Yes. He's looking into some things.

Blackhawk: That sounds promising.

Oblivion: Yeah, I guess. Her birthday was yesterday and it just feels weird not celebrating with her. That's two I've missed now.

Blackhawk: Time is a construct. When you're reunited, it won't feel like any has passed.

Oblivion: Yeah, I hope so. It feels like it's too much to wish for.

Blackhawk: You deserve all the things, little hacker. In fact, I want to send you something.

Oblivion: Isn't that against the rules. No personal information.

Blackhawk: Which is why I have an idea. Have you ever heard of a virtual address?

Oblivion: No, what is it?

Blackhawk: There are some sites where you can have a virtual address and use it to avoid huge shipping fees on things for international. Then once you've accumulated a certain amount in your storage container, it's shipped to you all at once. How about we both sign up for one and it keeps us still in the spirit of the program?

Oblivion: Um, sure.

Blackhawk: Until then, little hacker. We always have Raven.

Thirteen

FINLEY

THE FIRST HOUR HAD BEEN QUIET AS WE SETTLED INTO THE DRIVE, listening to the GPS navigate us out of the city. The early morning combined with the last few days caught up with me, and my head leaned against the window as my eyes drew heavy.

I'd fallen into that weird conscious, but unconscious state, where I knew I was asleep, but I wasn't dead to the world. So when the dream started, it felt like I was watching it play out like a movie, reliving the past, but I was unable to stop it or make any different choices.

"What is this place?" I asked as I managed to crawl through a window into the basement. I tumbled into a few boxes as I landed and I quickly jumped up to see if anyone had heard me.

"It's an abandoned house. Does it matter?" Obsidian said through my earbud. I'd remembered to bring them this time, meaning I didn't have to have it on speaker. Which was good when I was meant to be stealthy.

"I guess not. It's just kind of an odd request."

"I thought that too," Blackhawk started, but was cut off by Obsidian.

"Listen, as team leader, I pick from the pool of tasks I think we can do and which will give us the best opportunity to make it."

"Yeah, yeah," I grumbled, brushing off the dust I'd collected on me. "Why am I the only one who breaks into places?"

"Because you're the best at it."

"Flattery will get you nowhere," I teased, but secretly liking that Blackhawk noticed my skills.

"With us being only three members now, we have to make a splash," Obsidian continued, ignoring the flirting. He'd gotten pretty good at doing that.

"Ugh, don't remind me. I can't believe Mongoose bailed on us." Sighing, I pulled out the mini flashlight and looked around the room. "I don't see anything other than boxes. What should I take to show we were here?"

"Are there any files, or I don't know brochures? Just something with a logo on it."

"Sure, let me pull up the mystery place's Wikipedia and see what's in each box," I sassed, rolling my eyes.

A deep chuckle came across the app, and even distorted, I knew it was Blackhawk's. Spotting a box that said office, I walked over to it and began to open it. Thankfully, there was a brochure on top, so I plucked it and hoped it was for this place. Smoothing it out, I shined the light onto it.

"Magnolia House," I murmured. "Found something. Okay, I'm getting out of here."

"Grab a file too. I'm curious," Obsidian said. Sighing, I grabbed a couple of folders off the top and shoved them down the back of my pants, pulling my shirt over them.

"Got it. Now, I'm leaving. This place gives me the creeps and it stinks."

"Be careful, little hacker. We need you on our team."

Smiling, I climbed out the window and closed it as I dashed off toward the street I'd parked on. Pulling my disguise off, I went to sign out of the app when I noticed a message in my inbox. Clicking on it, I was surprised by who it was from.

Mongoose: Oblivion, I need your help. Can we talk?

Jerking up, it took a few moments for me to realize we were still in the car. Peering around, I found Cohen still driving. He peeked over at me, a concerned look on his face.

"You okay, sweetheart?"

Wiping my mouth, I nodded, trying to rid myself of the dream. It felt like I'd been right back there.

"Yeah, just a weird dream."

He reached over and squeezed my leg, giving me some comfort. I looked back and found Asa had his eyes closed on the seat, so I turned back to the front. Music played softly as we drove, and thoughts I'd been trying to ignore about the two men in the car began to filter through. It was like my brain was going to make me think about one thing or the other. I couldn't ignore both.

The guys seemed to have accepted what I'd shared with them about my past and why I'd left, but would they when I told them everything?

Was I only asking for heartache getting involved with Cohen, too? I think I had it best when I just focused on one boy. Less likely to screw it up that way.

Twisting my body to get comfortable, I jumped when a hand clamped down on my thigh. I followed the arm up to find it belonged to Cohen.

"Stop whatever torture you're putting yourself through right now. Quit trying to predict everything and just let things happen."

"I—"

"You were. You forget that we both know you," Asa piped in from the back, apparently not as asleep as I'd assumed. He leaned forward, poking his head between the seats. "Trust, babe."

"How did you know?" I asked, noticing that Cohen wasn't in any hurry to move his hand.

"You've moved every two seconds and have sighed or huffed every three."

Chuckling, I tried not to think about how hot my face was getting. "Sorry." I turned my head to look out the window, needing a little space. Asa had insisted on letting me sit up here, but it felt like I was under a spotlight.

"How about we play a game to get to know one another better?" Asa asked, pulling me back to face him.

"What kind of game?" The mention of games had me souring, the ones with Blackhawk not ending how I ever thought they would.

"Since we're in a car, we could do something like 20 Questions or two truths and a lie."

"Two truths and a lie?" I asked, not having heard of it before.

"It's exactly as it sounds. You give two truths and one lie, and we have to try to figure out which one is the lie."

"Huh, okay, that sounds interesting. You first, though," I teased, giving him a peck on the lips.

Asa smiled brightly, warming my insides. I swear, he had the power to light the whole world, or at least mine.

"You in, Cohen?" Asa asked.

"Yeah, sure, why not." He shrugged, and I realized his thumb had started to rub on the inside of my leg. Swallowing, I debated moving so it would make his hand move, but I hadn't found the willpower yet to do it.

"Hmm, okay. I've got it. I once met Hulk Hogan. I'm allergic to strawberries. I've never roller skated." He ticked them off on his fingers, saying them all with the same tone of voice, giving nothing away. It had me looking at my boyfriend in a whole new way. I observed his facial features as he stared at me, grinning.

"Hmm." I tapped my finger on my lips as I debated.

"I know," Cohen said smugly. "You guess first, sweetheart."

My cheeks warmed, and I didn't know if I hated or loved when he called me that. "Fine, turd." I stuck out my tongue, again trying to take their attention away from my ever-heating cheeks.

"Geesh, I feel like a horrible girlfriend. I'm going to go with Hulk Hogan." I sat back, looking over at Cohen. He still had his smug face as he navigated around a car, turning his blinker on. He had to move his hand to grab the wheel, and I hated how much I missed it already.

"Nope, it's roller skating," he answered, peering into the rearview mirror. His smug smile grew at whatever he saw there, and I whipped my head around to look at Asa.

"He's right?" I asked a slight screech to my voice.

"Yup," Asa said, laughing.

"But… but…" I sputtered, not understanding. "You've met Hulk Hogan? I knew about the strawberries, thank God, or I'd be a worthless girlfriend."

"Hey," Asa said, grabbing my face, stopping me from spiraling. "It's a game to get to know one another. I picked things I knew you wouldn't know. It's not meant to make you feel bad." His palms cupped my whole face, the rough sides of his hands feeling comforting as he stared into my eyes. Eventually, I nodded, licking my lips.

"Okay. You're right. Will you tell me about it?"

He smiled, leaning forward to press his lips softly against mine. "I'd love to." He sat back and told Cohen and me about the time he was at laser tag with his school friends and ran into Hulk Hogan, who was there for a birthday party for his son.

"He was really cool. He took a picture with us and everything. I thought I was the optimum of cool for years, and then no one knew who he was, and it no longer mattered." We all laughed, the sound filling the car. "You're up, Cohen, since you guessed right. How'd you know?"

"I'm not giving my secret away, dude." He smirked, glancing up at the mirror again. "And I've got the perfect three. You guys ready?"

We nodded, and I leaned forward, turning in my seat with my leg bent as I peered at the two guys. I wasn't trying to bring my body closer, so he'd touch me again. Nope, not at all.

"I was once stood up because I was too edgy. I have a sister I've never met. I'm a millionaire."

I thought over the things he said, trying to hear them how he told them to see if he'd gone up any on certain words. But like Asa, I couldn't tell any of them from the other. Deciding to go with the most far-fetched, I glanced up, finding he was looking at me out of the corner of his eye.

"What do you think, Fin?"

"Millionaire is a lie."

He didn't say anything, looking at Asa to give his response. "Your guess, man?"

"Sister." Asa nodded like he was trying to sound more sure of the answer himself.

"I'm hurt, you guys," Cohen said. "To think you both believe I've been stood up! Obviously, I need to up my game if you both assume that to be true."

"Wait… so you are a millionaire?" I asked, gasping.

He turned his head to glance at me quickly before focusing on the road. "Um, yeah. I was a genius hacker, remember? What did you think I was doing?"

"But… I guess…" My brain stopped. "You kept the money? It made me feel dirty, and after everything went down, I used it to repay for some of the damage I caused." I swallowed, not wanting to go into details yet. I wasn't ready to face that dark secret.

"In the beginning, I wasn't on the right side of things. I got caught once, too, you know. When I was twelve, I hacked into an organization, and they caught me. Instead of pressing charges, they gave me a job."

"At twelve? I feel like I don't really know you," I admitted.

"Yes, at twelve. They gave me training, a home, really."

"So, when we met, when you worked for my dad, you were what… undercover? Isn't that illegal? Corporate Espionage?"

"Whoa there, firecracker. You're jumping to conclusions. I did things off and on and lived my life as I wanted in the meantime. School and working as an intern were all part of my training for my masters."

"You have a master's? Why…" I shook my head. "I don't really know you."

"I actually have my doctorate now," he said sheepishly.

Cohen pulled off at the next exit, stopping at a gas station. He turned the car off, the sound of it clicking the only thing we could hear as we all sat there. Cohen turned in his seat, taking my hands.

"Fin, we do know one another. We just need to learn the details of things. But I know who you are to your core, and you know me. We spent hours getting to know the real parts of us as we chatted and became friends. The facts of my life are things anyone can learn from a simple google search, but the aspects of my personality, which Spice Girl was my favorite, and my all-time favorite movie, are the things that really define me. Those are the things you know, and not many others do."

I could hear the sincerity as he spoke, and I knew I was probably freaking out about something that didn't matter, but the mere fact that I didn't know these things made the perfectionist in me feel like a failure.

"So, you do have a sister you've never met?" I asked. He nodded, his eyes closing as emotion seemed to take hold of his body.

"Yeah." He opened his eyes, swallowing. "I was adopted by an amazing couple, but I felt like I was still missing something. I looked into my family history when I first started hacking and found that my biological family had been killed in a car crash. I had an older sister. She was five years old when she died. I'd been left with a sitter at the time."

"Oh my God. I'm so sorry, Cohen." I moved my hands to cup

his face. His scruff felt nice under my palms, and I traced my thumb over his cheek.

"It's okay. It's hard to miss a family you never knew. But it explained why I felt like a part of me was gone. I was convinced it wasn't an accident, my brain wanting to find a conspiracy, but it was. Just a drunk driver. Wrong place, wrong time, type of thing."

He shrugged his shoulders, and even though he said he was fine and over it, I felt like it was only partially the truth. Pulling him to me, I wrapped my arms around him in an embrace, wanting him to know he wasn't alone. After a while, we pulled back, and he looked lighter.

"Thanks," he whispered. Cohen cleared his throat, turning to Asa. "How'd you know I was a millionaire?"

Asa laughed, raising one shoulder. "I gotta keep my secrets, man." Cohen broke out into laughter, lifting his fist to Asa's.

"Fair enough. Alright, I'm going to get gas. It's your chance to get any snacks and go to the restroom."

Asa and I climbed out, stretching as we made our way in. After a quick pit stop, I grabbed a soda and a few sweets and headed to the counter. Cohen was already there waiting. I placed them on the counter and pulled his face down toward mine. I pecked his lips before I walked out, swishing my hips. I stopped at the door, looking over my shoulder at him.

Both Cohen and Asa were watching me. Cohen had a look of shock that turned to glee as he regained his composure. Asa seemed to be delighted, looking at me with love. Blowing a kiss, I headed out to the car, leaving them to take care of the snacks.

They joined me a few seconds later, handing out the goodies, and we got back on the road. The game never picked back up after that, but the atmosphere felt lighter as we took turns being the DJ and singing along.

It was late into the evening when we pulled up to a hotel. Cohen got out to get our room, and I sat back, realizing I was beginning to hate hotel rooms.

"You okay, Fin?" Asa asked, leaning forward again.

"Yeah, I think so. I'm glad you're here."

"Me too," he said. Asa opened his mouth to say something else, but the door opening had him closing it, and we exited, grabbing our meager belongings. We'd stopped and picked up a few things for me, so I at least had clean clothes, but they wouldn't last long if my track record was anything to go by.

Jumping up on Asa's back, I smiled, hugging him as he carried me up the stairs. Thoughts of Blackhawk began to flood me again, the hope I'd catch him on Tuesday filling me with glee. At least this time, I wouldn't be alone, which felt like all the difference.

Fourteen

FINLEY

I WAS RUNNING THROUGH A MAZE. I WAS BEING CHASED BY A GOOSE and it kept poking me in the back. Knocking it away, I kept running until I fell over, tripping on a log. I jumped when I landed, my body twitching, making my eyes open. That was when I realized it had been a dream and I wasn't actually being chased in a maze.

My heart started to slow at the knowledge, my breathing evening out. It took me a few seconds to realize where I was and who I was with. Two bodies pressed against me in the dim light. Unlike yesterday morning, they were both still in bed with me.

Yes, both.

I wanted to laugh at the fact that Cohen had gotten a room with only one bed, but it also didn't surprise me. He was mischievous to his core, and I knew it was his way of pushing my boundaries a little. I couldn't say I minded.

Snuggling back into the chest and arms wrapped around me, I realized, too late, that the poking hadn't been part of my dream but my reality.

A soft moan sounded out, and the body moved, rubbing itself against me. My breath caught as I felt their hand grip my stomach.

Opening my eyes, I realized Asa was in front of me. Which meant… at some point in the night, I'd rolled over into Cohen's arms.

And now he was stabbing me with his very prominent morning wood.

Fingers splayed out across my tummy, pressing into me with a firm touch. They stayed there for a few seconds before they shifted slightly, moving lower, and I knew he was no longer asleep. Biting my lip, I debated if I was ready for this.

I knew Cohen. I liked Cohen. I always had, but something kept making me stall.

Was it just fear? Keeping me on this side of what I thought was okay? Or was it something more? The hard part was I wasn't sure. Years of suppressed emotions made me unable to know what I was genuinely feeling now.

I felt him move closer, his embrace feeling so safe that my body naturally relaxed into his arms. Deciding to let go and live, I didn't stop him. They both wanted me to trust them, which started with trusting myself.

When he stalled a second later, I placed my hand over his, moving it down to the hem of my sleep shorts. His tongue brushed the nape of my neck, eliciting shivers throughout me. Goosebumps spread over my arms, my nipples pebbled as they rubbed against the tee-shirt, and I bit down on my lip harder to contain a moan that wanted to slip out.

His hot breath came out in puffs as he began to creep ever so slowly beneath the elastic band. I'd never cursed myself so much for wearing shorts to bed. At the time, it seemed like the sensible thing to do. But when I wanted the boy I was too afraid to admit I liked to touch me, they felt like the world's largest chastity belt.

Cohen's pinky brushed against the cotton of my panties, no doubt feeling the wetness already present. I couldn't hide how turned on I was from the simple touch he'd given me. I was so wound up that I felt ready to combust. Holding my breath, it felt like a lifetime as he peeked his finger around the material and touched my folds.

My body responded in kind, and I bucked back into him, rubbing against his hard length. The moan I'd been trying to contain slipped out, and I re-opened my eyes to find Asa watching me. Guilt crept up my spine, and I locked my legs, my body tensing. Cohen froze, feeling me shift. My eyes grew huge, but Asa moved closer and grabbed my chin, bringing our faces closer.

"Relax, Fin." He kissed me, and I melted, my body doing as he said into the arms of Cohen, who responded in kind. But as Asa's hands weaved into my hair, kissing me like a man starved, he slowly began to move.

Asa kissed me deeply, wrapping his tongue around mine in a passionate caress. It had only been a month since I'd last kissed him this way, our earlier ones mere pecks to the panty-melting one he was giving me now. As our tongues battled, I mourned for the time we'd lost. It might have only been a month, but it felt longer. Probably because even though I'd been with him, I'd been pulling away for months.

Having shared some of the sins of my past mistakes, it had taken a wall down between us I hadn't realized was there. Kissing Asa now almost felt like the first time because I was kissing him as me and not the girl I was pretending to be.

Cohen's hand began to graze between my lower lips, pulling some of the wetness with him as he moved up and down. The teasing was driving me wild, and I tried to move closer to make him touch me more. His other hand gripped my hip, holding me still.

"Patience, sweetheart."

I groaned, making Asa chuckle as he pulled away and lifted my shirt. His tongue began to peek out, licking my stiff peaks, teasing me along with Cohen.

"If one of you doesn't fully touch me, I'm boycotting you both."

"Oh, I think someone doesn't like us teaming up," Cohen teased, biting my earlobe.

"This wasn't the type of team-up I had in mind," I gritted out.

Cohen's grip on my hip tightened, and he pulled me back into his cock, the hard length rubbing against my ass. Gasping, I clamped down the urge to rock more, hoping he'd reward me if I stayed the course. His finger dipped between my pussy lips, flicking over my clit, and I bit my lip, praying he'd finally push further.

Asa moved closer, taking my breast into his mouth; my back arched, making Cohen's finger slip further into my core. When he finally moved it in and out, it was the sweetest pressure, making me want to weep in relief. His thumb found my clit, and his finger began to plunge in me deeply as Asa sucked my nipple. I rocked into them both, wanting more but knowing we weren't there yet. This was a huge first step, and I needed to take it for what it was and not push myself too much too soon, even if my body was screaming for more.

It didn't take long once Cohen began to spear me, and I found myself grasping Asa's head to my chest as I began to spasm, a cry of pleasure leaving my mouth.

"Fuck, sweetheart, you make the sweetest sounds. I can't wait to hear more," Cohen whispered, licking up my neck again. I shivered, no longer trying to hide how my body responded to him. He pulled his finger out slowly, the sensation making my eyes roll back, and for some reason, I wasn't surprised when he sucked down my juices like a desperate man. It was primal and seductive, making me wish they were still in me so I could ride them again.

"Good morning," Asa whispered, pulling me closer, not caring at all about Cohen. It eased the last shred of hesitancy I had out of me that he was being honest about his feelings. I guess I owed it to myself to be real then. If Asa was willing to let me be open with my heart, then I needed to brave and open it and stop hiding behind him.

"I'm not sure which is better to wake up to," I said, a smile on my face. "An orgasm, or coffee and donuts."

The boys snickered, knowing I was full of shit, but it eased the tension as we got out of bed and dressed. It was time to find Blackhawk.

Screams of joy and the rush of rides as they went around, hit us as we walked into the Raven Time theme park. It took a minute to orient myself to the surroundings, the environment so different from what I was used to.

"It's very loud," Cohen said, his nose scrunching up as he looked around. "And bright."

Asa had a massive smile on his face as he took it all in. "That's because you tend to be more of a vampire hermit and only come out at night. Come on, we have a bit of time before we need to meet him. Let's scope out the area and maybe go on a few rides. Might as well have some fun while we're here."

He bounded off, full of energy, and it was at times like this that I wondered how he dated me. While he had the energy of Sawyer, my best friend, Asa, also had a lightness about him that was utterly him.

"Is it me, or is it weird how happy he is all the time?"

Snorting, I hit him in the stomach. "You're the weird one. Asa is a good one. Don't knock it."

Cohen rolled his eyes but smiled, tugging me along as we followed Asa. He stopped and looked at each sign, reading everything and taking it all in. It was cute.

"Oh, this!" he said, pointing to a pretty empty line. I looked at the sign, trying to read what it was.

"Rock-n-Roll Riders?" I shrugged, the name doing nothing to tell me what the ride was about. Cohen sighed but agreed and followed us into the line. We didn't have to wait long as we made it to the front and stood behind the metal bars until the ride appeared. Everyone who got off seemed happy and full of smiles, so I took that as a good sign.

Asa pulled my hand, going for the front of the ride when we were allowed to enter. Cohen dragged his feet behind us, and I didn't know if it was because he wasn't used to being up this early or something else. It was a three-person cart, so we slid in, with me in the middle. Asa pulled the bar down, an excited look on his face as he peered over at me. When he looked at Cohen, though, he frowned, and I turned to see what it was about.

"You okay, man?" he asked. "You don't look so good."

"Hmm, mm," he replied, his eyes shut tight. Grasping his hand, I threaded our fingers together and pulled his head to look at me.

"You okay?"

"So, confession time. I've never been on a roller coaster, and I'm kind of afraid of heights."

Sympathy for him filled me, and I squeezed his hand. "You can get off," I started, right as the attendant came and tugged our bar, deeming it was good.

"You're good," he said, tapping the cart, and in the next second, we were off. I turned back to the front, holding Asa's hand as the ride began to move. It was slow at first as it crept up, and I peeked over at Cohen, his eyes still closed tight.

I could feel us climbing, and I knew a big dip was coming, so I decided to be brave. Taking a breath, I quickly kissed Asa on the cheek and let go of his hand. He smiled, nodding, having figured out what I was going to do.

I cupped Cohen's face as we came to the top, his eyes remaining closed. "Cohen, look."

He shook his head, so I decided to go all in. As we began to crest over the edge, I pulled his lips to mine. I kept my eyes open, wanting to see if he would look. Pressing my lips into his, he stayed frozen for a few seconds, and I felt us beginning to plummet down.

Shouts of glee rang out around us, my stomach climbing to my throat as we dropped, but I kept pressing, holding him to me.

After a few seconds, he opened his eyes, and I felt as if I had seen Cohen Campbell for the first time. There were no barriers, no banter to hide behind, just raw vulnerability.

He stared back, and something in him switched, and I caught a fire burning. His hands swept up into my hair, pulling me closer to him as the roller coaster turned and wheeled around bends. Asa's hand gripped my leg, but outside of that touch, I felt like I was floating as Cohen kissed me back.

It was aggressive and rough; his tongue sought dominance as he took over the kiss, not asking for permission but taking the kiss he wanted. When we started to slow, he drew back, panting a little as we stared.

"I think roller coasters just became my favorite thing," he said, his eyes bright and his smile wide as he peered back at me.

"Me too."

The three of us climbed off, rode a few other rides, played a couple of games, and grabbed food as we walked around. When the sun began to shift lower, I knew the time for fun and games was over.

"I guess we should head to the funhouse," I said, sighing.

"The fact he picked a funhouse is creepy within itself," Asa said, swinging my hand. I'd been holding hands with both of them all day, not caring as people would stop and look. It felt nice to not let other people dictate how I should act.

"That wasn't in the book, was it?" Cohen asked.

"No. I don't recall it being there. They went to the Ferris wheel and ate cotton candy." I shrugged.

The sign for the funhouse grew bigger the closer we got, a new pit forming in my stomach. It felt wrong somehow. Everything Blackhawk and I had up until this point had felt more, but maybe that was my misguided attempt to not feel like I'd been duped like the world's biggest loser.

"You ready?" Asa asked, looking at me.

"I dunno. It feels strange. What if we didn't get the clue right?"

"Then we go back and reassess. You're not in this alone."

Taking a big breath in, I nodded, feeling confident with their presence that this time it wouldn't be too late.

"One at a time," the attendant said, stopping Asa from following me.

"We'll be right behind you," he said, and I swallowed.

Stepping into the funhouse, I took hold of the railing as it began to tilt, throwing my balance off-center. Mirrors and lights around me began to move, making my depth perception off, and I struggled to walk in a straight line.

I couldn't turn to see how the guys were doing, so I focused on taking one step at a time, looking only at the ground. When I got to a hallway, I sighed in relief, the topsy-turvy feeling dissipating. Turning, I was surprised when I found myself alone and when I took a step, I smacked into a mirror.

"Ow! How?"

What I thought had been the way I'd come was now closed off, a mirror in its place. I spun around, all the mirrors showing different reflections of me in a kaleidoscope of Fin's.

Frantically, I began to stumble as I searched for a way out, a way back to the guys. My breathing became ragged as anxiety began to overtake me, and flashbacks of past times began to collide with reality, making me confused about what was real and what wasn't.

I caught a flash of black out of the corner of my eye, and I turned, searching for it. Tears streamed down my face as I tried to find someone. I was so dizzy, I could barely see.

"Please, I don't want to be here."

A body pressed up against my back, a hand covering my mouth, and I began to thrash. I felt something begin to prick my neck, a cold feeling settling in me that I was being drugged again. But when I blinked, it was gone, and the body left me.

Sucking in a breath, I took the chance and darted forward, finally seeing my way out.

But I'd been wrong. Again.

Smacking my face into the mirror, I saw two figures fighting, but I didn't know if that was my imagination, or reality once again. Before I could investigate, the pain encompassed me, my eyes sliding closed as everything went dark.

Fifteen

MILO

M y life had never been easy, so debating the dilemma I was currently faced with should've been effortless. But I was finding Finley Reyes to be anything but easy.

From the moment I met her, I felt a spark ignite in me that hadn't been lit in years. Being a Bellamy, expectations were placed on my shoulders from birth. As I grew, I bucked against them as much as possible, trying to find my own path. Over time, having to fight for the simplest thing wore me down. I hadn't realized how tired and stagnant I'd become until I was helping two girls who'd been taken against their will and being forced to be part of a human auction.

It was at that moment I knew I couldn't continue down the path I was on, attempting to play both sides—living the life I wanted by becoming a doctor and fulfilling family commitments when called upon. I'd ignored the more sinister side of things, pretending they didn't exist, but I couldn't ignore it any longer in that dark underground facility.

The Bellamys were criminals, and if I turned my head, I was just as bad.

Helping Finley was the first step in taking a stand against them and separating myself from my family. Over the past year, I'd become financially independent, setting myself apart from the Bellamys. After the Council had been taken down, it was necessary as everything connected to them was seized by the authorities, leaving the once flourishing Bellamy line barren.

And today, I would make the last stand against them, finalizing my separation from a family of crooks and murderers.

"Dr. Milo Bellamy," the chancellor announced, and I smiled, walking up the stage to shake his hand. He handed me my diploma, and I walked over a few feet, moving my tassel to the other side. Posing for the photographer, I smiled into the camera, the weight of my achievements sitting proudly on my shoulders.

I'd done it. This had been all me.

Walking back down the steps, I shook hands with a few of my professors before making it back to my seat. Some of my classmates congratulated me in passing, patting me on the back. I wasn't that close with most of them, having kept to myself, too afraid of being used for my family. It was a lonely life, always being mistrustful of others.

It was why Finley had been such a breath of fresh air. But as that one '90s song went, as soon as I thought I'd met the girl of my dreams, I was introduced to her perfect boyfriend. It was ironic that the first girl I liked was someone I had to rescue from my family.

Since then, I'd been wrestling with my feelings, while trying to be the friend she needed. It was nice, actually, because I got to be in her life without much commitment.

But for the first time, I wanted more. I wanted her to expect things from me. I wanted to be counted on. This past month, I wondered if I'd finally have a chance.

She'd reached out to *me*, needing *my* help.

Finley Reyes made it easy to ride in on the white horse and rescue her.

"Congratulations, graduates!" the chancellor cheered, and

everyone rose to their feet, tossing their caps into the air. I followed suit, but I couldn't deny it felt lonely. I'd worked so hard to be seen as a nobody, so I wouldn't be taken advantage of, that now, when I'd succeeded, I realized how sucky it actually felt to be alone.

Perhaps it was time to step up my game. I didn't know what was going on with Fin, but I couldn't deny my feelings for her had grown. This could be my one chance to show her I could be depended on as more than her friend.

Decision made and my dilemma over, I headed to my car, not even bothering with pleasantries as I made my way there. It would be unlikely that I'd see any of my classmates again, especially since my residency was on the West Coast. There wasn't anything left for me in Boston.

Tossing the black gown and diploma case into the passenger seat of my car, I revved the engine as I pulled out my phone and clicked on the icon for Fin. She didn't know I'd done this, but it felt like the safest bet to keep tabs on her with no one else knowing where she was currently. It was merely for her safety.

Yeah, I didn't buy it either.

When her location showed her only a few hours away at an amusement park, I became even more curious about what she was up to. It would take too long to drive, even in my sports car, so I made a left at the end of the road and headed toward the airport. As much as I hated my family at times, I couldn't deny that I'd learned to use my resources wisely. It was time to use some of my money to charter a jet. For some reason, I had a weird sensation that it was crucial I made it to her location today.

THE SUN WAS STARTING TO SET AS I STEPPED INTO RAVEN TIME. EVEN though the park closed soon, it was still full of families and teenagers as they hurriedly rushed from one side to the next, desperate to get in one more go before the rides shut down. The smell of cotton candy, funnel cakes, and fried chicken filled the space as I walked through the park, looking for the woman who'd stolen my heart.

In a naive way, I'd thought I'd be able to feel her, my body being automatically drawn to hers. But I didn't see her anywhere, so I pulled out my phone in desperation, hoping I could pinpoint a more precise location.

"That can't be right," I muttered, looking around since the damn thing said I was right where she was. The only thing here was a funhouse and a hot dog stand, and Finley wasn't anywhere. Shouting at the front of the line drew my attention, and I recognized the two guys. They were fighting with the attendant to let them through, saying they were with the girl who'd gone in already.

"Sorry, it's full. You have to wait until that party is out." The kid didn't care that two guys twice his size were demanding to be let in. I'd respect the kid if it wasn't at Fin's expense.

Knowing that nothing good could be occurring if Asa and Cohen were blocked off from the front, I made a split-second decision to circumvent the line and go around to the back. It might be selfish not to let them know I was here or that I was finding a different route, but I couldn't deny I wanted to be the one to rush in.

Fuck, I really needed to find another way to show her I cared. I'd think about it later when I knew she wasn't in danger.

The loud generator blocked all sound from the front as I looked around the building. Trash littered the ground as I made my way around it. A little way down, I discovered a side door standing ajar, so I peeked in. Finding no one around, I slipped in and took a few seconds to orient myself to the darkness.

Music could be heard from the front, so I followed it, realizing I was behind the attractions. Every so often, there would be a door, so I'd open it and look in to see if it was where Fin was. I found myself in the mirrors at the third door, and I instantly cringed as a hundred different versions of me glared back.

It made it more difficult to look around with all the distortions. Squinting, I saw a shape lying on the ground, but it was far away. Closing the door I'd opened, I quickly went to the next to find two guys fighting. Shutting it, I kept going, praying that one of them would open closer to the prone figure.

On the fifth one, I struck gold and was able to see the person lying on the ground better. Making my way around a few mirrors, I kneeled down, brushing the hair back. A spike of fear rushed through me when I realized it was Fin. The two figures I'd seen earlier moved closer, and I had an odd feeling they were fighting over the girl lying on the ground.

Picking her up, I made my way back to the door, thankful I'd remembered which turns I'd made since it looked the same in the mirror maze. When the door shut, the music was dulled, giving me a slight reprieve to look down at the girl in my arms. She made a small moan, but it was enough to let me know she was still alive. Going back the way I'd come, I counted the doors as I passed until I went to the one on the opposite side that led outside.

When I exited the house of horrors, I looked around, searching for a place to lay her down. A nearby picnic table by the hot dog stand caught my eye, and I walked over, laying her on top of it. The yelling at the front of the line was still going on, and I realized Asa and Cohen were still trying to get inside. Placing my fingers in my mouth, I let out a big whistle, drawing their attention.

I motioned for them to come over, pointing at the table. It took them a few seconds to recognize me, but once they saw Fin's prone body, they quickly gave up their quest to argue with the teenage attendant and jumped over the railing to get out of line.

While they made their way to me, I checked Fin over, taking her pulse and inspecting her body for any signs of injury. There didn't seem to be any visible signs of trauma outside a knot on her forehead.

"Milo?" Asa asked, slightly out of breath as he reached me. "How?" he started, but then shook his head. "Actually, explain later. Is she okay?"

"I think so. She was unconscious when I found her. It looks like she might've hit her head. Her pulse is a little fast, and she's pale, but that could be from passing out." I lifted her eyelids, finding her pupils responded to the light, and a sigh of relief fell from my lips. "I think she's okay, for the most part."

I looked up, meeting the two guys who were watching me. They didn't look pissed, so I relaxed, no longer worried I'd get a black eye.

"I can tell you both have questions, but the fact that you were both still out there and that when I found her, two other guys were fighting, I'd suggest we go somewhere else for the conversation."

Whatever they'd been about to say died off, and they both went into hyperdrive, focused on Fin. I appreciated that they took what I was saying seriously and didn't hesitate to respond. Maybe this wouldn't be as horrible as I imagined.

Though I hadn't expected two other guys to be present when I shared my heart, it seemed like I'd have to get used to it or move on. I was beginning to realize I couldn't move on.

Asa bent down and picked up Fin into his arms. I wanted to pout for losing the opportunity to do so, but this wasn't the time. I followed them out of the park, and I peeked back, something drawing my attention as we turned the corner. I couldn't be sure, but it looked like one of the figures from the tussle was standing in the shadows, watching us.

Stopping, I looked closer, but nothing but darkness greeted me, the last light of the sun having disappeared.

"Milo?" Cohen shouted, and I turned back, jogging to catch up to where they'd stopped.

"Nothing, I thought I saw something," I said in response to their looks. The three of us made our way out of the park with nothing more to say, ignoring looks as Asa carried Finley.

I'd come here thinking I'd share my heart with a girl, praying I wouldn't be rejected. And instead, I was possibly finding myself part of something bigger. All I knew was if Fin was involved, I was all in. It was time I stopped being just her rescuer and showed her I was here to stay.

Sixteen

FINLEY

Pain throbbed in my temple, and I wanted to move so I could make it stop, but my arms were banded to my sides by a strong force. Voices shouted nearby, and I tried to recall the last thing that had happened, but nothing outside of the pain filtered through.

A whimper left my lips, acting as a warning sign to the noise as it abruptly stopped. The tightness holding me shifted, a warm sensation spreading over my forehead.

"Fin, sweetheart, you awake?" a voice asked, sounding miles away. I felt like a kid with a string and a can, waiting for the garbled message to reach me, but it didn't make sense when it did.

Painfully, I used all my strength to lift one eye open, only to be blinded by a light shining into it. Wincing, I drew back, smacking into the hard object that held me. Another whimper left me as I tried to figure out what was happening. Memories coursed through my head of my kidnapping as fear rose up in me, coating my skin in a cold sweat.

"No!" I shouted, but the sound only came out as a muffled scream.

Soothing sounds and soft touches bracketed my face as the pressure from behind let up. The now gentle compression felt nice, calming my racing heart and breathing. As I began to feel more like myself, I decided to try opening my eyes again. Slowly, I lifted my eyelid, thankful that I wasn't blinded by light this time. A face swam into focus, the edges of a smile playing on their lips.

"Asa," I sighed, my body relaxing. His comforting smell of rain and cotton filled my nostrils as I breathed him in. My hands reached out, clasping onto him, not wanting to be left alone.

"You're okay, Fin. You're safe. We got you," a voice behind me said, reminding me that there had been someone there. I peeked over my shoulder to find Cohen smiling at me.

"What happened?"

"What do you remember?" a third voice asked. Asa leaned to the left, and the owner of the little flashlight came into view.

"Milo! You're here?"

I tried to sit up, but Cohen's arms had reclaimed their position around me, keeping me pressed to his chest. It felt awkward to be held by him in front of Milo, and I didn't know why. I reasoned that I didn't want Milo to feel uncomfortable, but even that sounded off to my own mind.

"He's the one that found you, sweetheart," Cohen cooed, brushing my hair behind my ear as he whispered into it. "He saved you."

"That sounds about right," I mumbled. Dropping my eyes, I looked at the bedspread, trying to place where we were. It looked like the one from our hotel room. That knowledge seemed to help me relax completely, and my brain began to think again.

I was safe. I was safe. I was safe.

Now that I knew I wasn't being kidnapped again, the flashes of memory began to trickle through. The funhouse and the masked man that'd grabbed me.

"Where did you find me?" I asked, needing to know more information.

"You were unconscious in the middle of a funhouse," Milo

answered, sitting on the bed. I watched as his hand flexed, almost like he wanted to reach out and take mine. Deciding he'd earned a little hand-holding, I reached out and took his before remembering he wasn't part of the dating deal.

I sucked in a breath, watching out of the corner of my eye to see what the others would do. When no one tensed, got angry, or punched Milo, I decided to take it as a win for now and would deal with it more later. Milo appeared to be on the same page as his grip tightened in mine.

"Okay, well, I guess that's good that I didn't get taken far. So, were you the one who attacked Blackhawk?"

"Blackhawk?" he asked before shaking his head. "I don't know who that is, but I didn't attack anyone. Two guys were fighting when I found you. I didn't stop to ask them their names."

Something about the way he said that had a giggle leaving my lips, and his shoulders relaxed, a smile spreading across his handsome face. I took him in, noticing him in more detail. He was dressed in a button-down shirt, bow tie, and dress pants. He looked really handsome, not helping with my 'wanting more than I should' problem.

"You look really nice," I blurted, my cheeks heating. Cheese cracker! I was turning into Sawyer.

"Oh, thanks." He glanced down like he'd just realized what he was wearing. "I didn't really have time to change before heading here."

"How did you know to come?" I asked, finally realizing how odd it was he was here. "And what were you doing beforehand?" I scrunched my nose, groaning when it hurt, remembering the throbbing from earlier. My hand reached up to touch the spot, but Asa grabbed it, locking it in his. I was now being touched by three guys, and my vagina started to get ideas.

"I, uh…" He blushed even more, and I wondered if he could read my thoughts or if I'd voiced it all out loud, and my own face began to redden in response.

"It's kind of an embarrassing story. Can we maybe talk about what happened to you first? I want to make sure you're okay."

"After you went into the funhouse, the attendant wouldn't let us through," Asa began, pulling us back to the topic. "He kept saying that the party was full and we had to wait. What happened once you were inside?"

I blinked, trying to recall the events. They all slammed into me, my eyes closing at the onslaught.

"It was weird. Everything was trippy, and it took me a while to get my equilibrium. The mirrors played tricks, and I thought it was one of you, but then a guy was behind me. I don't remember much other than him placing a hand over my mouth. There was a little pinch in my neck, but then it was gone. I thought one of you had come in, so I took the chance to run. What I assumed was the way out wasn't, and I smacked into the mirror at full speed. I'm guessing that's where I got this." I tilted my head since I didn't have the use of my hands. "Your turn."

The guys all looked at each other, apparently not knowing who I was speaking to. A smile spread across my face, and despite the situation, it felt nice to be surrounded by them all. But as soon as the thought entered my head, I pushed it away. I couldn't get too comfortable thinking I could keep all three.

The realization had me sobering, and I dropped a hand to tap Cohen's arm. He made a grumble, the possessiveness doing something to my insides.

"Can I sit up, please?"

"Fine," he replied, the sound more like a growl than a real answer. He let go of me, and everyone repositioned themselves on the bed as I sat up. I briefly glanced around, trying to buy time as I took in the details of our room.

Putting my hands in my lap, I peered back at Cohen and Asa. "Did you get a good look at Blackhawk? Where is he? Did he get away?"

They both seemed to drop their eyes as Asa shook his head. "We didn't get him."

"But, I thought…" Cohen sighed, his whole body collapsing like a deflated balloon.

"We never made it inside. We don't know who the other person was."

The knowledge that an unknown person had saved me felt odd. Was it coincidental? Had they been trailing Blackhawk too? Or was it just a good Samaritan?

"Oh," I finally said, playing with the cover. "Hmm, so." Looking up at the guys, I noticed their faces reflected mine. "Yeah, I got nothing. Okay, so first Milo tells us where he was and how he found me, and then Cohen and I will see if we can find anything out from any cameras."

"Already ahead of you there. They were turned off during that time frame. Which makes me think it was Blackhawk, at least. He'd know how to do that."

My shoulders slumped, and I drew in a deep breath. "Right, fine, we'll worry about that later. Milo?"

He smiled, shaking his head as his cheeks heated again. "You're not going to let it go, are you?"

"Nope. Sorry, but it's easier to focus on that than almost being kidnapped again." That seemed to sober the guys and Milo nodded, exhaling.

"First, I, um, kind of graduated today." He brushed his fingers through his hair in a nervous gesture, and I felt jealous of them.

"Wow, congratulations, man!" Asa cheered, slapping him on the back. And once again, my perfect boyfriend reminded me what the proper response was in this situation, and it wasn't fixating on fingers.

"Congrats, Milo. Or, I guess, Dr. Milo. I'm so happy for you." He smiled at me, some relief on his face.

"Yeah, well, it feels good to do something outside of my family.

But when I looked around the crowd, I realized how well I'd done at pushing everyone away so they couldn't take advantage of me. I was there, alone, with no one to take a picture with. And it just felt like it didn't even matter. If no one witnesses your success, is it a success?"

"Of course it is. Don't let them take this from you too. We should celebrate."

"You're right, and that's how I ended up here. I knew who I wanted to celebrate with." He ducked his head, his cheeks returning to that adorable shade of red.

"How did you know where I was, though?"

I conveniently ignored the other part that, out of all the people in the world, I was the one he wanted to celebrate his accomplishment with.

"Does it matter?" Asa asked. He looked at me, a serious look in his eyes. "He saved you. Without him," he shuddered, stopping his words as thoughts flitted across his eyelids, "you might not be sitting here with us now. So, you two can talk about it later, but I'm glad he showed up when he did. And personally, I think that calls for some pizza and beer. How does that sound for a mini-celebration tonight?" he asked, turning to Milo.

It was killing me not knowing the answer, but I recognized what Asa was saying and doing. He was including Milo in our little circle, and I needed to honor what that meant. I could talk with Milo later, but maybe Asa was right about not needing to know as well.

Looking up, I found that Milo had been watching me. I gave him a soft smile, letting him know I wasn't angry. It seemed to be what he needed as he turned to Asa, and they started to talk about pizza toppings. Cohen took the opportunity to pull me back to his chest.

Tilting my head, I looked at the man I was getting to know on a whole new level. "I never took you as a cuddle person."

"Oh? Was it the stellar wit that keeps people at arm's length or the all-black attire that made you take that leap?" he asked, smirking at me.

Snuggling into his arms, I found him to be rather comfortable. "Hm, more of the 'I'm too cool for school' attitude."

Cohen laughed, his breath making the top of my hair move. "Yeah, well, it's probably a lot of things. I kept people at arm's length on purpose. But deep down, I'm a big softie who's a physical person. I knew if I ever let myself get too close then, I wouldn't be able to let you go, and for the longest time, I didn't think you were an option."

"I'm glad you didn't run away," I whispered, my eyes drawing heavy again as I listened to his heartbeat.

"Everywhere I ran, it always led me back to you. I'm not going anywhere, sweetheart. I will cuddle your ass until you're old and gray."

"That's kind of sweet in a morbid way." I yawned, shifting a little.

"Ssh, close your eyes. I'll wake you when the food is here."

He pressed his lips to my forehead, and I took his advice, letting myself fall back under. At least this time, I was safe and surrounded by three guys who would do whatever it took to protect me. Like Milo, I was learning that some things were better with people. And this was definitely one of them.

Seventeen

FINLEY

The smell of melted cheese and pepperoni tickled my nose, waking me. Cohen's warm body still pressed into me, and I stayed still for a moment, enjoying the comfort of his embrace.

"Where should we eat it?" one of the guys asked quietly. "The table is only big enough for the box."

"True, it looks like the bed or floor then."

I heard them gathering things, and I debated if I should get up and help. Usually, that was my role, the one who made sure everything was taken care of and ready to go. But I couldn't deny that it felt nice to let someone else take charge for once.

"I know you're awake, sweetheart."

Turning my head into his chest, I felt his laugh rumble through me. "You're comfy." I yawned, nuzzling down in him.

"Good to know. Pizza's here." I could practically hear the smirk in his voice.

"Mm," I mumbled, shaking my head.

When my stomach growled, I sighed, moving to sit up, no longer able to ignore the hunger. I found all three guys focused on me when I opened my eyes. Blinking, I realized that sleeping as many times as I did in my contacts wasn't cutting it anymore, and they were dry as a bone.

"Um, give me a minute."

I slid off the bed and padded over to the bathroom. Shutting the door behind me, I leaned against it for a second. There were so many emotions racing through me that I didn't know where to start.

"Right, first deal with the most pressing matters," I said aloud, the habit not completely broken yet.

Taking a second to relieve myself, I quickly took out my contacts and tossed them into the trash. Placing my glasses on my face, I looked at myself in the mirror, taking in my features. My skin was pale, the bump standing out on my forehead. Brushing my hair over, I covered it for the most part. My nose stud shined in the light as I turned back and forth. Despite my paleness, my eyes seemed bright and alert, and I could only attribute that to the three men in the other room.

Pushing my shoulders back, I took a deep breath and left the relative safety of the bathroom. Their chatter stopped when I emerged, both making me happy and suspicious. I was glad they weren't at odds, but what did three guys who were practically strangers have to talk about besides me?

Which led me to believe they were talking about me.

"Um, it smells good. Shall we?" I asked, sitting back in my spot on the bed. Asa nodded, lifting the lid. He frowned, leaning closer.

"Did they put on the wrong toppings?" Cohen asked.

Milo leaned with him, his eyes widened before glancing up at me. I was beyond curious at this point, so I peered around the raised lid, pulling it back.

"Did we get pizza boobs? Sawyer got cake boobs once."

Asa let it fall, making me appreciate the fact he wasn't trying to hide this. An envelope with my name was taped to the inside of the box. So, not boobs.

"Wow, that's not creepy," I said.

"I don't even want to know what cake boobs are," Asa said grimacing.

Laughing at his discomfort, I ripped off the envelope and held it in my hand. I knew it had to be from *him*. The weight of that knowledge felt heavy in my hands, and I debated if I wanted to open this or not. I hadn't processed what happened at the funhouse yet, but clearly, if he was willing to drug me and take me, we weren't playing on the same levels anymore.

Was it even worth continuing this fight? Did I want to risk my life to get my revenge? Maybe I needed to accept I was out of my league and move on.

"Are you going to open it?" Cohen asked, squeezing my leg close to him.

I looked up, shrugging. "I don't know. I think I should just stop. It doesn't feel as worth it anymore. The stakes are too high." I tapped the letter on my knee, the corner poking into my skin. The slight pressure helped ground me so I didn't spiral into a million places.

"Did you see who delivered the pizza?" Cohen asked, not responding to me.

"It was just left at the front desk," Asa said, frowning as he began to think. I watched as he ran his hand through his blond locks, his green eyes staring off into the distance.

Cohen jumped off the bed, grabbing his computer and bringing it back over. He started to type in some things as I stared back at the envelope. Milo nudged my foot, making me look up. The pizza box in between us had been left abandoned. I wasn't sure if it was even safe to eat it at this point. It was sad to waste pizza.

"You want me to read it with you?" he asked. I peered into his dark brown eyes behind his silver frames, wondering if when two people who wore glasses kissed, they scratched one another.

He grasped my foot this time, shaking it again. "Fin?"

"Huh?" Oh, right, he'd asked me a question, and I'd gotten distracted by thoughts of kissing. "Yeah, I guess."

I shrugged, not really knowing how to feel at this point. He moved over, our thighs touching, and I liked how that felt. I couldn't deny that no matter what I got out of the end of this, I at least had faced my feelings.

His hand landed on my thigh, and he squeezed it, letting me know he was here. Taking a deep breath, I flipped it over and pushed my thumb under the flap, tearing it.

Once it was open, I stared at the folded paper, not yet quite ready to pull it out. Sucking in a breath, I let it out slowly, feeling more calm. Carefully, I slid out the paper, letting it fall to my lap. With each step, I seemed to need to stop and take a breath of courage, before I could move on to the next.

I unfolded the paper with trembling fingers, surprised when it was a letter. For some reason, I hadn't expected a letter, but more of a note with letters cut out of a magazine like a serial killer's ransom note.

Glancing over at Milo, I found his eyes watching me. He was confident and reassuring, giving me the courage to look down and read what Blackhawk had to say.

Oblivion,

I'm sorry for going to this extreme to get this to you. I promise, I only paid the guy to attach this letter. I didn't do anything to the pizza. If I know you like I think I do, that will be your first question.

I was afraid you wouldn't get online after what happened today if I didn't Send you something real.

First, congrats on figuring out the cluE. Your cleverness is one of the things I admire about you the most. I forgot how much fun we had with our puzzles and games, and *Forgotten Time* seemed like the best way to gain what we'd lost.

But something seems to have gone amiss.

You were almost hurt today, and that's never been part of the game.

I'm glad one of your suitors Could get you out in time. Whoever is working against me is smaRt. Too smart. I have an idea, but I need to finalize it before saying anything.

Until thEn, I don't think it's wise to continue our game. I hope you understand, but your safeTy is more important than just having fun. It would've been great to meet you in person today. You looked Stunning. You've grown up to be a beautiful woman, just like I thought you would.

I'll be in touch.

See you soon,

Blackhawk

I dropped the letter onto my lap, my mind whirling with questions. Why did it sound like he wasn't the one who'd attacked me? In fact, he acted like we were just having fun? That he hadn't betrayed me all those years ago.

"It doesn't make sense."

Milo watched me, then picked up the letter, rereading it. Asa walked back into the room, a new pizza in his hand. I hadn't realized he'd left or that it had taken me that long to build up the courage to read the letter.

He took the cold pizza off the bed, closing the lid. He observed me, looking for something. I gave him a lopsided smile, hoping it would help soothe whatever had made the crease between his eyes develop.

"Thank you for getting a new pizza. He said he hadn't touched it, but..." I shrugged.

"No problem. You okay? That feels like the wrong thing to ask, but I'm not sure what else to say."

"I'm not even sure what I am. It's kind of been a day."

Asa moved closer to the bed, sitting in front of me. He pulled my legs across his lap, and I was officially cocooned by the three of them. Cohen was still busy typing on his computer. When I peeked over, he was typing code so fast I couldn't follow it. Milo folded the letter and handed it to Asa.

"What do you think?" I asked, looking up at him.

"I don't know the whole story, but it seems like he wasn't the one who was trying to take you, but the other guy, fighting him off. I think…" he shook his head, clearing something.

"What?" I asked, realizing he'd stopped himself from saying something.

"It's nothing."

"It's something," Asa said, not letting it go either.

"It's just," he sighed, looking down at me. "When we were leaving, I looked back, and it looked like one of the guys was watching. It seemed like they were making sure we got out okay. I got the sense it was more out of concern instead of wanting to follow us."

"Fuck," Cohen grumbled, slamming his laptop closed. He rubbed his head, pulling at the wavy ends. "This guy is good. He's top-level. He covers all of his bases, leaving no trail behind. If he doesn't want you to find him, you won't. I'm sorry, sweetheart."

Cohen dropped his hands, turning to look over at me. Regret sat heavy in his eyes. Taking his hand, I linked our fingers together.

"Thank you for trying."

"So, where does that leave us?" Asa asked just as my stomach growled in demand. The guys laughed, and he got up, grabbing the pizza and napkins. He lifted the lid and pulled me a piece, placing it on a plate before handing it to me.

"Thank you," I said, smiling at him. Asa taking care of me was nice.

The guys dug into their food, making the room quiet as we all fell into our own thoughts as we ate. After finishing two slices, I set my plate aside, picking up the letter again.

Staring at it, I noticed something. "It's a password," I mumbled as the letter fell together. Every so often one would be capitalized randomly.

Cohen took the letter from me, reading it over, a smile spreading across his face as he seemed to pick up the same thing I had.

"You're right. Maybe it connects to something," he said, opening his computer. Before we could see where that led us to, a knock at the door had us all startling. Asa looked around at us, the three of us shrugging almost simultaneously, making us laugh.

Asa moved my legs from his lap and got up. I glanced over at Milo, and he had the same look I did—curiosity. Together, we crawled off the bed laughing, making it to the door just as Asa shut it. He turned, smirking when he saw we'd come to his rescue.

He lifted a black envelope, a gold script written on the outside. Moving closer, I realized it was my name.

"Another one?" I asked, reaching out for the card.

"The front desk said it was dropped off this morning with strict instructions to be delivered to our door at 8pm."

A weird feeling began to bubble up in my belly when I looked between the two. Just how out of my depth was I? I thought I could right the wrongs from my adolescence, but instead, I seemed to have stumbled into something bigger than I was capable of handling.

The three of us walked back toward the bed, catching Cohen's attention when I stopped at the foot of it with the card. I waved it awkwardly at him.

He gulped, his eyes going wide. "Um, where did you get that?"

"It was dropped off at the front desk to be delivered this evening," Asa replied. I glanced up at him, finding he was looking at Cohen oddly. Looking back, I noticed he was more sweaty than usual. I'd assumed it was about me, but maybe Asa was picking up on something I'd failed to see.

"Do you know what this is?" I asked, not taking my eyes off him. He nodded slowly, swallowing.

Tired of all the letters I'd received today, I flipped it over, pulling up the flap. The thick cardstock ripped satisfyingly. I pulled out the black card, blinking after, sure I'd misread it.

"You're part of the Order?" I asked, putting the pieces together.

Cohen's shoulders fell, and he nodded. "I am. That company I said that saved me? The one that offered me the job when I'd been caught?"

"Yeah," I said, my throat going dry.

"It was them."

"So, you've been working for the Order the whole time?"

"Yes, but not how you're thinking. You were never part of the job, Fin. I promise. It just happened to overlap at times. The Order is secretive. You can't talk about it. So even though I've been part of it, it's not like I have an office to go back to. I work for them by working other places."

"Does Samson know?" Asa asked, his arms crossed, his eyes narrow as he stared down Cohen.

"No." He shook his head. "No one knew. I don't know anyone outside of my training class who's in the Order. Just the people I've met while there, and that's limited. Everyone uses a code name online, so I don't know who people are. It's a safety measure. I've never even met my handler face to face."

"Why didn't you say anything?"

"I can't. If you think your phone or other smart devices are listening to you, the Order is bigger than that. They're in everything, bringing balance to the corruption where they can. They would've had me taken away the next day if I had told you. You never would've seen me again."

A sadness I hadn't expected filled me at never having seen Cohen again and despite my hatred of secrets, I was glad he hadn't told me if that was the consequence.

"So, why are you telling us now?" Milo asked Cohen, and I realized he hadn't read the card.

I lifted the card, handing it to him. "Because I've been invited to join their ranks."

Finely Reyes, you're cordially invited to join *Imperium in Imperio*. We'll trust your judgment on who you share it with. Be selective. This is your first test. You have forty-eight hours to respond.
The Order

Eighteen

FINLEY

THE WIND WHIPPED AROUND ME, TOSSING MY HAIR IN EVERY DIRECTION. I reached down to my wrist for the hair tie I kept there but came up empty. Sighing, I returned to staring out at the dark landscape, not really taking in any of the details. There was too much rushing through my mind for me to focus on anything else.

From almost being kidnapped again, the message from Black-hawk, and the invitation to join the Order, I was overloaded.

Knowing there was only one person I wanted to talk to, I pulled out my phone and dialed my best friend.

"Fin! Oh my goodness, it's so good to hear from you. I've missed you so much. I know we just talked the other day, but I was angry then. How are you? How are you doing with Cohen and Asa?" she rushed out in her typical Sawyer way.

Laughing, I wiped a tear that had escaped, already feeling better from just hearing her voice. "Slow down, Sawyer."

"Oh, no. I know that voice. What happened?"

Sitting down in a chair, I spilled everything to her, not holding any details back this time. I was tired of limiting myself. It was time

I let people help me. I sat back, a big breath leaving me when I was done.

"Wow, I didn't realize how good it would feel to say all that."

"Girl! It's about time you did. I can't believe you've been dealing with all of this on your own. I'm glad you finally trusted me enough to share."

Remorse filled me as I heard the pain in her voice. "No, Sawyer, it wasn't about trusting you. It was about trusting myself to not have to control everything. Ugh, I think I should start seeing my therapist again. I hadn't realized how much I'd been carrying around, trying to manage it all on my own. And now, I'm in this mess."

"Which sounds kind of cool. From what Isla told me, this Order is legit. They don't ask just anyone. It was their creed that saved me with the Council."

"Yeah, I forgot about that. That actually makes me feel a little better. But… what about Cohen working for them?"

"So? He never lied, and it wasn't like he was spying on *you*. And it sounds like there were serious consequences if he said anything. You can focus on that, or you can give him the benefit of the doubt. I think he's earned it."

"You make it sound so simple." I sighed, rubbing my head.

"If I learned anything in the past year, the things you want your life to be based around are simple. Grab hold of those you love and follow your heart. You might get hurt, but the journey is usually worth it. Henry and I wouldn't have another chance at the Olympics if we hadn't taken the risk."

"Wait, what?" I shrieked, standing up and almost dropping my phone.

"You didn't know?" she asked, her voice small, making me realize just how much I was hurting those I loved.

"I'm sorry. I've been a shit friend. Tell me all about it."

Listening to Sawyer tell me about her show and how the rest of our friends and family had shown up to be there made me miss her more. I was happy for her and my brother. But as the sinking feeling of not being accepted started to filter through, I knew I had to finish what I'd come to do. I just needed to go about it differently.

"I miss you so much," I said, not hiding that I was wiping the tears. "I promise to not run away or keep things from you ever again. Can you forgive me?"

"Of course, Fin. You're my sister. I love you. And if anyone understands what it means to fight a battle from the past, it's me. Just remember that it works better with others." I heard some ruffling and mumbling, and it sounded like Sawyer had placed her hand over the receiver. "Sorry, there's someone who wants to talk to you," she huffed before handing the phone over.

"Fin," Rhett grunted, and I knew I was in trouble.

"Hey…" I cringed even though he couldn't see me.

"Don't 'hey' me. Tell me that you're done being a martyr and that you will let people help you."

"I promise. Cohen, Milo, and Asa are here. Even if I wanted to run away, they'd find me. Heck, I'm pretty sure Milo has placed a tracker on me already," I grumbled, rubbing my forehead.

"Good," he huffed, a pleased tone to his voice. "I gave you a pass last year, but not anymore. You hurt Sawyer, and I won't let you do that again."

"I know. And you're right. It was selfish of me. I was just in such a dark place, it felt like the only way out. Can you forgive me? I'm sorry I left on your birthday and used that as an excuse to sneak away. I'm the worst friend, and I promise to make it up to you when I'm back."

"You better. I think a chick-flick marathon is in order."

I smiled, my shoulders dropping. Rhett might seem like an oversized bear to most people, grumbling at them to get out of his way, but he was a true romantic at heart and had been my movie-watching companion for a few years.

"You bet. Thanks for caring and looking out for Sawyer. I'm glad she has you."

"Hmph, well, I'm glad to have her. We both need you too. You're our friend. Don't forget what that means to someone like me."

Nodding, I realized he couldn't see me. "Yeah, you're right. Is Henry around?" I asked, knowing I needed to talk to him too.

"No, he's out with Soren. They went to hear Shadows of Mayhem. I think Henry might write a song for them."

"Wow! That's so cool, I didn't realize they'd contacted one another. Shit. Okay, I feel like I'm missing so much. Maybe I should just come home?" I bit my lip, knowing Rhett wouldn't spare my feelings from the truth.

"Take care of what you need to, Fin. Everything will still be here when you return. But if you don't deal with it, you'll just find yourself back to where you are now, missing out on everything. So, it's better to handle it now."

Taking a deep breath, I accepted what he had to say. "You're wise, Rhett Taylor. Can I say goodbye to Sawyer?"

"Be safe, Fin," he grunted.

"I will." Smiling, knowing that was his way of saying he cared.

I waited until my bestie returned, already feeling lighter from talking to them both. Once we said our goodbyes and I promised to check in every few days, we hung up. Leaning my head back against the chair rest, I took a deep breath and then exhaled, the stress falling away as the air left my body.

"How's my sister?"

Jumping, I peeked over my shoulder, finding Asa leaning against the glass door. I hadn't realized he'd come outside. Blushing, I hoped he couldn't see it and hadn't heard all the boy drama I'd spilled to Sawyer.

"Um, good. She's excited about qualifying for nationals. One step closer to the Olympics now."

Asa smiled, pride showing for his sister. "Yeah, did you see it?"

I shook my head, dropping my eyes. "No, I, uh, forgot." I began to fidget with the chair, picking at nothing just to distract myself.

"Hey, don't do that. I know you would've been right there if you could've. So do Sawyer and your brother. Let's just focus on doing what we need to do to return home. Okay?"

Glancing up, I found him watching me, nothing but love and warmth on his face. "Yeah, that sounds good. Um, do we have any more information? Sorry I just left. I kind of needed some air."

Asa walked in front of me, leaning against the balcony, facing me. "Yeah, Cohen spoke with his handler, and they've arranged for us all to be allowed to accompany you."

"Really?" I raised an eyebrow in question, wondering how that happened.

Asa chuckled, grabbing my hand. "Cohen said we were all going to be there anyway, so they might as well put Milo and me to work."

Smiling, I linked our fingers, raising our hands to peer at it. "So, Milo, too?"

"Yeah. He doesn't start at his residency until late summer, so he has some time off."

"And," I swallowed, dropping my eyes, "what do you think about him?"

"I think the better question is, what do you think about him? Or *feel* for him?"

Blowing out a breath, I lifted my eyes, knowing I needed to be looking at him when I talked about my feelings. "I like him. I was too afraid to admit it, but I do."

Asa kneeled down, placing both of his hands on my thighs. "Have I given you the idea that I wouldn't be open to the type of relationship my sister has? If I have, I'm sorry for making it where you couldn't talk to me."

Instantly, shame filled me, and I moved forward, taking his face into my hands. "Oh, Asa, no. I'm sorry you thought that for even a second. You've been the best boyfriend, hands down. I didn't think I deserved to be selfish and ask for myself. It was all me. Since I was a teenager, I've hated parts of myself, and I've tried to change, hide, or omit them so others would like me. It's my insecurity, and I'm sorry it leaked out onto you."

"Don't you get it, Fin? I'm not perfect. You act like I am, but I'm just as insecure, selfish, and cowardly as the next person. I knew you were struggling, but I didn't want to push you, afraid I'd lose you completely, so I let you be. I should've tried harder. Maybe then you wouldn't have felt you had to run away. I'm sorry."

"Ssh, you have nothing to be sorry about. Asa, babe, you're amazing. Even if you don't see yourself as perfect, you are to me. I love you so much. I'm sorry I made you doubt yourself. Can we promise to talk to one another about everything, even if it's uncomfortable?"

"I like the sound of that." He leaned forward, kissing me briefly. "And as far as the other two guys go. I know you have a connection with them both. I can see it when you're with them. I'm cool with Milo too. If you find you want to explore things, I'm not going to run away screaming. I'm here to stay, Finley. I waited a whole year just to ask you out. I'm not going to run off scared now that I got you."

"You really are the sweetest," I said, kissing him again. Wrapping my arms around his neck, I pulled him to me, needing his hug. Asa came willingly, and we held one another for a while, just content to be near each other.

When his hands started to roam, I couldn't deny that my lady parts were heating up. Lifting my head, I boldly watched him as he unbuttoned my shirt. Since he was still on his knees, I could see every move he made as his jaw tensed, his nostrils flared, and his pupils blew.

"Are you sure?" he asked, his hand wavering in the air between us.

"Yes. We'll just have to be quiet. But we're high enough up here that I don't think anyone would be able to see us."

"I kind of like the thought that they could." Asa grinned, showing me a whole new side to himself.

Dropping my shoulders down, the shirt slid off, leaving me only in my bra. Slowly, I reached forward, unsnapping the front clasp, glad I'd decided to wear this one today. As soon as my breasts were displayed, my nipples pebbled from the breeze, drawing Asa's eyes to them. He licked his lips, and I knew he was a second away from striking.

Reaching down, I unbuttoned my shorts, the movement snapping him out of his staring contest with my tits. Asa jumped up, pulling his clothes off in quick succession as I pushed my shorts and panties to the ground. At this angle, his cock jutted out at eye level as it began to harden right in front of me, rising up like it was saying hello. Leaning forward, I lifted my eyes to watch Asa as I kissed the tip.

He sucked in a breath, hissing as my warm tongue swirled around it. I moved to take more of him into my mouth when his hands shot out, lifting me under my armpits.

"I don't think I can wait tonight. I need you, Fin."

Sucking in a breath at the desire in his voice, I barely nodded before I was spun around, and my hands caught the railing I'd been standing against earlier. Asa's hands skated down my body, leaving a trail of goosebumps in their wake. The cold air kissed my skin as I breathed in anticipation of what would come next.

Tilting my head back, he bent down to kiss me, his tongue swirling with mine in a passionate embrace. His hands trailed over my breasts, pinching and teasing the mounds as he explored my body. The world around us ceased to exist as he mapped out my body with his touch.

"More," I gasped, breaking the kiss to state my claim. A sound similar to a growl left his lips as he pulled my hips closer to him, his hard cock nesting between my ass cheeks. His fingers lowered to my pussy, finding me warm and waiting for him.

He began to lightly touch my clit, giving me only teasing caresses as I pushed forward, wanting more friction. A frustrated sigh left me as he kept moving his fingers away each time I tried.

"Asa," I begged, hoping he'd take mercy on me.

His head bent, nipping lightly on my neck as he whispered in my ear. "I like it when you say my name so full of need."

Before I could respond, he gave me what I wanted, plunging his fingers into me and making my knees buckle as they filled me.

Biting my lip, I barely contained the moan that wanted to escape. Pushing against the railing, I rubbed against his cock, no longer satisfied with his fingers. Spreading my legs wider, I arched my back, hoping my core would be closer so he could slip in.

Asa chuckled, taking the sign for what it was, and moved his hand, positioning it on my hip as he tilted me the rest of the way. I helped him move into the right spot by going up on my tiptoes. As he slipped into me, I let go of everything I'd been holding, allowing it to escape into the night air around me, my moan becoming one with the breeze.

Together, we found a rhythm as he plunged his hard length into me, easily sliding in and out. The sounds of skin slapped against one another, adding to the night sounds. Little gasps and puffs of air were all that could be heard as we let our desire take over.

"I can't last much longer," he groaned, and I nodded, needing him to tip me over the edge.

"I'm ready."

"Fuck, I didn't put on a condom," Asa groaned, stopping his movement.

"Don't you dare stop, Asa! We're good. You know we are."

A little chuckle left his lips before he bent and kissed the dip between my neck and shoulder. His fingers tightening on my hips was the only warning I got before he plunged back into me, pushing a gasp from me. One hand moved around to the front, finding my clit, and he rubbed in circles as he pistoned in and out. It was all I needed before I felt my body tensing up and everything exploded as I came.

My head dropped back, and he sealed his lips to mine, stealing the moan from my mouth. A few seconds later, he stuttered as his hips slammed into me one last time, and he held himself tightly to me as he jerked inside. Pulling our lips apart, we stared at one another in the darkness, and I knew that everything he'd said was true. There weren't any more secrets between us, and I looked at him for the first time as my true self.

"I love you," I whispered, needing to put it out into the world, adding to the sounds of our love in the night.

"I love you." He smiled, pecking my lips before he slowly pulled out. My calves screamed at me from the position as I lowered back to the ground.

"You ready to face them?" he asked as he picked up our clothes, handing me mine first.

"Yeah. Plus, I'm starting to get cold, and if we stay out here much longer, I doubt we'll get away with what we did."

"It's cute you think we did."

Laughing, I got dressed and found Asa holding out his hand for me when I was done. Placing mine in his, we walked into the hotel room together, ready to face our next adventure.

We found Milo asleep on the bed, while Cohen busily worked on his laptop. He looked up at our entrance, closing the lid and moving around the bed toward us. He stopped in front of me, worry etched on his brow as he searched my eyes for something.

"I promise, there aren't any other secrets. I told my handler that I wouldn't keep anything from you anymore. He agreed as long as I can get you to come to the Order and see it for yourself before you make up your mind."

"Okay," I said, stopping whatever speech he had planned.

"Wait, you're not going to fight me on this?" His brow arched up as he looked between Asa and I.

"No. I'll see what they have to say. If they can help, then I'm willing to listen. Did you discover anything on the IP address?"

"It's running through a program that's looking for all possibilities. I'm beginning to wonder though if maybe it's not an IP address but a location of a server."

"What makes you think that?" I asked, just as I yawned. "You know what, never mind. Let's get some sleep. I'm tired. We can discuss it in the morning. There's been a lot to unpack today,"

"Seems like you unpacked something on the balcony," he teased and I rolled my eyes, trying to hide the blush.

Walking into the bathroom, I quickly washed my face, peed, and cleaned myself up before I got ready for bed, changing my clothes. When I found both Asa and Cohen standing at the foot of the bed when I emerged, I wasn't sure what the problem was.

"Everything okay?" I asked, adjusting my glasses.

"Yeah, it's just..." Asa pointed toward the bed, and I realized that Milo had spread out in our absence. "He looks so peaceful. How do we tell him to move?"

Giggling, I walked over and took Milo's glasses, which had gone crooked in his sleep. Brushing his hair over, I waited for him to wake up.

He blinked slowly, looking at me with adoration I didn't feel I deserved, but Sawyer's words to embrace the affection and let the guys tell me how they felt helped me not dismiss it.

"You want to change into something more comfortable? I'm sure the guys can give you something." I peeked over my shoulder, finding Asa already holding out a pair of sweats and a shirt. Taking it from him, I placed it on Milo's chest. His hands clasped onto mine, holding them for a second.

"Did you decide what you're going to do?" he asked as he began to sit up. I went to hand him his glasses but stopped when he started to untie his bowtie and unbutton his shirt. When I didn't say anything, he stopped, looking up at me. I didn't know how good his vision was without his glasses, so I tried to school my features to make it less obvious I was checking him out.

"Hm?" I asked, the guys chuckling behind me. I'd somehow forgotten that even though Milo might not be able to see me, Asa and Cohen could. "Oh, right, yes, I guess we're all going in the morning."

"Me too?" he asked.

"Yes, I'd like for you to if you wanted. Asa said you had some time off?"

"I do. I just didn't want to assume."

"Oh, well, yes, mmhmm." After confirming him joining us, Milo continued undressing, stripping down to his boxers.

"Is this okay?" he asked, looking around the room. "I usually sleep naked, but I figured that wouldn't be appreciated."

"Speak for yourself," Cohen mumbled, making me smile.

"Yeah, it's um, fine with me," I said, a little too brightly. "You okay to share with us? It might be a tight squeeze."

"I bet it is," Cohen whispered, making my cheeks red. I couldn't take his commentary any longer, so I turned, narrowing my eyes at him. He played it off, whistling like he hadn't been saying anything.

Setting the clothes Asa had given me on the table, I looked between the three guys, trying to figure out what order. "Um, anyone okay with being guy to guy? What do we do, butts to butts? Feet to head?"

Asa chuckled, stepping forward and putting me out of my rambling misery. "I'll sleep at the end. You can be the middle. I already got my cream," he whispered before kissing my forehead, and plopping down at the foot of the bed. Cohen tossed him a pillow, and he shoved it under his head, crossing his feet over one another, looking completely relaxed.

Sighing, I turned back to the guys. Cohen had taken Asa's decision as his cue to slide into the other side of the bed, leaving me to climb over one of them. Milo saw my dilemma, making me think he must've noticed my ogling of him, and picked me up, placing me in the middle.

Everyone settled down, the room going dark as Cohen turned out the light. Breathing could be heard as everything quieted, the sounds of three people making me hyperaware of every move I made. Eventually, I was able to fall asleep, and I wondered if I'd wake up with something poking me in the back again.

Though, I couldn't say I minded how that had ended.

Nineteen

FINLEY

Unconsciously, I worried things would be weird when I woke, but surprisingly they were so normal that I was beginning to wonder if I'd woken up in a different life. The guys had all seemed to bond and were working together better than some pit crews. Breakfast this morning had been an enormous spread they'd managed to put together, and now they were dividing the tasks for the day before we left like soccer moms before a tournament.

It was scary how sexy I found their organization and team spirit. Hopefully, they remembered to get me some new underwear, or I was doomed.

When Cohen brushed against my leg for the third time, I could no longer take it, and I gasped as I shifted.

"Yes, sweetheart?" he asked, his fingers trailing up my leg.

"I didn't know my legs were a keyboard," I hissed when his fingers got to the hem of the oversized t-shirt I was wearing. I'd gambled that I'd be okay for a few hours while I waited for Asa and Milo to return with clean clothes. It seemed like Cohen would cash in on that bet and tease me until I caved.

The joke was on him. I was a horrible gambler and always folded. I was practically putty in his hands if he dared to take it.

Looking up at him, I found him closer than I remembered as he hovered over me, his stubble brushing against my cheek. His stormy blue eyes bore into me with such an intensity that I forgot to breathe.

He didn't waste words asking, descending down onto my lips like it was the most natural thing for us. And perhaps for us, it was. Cohen was the boy I'd known in a different form for over five years now. Kissing him felt like the answer to all the nights I'd wondered if a boy would ever notice me.

The laptop was moved from Cohen's lap, and I quickly replaced it as he shifted me. Straddling him, I brought my hands to his hair, weaving them into the tresses. He groaned beneath me as I began to rock into him. When Cohen's hands dropped down to my shirt, and he began to lift it, I pulled back, biting my lip as I watched him. Raising my arms, I dared him with my eyes to proceed.

Smirking, he pulled the shirt over my head and then stared, his eyes wide. "Fuck, sweetheart. You've been sitting next to me all morning practically naked?"

Lifting a shoulder up, I smiled. "I like to live on the dangerous side."

Cohen coughed on my words as he began to grow harder beneath me. "How dangerous do you feel like being today?" he asked, skimming his finger over the top of my breast. His eyes dropped, watching his finger as it dipped and lowered around the other.

Reaching down, I unzipped his pants as I watched him. When my hand grazed the waistband of his boxers, his eyes jumped to mine, no longer focused on my breasts. "Very," I said, tucking my fingers under the elastic band. Coarse hair greeted me as I lowered my hand, finding his hard cock waiting for me.

Stroking it, I gripped it firmly in my grasp as he sucked in a breath, waiting to see what I would do next. Pulling his boxers lower, I freed him. It was kind of hot being completely naked with Cohen still dressed, only his cock out on display.

Taking his dick into my hand again, I rolled it around as I looked at it closely. It was girthy, and I hoped I'd be able to take it. Licking my lips, I debated bending over and kissing it.

"If you do that, I'll be a goner," he rasped, his voice hoarse.

Peering up at him from under my eyelashes, I decided to do as I said and live a little dangerously. Lifting up on my knees, I gripped his cock with one hand as I positioned him at my entrance.

"Shit," he mumbled, his body tensing as he waited for me to move. I could see how much he was holding back, giving me this moment to own. It seemed Cohen knew me better than I'd ever imagined.

"Are you sure you're ready?" he asked, giving me one last out.

Nodding, I leaned forward, kissing him as I slowly lowered myself onto him. His thick cock stretched me more than I'd ever been, and I sucked in a breath as he continued filling me. When I was fully seated, I pulled back, taking in a breath. Cohen's eyes drilled into me, begging me to move.

Rising up, I quickly slammed myself back down, hoping if I did it quicker, I'd adjust faster. Gasping, I held onto his shoulders as he cursed. I could feel parts of his zipper biting into my bare backside, giving me a reprieve from the feeling of him filling me up.

"You're doing so good, Fin. Do you want help?"

I started to nod just as we heard a beep at the door. Eyes wide, I stared at Cohen for half a second before he was lifting me off him and pulled my shirt over my head. Quickly, I tucked it under me just as he pulled the laptop into his lap when the door opened. His pants were still undone, but the computer covered them for now.

Our breathing was quick, so I focused on the screen as I tried to calm my racing heart. Was what we did wrong? Was he having second thoughts?

"Stop whatever you're thinking. I just panicked about being

found in a compromising position, not about the act itself," he whispered just as Asa walked into view.

"Clothes have been dropped off. They'll bring them up when they're clean. In the meantime, I got you a few things," Asa announced, smiling at us. I peeked up and discovered Asa standing with a few bags. I looked behind him to see if Milo had returned, but found it empty.

"He had one more stop to make and wanted to do it on his own," he said in answer to my look. Nodding, I focused back on the bags in his hands, trying to ignore the slickness between my legs as giddiness filled me at the prospect of new clothes. Rubbing my hands together, I started to bounce at what lay inside them.

"Damn, if that's the response clothes get, I want to buy them next time. Go on, give us a show," Cohen said, chuckling as he nudged me toward Asa, a slight dare in his voice.

Glancing at him, I raised my eyebrow as we stared at one another, seeing who'd cave first. This time, I had a feeling I'd win. With a squeal, I hopped up on my knees, clapping as I smiled at the pretty things. With a wink, I began to crawl forward, knowing full well that my pussy, which had to be glistening at this point, would be on full display for Cohen.

A curse and a shift of the laptop had me smirking as I snatched the bag and dumped it onto the bed, finding a few tops, jeans, and best of all, some underwear and a bra. I fingered all the items, the thrill of new things making me high as I began sorting the clothes into outfits while keeping my butt lifted, so Cohen had to stare at it.

"Thank you," I said, jumping up to kiss Asa. Wrapping my arms around his neck, the earlier heat returned, and I got the idea to see how far I could push our newfound relationship. Nipping his ear, I leaned forward to whisper.

"Were you serious about seeing where this leads us?"

He pulled back, looking me in the eyes. "Yes. I'm not scared. Why?" he whispered, never dropping his green orbs from mine.

I peered over my shoulder and saw the pure need on Cohen's

face, the want still present. It seemed we were all going to find out if we were okay with everything we'd said.

"You should check out what Cohen and I got up to while you were gone."

"Okay," Asa said, looking over my shoulder. Taking his hand, I pushed it under the shirt and onto my pussy. His eyes widened as he looked back at me, a grin spreading across his face. "It seems I interrupted something." His fingers began to tease my labia, and I felt a body press into me from behind. "How can I help?" Asa asked, but it was clear it wasn't to me, but Cohen.

"I think Fin's done enough talking for today. Maybe you can give her something to occupy her mouth?"

Cohen's warm hands landed on my ass as he pushed the shirt over my head. I sucked in a breath as it was removed for the second time. Asa's eyes widened as he nodded enthusiastically. He grabbed the shirt I'd been wearing from Cohen and tossed it, unhooking his pants as he watched Cohen fondle my naked body.

His hands gripped my hips, and I felt his cock slide between my legs, rubbing against my pussy. With a moan, I lowered onto my elbows, lifting my ass higher for him to enter me. Cohen didn't hesitate, pulling me onto him in one go, my garbled scream lost in the bed as my head fell forward at the force.

"Holy fuck, Batman!" I shouted as he began to thrust into me, no longer taking it slow but showing me just how good it could feel as he plunged deep.

Lifting my head, I found Asa stroking himself as he watched the show before him. It was hotter than I imagined seeing him get off on me being impaled by another man.

"Don't forget your role, Asa. Stuff her mouth," Cohen growled, reaching down to pinch my nipple with one hand. Moaning, I opened my mouth as he stepped forward, ready to take him. It was odd at first, as Cohen's thrusts pushed me further onto Asa's dick, but I soon lost track of what was happening when my body began to race toward an orgasm. I'd never come this quickly before, and the knowledge of that scared and excited me.

Asa held my head in his hands as he used the momentum of Cohen to fuck my mouth. Looking up, I checked again, worried I'd find him mortified by what he was participating in, but as usual, Asa surprised me. Nothing but love and lust stared back at me as he peered down. The last of my resolve fled, and I allowed myself to let go and throw the worrying out the window. I toppled over as soon as I did, my body following behind my mind as waves of pleasure crashed into me.

Body spasming, I closed my eyes as what felt like a million white stars exploded around me. With a grunt, I felt Cohen tighten his grip on me as he thrust harder, holding me to him. I moaned, the vibration being all Asa needed as he erupted down my throat. Swallowing him down, I panted when he removed his cock from my lips, my body no longer able to hold itself up; my muscles had turned to jelly.

The guys laughed as I fell onto the pile of clothes, feeling completely at ease being naked. Asa scooped me up a few minutes later and walked me into the bathroom. With great care, he washed me off in the shower, paying extra attention to my hair. Each gentle caress made me love him even more.

"Thank you," I whispered later as he draped a towel around me.

"You don't have to thank me, but you're welcome."

"It's more than just the shower. You take care of me in a way I've never been taken care of before. I didn't even know I desired that, so thank you. You haven't once admonished me for caring about more than one guy, and even though this revenge quest has nothing to do with you, you're here, supporting my crazy mission. So, thank you. I love you, Asa."

"I hope you realize one day that you don't have to thank me for those things, Fin. I love you. Your crazy is my crazy. I'm not going anywhere." Kissing my lips, I had to stop myself from melting into a pool of goo.

"Now, I believe we're owed a fashion show," he teased, waggling his eyebrows. Grinning, I raced out into the room, grabbing the new things he'd bought me. Cohen laughed but set the computer aside, eager for the show, apparently.

That was how Milo found us a few minutes later as I pretended to walk the catwalk in a pair of black jeans, a scoop neck top, and my boots. He grinned as he walked in, placing his bags down onto the dresser and waiting until I was finished to tell us what was in the bags.

"So?" I asked, no longer able to wait. He smirked, looking over at Cohen.

"Well, Cohen and I thought it would be a good idea for us all to be connected. So, I got us some smartwatches, and he's going to program them so we can always find one another no matter where we go. It only works if we wear them, but it's better than nothing."

"You did that for me?" I asked, looking between Cohen and Milo.

"Of course, sweetheart. I trust the Order, but it doesn't mean there's not something going on where we're worried about your safety. I've programmed a lot of cool features where you can reach out to any of us and let us know if you're in trouble, need help, etc."

We spent the rest of the night going over the tech, and like the nerd I was, I couldn't wait to play around with it. Before too long, it was time to pack and get some sleep before we started on our long journey. I hadn't expected my mission to turn out this way, but as I smiled into my pillow, I knew I was glad. Now, if I could only figure out what Blackhawk's message meant.

Twenty

FINLEY

 onto the nearest soft surface. It had nothing to do with the increase in my sex life. Nope.

We'd only gotten a few hours of sleep before the alarm went off, spurring us all into motion as we got ready. First up had been a flight on a private plane, which was my new favorite way to fly, taking us up north. From there, it was a three-hour drive by car through mountains, firmly making it my least favorite way to travel. I'd be happy if I never saw a sign for a switchback curve again.

When we all finally stepped out of the SUV, I didn't know who was happier to have it over with. We all looked a little green around the edges from motion sickness, except for Cohen, who'd been driving and seemed to take delight in our plight.

"Come on, I'm famished," he said, patting his stomach. The thought of food had me clutching my stomach again as nausea rolled through me.

"Yeah, pass."

Cohen chuckled, walking toward me. "Come on, sweetheart."

He took my hand, leading me toward the ominous-looking building. Though, if I imagined a secret facility for a place, this wasn't exactly what I had envisioned. It was concrete and looked like a place people went to die a slow death as a taxidermist or something.

Asa and Milo trailed behind us, both quiet as well. I didn't know if we were all nervous, nauseous, or just plain tired, but the conversation had been at a minimum all day as we'd traveled. I'd been sucked into my own thoughts, so I wouldn't focus on all the varying reasons why no one was speaking. Nope, I wasn't going to spiral in a million directions. I wasn't going to do it.

"You ready?" Cohen asked, breaking my cycle of thoughts.

"Yeah." I glanced over my shoulder, finding Asa and Milo nodding.

Cohen squeezed my hand and knocked on the door. A screen appeared, surprising me. But when I really thought about it, it shouldn't have. If this place was as high-tech as I expected, they would have the most advanced technology.

Cohen's face was scanned, and then he placed his hand on the pad. Once he was done, he turned, looking at all of us. "You'll need to scan as well. Biometrics of everyone in the building are recorded for safety precautions."

Nodding, I stepped up, the screen flashing over my face. I could feel the warmth of the laser as it scanned, and I hoped it wasn't exposing me to radiation or anything. Once it beeped, an outline of a hand popped up, and I placed mine over the screen. Once it was done, my name appeared with my date of birth on the screen.

Stepping back, I made room for Asa and Milo to go through the process. Once the four of us had passed, the door beeped louder, a hissing sound emerging as it opened.

"Was that sealed?" I asked, and Cohen looked at me, nodding. He had a smile on his face I hadn't seen before, and I could tell he was happy to be here.

"Yeah. Security is top-notch. All the tech here is absurd. I can't wait to show you some of it. Come on." Again, he grabbed my hand, pulling me over the threshold. Excitement vibrated through his whole body. I wondered if he'd been electrocuted for a second.

The interior didn't match what I expected, either. It was a stainless steel room with no personal effects. There wasn't a desk or any furniture. Just an elevator bay at the back. Cohen walked toward it, and I peeked over my shoulder at the other two. They were both looking around as I had, looks of confusion plastered on their faces. Asa caught me watching and raised his shoulders.

The elevator opened as we approached, and we stepped in. There weren't any buttons to push, so it was a little unnerving when the doors shut and it began to move. Cohen watched me, a smile on his lips. Scrunching up my face, I gave up, trying to figure it out, and sighed.

"How?"

With a short laugh, he pointed to the camera in the elevator's corner. "Someone is watching and knows where people are meant to be. It will only go to the floor you're authorized to be on at a specific time."

"Phew, I was beginning to think it was a magic elevator or something," Milo said, blushing.

"I mean, it kind of is," Asa replied. "Who's to say tech isn't magic in some form?" He shrugged his shoulders, completely serious.

"You're a nerd," I gasped, slapping his muscular arm. "I never realized it because you hide it so well. But under all the brawn and goldness is a bona fide nerd!"

This time, it was Asa's turn to blush as he shrugged his shoulders, not responding. The elevator began to slow, and we all stopped talking, unsure of what to expect when the doors opened. So far, it had been sterile, quiet, and devoid of people. I couldn't imagine an entire order being that way. There had to be people somewhere, right?

The elevator stopped, and I sucked in a breath as I waited. It felt like forever, but the doors began to open, revealing what lay beyond. Noise greeted us as it opened into what appeared to be a common room. It was so different from upstairs that I almost felt like I'd stepped off into a different world. Maybe the elevator *was* magic after all, because I definitely felt like an outsider stepping into this setting.

People stopped talking when they heard the elevator, and they turned to look at us. Cohen exited first and was greeted with a loud welcome as people began to converge on him. I stayed back with Asa and Milo as we watched it unfold.

"Is it me, or does it seem like he's really popular here?" Milo whispered.

"No, I agree. I mean, he's a friendly guy, that's not the weird part, but I never took him as this..." Asa said, waving his hand around.

Nodding, I couldn't help but agree. It was a whole new side of Cohen, but I didn't hate it. He'd always been friendly and outgoing with me online. I hadn't known when we met in person if it was the circumstances or if he was just more reserved face to face. With this new information, I had to guess it was the situation. Or maybe it was the fact he had to keep this part of his life hidden. I knew from experience that when you had to hide something, it began to bleed over into other areas, making you forget what you were hiding to start with after a while.

Cohen seemed to have noticed we'd stopped, turning to reach out a hand for me. I walked forward, waving awkwardly at the crowd.

"Fin, meet some of my old friends. This is Kristina, Asher, and Caleb. We went through training together." A girl and two guys smiled back at me, assessing every part of me, making me feel like I was under a microscope.

"It's nice to meet you all. This is Asa and Milo," I said, wanting the attention off of me, and pointed to the two tall guys behind me. It worked as the trio began to observe the new guys, but I realized my mistake when I caught an interested gleam in Kristina's eyes. "They're mine," I blurted, my face heating. "I mean, with me. Asa's my boyfriend, and um..."

The guys chuckled. I could feel them all shuffling closer, so it didn't seem to make them mad I'd just awkwardly claimed them in front of people without even discussing anything. I didn't even know what we were, but I knew I wanted the chance to figure that out before other people began to make it messier.

Kristina smiled at me, making me feel less awkward. "It's nice to meet you. We haven't gotten to see Cohen in such a long time. I'm glad he was able to return and bring you. He used to talk about you all the time."

I peered up at the man in question, finding him blushing; despite his insistence, he didn't do that.

"Oh, really?" I teased, liking her now that she wasn't drooling all over my men. Fuck, I needed to quit assuming things, but I couldn't deny how nice it sounded and felt to claim them. Sawyer was right again; I needed to stop being scared and take what I wanted.

"Come on, let's show you to your quarters and then grab some food. You must be starving after the trip. It's never fun the first time coming up that mountain," Asher offered, motioning for us to follow.

The other people gathered nodded, saying hello to Cohen and us as we passed. Most of the people were around our age, with a few younger and older mixed throughout. All in all, I'd guess there were about twenty people spread out in the room as we passed through it.

We stopped at a door, and once again, we had to scan our hands to get through it. Cohen hadn't been kidding when he said they had this place wired with biometrics. Stopping at another one about ten down, Cohen placed his hand on the panel and then stepped back.

"Go ahead and scan yours. This door will be set up to allow

only us entrance." The three of us nodded, used to the drill now, and scanned our palms. Once that was done, it beeped, and the door opened.

"I'll see you guys in the canteen," Asher said, letting us walk into our quarters. I liked how much they respected privacy here. None of us had brought in our bags, considering we had such few things, so we walked in and looked around, but it didn't take us long to take in the small kitchen, living room, bathroom, and two bedrooms.

"It's nice."

"You haven't seen the best part," Cohen said, grinning. He grabbed my hand, pulling me out of the room and down the hall toward another door. This one didn't require a handprint, so he opened the door, and I was immediately greeted by the smell of detergent and dryer sheets.

"Yes!" I jumped up and down, the excitement coursing through me. "This is my new favorite room." The guys laughed, but I'd gone so long without being able to clean clothes I was desperate for the easy access.

"You can do a load whenever you want. It's free use for all. I know you just did some, but if you need to do anything, our bags should be in our rooms after we eat, once they've gone through checks."

"Oh, I thought we were just waiting, but I guess that makes sense." I shrugged, following them out of the laundry room, a contented sigh leaving me.

"Man, I've never known anyone to get so excited about laundry," Milo whispered to Asa, making him chuckle.

"Fin loves her clothes, and having clean clothes is one of her favorite things."

"I like having all the options laid out for me when deciding what to wear. It's the worst thing in the world when I need a certain top to pull a look together, and it's dirty! The travesty!"

The guys laughed, but I was serious. Fashion emergencies were no joke. Henry could attest to how many I'd had.

When food smells began to reach us, my stomach growled, no longer angry about all the switchback curves now that I'd settled. The canteen was full of people gathered around tables. It was set up like a restaurant that included a hostess station at the front, tables and booths around it, a bar to the side, and a stage in the back. It was lively, and I loved the energy of the place.

"Wow, this is awesome," Asa said, echoing my thoughts. Cohen smiled that look again, like he'd won the lottery, leading us to the hostess. I finally realized what the look on his face meant. He was home, and he was proud to show it to us, introducing us to people he cared about.

"Cohen! It's been so long. Give me a hug," the woman at the front said, walking around to pull him into an embrace.

"Hey, Grams. I have some people for you to meet." She pulled back, patting his face before turning to us.

"Oh, this must be the lovely Finley I've heard about." She reached out a hand for me, and I grasped it, not realizing she would pull me into her. I went easily, her hugs reminding me of a grandmother I hadn't seen in ages, and her name made sense. She must be the grandmother to all the people here.

"It's nice to meet you."

"It's Karen, but most people call me Grams. Especially after that horrible meme-making my name synonymous with a dumpster fire," she huffed, letting me go.

"Dumpster fire?" Milo whispered, making me laugh.

"Well, I like Grams. I'd be happy to call you that."

"I knew you were the real deal the moment you walked in. I have a knack for that. Now, introduce me to the other two lovely fellas you have here." She lifted an eyebrow, and I had a feeling she knew they were more than just casual acquaintances.

"This is Asa, my boyfriend, and Milo."

They both stepped forward, receiving their own smothering hug. I noticed how Milo melted into her embrace, and I knew I'd need to give him more attention. With what I'd gathered of his family, being part of the Council couldn't have meant they were touchy-feely.

"Welcome to the Canteen. Let me show you to a table." She smiled at us, leading us over to a somewhat private area. It had a wraparound booth that opened to the side of the stage. There wasn't anyone up there yet, just some soft music playing over the speakers. Once we were all seated with me between Asa and Cohen, I looked at him, wondering what we do next.

"So?"

"Someone will be out to ask us what we want in a minute. They usually have two meat options and a vegetarian one each meal."

"Great, I'm starved," Asa said, patting his stomach.

Cohen's phone beeped as someone approached us, and he pulled it out, scrunching up his face. He put it away as the waiter neared, taking over for us.

"Good evening, tonight we have a chicken curry or steak stroganoff. Unless anyone would like to hear the gluten or vegetarian options?" he looked around at us, but we shook our heads. "Excellent. Would you care to start, Miss?"

"Oh, um, sure. I'll have the chicken."

The others went around the table, ordering their food, and we fell into an easy silence as we waited. I didn't know about the guys, but I was busy processing all the new information from the moment we'd stepped out of the SUV. There was a lot to filter through, and my brain was verging on overstimulation.

"Who texted?" Asa asked a few minutes later, reminding me that Cohen had pulled out his phone.

"My handler, he wants to meet."

"Why is that bad?" I asked, noticing the frown on his face.

"In all the years I've been part of the order, I've never met him face to face. Or, well, I might have. You see, everyone here has a code name. Online, we go by those, in person, our real names. We never share our identities to help keep them separate and secret. It also helps build camaraderie. We can form connections with people without feeling competitive with them."

"I don't understand why it's bad then." I reached over, taking his hand.

"Because it goes against everything. So, does that mean I'm no longer going to be part of the Order? Or am I heading into something more dangerous and the information won't matter if I know it because it dies with me?"

The realization of what he said struck me, and I began to look around at everyone, wondering just who they were online. The food arrived, and we all ate in silence, too consumed by what this meant for us to engage in conversation.

Twenty-One

COHEN

We all trailed back to the room, the earlier excitement of returning to a place that had felt like my only home for years drained with each step. They wouldn't kick me out now, after all this time?

Granted, I hadn't been the best Order agent, but I'd always done my job. Just when it had come to Finley, I'd looked for ways to circumvent the mission. I'd even been shirking them for the past six months, much to my handler's annoyance. When he'd finally told me to approach her, it felt like my life was coming full circle, and I could have the life I'd always wanted.

But what if that was all a lie?

I'd blindly trusted the Order because of who they had been to me, but what if that was childish ignorance coming into play?

"Hey, what if we play some games and not think about death and stalkers for one night?" Fin asked as we stepped into our suite.

"Sounds like a great idea, babe," Asa said, pulling her into his side and kissing her effortlessly on the forehead. It no longer made me envious as I watched their easy affection. She was mine now, and I wouldn't let her go.

"Yeah, there should be some board games in the closet. If not, there will be some out in the common room. We could even see if the others want to join, or just keep it us?" I asked, checking my phone as a message came in. "Actually, our bags are ready. If someone comes with me to grab them, we can look at the games?" I asked, looking up.

"Let's just keep it us. I don't think I can socialize anymore tonight," Fin said, twisting her shirt, and I noticed how tired she did look.

"Of course, sweetheart."

"I'll help," Milo suggested, walking toward the door with me.

"We'll be right back."

Asa and Fin already had the door open to the closet, scrounging through it before we even exited. Laughing, I shook my head as Milo and I fell into a leisurely pace. We were quiet as we made our way to the elevator. I didn't know him as well as Asa, so I debated whether I should wait him out or just lay it all out there. Thankfully, it seemed Milo was ready to talk, making my decision easy.

"Am I dumb for being here? My whole life has been careful decisions laid out to reach a goal that was far away from anything I'd grown up around. I can't say I've been that same guy the last year."

I looked over at him as the elevator moved, assessing what he wasn't saying. "I think the real question is, did you like that person? You said you were tired of being alone, and you can't deny that Fin makes you feel alive in a way only Fin can."

He thought about my words before he slumped against the wall. "Yeah, you're right. I just had a moment of freaking out. I guess I worry I won't have a place with you guys. The three of you already feel so united."

"I understand feeling insecure in your role and place. I do. I've waited years to find it with Fin. The one thing I learned was that you can't stay on the sidelines. If Fin says she wants you here and you want a chance at being a part of her life, then trust that. She's not pulling you along just for fun. That's not who she is."

"Yeah?" he asked, looking at me with hope.

"For sure. Finley is as amazing as you think she is. It's not an act. Tell her if you want to be part of her life."

"Thanks, I think I will."

The elevator dinged as the doors opened, and I clapped him on the shoulder as I moved out of the space. I turned to the right, knowing where I was headed, and walked toward the surveillance room. Rounding the corner, I froze when I saw who was up ahead. I quickly pulled Milo into the first door that would open. Closing it, I leaned against it, waiting for the footsteps to pass.

"Um, what's that about?" he asked, looking at me quizzically. I realized I was still clutching his shirt in my hands, so I dropped it, smoothing out the material.

"Sorry. Just an old flame I don't want to deal with at the moment."

"Ah, okay. Do you think it's clear now?"

Taking a deep breath, I waited for my heart to slow before peeking my head out the door, looking both ways. When I didn't spot anyone, I nodded, and we both stepped out. We made it to the surveillance room a few more doors down without interruption, making my heart slow the rest of the way.

"Agent Campbell," one of the guards greeted, picking up a clipboard for me to sign. I quickly initialed all of our belongings, scanning them to see if anything had been kept out. It seemed all our items had passed, so I handed the clipboard back to the man.

Milo was looking around at all the computer screens, a look of awe on his face. "This is impressive, and I'm not one who geeks out about this stuff," he said. Laughing at him, I turned to the beeping door as the guard carted our bags out.

"Here you go," he said, returning to the screens. Picking up two, Milo picked up the others, and we made our way back toward the elevator. The corridor was empty, and I sighed, the rest of my body relaxing. Tonight was not the time for an awkward reunion.

The trip back was quiet, both of us consumed in our thoughts, so when the elevator dinged, I jumped slightly. In the common room, Milo followed me over to the bookcase that was overflowing with board games. A few people were still out, playing some, nodding to us in greeting as we passed.

Selecting a few that I liked, I handed one to Milo, and we headed back to our crew. "I'm serious. You should talk to Fin. I thought I could walk away and let her be happy, but I knew I was only lying to myself when I saw her. She's brought me into her life now, and I hate that I waited so long to step forward. So, if my misery can teach us anything, it's that you shouldn't wait."

Milo nodded, and I placed my hand on the scanner, and we waited for it to beep. When we entered, we found Asa and Fin sitting around a coffee table, snacks and drinks ready for us. They both smiled as we entered, cementing the things I'd said. Asa had become like a brother to me, and I was grateful for his friendship. If I was honest with myself, it was one I hadn't ever let myself have with anyone. I slept around, flitted from city to city, telling myself I wanted it that way. In reality, I was lonely and pining for the type of family I had always wanted.

I had a chance to have everything I dreamed of, and it was right in front of me.

"What did you find?" I asked, looking at the stack of games.

"Connect Four, Sorry, and Monopoly!" Fin cheered, leaning up on her knees to see what we had. She looked so cute in her glasses and short shorts. I was about to suggest another game when I remembered she wasn't there in her relationship with Milo.

Setting the bags down, I placed the games on the table and then took the bags and put them in one of the bedrooms. I pulled out my computer, checking that the Order hadn't placed any new software on it while they had it. After a quick scan, I carried it out to the other room and sat in a chair while they discussed what games to play.

Opening up the program I had running on the code Blackhawk had left us, I found it was still only 40% through all the possibilities. Sighing, I set it aside and focused on the group in front of me.

"What's it going to be, sweetheart?" I asked, focusing on my girl.

"I think we should have a Speed Connect Four tournament, and then maybe a group game?"

"I'm game," Asa said, then laughed at his unintentional joke. Settling down on the couch, I faced off my opponent, who happened to be Fin first.

"No cheating, sweetheart."

"I'd never!" she exclaimed, but smiled, lifting only the corner of her mouth. Laughing, I placed my red piece into a slot, and she followed quickly. Over the next few seconds, we both put tokens into the spaces, trying to find our way to four.

"Ah!" one of the guys said next to us, but I didn't look away, needing to focus on beating Finley. She leaned forward, her shirt dipping a little to show her cleavage. I knew it was a ploy, but like the hungry man I was for her, I fell into her trap willingly and placed my piece without looking.

When she smirked, moving back, I knew she'd won, but I couldn't say I cared anymore.

"I win!" she cheered, giggling.

"No, I'm pretty sure I won, sweetheart." Fin peered up, meeting my eyes, and I watched as she licked her lips, her pupils going wide at my meaning.

"My turn. Championship round," Asa said, interrupting our eye fucking. Milo traded places, and I found the game much easier to concentrate on without Fin as my opponent.

After that, we played Sorry and then finished with a wild game of Uno, where it spit cards at us. I called it when we all started to yawn, knowing that tomorrow would come early.

"Come on, let's go to bed. We should be rested for whatever tomorrow brings."

Everyone nodded, and despite having two rooms, we all ended up in the same bed again, with Milo sleeping at the foot. Cuddling up to Fin, I held her in my arms, happy to be here.

"We'll deal with it together," she said, smoothing her hand over my face. "You taught me that."

Dipping my head down to hers, I breathed her in, feeling my whole being relax. "Thank you for reminding me, sweetheart." Kissing her nose, I snuggled her close, not even caring that Asa's arms were wrapped tight around her from behind.

Dodging an ex, decoding mysterious clues, and facing my handler were all things we'd do together, and I found myself liking the sound of that more and more.

Beeping woke me a few hours later, and I realized the program had found a match. Slipping out of bed, I crept over to the computer and picked it up, the flashing message making me giddy. This was the part I loved. Using my systems and knowledge to crack things, finding the impossible.

I hesitated for a second as I sat in the chair and looked over at Fin sleeping. She looked so peaceful; I hated to wake her. It might be better for me to comb through everything and then condense it for her so she didn't have to sift through all the boring things.

Part of me knew that was a lame excuse, but I carried on, clicking the cursor to follow the program. My earlier guess that it might be more than an IP address turned out to be correct. It was more of a web address to a secret folder. When I typed in the key, it opened, and I found what looked to be conversations. When I saw Blackhawk and Oblivion and another screen name, I paused, the urge to stop filling me, but my need to know what I needed to protect her from overtook my common sense, and I opened it.

Obsidian: It can't be him.

Oblivion: Are you sure? I thought you said that place was abandoned. How did this happen?

Blackhawk: You both are jumping to conclusions. Mongoose is fine. I promise.

Oblivion: Then who was it? If not him, then who? Do you not care that someone died?

Blackhawk: Of course, I care, little hacker. I'm just saying we're not responsible.

Obsidian: This is messed up. What did you say to him?

Oblivion: Nothing. He just said he needed help. When I asked him what, he returned and said not to worry about it. That he had figured it out and knew how to make things right. I haven't heard from him in days.

Blackhawk: What could going back to the house prove? It doesn't make sense, so the likely reason is that it's not Mongoose.

Oblivion: But what if it is and we do nothing?

Obsidian: Hawk's right. What can we do? We don't know his real name, where he lives or even what he looks like. There's nothing for us to report. If we say anything, we could be seen as accomplices.

Oblivion: But we didn't do anything with this fire.

Obsidian: So, you're just going to say, "Sorry, officer, we had to break into this place for an illegal hacking club on the dark web and just take a file?" Yeah. He'd lock you up so fast you wouldn't even get to ask for a lawyer.

Oblivion: I don't know if I can just ignore this.

Blackhawk: You have to. As far as MKG is concerned, he left a month ago. We have no connection to him. From this point forward, we don't talk about him. He left our team because of his mistakes that almost cost you Oblivion. We have another mission tonight. I'll take point. You can be security this time, Oblivion. You've earned the break. Do we all agree?

Obsidian: I'm good. You're right. He hasn't talked to any of us. There's no way to know if it's him, so no use concerning ourselves.

Blackhawk: Little hacker?

Oblivion: Yeah, fine. No more thoughts.

Blackhawk: We reconvene in four hours. Be ready.

I clicked on a few more, barely reading them as my mind processed the new information. Fin had briefly mentioned that they'd been a foursome at one point, but she hadn't said why they weren't at the end. Could this be the masked man who had attacked her? Coming back for vengeance after all these years? I skimmed through the messages, but the more flirty they became, the more I felt like I was invading her privacy. Copying all the files onto my own drive, I exited the site with the intention of returning to bed.

Something nagged me during the conversation, though, and I clicked onto one of the secure Order servers of back missions. After an hour of scrolling through files, my eyes closed, and I decided to call it quits. Just as I was about to shut the computer, my cursor moved over a folder, and I blinked, thinking I was reading it wrong.

Magnolia safe house-explosion

Opening the folder, I read the report but found no information that made sense. If it was a safe house, it couldn't have been the same place Fin had broken into. Right?

Crawling back into bed, thoughts plagued me as I tried to put the pieces together. Something wasn't right, and I was determined to figure it out. Fin's life might depend on it.

Twenty~Two

RYKER

I watched on the screen as they walked the complex. I'd been watching every single move since they'd arrived yesterday. I was fascinated by them. Every little thing they did made me wonder, and I pondered what it meant. Finley had always been a curiosity of mine, and having her resurface after all these years had me even more desperate to learn as much as I could about her. I hadn't realized how much I'd needed her until she'd disappeared.

Our games had been fun, and I'd gotten back a part of myself I thought had been lost years ago. And after all this time, it seemed like we'd finally be face to face. Nerves filled me, and I didn't know why. I shouldn't be this nervous, but I was. We'd come so close to meeting before, but things were different this time. It wasn't on my terms, but it was necessary. Someone was trying to hurt her, and I couldn't hide any longer.

When they entered their apartment, I knew it was time. Standing, I smoothed down the black button-down shirt. It wasn't what I usually wore, but it felt like I needed it. Though, paired with my black jeans with holes in the knees and combat boots, I didn't know who I was trying to fool with my shirt. Maybe myself more than I realized.

I'd looked into the other two guys who'd tagged along, needing to know who my competition was. Milo was a descendent of a Council family, but based on what I found, he was clean, never having participated in any of their criminal dealings. I could respect a man who'd bucked family tradition to find his own path. I knew firsthand how difficult it could be to turn away from the sinister side of things. With his recent doctorate and killer fashion sense, I felt intimidated by the man I'd never even met. He had the wealth and prestige to provide a good life for Finley and a respectful career path.

But it was Asa who struck me as the biggest obstacle. While Milo had wealth and an honorable career, Asa was her boyfriend. He was clean-cut, an all-star hockey player, and had connections to her best friend. They'd been dating for almost a year, and I knew he cared for her. I just wasn't sure how much and whether that could be tested.

Cohen was a surprise for me. I'd known him for years as his handler, a fellow trainee of the Order, and even longer online as Chaos. Our relationship was long and filled with pitfalls that would need to be dealt with. I knew it would be a surprise for him when we came face to face. The secrecy had felt necessary all those years ago, but now I wondered if I hadn't kept it from him for other reasons. Seeing him holding Finley's hand, though, had sent a spike of jealousy through me I hadn't been prepared for.

Knowing I couldn't put this off any longer, I sucked it up and moved toward the door. Walking through the hall, I blanked my face, needing to keep my features neutral amongst the others. Only a select few knew my true role in the Order, and I wanted to keep it that way.

Imperium in Imperio, or the Order as we called it, had been created as a way to bring order to all the agencies around the world. As our founders had known, any time power was involved, it could be easily corrupted, morphing the organism into something it was never meant to be. The Order was there to bring balance back to the fold. And we'd been doing it undercover for decades.

Nodding at a few people, I turned down the hall toward their quarters. This was it. I stopped in front, debating if I should knock or just enter. With my position in the Order, I had access to every room, but I didn't know if I wanted them to know that yet. Letting out a deep breath, I raised my fist and knocked on the door, the chatter inside stopping at the sound.

Footsteps sounded, my trademark smirk crossing my face as I heard the handle turning. A retort to reprimand them for not using the camera crossed my mind, but I held it at bay. This would work better anyway. I wasn't sure if Cohen would open the door if he saw my face.

The former Council heir was the one on the other side, assessing me as he opened it. "Can we help you?" he asked.

I didn't drop my smirk, the role too comfortable to let go of. "I'm here for Finley." It wasn't what I meant to say, but it was true.

His eyes narrowed as he tried to decipher my meaning. Whether or not he took it as the threat it was, was up to him. I would make Finley mine.

"Name?" he asked, not moving, making me respect him.

"Ryker Jenson."

"Don't let him in," a voice said behind Milo, and I peered up to find Cohen staring me down. I looked around him but still didn't see my little hacker anywhere.

"Ah, Cohen, that's no way to greet your *superior*." Cohen's face paled, and Milo looked between the two of us before stepping back and letting me in.

Just as the door closed, the other two walked out of a bedroom with a basket of dirty clothes. "Who was at the door?" Finley asked before stopping and looked up to meet my eyes.

Smirk in place, I waited for her to rush toward me, showing all these guys the bond we had. She dropped the basket, running for me, and I felt like I'd been waiting my whole life for this moment. I opened my arms and waited for her to sweep into them and give me the kiss I'd been dreaming of for five years. When a pain seared me, I blinked, not understanding.

Bending over, I blinked more, looking at my little hacker as tears trailed down my face. Her face was red, and she was breathing hard as she seared me with hatred. I looked up to make sure I'd come to the right place. Asa and Milo looked on in shock, slightly cringing in discomfort. Cohen had a mix of disbelief, fear, and satisfaction at my plight as he stared down at me.

"What the hell, Finley?"

She moved closer, her hands on her hips as she stared me down. "Don't what the hell me! What are you doing here?"

Cohen moved closer, pulling her further away from me. "Sweetheart, not that I don't appreciate the gesture. But is there a reason why you kicked my *superior*?" he ground out, the word sounding sour to my ears, breaking something in me.

"Your superior?" she asked, shaking her head in disbelief. "No, this is Blackhawk."

At the name, the guys stopped, their faces changing to ones of rage. Backing up, I lifted one hand, still cupping my balls with the other as they throbbed in pain.

"Wait a minute. I think there's a misunderstanding. Yes, I'm Blackhawk, but I'm not the bad guy here."

"That's rich coming from you," Cohen seethed, no longer caring that I was his boss.

"Stop. I think we need to take a minute and talk about things. We're clearly all missing some information."

Finley shook her head, hurt and rage on her face that made me stop, wondering what I'd done to make her look that way.

"I don't understand. Finley, I thought we were playing a game. I didn't mean for you to get hurt. That's why I called you here. The MKG has grown too big, and we need to stop them."

"MidKnight Guild? They're still out there?" She shook her head, clearing her thoughts. "The only person I have a vendetta against is you. You're the one who ruined my life, and I want my revenge."

I stared, not understanding. But before I could explain, the door to the room opened as three operatives swarmed the space, raising guns at the four of them.

"Halt. Come no closer. Sir, are you okay?" the leader asked.

"Yes, I'm fine. It's a misunderstanding. They're not a threat."

At my directive, they lowered their weapons but didn't exit yet, still waiting for my command as they assessed the situation.

"Sorry, sir, your vitals increased, and we could tell you were in pain. We thought you were under threat. Shall we leave?"

"Yes, I'm fine. Nothing an ice pack won't cure." The three guards nodded, taking their leave.

"Why did they come to your rescue?" Cohen asked, looking at me differently than he ever had before.

Sighing, I closed the door, leaning against it. "Because I'm not only your handler but the leader of the Order."

Cohen's face paled again as he took in the information. His hand shot out to grab the table, and he slumped down into a chair. The others followed suit, Finley watching me with narrowed eyes. I stayed where I was, predicting the space between us was a good thing for the time being. At least for my balls' sake.

"I think you have some things to explain. First, how about the night you had me arrested?"

She crossed her arms, and I was momentarily distracted by her tits, so when the words sunk in, I stared, sure I'd heard her wrong.

"I'm sorry, what? I haven't gotten anyone arrested."

"Yes, you did!" she screamed, some of her fire emerging, and I reflexively covered my balls, afraid of a second attack.

"I promise you, I did no such thing. Can you please share what you're accusing me of?"

She laughed, the noise appearing off. "Fine. Play it that way. I have nothing to say to you, and if you run this place, I want nothing to do with the Order. This was a mistake."

Fear rushed through me at possibly losing my chance to finally have Finley in my life. So, I did the only thing I could think of at that moment.

"Well, I'm sorry to hear you feel that way. If you don't want to share what I'm accused of, then maybe a few days to cool off is in order." I smiled at my pun, moving to open the door. Standing in the middle of it, I turned and looked at them. "I'm sorry it's come to this."

Shutting the door, I punched in my code, sealing them inside until I unlocked it again. I heard the knob turn and a scream when it didn't open. Fire filled my veins as I walked back to my office, determined to make Finley talk to me and realize I was the man for her.

Twenty-Three

FINLEY

The door slammed closed, and we all stood there, staring. I rushed toward it, twisting it. Screaming, I backed away. My breathing was coming out ragged as I tried to put all the puzzle pieces together.

MKG still existed.

Blackhawk was Cohen's handler.

He wanted me as part of the Order.

The air left me, and I sunk down to the ground, no longer able to keep standing. The memory I'd tried so hard to ignore, the one where everything had culminated, rose to the surface, and I could no longer deny it existed.

If MKG was still operating, what did that mean? Was this Obsidian? Mongoose's ghost? Were they after us? Were any of us safe?

"Fin?" a voice beckoned, but I was too stunned, too overwhelmed, to hear it. The realization that a long-forgotten ghost had emerged had me withdrawing. I couldn't do this. I was too weak to deal with this. It would be better if I just checked out. I didn't deserve love. I wasn't owed anything.

The things I'd done meant I was destined to live a life of solitude, never able to repair the damage I'd caused.

There was no redemption to be found here. I was deluding myself into believing I could. It didn't matter that I'd found Blackhawk. He might've been the one to set me up, but he wasn't the one with blood on his hands. That honor lay only with me.

I'd killed Mongoose, and then conveniently forgot about it to appease my guilt.

"She's in shock. The door's locked. Cohen, can you hack it?"

"Unlikely, if the Order designed it that way, there's no way I'm getting through it."

"Call him back. She needs help. Do it! *Now!*"

The disembodied voices floated around me. I knew the familiar sounds, but it didn't seem to matter. Nothing mattered.

I'd killed someone, and when my family knew, they'd toss me out like I deserved. There was no hope for me. I should've taken that bottle of pills all those years ago. Maybe then I would've saved someone from dying.

Closing my eyes, I let the blackness take me, praying it would all be over soon. There was no redemption for the broken and downtrodden. Happiness and love were a lie I told myself to wake up every morning. But I didn't deserve to wake up.

Twenty-Four

ASA

Panic surged through me, and I glanced around, trying to figure out what to do. Everything had spiraled in the last ten minutes, and I felt like someone had hit me in the head with a hockey puck. Milo hovered over Fin where she'd passed out on the floor. Cohen angrily paced back and forth as he tried to reach someone on the phone and I stood there, useless as I tried not to pee my pants.

Fin thought I was perfect, but this was where I failed. I didn't know how to handle things like this. I'd been faced with that realization when she'd been taken, and as she laid on the ground, going into shock, I was hit with it again.

I wasn't enough, and ultimately it was why I realized I needed the other guys. Because at some point, she would've realized it too, and then she would leave.

I was always the one who was left behind.

It had happened since birth when my twin was taken from me. I could feel a part of me missing, and I unconsciously overcompensated for that loss with my parents until finally, I wasn't enough to engage my father's interest, and he abandoned me altogether. My mother was easier to appease, but I could tell she was missing part of her heart. When I found Sawyer, I felt whole again. Everything felt like it was aligning.

But then Fin had been taken, and I realized my flaw.

I wasn't good in a crisis. I couldn't do anything. I had no discernible skills outside of hockey. It was just a waiting game until everyone else figured it out.

The self-defeating thoughts threatened to take over when I looked down at the woman I loved. I would lose her. I would lose them all. Two guys I'd come to feel true friendship with.

Milo and Cohen both said something, looking at me for the answer. My breathing quickened, and I knew I would pass out if I didn't stop it.

"Asa! Snap out of it. This isn't the time to freak out. Fin needs you," Cohen bellowed.

I shook my head, the decision made. "No, I'm just in the way."

Cohen walked over, his own panic evident in his eyes. I waited for him to tell me I was right and that he'd take care of Finley. Dropping my head, I inadvertently placed my face in the path of his fist, and I stumbled back as pain filled me.

The throbbing in my jaw and cheek helped center me, and I peered up, finding Cohen watching me. He shook out his hand, his knuckles red as he watched me. Cracking my jaw, I raised a hand, touching the spot and wincing. The pain filled me, and I held onto it, knowing it was the only thing keeping me from spiraling back into those thoughts.

"Thanks." I nodded, relaxing Cohen, who'd probably wondered if I would retaliate.

"I need your help, don't leave us, man." He stepped forward, squeezing my shoulder and staring me in the eyes. "I know this is fucked up, but whatever demons you're fighting, leave them for now. We'll figure them out later. The woman we both care for is hurting, and right now, that's our focus. She needs all three of us. Maybe... even four. I'm still trying to get my head around the fact

that my handler is the leader of the Order *and* Blackhawk, and…
well, yeah."

He cleared his throat, and I noticed some of his own demons
surfacing. Cohen was right; we could deal with them later when
Finley was awake. Taking a deep breath, I slowed my heart and
cleared my head. When I opened my eyes, I found that his eyes
were clearer.

"Okay, what can I do?"

"If you can call *Ryker*," he sneered, "and help Milo, I'll keep
trying to break through the encryption."

Nodding, he handed me his phone, the five unanswered calls
showing. Hitting the dial button, I placed it on speaker and kneeled
down toward Milo. He was taking her pulse and muttering under
his breath.

"What do you need?"

"What don't I need," he snapped, closing his eyes. He looked
up, an apology on his face as his eyes filled with remorse. I didn't
need to hear it, though. We were all stressed, so I stopped him.

"It's okay. Better question. What can I do to help you?"

"What?" bellowed over the phone speaker, and we both
stopped to stare at it.

"Um, Mr. Ryker?" I asked, picking it up closer. "This is Asa."

"It's just Ryker. Fin ready to tell me?" he asked. I could almost
hear the smug smile he had to be wearing.

"Not exactly, um—"

"Listen, until she's ready to tell me, and we can have a conversation. I have a secret order to run," he interrupted, cutting me off.

"Do you have a medical wing?" Milo blurted, ignoring the
man's rudeness. "We need to get her to one before she deprives all
of her organs of oxygen and dies. Is that urgent enough for you?"
he shouted. It was the first time I'd witnessed the usually calm and
collected man irate, and I had to say, I liked it.

"What happened?" Ryker asked as the sounds of his movement
echoed through the phone.

"We don't know. She's in shock. Something you said made her go pale, and then she collapsed to the floor, staring off into space. She didn't even know who any of us were before she passed out."

"Fuck, okay, listen, I'm on my way. Tell Cohen the encryption key is 02141995."

I looked up as the phone clicked off and found Cohen nodding that he heard it as he entered it. The door clicked open, and Milo picked up Fin as we hurried out of the room. Turning in both directions, Cohen took off to the left, hopefully leading us to the medical wing. His face was a little ashen, and it helped me not feel so scared, knowing that we all were.

We turned down another hallway, coming to a door, and found Ryker standing in front of it. "Come on," he urged, motioning for us to enter. Medical staff awaited us, taking Finley and quickly hooking her up to monitors. Cohen and I stepped back, letting them do what was needed, but Milo stayed, and I think it helped ease our minds knowing he was there.

When they shut the curtain, we stood with Ryker, whose cocky expression had changed to one of concern. Perhaps he wasn't so bad if he cared for Finley that much.

"Why is MKG bad?" I asked, bringing his eyes to mine. He sighed, looking at Cohen briefly before finding my gaze again.

"I've handled this all wrong. We've gotten off to a wrong start, and I'm not even sure I know what's really going on. I thought Fin and I were playing our games like we used to. It was how we flirted, but it seems like it's something more than that. Why does she hate me?" he asked, looking serious.

"You're Blackhawk, right, from the club she joined to find my sister?"

"Your sister… so she did find her friend then?"

"No, that's a whole other story, they found each other, but that's who you are, yes?"

"Yeah. I went by the name Blackhawk at the time. Why?"

"Well, she hates you because of what you did on that final test."

He blinked, shaking his head. "I don't understand. She messaged the night of the last test, saying she wasn't feeling well, and had gotten grounded, so she couldn't complete it anyway. She stated she'd reapply and go through it again on the next round. But I never heard from Oblivion again after that. Not until a month ago."

Glancing at Cohen, his face held the same disbelief mine did. "Yeah, that's not what happened at all," I said, knowing Fin wouldn't lie about one of the worst nights in her life.

"Denial," Cohen coughed into his hands, though how hard he tried to cover it up was debatable since we both clearly heard it.

"I'm not in denial," Ryker protested, crossing his arms. "That *is* what happened. I waited and waited. I even searched, but no one else had ever heard from her again."

"Yeah, right," Cohen huffed, rolling his eyes.

"What's your problem?" Ryker barked.

"Nothing. It's just not surprising you're lying and think you're so blameless."

Ryker started to argue when Milo stepped out, halting their debate. "She's stable. She'll be okay."

We all sighed in relief, and Milo walked over to take the seat next to me. "And she hates you because you're the reason she was arrested. Just own it, dude," Milo said, closing his eyes as he leaned his head back against the wall.

"What the fuck are you talking about?" Ryker shouted, standing to look at the three of us.

"Fin. She was arrested during the third trial. You set her up," I repeated, narrowing my eyes at the guy. I wouldn't let him dismiss this.

"No, I most certainly *did not*."

"Well, someone's lying. There can't be two versions of the truth, and I believe Fin. Her getting arrested was a turning point for her. She wouldn't lie about it," I said, not backing down.

"And I was there that summer when she did her community service."

"I'm not saying she couldn't have been arrested," Ryker said, waving his hands. "I'm saying I had nothing to do with it."

"Maybe there can be two versions of the truth," Milo said as the rest of us started to argue again.

"How so?" I asked.

"There were other people in your group, right?" Milo asked Ryker.

"Yeah, it was Dex and me with Finley."

"Dex?" Cohen asked, shifting his feet, and I wondered if he knew something he wasn't saying.

"Yeah, he went by Obsidian. We were roommates at the time, but after that year, he transferred schools. He got out of the hacking business, but we're still close friends."

"We need to ask him what his version of the night is then. He might have the missing piece."

"Fine. I don't know what this has to do with anything, but I'll call him. I know what happened, though, and Fin bailed on us."

"That's where you're wrong," a small voice said. We all turned, finding Finley in a wheelchair, an IV attached. The nurse shrugged when we all looked at her.

"She insisted. She's quite convincing."

Smiling, I walked over to her, needing to touch her to know she was okay. "Hey."

She looked up at me, relief in her eyes as she took me in. "Hi, I'm sorry. Everything was just too much."

"I think we all need to have a conversation. A real one," Ryker said, frowning at us.

"Fine," Finley said, sighing. "Can it wait until morning? I'm exhausted."

"Sure. I'll have breakfast sent up and meet you in your rooms."

"You're not going to lock us in again, are you?" Cohen asked, narrowing his eyes.

"No. I won't. Get some sleep. You've had a long couple of days."

The three of us walked back to our rooms, pushing Finley in the wheelchair. We quickly got ready for bed, all of us eager to get some rest after the day.

As I lay there, listening to Finley's breathing, I vowed that I would be there for her no matter what was uncovered. I wasn't going to run away from this. I could be enough for her. She needed the guys and me, and I needed her. Together, we'd fight our demons.

Epilogue

My hand tightened on the stress ball as I squeezed, wishing it was something, or someone, else. Everything I'd planned for years was about to be ruined because one greedy little girl couldn't keep her nose out of my business. I'd have to make sure she got the message this time.

My phone flashed, his number displaying across the screen, and I squeezed harder. I needed to regroup before I spoke to him. I couldn't waste everything now on emotion. When jelly hit me in the face as a handful of beads exploded around me, I looked down, realizing I'd done it again. Another stress ball causality.

My assistant ran into my office with a worried look at the mess. "I'll clean it up, sir."

Scowling, I brushed the gunk off my once pristine shirt and knocked the squishy balls to the floor. She could deal with it. Standing, I walked over to the closet in the corner of my office and pulled out a shirt, the dry cleaning wrapper still on it. Tossing the soiled one into the hamper, I turned to find my assistant licking her lips as she took in my body.

Rolling my eyes, I ignored her lustful intentions and tore off the plastic before buttoning up the shirt. If she didn't get her daydreams of bedding the billionaire boss in check, I'd have to replace her. It wouldn't be the first time. If someone had told me in high school that the surefire way to get laid was to become a billionaire, I wouldn't have believed them. But here I was, ten years later, and I had more pussy options than I knew what to do with. Especially since pussy wasn't even my thing.

Sitting back at my desk, I clicked on a few windows to see if there had been any new developments. I didn't have time to keep monitoring their progress while putting my plan into place. I'd been this close to succeeding when Finley Reyes decided to get a conscience after all this time.

Pulling up the file of everything I'd gotten away with over the years, my cock started to get hard as I flipped through them. The true aphrodisiac was pulling off criminal actions and getting someone else to do the time. It got me going every time. By this point, I was a pro at it, able to ruin anyone's life with a few keystrokes. The only hurdle was the Order. Otherwise, I would've taken down Finley like I'd done all of my other foes. But she was protected by none other than *him*.

Turning to the framed picture on my desk, I rubbed the hard length in my pants as I stared at it.

"Anything else, sir?" my assistant asked, surprising me.

I turned to her, narrowing my eyes, hoping she'd go away. Instead, she simpered closer, batting her eyelashes.

"I can take care of that for you."

Staring at her, I tried to figure out what she was referring to when she leaned over, her hand outstretched toward my leg. Grasping her wrist, I tightened my grip as she cried out.

"Don't touch me," I seethed, dropping her arm. She fled from the space, giving me the space I'd been wanting. Stupid cunt and her ideas of grandeur.

The phone on my desk beeped, and I picked it up, staring out the window. "What?" I barked, not in the mood to handle any crises.

"The package you wanted has been secured."

Smiling, I felt life begin to surge through me again at the opportunity to make a scene. Yes, this was good.

"Thank you, Miguel. I'll be down shortly."

Picking up the phone, I quickly called HR to let them know I'd need a new assistant and to make sure she signed an NDA before she left.

"Make the next one old. I'm tired of these twenty-something girls trying to come onto me to fulfill some misguided fantasy. I just need someone to do the job and leave me alone."

"Yes, sir. I'll get on it," the voice said, and I hung up, not even caring who I'd just spoken to. The advantage of running your own company, everyone bowed to you and didn't bat an eye at your bad behavior. Though, I'd argue my behavior wasn't bad, just lacking social niceties. There were far too many things for me to conquer to make sure I didn't hurt someone's feelings during it.

Taking the elevator down to the secret floor, I went through the security measures to reach the level that wasn't documented on any blueprints. First, I scanned my hand, followed by a retina scan and then a voice activation.

"Purple tacos," I said, waiting for the screen to light up green. I changed the password daily to a random phrase, so it would be impossible for anyone to predict. My security was some of the best, and in fact, it was what had made me billions.

The elevator lowered and opened to the top-secret floor, revealing the stainless steel level. The guard at the elevator nodded to me as I stepped off and began my trek toward room #5. My shoes echoed on the floor, bouncing off all the walls with nothing to absorb the sound. It was an easy way to ensure no one could ever sneak up on anyone here if they were lucky enough to make it this far.

I passed the first room, the door shut tight. Each room had a different purpose, and the most sinister were closer to the elevator. Only one other person knew what went on behind that door.

The second door held my latest tech gadgets that I was developing for myself. If you couldn't keep the coolest shit for your own purpose, where was the fun in that? I'd taken on corporations and corrupt men with the things I'd developed, putting me into the position I was currently in today. I could hear the sounds of a saw as I passed, and I made a note to stop by and see their progress before I left.

Behind door three laid a server room that would make any geek jealous. It was how I managed to obtain ownership of MidKnight Guild, ferreting out all the secrets of the creators and, one by one, taking them from them. It had been fun to watch them implode on themselves. And now I ruled it all.

Door number four was perhaps my favorite, but I bypassed it as I came upon number five. It wouldn't do to get transfixed by the things in that room and forget my mission today. No, it would be better to not even peer at it.

The guard at the door nodded in greeting, but I barely paid attention to him. People below me were only good for the role they played. I didn't learn their names, remember their features, or know anything about their lives. It wasn't needed in my line of work, so I shoved all that non-essential stuff to the side and focused on the big picture.

A woman sat in the middle of the room, tied to a chair. She stared at me, not giving anything away as I approached. It seemed the Order taught their agents better than some other organizations I'd taken down.

Leaning against the desk, I watched her, assessing all of her weaknesses before speaking. "You, dear, were very hard to find. I'll give it to the Order for their secrecy. They really do have a knack for fading into the background."

She stared back, not offering anything. It would impress me if I was inclined to be impressed by such things. In my world, time was currency, and she was wasting mine.

"Okay then. If you have nothing to say, you're useless to me." Looking to my left at the guard, I nodded, indicating for him to follow protocol. It was always so fun watching them scramble. "When the gift is ready to send, I have a note to attach."

Saying nothing else, I left the woman alone with the guard, knowing the show was about to start. But as I neared door number four, my eyes drifted toward it, and I couldn't stop myself from walking over. Smoothing my hands over the door, even this part felt more significant than the others. Could a door be sexy?

Placing my thumb on the lock, I waited for the beep before the satisfying hiss of the air locked room emerged. Stepping inside quickly, I blinked a few times as my eyes adjusted to the red light. Wall to ceiling was covered in photos and conversations. Once I'd completed it, no one else had ever been allowed to step foot into this room. It was temperature-controlled and air locked when not in use to not disturb all the images.

Walking over to the couch, I began to strip down as I neared it, knowing I was too weak today to ignore the need coursing through me.

Laying back on the couch that was as old as me, I inhaled the pillow, still able to smell him. I might be a glutton for punishment, but it was one I would willingly accept.

Looking around at the photos, I zeroed in on my favorite as I began to stroke myself. Hitting play on the remote on the table, sounds of his moans I'd recorded filled the room, and it was like I was immersed in him.

His smell. His sounds. His body.

It might not be the real thing, but it was a close second. Quickly, I came, splashing my cum over his face that was plastered to the floor. Smiling, I kneeled down, wiping it over his lips and imagining him taking it.

"Soon, my love, soon."

The story continues in Lipstick Lies

Lipstick Lies

THE ORDER DUET BOOK TWO

Prologue

She emerged in a red dress and the shoes I'd sent to her. The heels clicked against the pavement as she walked across the parking lot. She moved with such freedom and optimism that it instantly made me want to squash it out of her.

And tonight, I'd get to do just that.

I'd been preparing for this over the past six months. At first, I assumed she'd flake out like all the others had and leave me to my mission. But Finley Reyes had proven to be more persistent and annoying than I'd bargained for. Especially when she started to encroach on *my* territory. I couldn't let her stand after that.

So, I waited and devised the perfect plan, infiltrating from the inside.

She pulled her phone out of her bag and I watched as she tapped into the app. One of my monitors lit up, showing me her message. I currently had three screens visible as I worked. One featured the app, logged into three different accounts after I'd cloned theirs, the middle displayed the video footage of Oblivion, and the last was the actual account we were hacking into.

Focusing on the first part of the sabotage, I responded to Finley from the cloned account.

Oblivion: I'm here. Are we set?
Blackhawk: We're all good. Ready on your count.

Switching monitors, I silenced the alarm for the school Finley was at and disabled the one for the true test back to back. It was a lot to manage all at once, but I'd been preparing for this night for months and I was ready. Every step had been outlined in my notebook of when and what I needed to do so I wouldn't accidentally screw up my chances to get into the MidKnight Guild while I thwarted Oblivion. If tonight didn't go as planned, I'd have to try a different approach. But with everything meticulously scheduled to the minute, along with my skills and expertise, it should all go off without a hitch.

A message popped up on the actual server, and I clicked over, triple checking I was on the right one. I'd even colored-coded each one to distinguish them apart and keep them separate. It would only take one stray message sent to the wrong person to screw it all up. Not that there hadn't been close calls in the past, but everything hinged on tonight's mission.

Blackhawk: I'm in position. Alarms?
Obsidian: Good to go.
Blackhawk: Any update from Oblivion? She should be here by now.
Obsidian: Nope. Guess she couldn't hack it in the end. Being grounded is a rookie move and not an excuse if you want to be a Knight.

I wanted to laugh at my joke, but there was no one here to hear it, so I chuckled softly to myself, enjoying my own humor.

Blackhawk: I thought she had what it took. Keep trying to get a hold of her.

Blackhawk: I'm in. Going silent.

The need to punch something rose up in me at his words, and I calmed my breathing, remembering it would all be over after tonight, and he'd be mine, once and for all.

Obsidian: Everything's clear. You got it.

Quickly, I zoomed back over to the other monitor, checking in on Finley. She walked toward the main office, not even realizing the alarm was going off the whole time. I snickered at my ingenuity as she set her own trap. Loading some pre-written text, I added it to the voice app for it to say. I'd already set it to wait a few seconds between each voice and change the octaves on the voice manipulation to help distinguish between us.

The most amazing thing to come out of this past year was the tech that I'd created. Finley had been a big help to motivate me to design something I could use to manipulate her. I'd even gotten off on the fact she'd developed some of the specs. I didn't know what that said about me, but I also didn't care. I'd use whatever advantage I could to get ahead.

I was twenty-one, had spent most of my life alone, and had finally found what I was good at. I wouldn't apologize for going after what I wanted at whatever cost. Too many people had discarded me, used me, or dismissed me over the years for me to have any empathy for others. The world was brutal, and the sooner she learned that, the better off she'd be. In fact, I was helping her understand the world before she let too much of her optimism out. She needed to buck up and see the world for what it truly was.

And now that I knew what I was good at, I didn't want anyone else coming in and stealing it. There was only one person I cared about, and I wouldn't let him be swayed by an underage girl who thought she could steal him from me. This was an act of kindness that I was doing for both of them.

> **Blackhawk**: I got the files. Can you make sure the cameras are wiped? I'm headed out.
> **Obsidian**: Already done. See you back at home base.
> **Blackhawk**: Still nothing from Fin? Maybe she got caught on her way out?
> **Obsidian**: Nothing. It's probably for the best, anyway. She never even realized we were all in the same city. How good of a hacker could she be?
> **Blackhawk**: That's not fair. We concealed our location on purpose.
> **Obsidian**: We found hers. She should've been able to do the same. We can talk about this later.
> **Blackhawk**: Fine. Losing both Mongoose and Oblivion. It just feels like we failed.
> **Blackhawk**: At the bike. Going off.

I watched as he mounted his bike, knowing he wouldn't drop this anytime soon. I'd have to be vigilant about making sure she wasn't able to reach out. I needed her to hate him. Good thing I'd already planned for that with the gifts and messages.

As the red and blue lights flickered on the monitor, the last piece of my plan fell into place. She'd have a hard time contacting us now. I knew she'd been picked up before for minor things, but there wasn't a judge in the state that would let her off the hook for breaking and entering. If only I'd thought ahead of time about pinning Mongoose's murder on her. Then I really wouldn't have to deal with her.

He'd been a liability I hadn't seen coming. Oh well, in the end, he'd gotten himself killed. I only wish I'd had more time to prepare so I could've used it more to my advantage.

As they escorted Finley to a police car, I began to wipe the clone accounts and closed out all the tabs I had opened. The tracker on Ryker's phone alerted me to him arriving, so I finished up all the back-end things as I waited.

When the door to our room opened, I spun around and smiled as he entered. Standing, I walked over to him, picking up the bottle of tequila we'd been saving. I couldn't stop the smile from spreading across my face.

"I think a shot is in order?"

He peered up at me, sighing. "Let's get it all submitted first. I don't want to count our chickens too soon."

Rolling my eyes, I set it down and spread out all the information we'd collected over the past year. This was part of the initiation we hadn't shared with Mongoose or Oblivion either, leading me to believe he hadn't wanted to from the start, planning on cutting them out, to begin with. It was only because Oblivion turned out to be a girl that Ryker had changed his mind.

"What do you think they're going to do with it all?" he asked.

I shrugged my shoulders. "Does it matter? We were asked to find information on some safe houses, troubled kids, and organizations that could be exploited. We have it. Now, we turn it over."

"I know, but it feels wrong." He peered up at me, and I saw the doubt that had been creeping more and more into his eyes reflected there.

"This is everything we've been working on for the past two years! Don't fall apart on me now. We'll be rich and have more power than we could've dreamed of. This is it, man. Just think of all the things you can buy. The freedom of never being hungry or worrying about which bill to pay this month."

Ryker sighed, dropping his head and letting out a long breath. He raised it after a few seconds, a smile spreading across it. "You're right. I've just been distracted. This is it. No more worries."

We scanned everything in and hit submit. I ignored how he hesitated when he entered the team members present for the last test. Once it was final, he scooted back, grinning.

"Shot time?"

"Shot time."

Picking up the bottle, I poured us both one, and we tapped them together before downing the liquid. It only burned slightly and we laughed at the feeling. Sitting on the ground, we passed the bottle between us, toasting our success and the things we planned to do with our money once our tech went live.

"I want the freedom to walk into almost any store and just be able to be like, yes, I want that and not have to worry about it," Ryker said.

Scoffing, I moved closer to him, falling as I went to grab the bottle and landed on his shoulder. "You can do better than that. I want a flashy car and a house with so many rooms, I forget about them."

His hand brushed mine as he grabbed the bottle, and I blamed the tequila for my lack of inhibitions. My love for Ryker wasn't anything new, but doing something about it was. Combined with the success of the evening in both getting rid of Finley Reyes and passing initiation for MKG, I decided to take my chance.

Leaning forward, I pressed my lips against his. He didn't move away, so I took the opportunity to push harder, my tongue sweeping out to ask for entrance. When he opened for me, I cried joyfully and pressed further, owning his mouth like I'd always wanted.

Things escalated quickly as we both got naked, rolling around on the ground, the empty bottle of tequila next to us. Reaching down, I pulled on his hard cock, knowing I wanted it more than anything else.

We didn't say anything as he plunged into me, the pain of the intrusion lasting for a moment before he was pumping with drunken movements. Neither of us lasted long, spilling out onto the floor, adding to the spilled remains of our shot glasses. Ryker rolled over, a snore leaving him a moment later, and I soon followed, too high on the success of a job well done.

I'd gotten everything I wanted in one evening. Ryker. Money. Prestige.

Which meant that it all had to fall down around me in the morning leading me to transfer schools.

But I never forgot Ryker. If anything, my obsession for him only grew, and I vowed to become so powerful he'd never be able to push me aside ever again.

Ryker would be mine or no one's.

One

FINLEY

WHEN MORNING CAME, I STAYED STILL, NOT WANTING TO FACE THE day. I'd been awake for several hours now but hadn't moved. Everything felt heavy, and I wondered if it was the drugs… or me.

Someone had gotten up a while ago, but I was too focused on myself to figure it out. I'd been held in a pair of arms all night. It was the only thing that kept me from falling apart. My mind kept replaying three things.

Blackhawk had a name, and it was Ryker.

Ryker was the leader of The Order and Cohen's handler.

He claimed he hadn't set me up.

I'd heard them talking as the nurses hooked me up to the IV, but I hadn't wanted to believe it. I'd been able to push it off until this morning, but I would have to face it soon. Suddenly, the thought of knowing the truth seemed like the last thing I wanted. What if everything I'd thought for the past six years had been a lie? Where did that leave me then?

I'd never felt so lost in all my life.

"Babe, I can hear your thoughts running a mile a minute. I

promise, whatever is said, I'll be there to help you figure it out. We've got this. Together."

Asa's soft words soothed me, and I relaxed for the first time in hours. Carefully, he turned me, bringing me to face him. It was then I realized that we were the only two people left in the bed.

"Hey," he said, tracing his thumb across my cheek. "How are you feeling?"

Licking my lips, I swallowed, wetting my dry throat so I could speak. I was too worried to care about morning breath. "Physically? A bit tired, but otherwise, I think I'm okay. I feel so embarrassed that I passed out."

"You went into shock, Fin. It was more than passing out. You don't have to be so hard on yourself all the time."

"It's the only way I know how to be," I admitted, closing my eyes. "It's easier than letting others do it."

"I don't think you really believe that," Asa whispered, pulling my chin up. My eyes naturally opened at the move, finding his green ones. They were so full of hope, love, and reassurance that I wished I could bathe in them. "What are you worried about discovering?" he asked when I didn't contradict him.

"That the past six years have been a complete joke and waste of time. Everything I thought I knew was wrong, and I'm nothing but a failure." Tears began to build, threatening to spill over my eyelids. Saying it out loud felt different than it just running around in my head.

Asa pulled me closer, his body practically wrapping around me as he held me to him. He dropped kisses on my eyes, nose, forehead, and hairline as the tears began to fall.

"You are magnificent and the furthest thing from a failure, Finley Reyes. You show me every day what it means to be strong. You strive for your best, showing others they can too. You care deeply for people, almost to the detriment of yourself, and you're always willing to be there for a friend. You're the most selfless person I know. If that is what a failure looks like, I want to be a failure too. But you haven't failed, my love. Not at all. Sometimes we just have to take a moment to readjust. Absorb the new information and recalculate our next move. It doesn't mean the last effort was worth anything less."

Peering at him through my tear-filled eyes, I grasped ahold of him, needing to feel his solid presence. The moment my hand touched him, I felt something settle, anchoring this man to me.

"I'm so glad I found you, Asa. You're a dose of pure sunshine combined with the strength of an unwavering force. I love you so much."

Gently, I pressed my lips to his, knowing I wasn't ready for anything more this morning, but I needed that small connection to remind me that I had him.

Asa pulled me to his chest, and I lay there, crying as the morning sun began to fill the room. At that thought, I realized we were underground and there shouldn't be sunlight coming into our windows.

"Wait, are we still at The Order?" I drew back, taking in the room. It looked like the same place I'd brought my bag to yesterday.

"It's artificial sunlight," Cohen said, and I turned toward the door, finding him watching me. When he saw I was looking, he came closer, sitting on the end of the bed. "How are you feeling?"

"Tired, but otherwise okay. What do you mean artificial sunlight?" I asked, sitting up. Asa followed, the cover falling and reminding me of his gorgeous chest of muscles. My hand lifted, and I realized I was about to pet him. Clasping it in my other hand, I dropped them onto the bed and looked at Cohen. He smiled at me but took pity and didn't comment on my near groping.

"Since a lot of the people here don't go up top a lot, they had screens made that mimic the natural environment." He got up and walked over to the wall where the curtains were drawn halfway over a window. There was a remote on the sill, and he picked it up, pointing it at the window, or I guess, screen. "You can set it to whatever time zone you like, part of the world, and season. Some people get tired of winter, so they have it set to more of the east coast and get all the seasons. I just have it on neutral, so it mimics what is outside the building."

"Wow, that's some smart tech. I bet it does wonders for people stuck down here for long periods."

"It's reduced a lot of seasonal depression. There are even sunrooms where people can go and get vitamin D."

"Oh, that sounds cool. I wouldn't mind checking it out. Could we do a tour later?"

"Absolutely." Cohen smiled, sitting back down and practically petting my foot under the blanket. He sighed, his face changing, and I knew I needed to check in with him. "Ryker called to say he'll be here in about thirty minutes. So, now's your time to grab a shower if you want one." He'd practically gritted out that last part, confirming my suspicions.

"You know what?" Asa started, looking at me before glancing back up. "I don't think she should be alone. You should join her to monitor. I want to check out the weight room, so I'll grab one later."

Cohen swallowed, watching me. Smiling over at Asa, I squeezed his hand, knowing he'd seen the same emotions I had and was giving me this time with Cohen to make sure he was okay. Climbing out from under the covers, I crawled over to Cohen. His face lit up at the gesture. I forgot that his confidence was a mask for his insecurities. I leaped, falling into his arms, taking a chance to see him smile.

He stood up, swinging me around with his momentum. Laughing, I held on as he carried me to the bathroom. I peeked over his shoulder, finding Milo watching me from the small kitchen area. I waved, offering him a small smile. He seemed to relax at the gesture, and I decided if I was going to make this work, I needed to spend some one-on-one time with him too.

Cohen sat me on the counter as he shut the door and turned on the light and fan. He set about getting the water ready before turning and looking at me. "I'll just sit out here in case you need me."

His cheeks were red, and I couldn't fathom what was embarrassing him. "You're not suddenly being shy, are you, Co-bear?" I batted my eyelashes at him, reaching for his hand.

"Co-bear?" He laughed, coming toward me, keeping his head down.

"Yeah. It's like Care Bear, but Co because you're Cohen. It's dumb. I'll find another nickname for you."

"No, I like it." He peered up finally, his hands moving to bracket my face. He sat his forehead against mine, closing his eyes as he breathed me in for a minute. "I was so scared I'd lost you, Fin. Everything happened so fast, and then you were on the ground. I'm so sorry that happened. I had no idea that Ryker was Blackhawk."

"It sounds like there's a story there. Let's get in the water before it runs cold, and you can tell me about it."

He gulped, his eyes opening. "You want me to join you?"

"Yeah." I smiled, pushing back as I lifted the shirt I was wearing over my head. His eyes dropped to my breasts, and he stepped back, quickly removing his clothes. I hopped down from the counter and slipped my panties off. I couldn't help but take in every inch of Cohen as he discarded the last of his clothes.

His cock was already jutting out as he eyed me. Taking his hand, I stepped into the shower, realizing how small it was when we were both there. Laughing, I stepped under the water as I took in all the ways his muscles dipped. I spotted a few tattoos, and I couldn't wait to check them out more. Our first time together had been so spur of the moment that I hadn't been able to fully appreciate the gorgeous specimen that he was.

"You're hot, Co-bear." I couldn't be sure under the water, but I could've sworn that his cheeks heated more. "Hand me the shampoo."

"Let me wash your hair?"

Smiling, I nodded and turned around. Softly, he began to massage the shampoo into my hair, taking care of each strand. I wasn't surprised when he started to talk. Cohen seemed to be the type that needed to be doing something when he shared deep things.

"Seeing Ryker was a shock to me yesterday. I hadn't seen him face to face in a few years. In fact, I'd actively been avoiding running into him. It seemed to work, as he didn't seek me out either. Which, of course, relieved and infuriated me at the same time." He made a noise that sounded like he was letting out a breath as he turned my head, massaging different parts.

"Ryker was the first guy I felt anything more than just a passing fancy toward. We went through training together when we were of age and instantly hit it off as friends. We were inseparable there in the beginning. We did a few missions together and worked on projects. My sexuality had always been a bit of a mystery to me. I'd experimented with both guys and girls, but nothing ever felt right. Then I met you, and it felt like my heart was on fire, so I assumed I was hetero. The label didn't feel right though, but I couldn't deny how you made me feel. So when I started to feel attracted to him, it took me by surprise. I tried to deny it because I didn't know what that would mean. One night, he made the first move when we were hanging out by kissing me."

He paused, dipping my head under the water before turning me, his eyes snagging mine with heat, but there was more there than just lust. Cohen held so much emotion in his eyes that it made me reach out to him, wanting to protect him from whatever he was about to share. He didn't stop me but grabbed the washcloth and began to soap it up. He started to wash me in soothing gestures before he spoke again.

"In my gut, I knew it was just a fling for him. He had a reputation, after all, but I thought I was different. It was both the best and worst relationship of my life. When it ended, I took a leave of absence and did some freelance jobs. When The Order reached out to me, I said I wasn't ready to return to the facility. They brokered an agreement that I didn't need to return, except once a year for annual training and a physical. I was also told I had a new handler and that they would communicate only through text or email. I wouldn't need to meet or do any check-ins. It felt like the best way forward, so I accepted."

He'd carefully washed me from head to toe while he spoke. He grabbed some conditioner off the shelf and held it out for me, asking if I wanted it. I nodded, and he turned me back, putting it in my hair.

"Since then, I haven't kept a serious relationship, my heart too battered to try again. I kept flirting with you online, which was enough for a while, but I wanted more. That night, I was going to ask you, finally having the guts to do it, only to find out you'd been kidnapped and had a boyfriend. But then the crazy thing of belonging with that group happened. Sawyer's relationship intrigued me, and I began to feel part of me coming back alive again. At first, I thought about stealing you from Asa, but he turned out to be a great guy. Then it felt like there might be a possibility for me, but I wasn't sure how to get it. I'd almost given up trying, wanting you to be happy with Asa and not interfere with that when you left again. My heart couldn't take losing you, so I went to Asa, planning on only helping him find you and then disappearing."

I sucked in a breath, turning to look at him. "You were going to give up?"

"Yeah." He nodded, sadness in his stance. "But I couldn't ever walk away. I kept telling myself, after this, or after that. I'd planned to walk away that moment in the hotel room when Asa arrived. But then I had to finally admit that I didn't want to. Asa and I had talked, but I wasn't sure how much of that was just him wanting to find you and saying whatever it took to make it happen. Hope speared me when he seemed to be upholding his words, and I knew I was a goner. I know it's too early for you, but I love you,

Finley. I have for years, and I just wanted you to know before it was too late."

I pulled his face down, needing to kiss him after he'd shared all of his heart with me. He was right that I didn't know how I felt about him yet. I cared about him a lot, but I didn't think I was at the love stage yet. So, I was glad he wasn't expecting me to say it. When we pulled back, I held his head close, wanting him to hear everything I had to say.

"I can't say those words yet. But I know I will, one day, if you give me a chance."

"That's more than I ever dreamed of." He lifted me up, my legs going around his waist. I could feel his hard cock against my stomach, and I rocked against it as he moved us toward the water so he could rinse the conditioner out.

"Fuck," he cursed, almost stumbling as I did it again. "I wish this shower was bigger so I could show you what happens to naughty girls, sweetheart."

I sucked in a breath, biting my lip, wanting to know what that was. But he was right. This shower was too small, and we'd be more likely to fall and hurt ourselves than enjoy it.

"How do you feel about Ryker now?" I asked when he set me back down, so he could wash his own hair really fast.

"Probably the same as you," he said, giving me a knowing look.

"Like you want to smack his face but kiss it simultaneously?" I asked with a laugh.

"Yep, that sounds about right." He shut off the water, pulling open the curtain. Cohen stepped out first and grabbed a towel. "The one nice thing is I finally figured out what I am. Talking with your brother and Soren helped me with it. I think I'm a pansexual. It's more about the person and my relationship with them."

"Oh? I can see that," I said, trying not to moan as he carefully dried me. "You know I accept you no matter what, right?"

He peered up, some lightness seeping in. "Yeah, babe, I know. Thank you for that, though."

"So, what do we do now?" I asked, wrapping the towel around me as he dried himself. The arousal was starting to climb again, and I knew if we didn't get out of this bathroom soon, I was about to say fuck it and let him have his way with me up against the counter and make Ryker wait for us.

"I guess we hear him out and then go from there. As my handler, I trust him and have a bond I can't describe. He was also a good friend before things ended romantically with us. I don't know if I could forgive him or trust him again in the other area though."

"Yeah, I know what you mean. We had a good relationship online, but then he hurt me. I don't know how I'll feel if that's brought to a different light."

"Well, the only way to know is to find out. Come on."

He pulled me out, and we both dressed in the room. I popped back into the bathroom and quickly dried my hair, putting on some makeup. I wouldn't usually care, but it felt essential to have it on with Ryker coming over.

It wasn't to look nice. Nope. It was to feel invincible.

Yeah, we'd go with that.

Two

FINLEY

I'D BEEN EATING THE SAME BITE OF BAGEL FOR THE PAST FIVE MINUTES. Chewing it to the point that it was basically molecules. The conversations I'd had with Cohen and Asa had been good for me, but it didn't change the fact that I was about to face the man I blamed a lot of my shame on.

"Would you like some tea or coffee?" Milo asked, drawing my attention.

"Yeah, sure. Coffee would be nice." He smiled, standing, looking pleased to have something to do. He set a mug down in front of me a minute later, fixed precisely how I liked it. I shouldn't have been surprised, but it seemed Milo kept shocking me.

"Wow, that's perfect. How did you know?" I asked, needing something else to focus on more than the need to know.

"I pay attention." His cheeks tinted a smidge, and I smiled at the effort.

"Well, thank you. I appreciate it." I took another sip, liking having something to do, so I searched my brain for a new topic that didn't deal with me or my drama.

"So, where will you be starting your residency?" I asked,

keeping my fingers wrapped around the mug. The warmth and familiar gesture were both grounding me.

"Um, well, I'll actually be working in the health clinic at Lux Brumalis. The doctor there is leaving, so I'll be starting in his place. I'll be supervised by one of the doctors at the hospital in Salt Lake."

I gulped, burning my throat in an attempt to not spit out the hot liquid. In hindsight, it might have been better than scorching my esophagus.

"Oh, wow," I coughed. Trying to relieve some of my throat's pain, I grabbed the glass of water and drank it down. The cool liquid felt nice on my throat, and I breathed a sigh of relief. "Sorry. That took me a little by surprise. Um, can I ask what made you pick Lux?"

His cheeks went full-blown red, his ears even turning pink at the top. "Um, well," he sputtered, rubbing the back of his neck as he tried to find the words. "It just seemed like a nice place, and the opportunity came, and I thought I could do with something less stressful."

"Have you worked with athletes before? They're high mainte-nance," Asa bellowed, his laugh filling the space.

"Yeah, well, it will be a good learning experience. I think Utah is nice."

"Just admit you did it to be closer to Fin. We won't hold it against you… too much," Cohen teased, picking up his tenth piece of bacon.

"Oh, um, well…" Milo began to mutter, and I took mercy on him.

"No matter the reason, I'm glad you'll be closer. It will be nice to get to see you more and spend time together. If that's what you want, I mean."

"Oh, yes. I'd like that." He seemed to finally find his words and stopped his stuttering with my proclamation, and I felt things might be okay with us. A knock at the door had us all tensing as Cohen got up, taking the few steps toward it.

I watched as he took a few deep breaths before squaring his shoulders and opening the door. He stared at the man on the other side for a moment before stepping back and gesturing for him to enter. Ryker stepped in, and my body reacted. The man I'd met at the bar, who'd made my insides flutter, was standing right in front of me. It was hard to reconcile him with the guy I knew online who had broken my heart.

His intense eyes watched me, scanning from top to bottom, almost like he was checking me over. It wasn't sexual at the moment, but more of an assessment of my physical well-being.

"How are you doing today, Fin?" he asked, that dark and delicious voice bringing goosebumps to my skin.

"Better, thank you." I hadn't meant to sound so curt, but it rolled out of its own violation.

"You look beautiful," he said, and I only stared at him, lifting my coffee.

"I know," I finally said, not knowing why I was being so rude. He smiled, making me think he liked my sass, and I pushed that aside. I didn't need him to like anything.

"Should we gather around the couches? It might be more comfortable," he offered, gesturing toward the furniture.

Sighing, I acted put out to have to move, taking my cup of coffee, I rose and walked over. I sat in the middle, Asa and Milo on either side, and I felt safe. Cohen remained standing, leaning against the wall, ensuring we were protected from all angles.

"What do you have to say for yourself, *Blackhawk*?" I said, narrowing my eyes at him. I wouldn't make this easy for him. He had a lot of explaining to do, and I wasn't going to let him off the hook just because he had nice eyes and a sexy voice.

"I think I should formally introduce myself. I'm Ryker Jenson. I first met you online as Oblivion. Over the course of that year, we became friends. There was a lot of flirting, and I thought things might change once you turned eighteen, but then I never heard from you before our last mission."

Fury rose up in me, and I was thankful to have the two men beside me, or I might've stood up and thrown my perfect coffee in his face, and it was too good to waste it that way. Rolling my eyes instead, I scoffed before taking a sip of my healing liquid.

"Have something to add?" he asked, almost like he was amused.

"That's rich coming from you."

"It seems we're back at the impasse of yesterday, little hacker. Care to explain what grievances I've caused?" he asked, calm and collected. He had the nerve to smile at me, daring me to fight him.

"First of all, you were the one who never showed up that night. I was there, and Obsidian was on comms with me until the police showed up. I was arrested and charged with breaking and entering. I got off with community service only because of my parent's connections. My whole future was almost washed down the drain that night because you set me up to take the fall. Don't even get me started on Mongoose."

Ryker's face hardened, and he moved closer, making my whole body tense. "Finley, that's not what happened. Dex was with me on comms, so I'm not sure how he could've been in two places unless he was lying to one of us. I waited for you, but I went ahead when you were thirty minutes late."

"Likely story. I'm not falling for it. I know what happened. I have the mug shot to prove it."

Ryker held his hands up, approaching me like a scared animal and pissing me off even more. I wasn't the one remembering things incorrectly.

"I'm not saying you're wrong. I believe that you were arrested. I just think there's a flaw in both of our stories. Where did you go that night? Let's start there."

"The high school. I was told to steal the budget for that school year."

Ryker tilted his head, observing me. "And who sent you that information?"

"You did." He shook his head, my hackles rising again at his dismissal.

"No, I'm not saying you're wrong. I'm saying it wasn't me. Did you happen to crack the code I sent you the other day? It was access to a drive with all our conversations on it. I thought I was showing you our history, but it seems it might be even more important than I realized."

I looked up at Cohen, who was shuffling his feet, scratching the back of his head. "Did you?" I asked. Observing him, I was certain he knew something.

"Um, yeah. Sorry, with everything that happened yesterday, I forgot to mention it. There are conversations, like he said. Here, I'll grab them."

"It doesn't prove anything. You could've deleted things."

"You're right, but I didn't. But I can show you what I received from MKG on our last mission."

Huffing, I sat back, still cradling my mug. Taking another sip, it was more to have something to do while we waited. Asa put his arm around my shoulders, pulling me into his chest. Milo didn't overtly touch me, but his body pressed into mine, offering me comfort on both sides. Ryker's jaw tensed as he watched Asa and me, making me smile a little.

Cohen walked out with his laptop and sat on the coffee table. Once the server was open, he turned it around and handed me his computer. Ryker moved around the back of the couch, making me nervous now that I couldn't see him. He leaned over my shoulder, pointing to a folder.

"You can look at all of them later. I'm not hiding anything, but check this one first so we can clear this up between us."

I clicked on the folder, heaviness filling my chest. Seeing the server messages had my hand shaking as I clicked on them. A thousand memories and emotions slammed into me, things I'd long since forgotten, things I hadn't wanted to necessarily remember. I closed my eyes, breathing deeply as I tried to calm my heart. Panic was edging around the corners of my mind, threatening to send me spiraling again.

"Breathe with me, Fin. Remember how we did it before? Breathe in your favorite color and let it fill you up, taking over all the corners of your fear. Now, slowly release all that fear, exhaling a color you hate. Let it go, exiting you. Again, in. Now, hold it, and release."

I did it a few times, feeling my three guys around me. I listened to Milo's voice, his smooth timbre making me feel calm. I exhaled and opened my eyes, turning to look at him. Nodding my thanks, I focused back on the screen, trying to read the messages.

MKG admin: Your team's final mission is to obtain a file on the blueprints for the new city building. All members must participate to pass. You have until midnight.

But... no. That didn't make sense. I blinked, but the information didn't change. So, how could we both be right? We couldn't. And Ryker's looked legit. Which meant... mine had been a ruse. But why?

"You're certain the message came from me?" he asked, not moving from behind me. I turned slightly, forgetting he was close, and almost bumped into him.

"Yeah. I, um, saved them." I escaped his gaze, focusing on Cohen. "May I?" I asked, pointing to the laptop.

"Of course, sweetheart. I told you I have no more secrets." Blowing him a kiss, I typed the address to one of my secure servers. My fingers hesitated over the keys as I debated opening this can of worms. Ryker sighed, thinking I didn't want to share my password, and moved back.

"I can't see anything," he muttered, sounding put out. For some reason, that brought me joy and gave me the boost I needed to open up this scab and hopefully heal this wound once and for all. With a deep breath, I typed in the password and clicked on the folder.

"Here," I said, opening the conversation from that last night.

Obsidian: Thirty minutes to go. Anyone need a reminder of the plan?
Blackhawk: Nope. You watch our backs, and Oblivion and I do the badass stuff.
Oblivion: Oh? I like being badass. Where are we going? And you're here?
Blackhawk: Secrets, little hacker. I couldn't miss out on meeting you.
Oblivion: So, where are we meeting?
Obsidian: Are you ever not flirting? I'll be on comms guiding you through. I have some things to do. I'll catch you guys later. Tonight we become official Knights!
Oblivion: Wahoo! Talk to you later.
Blackhawk: Later, Sid.
Blackhawk: Are you familiar with Clark Pleasant High School?
Oblivion: You're kidding, right?
Blackhawk: I'll take that as a yes. Meet me there at 10pm. We have a small window to get in and out before it's due. Are you ready, little hacker?
Oblivion: Definitely. See you there. And thanks for the gift.
Oblivion: Sorry, I know I'm not supposed to mention it.
Blackhawk: Yeah, no problem. See you soon, little hacker.

"What the crap is this?" Ryker asked, looking at me like I'd grown a second head.

"The conversation we had." I stared at him, wondering how he'd become the head of a secret order if he couldn't decipher that.

"Yeah, I see that, except it never happened." He looked up at me, sincerity and truth ringing in his eyes.

"What do you mean?" Cohen asked. "If you didn't do it, then who?"

He gulped, looking back at the screen before he met my eyes. "Obsidian. He's the only one who was at both of our sites. He has to be the one that led us astray."

"But why? I thought Sid was my friend. Why would he want me to get arrested? He almost ruined my life."

My body deflated, and I sank into the couch. Ryker moved around to the front, handing Cohen his computer. He appeared nervous for the first time, wringing his hands as he debated something.

"I think I might know why. And if so, then you were right, Fin. It was my fault, and I'm so sorry for that."

Son of a biscuit eater. What now?

Three

FINLEY

Ryker stared at me, remorse and regret heavy on his features. None of the cockiness I'd witnessed before present, and if anything, he looked ashamed of what he was about to tell me. It was something I was all too familiar with, and it made me soften toward him.

Taking a deep breath, I let it out slowly, preparing my battle armor for whatever he had to unburden. When he saw I was ready, he came around and sat on the coffee table, bringing him much closer than he had been.

"I'd really fallen for you over that year. I kept telling myself you were too young, but my heart didn't care. On that last mission, I was looking forward to meeting you and putting a face to the person I'd been crushing on. So, when I got word you weren't showing, I was crushed. I'd had this whole thing planned where I'd ask you out for your birthday. I wanted to get you some shoes you'd like so you'd have them to always wear."

"You did give me some shoes. You sent them to me and told me to wear them to the last mission. "

"No." Ryker shook his head, his eyes wide as he stared at me. "I never got up the courage to purchase any. I could never decide between the black or red ones."

"I distinctively remember you sent me red ones. Unless…" I looked at him, swallowing. My hands felt clammy as I wiped them on my legs. "You don't think he did, do you? How long had he planned to sabotage me then?" Anxiety was heavy as it swirled in my gut and I wanted to scream and run far away from this conversation.

"I'm starting to wonder if I even knew Dex." Ryker dropped his head, running his palms over his face. I glanced at Cohen who was staring at his handler with mixed emotions. "I feel like an idiot. All this time, I've been thinking of you and wondering why you never reached out."

"You thought of me?" I asked, dipping my head a little. For some reason, it was too personal to take head-on after the other news.

"More than I should. It's partially why the remainder of that night is but a vague memory. I completed the mission, though barely, on my own. Not something I let Dex know. I had too much pride back then. When I returned to our room, he had shots ready. We toasted to a job well done and our invitation into MKG. Too many shots later and the heartache of losing you led to some poor decisions on my part." He sighed, scrubbing his hands down his pant legs, not making eye contact.

"What happened?" Asa asked when no one else spoke up.

"Dex made a move, and I didn't stop it. I was too drunk to care, and spending it being reckless felt like the right call at the time. Things went further than I'd intended, and I told him it was a mistake when we woke up the next morning. Something changed in him after that and the next year he transferred. We'd grown up together and had been on a few teams since we worked well with one another, but I hadn't ever considered him more than just a friend. But I guess…" He shrugged, his whole body deflating.

"Imagine that. You changing your mind in the morning," Cohen spat out before storming out of the room and slamming the door. I jumped at the noise, looking at the room he'd gone into, hoping he'd return. When he didn't, I turned my fury onto Ryker.

"Explain that!" I pointed, not letting him off the hook.

"Shit. Maybe I am a horrible person who deserves what is happening to him. I suck at relationships, okay? After things with you—"

"Nope, you don't get to use me as an excuse. Especially since it wasn't even my fault," I said, sitting up to fight him if I had to. Knowing the hurt Cohen felt made me want to go to battle for him. Shit, I think I *was* in love with the turd muffin. But what a hot muffin he was.

Thankfully, my weird thoughts gave me enough time to cool down and give Ryker a chance to talk before I kicked him in the groin again.

"You're right. I was hurt, but it didn't mean I couldn't have reached out or tried to talk to you. I let my past dictate how I felt and washed my hands of you, grouping you in with everyone else in my life that had left me. Needless to say, I have abandonment issues, or so my therapist tells me." He rolled his eyes, sighing. "Cohen and I met during training. We instantly became friends and worked well together. We teamed up on a few projects and had good success. After a tough case, I kissed him. I'd only meant for it to be a one-night thing. I'm embarrassed to admit I'd already been through most of the recruitment class that year. But it wasn't like the others, and that scared me. It lasted a little longer than most of my flings, but when I saw that he cared for me, I freaked out and ended our agreement. We've never been the same since. He left for a while, and I tried to forget him the same way I did you—working harder than anyone and only having one-night stands."

His phone pinged, and he pulled it out, sending a quick message before turning his attention back to me. It was apparent he was avoiding noticing the two guys next to me. I didn't know what his play was, but if it was to separate me from them, he had another thing coming. I wasn't even sure I liked him. He was attractive, but there was too much history for me to let him into my heart too soon.

Even though I knew that to be true, a small part of me whispered I wanted to. I shoved that thought away, knowing I couldn't entertain it at the moment. Cohen was hurting. I was hurting. That had to be remedied first and foremost.

"Sorry, I just pushed back a meeting. Where was I?" he asked.

"Something about your work ethic," Milo stated, twisting the last two words to the point they sounded rotten.

"Right." Ryker briefly looked over at him before returning back to me. "Avoiding my feelings led me to advance faster than anyone planned, and when the position became open, I stepped into the leadership role. I kept my post as Cohen's handler because it was a way for me to stay in his life at a safe distance. The anonymity within the organization allows me to live free among my peers without them knowing I'm their boss. Only a handful even know my real title."

"So how do I and MKG fit into all this?"

"The Order had recruited me like most of their initiatives when I was younger. That's how I knew Chaos and connected you. I didn't know he was Cohen until later when we met for training. After I made it into MKG, I worked with The Order to determine their end goal. Why was this group recruiting teens and young adults to steal information about schools, homeless shelters, and politicians? Why were they focusing on kids as their go-to members?"

I'd never thought about it that way. I hadn't thought about what their motive was for wanting me. At the time, it just felt like the answer I needed to get what I wanted.

"What did you find?" I asked, clearing my throat. Asa brushed his thumb against my hand, soothing me more.

"I don't have enough time to get into that now, but I was able to shut it down. I never told Dex that I was responsible. I graduated college a year later, and I came here for training. Things had been weird with us since that night, and I didn't do anything to make them better. We talked off and on, kept up to date with one another, and occasionally would get together for a meal when one of us was visiting. As far as he knew, I worked at a security firm in Colorado. I never would've imagined he could've done all of this. He wasn't very assertive and would often wilt under pressure. It doesn't fit with the man I know."

"If it's not him, then we're back to it being you. So, what's it going to be?" I asked, crossing my arms. I narrowed my eyes at him, letting him know to not even entertain the idea it was me. There was no world where I would volunteer to get myself arrested.

He smirked, holding up his hands in defense. "I know, I know. The Occam's razor principle—the simplest answer is probably the correct one. If it's not you and it isn't me, then it has to be Obsidian, aka Dex. It's the only other explanation unless we're entertaining the theory a ghost planned it all?"

I furrowed my brow, taking lessons from Rhett. Ryker chuckled, the sound deep, making me want to roll around in it. Ugh, stupid sexy man with his sexy deep voice.

"So, how do we get ahold of Dex?" Cohen asked from the side where he'd emerged, leaning in the doorway.

"I've been trying to since you mentioned it yesterday. He's not answering."

"And what does he have to do with MKG being back?"

"I'm not sure that he does. Right now, I'm not jumping to conclusions until we have all the facts. First, I'll talk to Dex and figure out why he would pretend to be me and send you to the wrong location. In the meantime, we focus on MKG as a separate entity. I was being honest when I invited you to join our ranks. We could use someone of your skill set. There's a training class that starts today. If you're interested, then Cohen can show you where to be."

"And if we're not?" I asked, trying to hide the thrill that had run through me at the prospect.

"Then we go our separate ways. I'll have to brainwash you so you forget our location and everything."

"Fuck that!" Asa shouted as Milo joined in with, "No way!"

"Funny," I deadpanned once the boys had quieted. "Be serious, Ryker."

A grin spread across his face, and he leaned forward a little, enough to bring the intoxicating scent of his closer to me.

"I like hearing you say my name, little hacker." He licked his lips, his eyes dilating a little.

Huffing, I crossed my legs, trying to ignore the throbbing between them. "Yeah, I'll remember that then. Answer the question before one of my boyfriends loses it on you, and your team has to rush in here again because your monitor shows you peed your pants." I smirked, his eyes narrowing at the use of boyfriends, plural.

"Then we'll discuss this on neutral grounds. Until then, you have a decision to make. I hope to see you at dinner. I'll have a private one set up for us."

He stood, his phone clutched back in his hand as he began to walk to the door, already typing on it.

"You owe Cohen an explanation too. Not just me."

He tensed, stopping briefly as his step stuttered before continuing to the door. I didn't think he would respond, but he turned, meeting my eyes and then Cohen's briefly, saying, "Fine," and then was out the door. The sound of it latching and then beeping as it relocked was the only thing we could hear for a solid thirty seconds until someone moved.

"Boyfriends?" Milo asked, looking at me sheepishly.

"Oh, um, yeah, sorry, I kind of lumped you into that. I'm um, well." My face heated, and I realized the pile of dog poo I'd just stepped into.

"How about Cohen and I get some laundry started and check out the gym for a bit?" Asa said, getting up from the couch as he pulled Cohen with him, barely remembering to pick up the basket we'd dropped yesterday before they left.

The quiet filled the air, and I forced myself to turn and look at Milo. He was watching me and thankfully didn't look upset.

"So, um…" I mumbled, not knowing where to start.

"I'd love to be your boyfriend, Fin. I think we should get to know one another better, though. I know you have something with Cohen and Asa, and I'm still trying to figure out my place in your life. I like you and think we'd be good together, so maybe we just start there?"

"I think I can get on board with that. So, we're kind of dating?"

"Sure." He smiled, moving his hand to cup my face. "As much as we can in an underground secret bunker."

"Oh, I imagine we can be creative. But first, how about we just start off with a kiss?" My question came out hesitant, not sure how he'd respond. When he smiled, it felt like my heart might beat out of my chest as it raced to catch up with what was happening.

Milo leaned forward, his hand gripping my face firmer as he neared my lips. I watched every movement, cataloging them so I could remember this later. The feel of his hands, soft against my skin. The stubble on his jaw. How his eyes shimmered in the light. How it looked like he held his breath as he moved closer. But my favorite was how his eyelashes fluttered closed at the last second behind his glasses as his lips met mine.

It was tender and sweet and everything I knew Milo to be.

Tentatively, I raised my hand, placing it at the back of his neck, feeling the coarse hairs as I laid it there. When I didn't pull away, he moved his lips, pressing in harder. I gave him what he wanted, meeting his movements with my own.

When he pulled away, a whimper left me, my cheeks flaming, but I didn't feel too embarrassed by the pleased smile that spread across Milo's face.

"I look forward to courting you, darling."

Someone call the swoon police because I about melted.

Four

COHEN

I ONLY MADE IT A FEW FEET OUT OF THE LAUNDRY ROOM BEFORE ASA opened his mouth, not letting me get away with anything. He'd been eyeing me the whole time while we sorted clothes, so I knew it was coming. I was just hoping I could outrun him and he'd forget. Didn't look like it was going to happen though.

"Sooo… how are you doing?" Asa observed me, his gaze earnest as he checked me over for any cracks in my foundation.

Blowing out a breath, I shoved my hands in my pockets as I kept walking. "Can we wait until we're not in the hallway?" I asked, deflecting.

"Sure, man."

I kept walking, leading him to the gym. We walked in, finding it empty for the moment. Asa spun around, taking it all in. It was a state-of-the-art gymnasium with every piece of workout equipment you could ever need, a boxing ring, a track that ran above the place, a shooting range, and several rooms for massages, ice tubs, saunas, and even a pool. Just about every sport was covered outside of the ice ones.

"Wow, this place is massive. I thought the hockey training rooms were cutting edge, but this is… I have no words."

"Yeah, it's pretty awesome." I smiled, enjoying his excitement. Of course, the gym brought with it a whole slew of emotions. Memories of my own training, sparring with Ryker, and my budding feelings for him plagued me, and I suddenly wondered if this was the best place to be at the moment.

"You okay?"

A sardonic laugh left me before I could stop it. "I don't think I can answer that."

"Okay, how about you start with how you feel about seeing Ryker." Asa walked over to the wall and slid down onto the mat. Sighing, I knew I could benefit from talking about my feelings, so I followed and joined him on the ground.

"I don't know where to start," I admitted, laying my head back against the wall. "When things ended with Ryker, I took some time away from The Order. When I returned, I was anxious about running into him, but after a few months, when that didn't happen, I felt relieved and sad. It hit home that I'd just been a fling for him, so I moved on. But now, to learn that he's been my handler this whole time in secret is confusing. Did he do it to mess with me? Or did he care, and it was his way of staying in my life? My brain is going around and around, and I can't seem to land anywhere."

"I think that's one of those things you might have to ask him yourself. You'll never know the real answer otherwise."

I snorted, shaking my head. "If only it was that easy to talk to Ryker. He's not one for communicating."

"I dunno. I think you're remembering the younger version of him. While he might have some areas with Fin and you to make up for, I took him as a mature and serious leader. He might surprise you that he's changed since your last liaison."

"Maybe," I sighed. "But does that erase everything? I'm not sure I want to open my heart to him."

"A conversation is just that, a conversation. It's not a requirement to trust someone or forgive. It's just a chance to clear the air. I think you owe yourself that much. What you do from there is up to you."

"Yeah, I suppose you're right. Not to change the subject, but what do you think about Milo?" I laughed, tilting my head slightly toward him.

He grinned, shaking his head. "I'm cool with it. Much like you, Milo has been hanging around for a while now, so I've kind of come to terms with it. Plus, he seems to bring something out in her neither of us does, and I like seeing that side of Fin."

"You're a lot more easygoing about this than I thought you'd be."

"I've thought about that myself, and as far as I can tell, I think being separated from my twin at birth broke something in me. My whole life, I've been searching for something to fit that space. I tried with my parents and only got pushed away by my father. I tried hockey, and it worked for a while. The team aspect was nice, and I instantly had a group of friends. It wasn't until I met Fin, Sawyer, and all the guys in her life that I finally felt like I belonged. I get that with you and Milo too. When we all worked together in the hotel the other day, it clicked for me. Together, we're all better with Fin, and I love that feeling."

I nodded, thinking it over. "Yeah, I think I know what you mean. The Order was that for me for a while, that place to belong. The fallout with Ryker had me feeling on the outside again. Working with Fin and Samson has been that home I think I was looking for. This past week has been the most natural my life has felt in ages."

"Which brings me back to the original topic… does Ryker fit into that? For you? For Fin?"

Taking a deep breath, I looked around the gym, hoping the answer would come to me. When it didn't, my shoulders slumped, and I turned back to Asa. "I don't know, and I can't answer that for

Fin. If she wants him, then that's something I guess I'll have to figure out separately."

"So, for now, should we go through this training program?"

I smiled, some glee at what awaited them filling me. "I don't think it would be a bad thing. It would give Fin and us some time to work through things in this jumbled mess of secrets and lies. Besides, it's two weeks, still plenty of time to return to school in the fall if you plan to."

"Do you think we've given them enough time to talk about their feelings?" Asa asked, standing.

"As much as I'm willing to give," I admitted, standing up. "He can't have all of her time."

Laughing, Asa slapped me on the back, and we headed back to the room. As we drew near our door, Ryker rushed around the corner from the opposite direction. His face was slack, devoid of emotions, but I saw it in his eyes.

"What is it? What happened?"

He stopped in his tracks, looking between the two of us. If I didn't know better, I could've sworn he was gauging whether we were together.

"I need to know what you decided first."

"We were just about to go find out," Asa replied, walking up to the door and looking over his shoulder at me. Nodding, I followed him, and he placed his palm on the scanner and it beeped to let us in. He poked his head around, probably to give them time, so we weren't walking in on anything indecent since we had Ryker with us.

"Ryker has some news but needs your decision first," he said, stepping in. I followed, finding the two of them on the couch. Their lips were puffy, but they looked like they'd been talking otherwise.

"What do you guys want to do?" Fin asked, checking with us.

"I'm okay with it. Milo?" Asa answered.

"It's not how I imagined spending my time, but I'm game."

"Cohen?" Finley asked me.

My eyes heated as I met hers. "As much as I appreciate your concern, sweetheart, I'm afraid I'll be one of your trainers, not an initiate."

"Oh," she said. I could've sworn her cheeks heated, and her pupils dilated, but it was quick and gone when she turned toward Ryker. She took some time assessing him and finally let out a long breath.

"I'm not sure where I stand with you or The Order, but I guess the training program would give us time to figure that out. It looks like we're all in. So, what's this news you have to tell us?"

Ryker seemed to relax at her statement, moving closer to the couch. When he looked like he was going to sit next to her, I jumped over the back of it, falling into the seat. Asa snickered into his hand, taking the chair on the opposite side.

"I guess that seat is taken," Ryker said, giving me a teasing look I didn't want to acknowledge. Narrowing my eyes, I crossed my arms, but Fin pulled them apart, taking my hand. Smugly, I linked our fingers together, lifting my eyebrows now at Ryker as he sat on the coffee table. It was still too close for my comfort, but at least it wasn't right next to her.

"Did you hear back from Dex?" Fin asked when Ryker didn't immediately start talking.

"I think so. Cohen, I wanted you to hear this from me first because I knew you were close. Kristina was taken hostage on a mission last night, and I fear she didn't survive."

Gulping, I sat back, the news surprising me. "What happened?"

"Her team went to reconnaissance a building when they were ambushed. It's too early to tell, but the intel might have been false, luring them there for this purpose. She was taken after her team was tranquilized. When they woke up, all their gear and vehicles had been tampered with. It took them four hours to walk back to the safe house. They called in an hour ago to report it."

I realized then it was the messages he'd received while meeting with us. It made me respect his role and how difficult it must be to balance it all.

"What are the next steps? Why tell us?" Fin asked, proving she was perfect for The Order.

Ryker turned to her, and I realized we'd been having a silent conversation when his eyes left mine. "I'm telling you because I believe she was taken by MKG. And based on the package that showed up soon after the team reported in, I'd put good money on the fact that Dex is behind it."

He pulled out his phone and clicked on something, pausing briefly before turning it. "What I'm about to show you isn't pretty. Are you sure you want to see it?"

"Yes, I think I need to," Fin replied, squeezing mine and Milo's hands. Ryker nodded, letting her decide her limits, and turned the phone.

At first, I wasn't sure what I was seeing was real. Lining the box were photos of Fin dressed in a red cocktail dress and red stilettos. She was younger, probably around the age I'd first met her. That was when it clicked that this must've been the night she was arrested. From every angle, there was a picture of her, and they pieced together in the box to highlight her face with a red circle around it like it was a sniper scope.

Finley gasped, her hands moving to her mouth as she took it in. I placed my arm around her, pulling her to me, hoping I was giving her some strength.

"That was the night I was sent to the wrong place."

Ryker's face softened at her words, something in him easing. "I'm glad to hear you believe me. Yes, I think this confirms that Dex was also behind that night. I'm not sure what his motive was. If he just wanted you off the team, there were easier ways to do it. Why did he deceive us both?"

"Because he's obsessed with you," Asa said, his eyes falling to us. He'd been sitting back with his hands steepled as he thought. When he noticed we were all looking at him, he leaned forward.

"You said he was a brilliant coder? Correct?"

Ryker nodded, focusing on Asa.

"You were roommates. He had access to your computer and phone and could hack any of your passwords. I've learned how easy it is to clone those things with the right access this past year. You'd never question it because he was your friend. I bet if we look back through some of the messages, there were more conversations neither of you had with the other. When did you start liking Oblivion where he would've noticed?"

Ryker thought about it, glancing at Fin before turning back. "Maybe after our third mission. It was probably about three months into it."

"It wasn't too long after that you found out I was a girl," she said, her voice quiet.

"So, you're saying that, he's what? Obsessed with me? So he went after Fin to keep us apart? That's ludicrous. We were only friends."

"To you, but he obviously wanted more," I spat, some of my anger coming out in my words.

Ryker hung his head, taking a few breaths. "I screwed up with you, Cohen, and I'm sorry for that. I got scared. I promise, though, it wasn't like that with Dex. It was a drunken mistake. You… you never were."

He held my eyes, sincerity shining through, but I didn't know if I could trust it. Turning my head, I tapped my fingers on my knee as I tried to figure out the piece we were missing.

"Why now?" I asked, interrupting whatever they'd been talking about.

"Pardon?" Ryker asked, giving me his full attention.

"Why is he just coming after Fin now? She's been living her life for six years without a peep from either of you. So, why now?"

"I don't know," Ryker said, leaning back to think. "I managed to assist The Order in shutting MKG down years ago, and the original people behind it are in jail. I even checked again today that they were still behind bars. From what I can gather, Dex has been quietly operating MKG from the dark web. It wasn't until the past month they even popped back up on The Order's radar. I didn't think it was too serious since they'd been gone for so long. When Fin initially messaged me on the old server, I worried it was connected, but after a few traces, I knew she was clean. I thought," he paused, clearing his throat. He sat up, reaching out a hand to Fin.

She peered at it, not sure what to do. Hesitantly, she placed her hand in his. I wanted to yank it away, but I wouldn't do that to her.

"I thought at first you were back to apologize for what happened. When you didn't say anything, I figured the best way to engage after so long was to play our game. I wanted you to join our ranks, but I needed to know for certain you were ready. So, I devised the tests."

She pulled her hand back. Her eyes narrowed as some of her sass rose to the surface. "By covering me in drinks, ruining my computer, and then dousing me in paint? Or was it the attempted drugging and abduction? Some game." She scoffed, rolling her eyes.

"That wasn't me. I saw the person follow you, and I intervened. I was fighting them off. I would never drug you or take you against your will, Fin."

She sat back, and I pulled her in tighter, happy to have her close to me. Ryker's jaw tightened at the embrace, and I smirked, unable to hide my enjoyment at his discomfort.

"It wasn't until then that I knew something else was at play."

"Do you think that was Dex?" Milo asked.

"Could've been, or one of his disciples from MKG sent on a mission. It was hard to gauge in that fun house."

"Speaking of, creepy place to meet," I said, unable to miss an opportunity to needle him some.

Ryker looked at me oddly. "I said the Ferris wheel, like in the book. But you sent back the funhouse."

"Fudge sauce!" Fin said, jumping up. "He planned that. He's

been manipulating our moves even now!" She began to tug at her hair as she paced the small space between the couch and table, stopping when she came to the legs of the three grown men. When she realized she had about two inches to pace, she fell into the couch, exasperated.

"I'm starting to believe you more," she admitted.

"We should thoroughly sweep our electronics and change any SIM cards just in case."

"I used burners the whole time. It has to be the server," Fin argued.

"You might be right. If he's head of MKG, he might have access to things on the dark web we hadn't considered. I need to meet with my team and debrief them on this new information. MKG is becoming slippery and more dangerous than we'd originally assessed."

"Will there be a team sent to retrieve Kristina?" I asked.

"As soon as we have a lead. I'll keep you apprised of it."

"Thank you. She was a friend. How are Ash and Caleb doing?"

"They're pretty shaken up. They're both in the infirmary if you wanted to visit."

Nodding, I gave him a grateful smile. "Thanks, I will."

Ryker stood, looking at the four of us. "Training starts in an hour. Good luck. I'll be in touch."

"Wait," Fin said as he made his way to the door. "Are we still having that meal together?"

Ryker's face lit up, and he nodded. "If you'd like to. I'd like the chance to talk without all this subterfuge hanging over us."

"I think that would be nice," she said, looking at me.

"Okay, I'll see you guys at dinner then."

He gave a half-wave before he opened the door, the sound of it latching close the only thing we heard for a few minutes as we all sat with our thoughts.

"So, what does one wear to training?" Fin asked, looking at me.

It was such a Fin question that it had me erupting in laughter, lightening the mood.

"Whatever you want, sweetheart. But maybe leave the stilettos for later?"

She slapped my chest, but I saw some of the fear from the picture lingering, and I vowed to do my damnedest to erase that from her.

We all changed clothes and headed to the gym, and for once, I looked forward to whipping some new initiates into shape.

Five

FINLEY

Staring around the room, I took in the other people present. It felt weird to call us initiates when I didn't even know if I wanted to do it. The group was a mixture of females and males—the females were outnumbered by only a few—in their early-to-late twenties. It was a diverse set of people, and something about that made me feel hopeful that I could belong somewhere.

Some of the group chatted as they stretched, while others stayed to themselves, eyeing everyone from the mats. The three of us were in the back dressed in athletic gear, Cohen giving nothing away on what to expect. He was up at the front with some of the other Order members. It was easier to pick out the trainers as they were dressed in all black and had a look about them like they were about to make us hurt and enjoy every second of it.

I glanced over to Asa as he touched his toes. "What do you think?"

"Not sure yet. Physically, I think we'll be okay. It's just if we have to do other tasks. Outside of you, I'm not sure what skills we have," he admitted, turning back to look at me sheepishly.

Leaning over, I kissed him, pushing some of his hair off his forehead. "Babe, you're amazing at everything. Don't underestimate yourself." He smiled, lighting my insides up.

"Well, I know first aid," Milo chimed in, making me chuckle.

"You know more as well." I turned to him, kissing his cheek. "I'm not worried about us working as a group. I'm curious if we'll have someone added and what this training entails since Co-bear wouldn't tell us anything," I huffed, crossing my arms as I stared at the man.

"Co-bear?" Asa laughed, slapping his leg. "Oh, I can't wait to tease him about that."

My cheeks flushed a little, but I shrugged. I wouldn't take it back.

"Alright, trainees. It's time to see what you're all made of. Line up."

Standing, I followed Asa with Milo behind me. I didn't know if they did it on purpose, but they kept me in between them at all times. I liked it too much to say anything.

Cohen's eyes never left us as we headed to the front. I couldn't tell if he was nervous or excited from this distance, but the smirk that grew as we neared didn't bode well.

"Today, we'll gauge your physical limits," a man in his thirties with brown hair said as he assessed the line. "Eight laps equals a mile. Go."

Sighing, I started running with the group as they took off. Asa looked over at me, but I could tell he was holding back. "Don't wait on my behalf. Do your best."

He looked pained, but nodded, picking up his pace. Milo stayed with me, but at least it seemed like it was his natural speed.

"Running is the purest form of torture," I said after completing our first lap. Milo gave a hearty chuckle, but I didn't miss the fact that he didn't disagree. It looked like I'd have at least one partner in the non-workout camp. I much preferred only getting sweaty if naked bodies were involved.

I ignored the people around us, even when it seemed like others were lapping us. I didn't even look over at Cohen, too worried about what I'd see there. Was he disappointed I wasn't more of a kick ass girl? I could be kick butt in other ways, just not with running. It was the worst.

"One more," Milo panted, making me feel slightly better that my chest felt like it was on fire.

Nodding because I didn't have the breath to speak, I kept my eyes on the space in front of me. When we crossed the finish line, I collapsed to the ground, falling into a starfish. My face felt beet-red, and I had sweat in places sweat shouldn't be. My body tingled, and my muscles ached. I was beginning to reconsider the whole agreement to do this training if it meant doing *that* again.

A body stood over me, shielding the overhead lights. Looking up, I found a hand, so I reached up, taking it. Sighing, I sat up, realizing it had been Cohen. He handed me a water bottle, and I took it eagerly, barely remembering to drink it slowly, so I didn't make myself sick.

Once half of it was downed, I looked around, taking in the others. I was surprised when there were a few people still running. I hadn't tracked if we were last or not but had assumed we were. Everyone else was sitting around, talking as they stretched and drank water. Most looked as bright-eyed and fresh as they did when they started. I found Asa on my other side, noticing he fit in with that crowd.

"I kind of hate you," I said, taking a swig of my water. "You don't even look like you broke a sweat."

"Professional athlete, babe. It's kind of my job. I wouldn't be good at it if I couldn't run a mile."

"Ugh, you make it sound like that wasn't hard." I began to pout, falling back onto the floor. The guys laughed at me, Asa's head moving over mine.

"I'm not saying it isn't. Sorry, that came out insensitive. I just meant that I do this every day."

Before I could retort, the man who'd taken the lead began

speaking again. "Not bad. You'll be running that every morning. Your speed should improve each day so that you've shaved minutes off your time by the end of the two weeks. Now, let's move over to the weights. I'm going to break you into two groups. One group will work on legs and the other arms. After thirty minutes, we'll switch. Stand when I call your name."

He looked down at a clipboard, and I prayed that I wouldn't be separated from Asa or Milo. He began to list names, and I breathed a little easier with each one when ours weren't called. "Michales, O'Connor, Green, Mitchell, Anderson, Guzman, Chang, Young, Lewis, and Sharp, you're with Bishop." They walked off toward a different section of the gymnasium before he looked down at the list. "The rest of you are with Cohen." He nodded toward my smirking boyfriend, and I prayed this wouldn't hurt too bad.

Who was I kidding? He'd make sure it did. I'd have to find a way to get back at him later. Thoughts of how I could punish him pushed me through the next hour as we rotated between arm and leg exercises. My body felt like jelly, but I was proud of myself for sticking it out. Asa still looked like he was one of the trainers, while Milo and I looked like the two people who'd be picked last for any group sport.

"That's it for physical today. Most of you did well. You get a few hours break before the night training. See your group leader for where to go. Dismissed." The leader, who I'd learned was Jack, walked off toward the locker room, a few of the other trainers following.

"I don't think I can move," I mumbled, attempting to pick up my arm.

Cohen chuckled before he bent over and picked me up into his arms. A few of the other recruits looked at our group as we exited, but I didn't care. Snuggling into Cohen's arms, I'd let him carry me wherever he wanted.

"Oh, is that so?"

Blinking, I realized I'd said that out loud, but I stood by it.

"Yep." I smiled, my eyes already closing. "Tell me that we have time for a nap before we have to meet Ryker?" I said around a yawn.

"You do, sweetheart. I'm just glad you're not mad at me."

"Oh, I am. I have plans of how to repay you for the torture. I'm just too tired at the moment. But it's coming."

I didn't hear his response as I gave in to sleep.

AFTER A NAP AND A SHOWER, I WAS FEELING MORE LIKE MYSELF. MY muscles still hurt, but they weren't as bad as I expected. Cohen was pouting, nervous about what torture I would give him, and offered to rub some cream into them later so that they wouldn't be killing me tomorrow. Looking at the contents of my suitcase, I was itching to make something new, but time didn't allow for it today. I'd have to see if there was access to a sewing machine at some point. I'd gone too long without touching one. I was having withdrawals.

Pulling out a nice pair of dark jeans, I matched it with a criss-cross top that tied in the back, leaving most of my back exposed, meaning no bra. I could get away with it since my boobs were small. Adding hoop earrings, black heels, and a drop necklace, I did one more turn in the mirror before taking in my look.

A whistle at the door had me peeking over my shoulder, finding Asa watching me. "You look amazing. I love how you can just pull an outfit together." He walked closer, his eyes heating up as he noticed the front. "Shit. Making it through this dinner just got harder. Pun intended." He smirked, wrapping his large hands around me.

Picking up my lipstick, I watched as Asa tracked every move I made as I finished off my look. I spread the bright red shine across my lips, feeling confident as I stared back at the person in the mirror. I hadn't really taken stock since arriving here, mostly because I'd passed out and then was hit with more information than I could process, but taking it in now, I realized that I did feel lighter.

I'd found Blackhawk and was getting answers for what happened that night.

It wasn't what I'd believed, but it was still making the things from my past right, which felt good. I no longer felt like a shadow was hovering over me, just waiting to swoop in and cover me the second I forgot to pretend I was happy.

And maybe that was the most considerable relief of all. I wasn't pretending.

Things with Asa were better, and I wasn't hiding how I felt about Cohen and Milo anymore. I wasn't alone. In fact, I had people in my corner helping me fight the ghosts from my past. While I hadn't made the best decision to run off on my own, it had led me here, which was oddly where I needed to be.

Things were coming together, and I found that part of me I'd pushed aside, coming alive again. The Order could be a chance to explore that and figure out who I was becoming. I couldn't deny that I was changing. My life was moving in a new direction, and it felt right.

"You look amazing," Asa whispered, his breath hitting my cheek. He'd dropped his head down to my shoulder during my musings.

"Thanks. I feel amazing."

He smiled at me, still making my insides flip. A knock at the door broke our eye contact in the mirror as we turned to find Cohen. He took me in, his Adam's apple dipping as his eyes trailed down my frame.

"Damn, sweetheart. I think we need to skip dinner."

"That's what I said." Asa chuckled, dropping his arms from me. Reaching down, he took my hand and pulled me toward Cohen. "But I think you both need this dinner to clear the air. I wasn't sure about Ryker at first, but I think he deserves to be heard. And whether either of you is ready to admit it, you want to. I'm not saying you have to let him back into your hearts, but you might find he's a good friend."

I sighed, nodding. "You're right. And I think I'm ready. I'm not as mad as I was, and I can admit that I might have been putting all my shame and regret onto him instead of dealing with it myself. This adventure has at least made me face my own inadequacies as painful as it was."

Asa kissed my head. "I'm proud of you, Fin."

"Guess it's time I get over myself too," Cohen sighed. "Let's do this."

We walked out into the open area, finding Milo waiting. He had on the bowtie he'd worn the first day, and I smiled, loving seeing him in it. Asa nudged me forward, so I dropped his hand and walked to Milo.

"You look handsome," I said, just as he said, "You're beautiful."

We both blushed, and I took his hand, leading him to the door. There were some nerves in my belly, but I knew no matter what else was disclosed tonight, I was proud of myself for how far I'd come, and I had three men to help me wrestle through it.

Six

FINLEY

around a huge table filled with food. Ryker wasn't here yet, making me even more nervous for some reason. A guard stood at the door, but other than him, the room was empty.

"Where do you think he is?" I asked, just as a door opened, revealing Ryker in a suit. I swallowed, not having expected to see him dressed up. It really was criminal the way he filled it out. He was dangerous in regular clothes, but in a tailored suit that fit him just right, he was downright lethal.

"No fear, little hacker, I'm here." His smug smile reminded me why I had to keep my guard up, so I let my mouth take over without thought.

"Not scared, just didn't want to waste this good food. Now that you're here, we can eat." I picked up my fork, shoved something into my mouth, and chewed. I smiled like it was the best thing I'd ever eaten, but in reality, I wasn't even sure what it was.

The guys shifted, attempting to hide smiles as Ryker only nodded, picking up his fork and taking a bite. When it became too

303

quiet, and I wasn't even able to enjoy the food, I broke, assenting to the fact that he'd won this round.

"Fine. You win. Talk. That's why I'm here. How is MKG back, and why didn't you know Obsidian or Dex was running it if you've been talking all these years?"

Cohen choked on his bite as he tried to hide his smile at me giving in. I stuck my tongue out at him, promising retribution for later. Ryker took his time finishing his bite, setting his fork and knife down, and then wiping the corners of his mouth. It was a stall tactic, and it was doing exactly as he intended—driving me crazy.

A hand clamped down on my leg, squeezing, and I tried to steal some comfort from Asa. His thumb stroked back and forth, sending tiny ripples through me. Sucking in a breath, I forced myself to count to ten before I let it out and glanced back up at Ryker.

He was watching me with concern on his face, and the act dropped. "I'm sorry, little hacker. Sometimes, it's easy for me to fall back into that role without realizing it. You push all my buttons, making me want to push yours in return. You're right; we're here to talk. Let me start at the beginning and give you the full scope." Sighing, he took a long drink of his tea before placing the glass back on the table.

"After a year undercover, The Order was able to shut MKG down. It was run by a crime lord who'd discovered that if he used teenagers and young adults, he not only had access to things he typically wouldn't, but they were naive enough to follow orders without questioning them if they were getting paid. Everyone wants to belong at that age, and MKG gave people that. He filled their pockets and kept them happy, and they, in return, were willing to look the other way or not question the things they were doing."

I took another bite of my food, pondering what he was saying. It rang true. I'd been so desperate for information I hadn't stopped to ask why I needed to steal things. And because of that recklessness, someone had died. I didn't know what Mongoose's story was, but it still haunted me today, and I felt responsible.

"That makes sense. So, how did you shut them down?"

"I moved my way up the ranks and discovered who the man behind it was. Cruz Ayers and two of his cronies were put away. When I checked this morning, they were still in prison. I'm not sure when Dex revitalized MKG. That's something I'm curious about as well."

He took another bite of his food, and I took the opportunity to do so too. Chewing over his words, I tried to sort them in my head and what I wanted to know next. It felt like this was the one chance I would have to ask him whatever I wanted, and I didn't want to waste it.

"How did you become the leader here?" I asked, realizing that was what I wanted to know most. The past was important, but it didn't feel as vital for some reason. This was odd for me since the past led me here, but now that I was, it felt like I'd been able to move beyond it for once and look ahead to the future. A future that was still uncertain.

Ryker sat his fork down, and I realized he was finished. He sat back, his arms relaxing on the arms of the chair. My brain struggled with putting together the guy from the bar, the man in front of me, and the boy I'd talked to online for a year. He seemed like a million different versions of himself, and I wasn't sure which one was true. I wanted to believe I knew the real him, but with espionage being his job, it felt naive to do that.

"It wasn't something I sought out to take on. The Order operates differently than most organizations. Our prime objective is to make sure no one becomes too powerful. 'We restore the balance.' But every organization needs a leader, or there will be chaos and it will collapse from within. So The Order created a shifting leadership position and kept it anonymous. It works to even the playing field amongst our agents, keeping allies and rivals out of our personal lives. I was approached two years ago to be the next leader. Each head of The Order serves two years unless in a crisis, then the board may elect to keep them on until things have calmed."

"So, your time is almost up? What happens then?"

He smiled, liking my question, and I couldn't understand why. "The board is a rotating selection of previous leaders. So, once I've served my two years, I'll make my recommendation for my replacement and then take my place on the board to serve as a mentor for the next leader."

"Does it work? Keeping corruption and power grabs from tainting The Order?" Milo asked. I turned, knowing he would be the best to understand the hierarchy of a secret organization being connected to the Council.

"It's the best I've seen try. There are other measures in place that I'm not at liberty to discuss, but over the years, The Order has kept their purpose of serving others and keeping the balance."

"How old are you?" I asked, instantly curious. "You never would tell me when we talked."

"That's because I felt like a huge perv falling for a seventeen-year-old girl." He sighed, shifting a little. I didn't focus on how his shirt tightened around his chest muscles. Nope. Not me.

"I'm 26, the same as Cohen."

I turned to Milo, instantly curious how old he was. He smirked at me, apparently knowing what I was about to ask.

"I'll be 26 in a few months."

"Hmm, I guess Asa and I are the babies at 22." I barely refrained from saying I apparently had a type for older guys. Strike that from your brain, Fin! I did not need to encourage Ryker. Three guys were enough to handle.

I looked up after scolding myself to find the table all observing me. I wiped my mouth, afraid I'd somehow smeared something when they all started to laugh. My cheeks heated when I realized they were just watching me. I wasn't used to this much male attention directed at me. It was weird.

"I know we still have a few things to discuss. How about we move to somewhere more comfortable? I think I'll need some drinks for the next part." Ryker looked around, and I realized everyone else had finished eating. I quickly shoved the last few bites of food into my mouth, my cheeks pouching like a chipmunk as I nodded.

Cohen laughed, his shoulders shaking as he got up and walked over to me. "Sweetheart, you could've taken your time."

Shrugging my shoulders, I took his hand, wanting to ask how he was doing as we followed Ryker. Once I had the food swallowed, I bumped him, getting him to look down at me. I pointed to Ryker, lifting my eyes. He smiled, one corner of his mouth lifting with the gesture before he shrugged. I watched his face for a few seconds before nodding that I understood. It was complicated, but he was okay for the time being.

Same, dude, same.

When we stepped into a smaller space, I was instantly hit with Ryker's smell making me realize this had to be his space. It was so concentrated it made my skin break out in goosebumps, and I wanted to do a full-body shudder at the intoxicating scent. Cohen's nostrils flared next to me, and in some weird way, it made me feel better that I wasn't being tortured alone.

Ryker directed us to a seating area, and I took a seat, Cohen on my left and Milo on my right. Asa took one of the chairs positioned where he could see the door. He might not be trained as a spy, but I could see some of his time with his dad was paying off. He was a natural.

Ryker pointed to a drink cart as he began to fix himself something. Cohen stood and walked over, making some drinks for the rest of us. I watched them as they stood close to one another, trying to figure out their relationship. Ryker's hand brushed against Cohen's as he handed him the tongs for the ice, his eyes immediately jumping to the man in question. When Ryker didn't do anything, Cohen took them and finished his drinks. I had no clue what he'd made, but I took it, thanking him. He looked somewhat frazzled, and I wondered if *he* even knew what he'd made.

Ryker sat in the other spinning chair across from Asa, shifting to look at the three of us on the couch. "So, I've told you about The Order and how it works. What's next?"

"You didn't know Dex was behind it?" Milo asked, bringing up the question from earlier.

"No, we talk every now and then, but it's been a while since I've seen him in person. He kind of went underground after MKG shut down. Once I graduated college, there wasn't anything that connected us. I realize now that might have been callous of me, but at the time, I was focused on The Order, and Dex wasn't part of it. We were friends of convenience, and outside that one time together, we didn't cross the line. That makes me a shitty friend, I suppose."

"I can understand things from your point of view," I said, twirling the glass around in my hand, too nervous to drink it. The condensation felt nice against my skin, helping to cool me. "But, it doesn't change the events that occurred. There are things we must own up to if we move forward."

"You blame yourself for Mongoose," Ryker said. I held his eyes, nodding. Tears began to fill in mine, but I didn't shy away from this. I had to own it. He deserved that much respect. "Mongoose wasn't your fault, Fin."

I wiped a tear, shaking my head. "He asked for help, and I left him on his own. I didn't tell him to go into that building, but I didn't tell him not to."

"Wait, is this about the Magnolia safe house?" Cohen asked, drawing my attention.

"Safe house? I thought it was a homeless shelter. How do you know about that?" I asked Cohen, but it was Ryker who answered.

"This was what I wanted to talk to you about. MKG had found a list of Order safe houses. Magnolia was one of them. Mongoose was being bullied by someone, and in an attempt to find out who they were, he almost ruined my cover. He got close to the truth, so

The Order made him a deal. I didn't learn about this until years later. They faked his death and helped him create a whole new identity."

"So, he's not dead?" I asked, hope blooming in my chest.

"Well, I don't know for sure his current well-being. But he didn't die in a house fire five years ago."

I sat with that knowledge for a few seconds, letting it course through me. The rest of the tears I'd been holding fell, and I breathed a sigh of relief. Maybe I wasn't so bad at this after all?

"Now that I've told you about myself over the past few years, what have you been up to?"

Smiling, I gave him a brief synopsis of how after juvie and community service, I turned to white hacking, helping people who needed it. I went to fashion school, graduated early, and followed Henry to TAS to design costumes and be their social media manager.

"I met Asa last year, and we became friends. When Sariah, or Sawyer as she goes by now, showed up, things got a little crazy. Turns out, she's Asa's twin sister. I learned about the Council and was almost sold in a human trafficking auction, but Milo saved me from that. Cohen was helping me find a pervert, and he stayed around after. I worked with the Agency and then Samson's security company after it was disbanded. It's been a crazy year, but I've learned a lot and grown. It's why I knew I had to come and face you, or well, the person I thought was responsible for getting me arrested."

"Now that you know it wasn't me, what do you plan to do?"

I looked to the guys, not knowing how to answer this. "I guess it depends on them. We agreed to do the two-week training course, so I guess I'm here for the next two weeks."

"Then I guess I have two weeks to convince you to stay."

"Stay?" I shook my head. "I don't know about all that. But what do you plan to do about MKG?"

"If Dex is behind it, then we'll go after him. MKG is dangerous, and if they're still operating, then that's bad news for everyone. Starting tomorrow morning, I'd like you to join the task force I'm creating to take them down. Each of your unique skills will give us an edge."

"I can't speak for them, but I started this journey for that reason, so I'd like to see it to the end." The guys watched me, and I wasn't sure what they would say. Cohen was the first to answer.

"I'll join. My other assignment ended, so you know I'm free." Ryker nodded, looking to Asa and Milo.

"If Fin's there, then so will I," Asa said like that was the answer to everything.

"Same," Milo said.

It filled me with an emotion I wasn't used to, and as my cheeks heated, I ducked my head, unsure if I liked it or if it was scary.

After chatting a little longer, we headed back to our room, I couldn't deny that Ryker wasn't the douchecanoe I thought he was. I didn't trust him entirely yet, but I was warming up to him more and more. That night as I lay in bed, I replayed everything that happened, looking for any sign of falsehood. After an hour, I had to admit I couldn't find any. It looked like Ryker was going to get a second chance. Knowing him, though, it wouldn't take long for him to muck it all up. A smile spread across my face, and I knew I was hoping he did. He was much easier to hate when he was in the doghouse.

Him and his stupid suits that smelled too good.

Seven

FINLEY

After an abbreviated training session in the gym, we were directed to a conference room. We'd been given fifteen minutes to shower and change. This whole spy life was not meshing well with my need to primp and accessorize. They were out of their minds if they thought I could wash, dry, and style my hair in fifteen minutes. Suffice to say, I barely managed to wash off, deodorize myself, and dress in basic leggings and a shirt in that time frame.

Huffing, I slunk down into an empty chair, attempting to braid my damp hair. Everyone else looked put together, making me instantly jealous of them. I took a moment to look around as they focused on the person at the front. The guys were behind me, having saved me the chair, so I smiled my thanks as I surveyed the group.

When Ryker walked in, I sat up straighter, smoothing down my shirt until I realized I was doing it and forced my hands into my lap. None of that. I did not need to primp for Ryker. The room grew quieter as he strolled to the front, his gaze assessing everyone. I tried not to let it bother me when it slid over me without a second glance. He couldn't play favorites. I knew that. But it still stung.

Dropping my eyes, I fiddled with my hands as I sucked in a deep breath. I couldn't let it affect me. This was a professional agency, and I didn't need to allow my feelings to muddy it. Pressing my palms down on my pants, I looked up, ready to listen. I caught Ryker's gaze just before he glanced away, and the concern there had me reassessing things. Okay, I could do this.

"Welcome, recruits. I'll be going over combat strategy today and then separating you into teams. You'll each be given a handler and objective. Your purpose is to complete your objective. The team that finishes first will be awarded a night off while the other teams rotate night watch."

An excited murmur started up around the room. I watched my peers, trying to figure them out, but they all blended together. Though, that might be the point. If there was nothing that distinguished them from the crowd, they were easily forgotten and able to sneak in and do what was needed while keeping a low profile.

If there was one thing about me, I was the oxymoron of a low profile. The fact I'd worn a red dress and stilettos to steal something confirmed it. In the past, that might've bugged me, but at this point, I owned the fact I was my own person. Even if that meant I didn't have a career as a professional spy, I was okay with that. I'd just have to figure out my adrenaline problem another way.

When I focused on the room, I realized they were already listing off teams. For Ryker's sake, he'd better have placed me with my guys, or I'd glitter bomb him so hard he'd be picking it out of his teeth for weeks.

"… Team three is Michales, Hemp, Doe, Young, and Black. See Bishop for details. This leaves our last team to Reyes, Welch, Bellamy, Sharp, and Guzman. You're with Campbell. Now strategy time."

Ryker rolled up his sleeves, exposing his tanned forearms, his veins popping as he flexed the muscles, and I had to physically remind myself to not get caught staring. I mean, to not check him out. Ew, gross. A snicker behind me made me believe I hadn't been as covert as I intended.

Over the next hour, Ryker displayed his knowledge and skill in how to approach a hostile situation. I'd managed to take notes, finding his pointers helpful. He had a natural flair for teaching, and I wondered if he'd ever considered another career path. He was only twenty-six. Surely this wasn't his end goal? Besides, he was about to retire, or whatever, and be a mentor. As much as people boasted about retiring early, I doubted anyone wanted to do that at twenty-six. I'd get bored so quickly; I'd be making outfits for everyone out of all the curtains and sending them off to sing as they skipped along.

Okay, so I might have a slight obsession with the *Sound of Music*, but it didn't make it any less true.

"Right, that covers what you'll be doing tonight. Any questions?"

A pretty brunette raised her hand, her eyes shining as she looked at Ryker, making me immediately want to stab her with my pen. Lying it flat, I sat back, hoping the homicidal urges would also lessen.

They did not.

Going to my happy place of no budget in Mood Fabrics as I perused the aisles to later being shouted at by Tim Gunn *"to make it work"* I almost missed it when the meeting was dismissed.

You're so right, Tim Gunn. I just need to make this work. I have this in the bag.

Scooting back in my chair, I found my three guys looking at me with a mixture of odd expressions on their faces. "What?" I asked, wiping my face in case I'd drooled from the no budget dream. I narrowed my eyes as I tried to figure out what had them looking at me that way.

"You were whispering to yourself," Milo said, taking pity on me. "Something about 'making it work,' and you wouldn't let Tim down?" He said it with a slight question in his voice, almost as if he wasn't sure if that was correct or not.

Asa laughed, placing his arm around me as we began to leave the conference room. "Tim Gunn is Fin's spirit guide. Whenever she's stressed, she watches him on repeat."

"How do you know that?" I asked, my cheeks tinging red at being called out.

"We've been dating for almost a year. I've caught you with it on when I've been over. I might not know the difference between Valentino and Tom Ford, but I know Project Runway is your safety blanket."

Sighing, I smiled, squeezing his hand that was draped over me. "Yeah, something about Tim Gunn yelling at other people really settles me."

Cohen and Milo laughed, but it was more in spirit and not at my expense, making me relax more. We followed who I suspected were the other two members of our team to a private room down the hallway. I glanced at the girl and guy who joined us, but like before, outside of noticing they were fit and attractive, my brain couldn't latch on to any details about them. In fact, once Cohen began talking, I forgot all about them.

"Alright, Team Campbell, I'll be your handler during this mission. My role is to supervise only. I won't step in unless someone is in danger. This is a real mission and should be treated as such. If you can't handle this, then you're not Order material."

Everyone nodded, and I crossed my legs, liking Cohen's take-charge voice a little too much if the zing in my lower regions was any indicator. He smirked at me briefly, catching my shifting, only flooding my panties a little more.

"Tim Gunn, Tim Gunn, Tim Gunn," I chanted, making sure it was only in my head this time.

Cohen flicked on a screen, and our objective popped up. "This is a bakery that one of our sources states has a very eclectic clientele.

Rough men and women come and go with pink boxes of cupcakes and pastries at all hours. Every day, like clockwork."

"You think it's a money-laundering scheme?" I asked, my brain already connecting the dots and the weak areas to exploit.

"Yes. We believe the cakes are used to disguise the money coming and going from the bakery. From our surveillance, a separate ledger is written into when these pink boxes are collected. That's what you're after. Get the ledger and provide evidence. Your only rule is to not get caught. You can use any of your talents; otherwise, I'll leave you to discuss. I'll be back in thirty minutes and expect to hear your plan. If it doesn't sound feasible, you fail before you even begin."

Swallowing, I thought through all the pitfalls as Cohen left, my brain running a mile a minute. As the others began to brainstorm, I took out my notebook, reviewing the notes that Ryker had given us. Some memories from MKG also surfaced, and I pulled on those strings of nights we discussed our plan of attack.

"It's easy. We go in, we punch them out, and take the book," the neutral male said, making me roll my eyes.

"You really think a bakery frequented by bikers and the like will let you just walk in and punch them? Please," I sighed as I focused on the paper, flipping through the screen until it showed the blueprints. "There is a small window of time when they're closed. We'll strike then. Here are our entry points. We'll need someone to disable the cameras and the alarm and stand guard. Two people will then enter the building and retrieve the book. If we do it right, we'll be in and out in under two minutes." I finished drawing the plan and looked up.

The girl was watching me and assessing my gaze on her as she pondered it over. Her male counterpart seemed to have a few screws loose as he scoffed, kicking his legs up on the table like he was king.

"Let me guess, princess, you're one of the two? I saw you eye-fucking our leaders. If you think you can get into The Order through your pussy then you're sorely mistaken."

Asa sat up, ready to strike, and I felt Milo tense next to me. I placed an arm across Asa's chest, stopping him. But before I could even retort, the girl punched him in the junk. The mouth-breather crumpled to the ground and I decided I liked her.

"That was awesome. What's your name?"

"Nicole Sharp." She stuck out her hand, and I took it, shaking it.

"Finley Reyes. So, that makes that mouth-breather, Guzman?"

She nodded, casting her eyes down at him like he was scum, making me like her even more. "Yep. He thinks that because his big brother is in The Order, he's a shoo-in. The tool can't keep his mouth shut long enough to keep himself out of trouble."

Chuckling, the guys settled back now that the douche was on the floor whimpering. "I'd offer to get you some ice, but yeah, suffer those purple balls. Anyway, I guess that means he's out. What about the rest of us? What are our skills?"

After a few tweaks, we decided I would disable the cameras and security system. Milo and Nicole would go in to retrieve the book while Asa stood guard outside. Guzman was relegated to van duty with me to monitor things. When Cohen appeared a few minutes later, we explained our plan to him, and he nodded, seeming pleased.

"You didn't want to be the inside person?" he asked me.

Shaking my head, I looked him in the eyes when I answered. "No, I know my skills and would be best at manning the systems. Based on the preliminary surveillance, they shouldn't be too difficult." He watched me, almost like he expected me to start laughing and say I was only joking and I'd be the one running into danger. When I didn't, he nodded, looking at the rest of the group. Guzman was now sitting at the table, scowling with his arms crossed, and I bet they were protectively covering his man berries as well.

"Alright. Sounds like you've all thought of everything. You

have two hours to eat and gather whatever you need. Meet on level 1 at 20:00. If you're late, it's a strike, and we leave without you."

Everyone nodded, gathering their things, and we headed out the door. Together as a unit, we walked to the cafeteria to grab some food, getting it to go. The guys were quiet as we walked back, and I wondered what they were thinking, but my mind was too focused on the task and the need to ensure this one succeeded.

Eight

ASA

Finley was eating her food, but I didn't think she was tasting it. She was lost in her thoughts as she ran over the plan in her mind. I knew this was important to her. She felt like she'd let people down in the past and failed; this was her chance to redeem part of her soul. But it didn't mean she had to do it alone.

"Babe?" I asked, nudging her.

"Hmm?" She looked over, but her gaze was far away.

"I think you need to get out of your head before tonight."

"What do you have in mind?" Cohen asked, a smirk beginning to form on his face.

I glanced to Milo, who was watching her, and I wondered how much I could push this. They were still figuring out one another and weren't there in their relationship yet. But it felt like we needed to be a solid unit to succeed.

My sister's relationship suddenly made sense to me. Not that I ever wanted to think about my twin being with seven guys, most of whom were my friends and teammates, but she'd created a family unit. She had an unbreakable bond with each of them, giving her the strength she needed to go up against our father and the Council.

We needed to forge ourselves together so nothing could come between us, and it felt like I was the commander of this ship. It was going to be me who brought us all together.

Standing, I held out my hand to Fin. She didn't hesitate, taking it, making my heart swell at her absolute trust. Smiling, I pulled her into my arms, holding her close for a hug. Dropping my head, I whispered my plan into her ear.

"I think you should let us bring you pleasure. You need to quit worrying about all the things that could go wrong and relax. You coming a couple of times should do the trick."

She sucked in a breath, pulling back to look at me. I showed her the heat in my eyes and nudged her with my erection. Lifting her chin, I dipped my head for the last bit.

"I know you're not there with Milo, so let him watch. Think of this as a group bonding project. One where the goal is to give you multiple orgasms."

"Let's try not to kill me," she teased, her eyes dancing with delight. My words had done the trick, and she was no longer locked away in her head. She glanced over at Milo, licking her lips as she nodded. "Okay."

Cohen and Milo looked at us, unsure what was going on. Taking my command seriously, I turned to them both.

"Our first mission tonight is to make Finley forget and to relax. The best course of action for that is several orgasms. You both game?"

Cohen stood and was stripping his clothes in the next second. Milo hesitated, and I could see the no on his tongue. Fin didn't need that right now.

"Your role is to watch and learn, Milo." He glanced at me, some slight fear in his eyes, and I wondered if I'd read the room wrong. Was he not interested in her that way? Maybe he didn't want to be part of a group scene? Didn't Sawyer say they all had a boundaries talk? Shit. Perhaps I should have started there.

Before I could spiral too far, he nodded, standing as he took a deep breath. He didn't take his clothes off like Cohen had, but followed him into the room. He tried to hide the bulge growing in his pants, making me feel marginally better about assuming things.

Picking Fin up, she giggled as I swung her in my arms, carrying her the rest of the way to the room. Even though this suite had two bedrooms, we'd all been bunking in the bigger one. It was another reason I'd assumed Milo would be okay with being with everyone. Cohen was already down to his boxers as he sprawled out on the bed, and I began to think about how I wanted this to happen. I was going to need to read some of those books like Soren so I could get some ideas on how all of this worked at this rate.

Tossing Fin on the bed, I grinned as she bounced, rolling into Cohen's legs. "Let me help you out of your clothes, sweetheart," he said, grabbing her.

While Cohen occupied Fin, I looked around the room, finding Milo nervously standing against the wall. Walking toward him, I tried to ease him from looking like a scared animal.

"If you're not ready for this, you don't have to stay. No one wants you to feel uncomfortable. I just didn't want you to feel left out. I probably should've asked you beforehand what you were comfortable with, but with everything going on, we haven't really had a chance to talk about it."

Milo looked at me, swallowing. "If you're all okay, then I'm okay. I just don't know what to do."

I shrugged one shoulder, glancing back at the two on the bed. "Whatever feels natural."

Tugging at the back of my shirt, I decided to take my own advice instead of working out logistics and go with what worked. Tossing the material to the ground, I slipped my shorts, boxers, and socks off as I walked the rest of the way to the bed. Fin and Cohen were kissing as she straddled him, parts of her clothing still on like they'd both gotten distracted midway through.

Running my hands up her back, I unclasped her bra and slid it off her shoulders. Moving down to her panties, I lifted her up a little as I moved them down one leg at a time. She adjusted with me but never broke her kiss, making me smile at their commitment and total loss of the world around them. Knowing that it was just as likely for me to do that, I turned to Milo as he settled into a chair.

"Set an alarm for thirty minutes before we need to be upstairs." He nodded, pulling out his phone, satisfying my concern, and I looked back to the two on the bed. Cupping her breasts in my hands, I fondled them between my fingers, tweaking her nipples.

Fin gasped, releasing her mouth from Cohen's as she peered back at me. "About these orgasms, you promised me." Her pupils were fully blown, lust driving her, which was beautiful to behold.

"I'm ready to deliver." Reaching into the drawer, I pulled out some condoms, tossing one to Cohen, who caught it in his hand. Fin looked at them, biting her lip.

"I was thinking…" she started before I cut her off with a kiss.

"Not today. We can talk about it later." She nodded, satisfied with the answer for now.

Rubbing my palms over her backside, I kissed her nape, nipping it as my tongue lavished her skin. Cohen's fingers were already pumping in her, and she writhed on them, bucking as she sought them out. I'd planned to start with oral, but at this rate, I didn't know if she'd last.

"More," she panted, and I glanced over, catching Cohen's eyes. At his nod, I slid on the condom with ease, my cock hard and waiting.

Nudging her ass checks with the head of my cock, I began to rock back and forth as I dragged it through her wet folds. Her moan was all the encouragement I needed as I pushed forward, slipping inside her. Her pussy fit around me like a glove, and I gripped her hips tight as I held back the need to slam into her.

"Fuck, Fin. You feel so good," I groaned. She wiggled as she whimpered, and I knew I needed to move for both our sakes.

Focusing on the task at hand, I eased back slowly and then pushed in. I kept it at a slow pace, driving us both wild with need, refusing to push it too soon.

"Please," she whimpered, "I need more."

Her cries were too much, and I gave in to the desire running through me. I didn't even notice the other two in the room at this point. The only thing I was focused on was Fin, and how her amazing pussy gripped my dick perfectly. Slamming into her this time, she grunted, wiggling back against me more.

"Yes, yes," she chanted, urging me on as I withdrew and thrust back in with significant force.

It felt like the whole bed was moving with each thrust, but I only focused on her ass and how it felt beneath my hands as I gripped it. Her legs began to tremble, and I knew I was close to completely losing control. Pulling her body up, I sealed my lips to hers for a searing kiss before letting go so I could slam into her one more time. My hands felt permanently attached to her hips, and I wondered briefly if there would be fingerprints left behind. As much as I didn't like to think of hurting her, the caveman part of me liked that I'd marked her as mine somehow.

Rearing back, I withdrew completely, lining myself up as I thrust in, feeling my balls draw up as I came with a roar. If these rooms weren't soundproofed, I was confident someone would be breaking in to make sure no one was hurt by how loud my shout was.

Her body trembled beneath me, the aftershocks coursing through her, and I slowly withdrew, falling to the bed with a groan. After a few seconds of panting, I opened my eyes once the blood had returned to my brain. I found Finley with her head tossed back as she rode Cohen, a look of pure ecstasy on her face and one I wanted to be cemented in my brain for all eternity. She looked free, happy, and sexually pleased. Something I hoped to always bring to her life.

Sliding off the bed, I carefully pulled off the condom and walked to the bathroom to dispose of it. Washing my hands, I quickly glanced in the mirror, finding my own eyes not far from Fin's. If I looked even a percentage of what she had, it only reaffirmed that this was the right course for us.

Walking back into the room, I grabbed the discarded shorts and slid them on. Glancing at Milo, I found him captivated by the show as he watched their bodies entwined intensely. I was impressed he didn't pleasure himself. The most he was doing was rubbing his erection outside his shorts, but everything was still on. Maybe he was shy, and I needed to give him some space.

Finley came again a few seconds later, and I walked back into the bathroom, warming the water as I ran a rag under it. When I walked back into the room, she was lying on the bed, a blissed-out expression on her face. Nodding to Cohen as he headed into the bathroom, I gently wiped the washcloth over her, hoping to soothe her. She moaned in relief, and I laid it on her.

Moving to climb off the bed, Fin caught my hand, pulling me back to the mattress. "Thank you, Asa. You're the best."

Grinning, I kissed her and covered her with a blanket before standing and walking out into the kitchen. I didn't know what Milo would do, but it felt like he could use a moment alone with her. Cohen joined me a minute later and worked with me to pick up the trash from lunch. Our space wasn't huge, so keeping it clean felt crucial to not losing our minds all living together.

"You good?" Cohen asked as we sat down on the couch a while later.

"With what occurred in the bedroom or the mission?"

Cohen lifted one corner of his mouth in response. "Both, I guess."

"I'm perfectly okay with the bedroom and feel ready for the mission. Any pointers?"

Cohen seemed to think it over for a few seconds but then shook his head. "Not really. You have good instincts. So follow them."

Nodding, we drifted off into silence as we relaxed. It felt like no time had passed when Milo poked his head out, holding up his phone.

"Thirty-minute warning."

With that, Cohen and I stood, heading to finish getting dressed. It was time to find out if we were Order material or not.

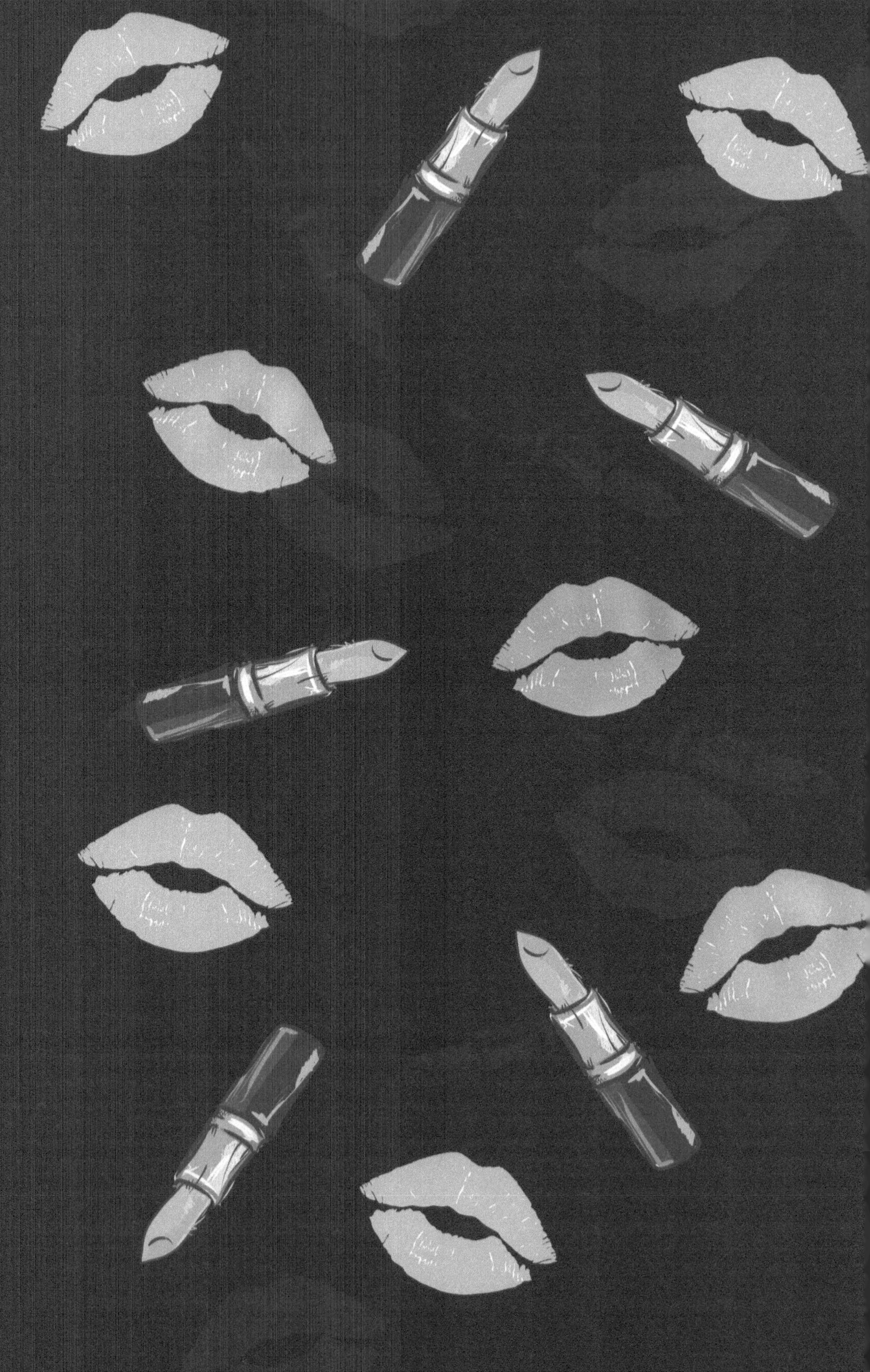

Nine

FINLEY

with Guzman as my companion. My fingers itched to do more, my leg bouncing up and down while I scanned footage. I'd been honest earlier when I said I was okay with staying back; it had made the most sense. But doing it sucked monkey balls.

The need to be the one on the front line coursed through me and I wondered if I had control issues. My brother seemed to think so. He reminded me every time I took over any event, deeming his skills lacking. Okay, maybe he had a point. But it didn't mean I was wrong about his ribbon curls.

Snorting, I focused back on the screen, knowing I needed to be the best lookout for Milo and Asa. Lord knew Guzman wasn't going to do it. He was currently crunching some chips and watching golf on ESPN. I wouldn't let us fail because I was bored… Okay, *jealous*. I didn't like being the lookout. There, I'd said it.

"How's it looking, Oblivion?" Cohen asked, using my code name over the comms, ignoring Guzman. Ryker had developed the app we'd used years ago into a more sophisticated one. With Bluetooth and smartwatches, it was practically seamless now.

"Clear so far. They've moved into position."

"Good, keep me updated." I could hear the apprehension in his voice, and I knew he at least understood how I was feeling. He hated being left behind to watch from the sidelines.

I zoomed in as I watched the three approaching the fire escape. Asa stayed back, manning surveillance from the ground as Milo and Nicole began to climb up. There was an air vent there where they were going to gain access, and shimmy their way down into the bakery. The place had been closed for an hour, and there hadn't been any movement or light since, giving them a fair chance at not running into anyone.

"We've made it to the roof," Nicole said, coming over the comms, slightly out of breath. I switched one of my screens to get a better view, keeping Asa on another. My heart rate started to increase as I watched them, worry for their well-being overcoming me. I couldn't lose them.

Keeping my eyes peeled, I watched as Milo and Nicole opened the vent and put on the rappelling equipment before shimmying down. Their helmets had mini cameras, so I turned them on, finding them as they began to descend into the bakery.

"Holy shit. I didn't think things like this existed," Nicole said, tilting her head down to show us.

Red lasers spread across the room. This bakery had better security than most banks.

"Um, Chaos," I said, switching comms so the team wouldn't hear. "We might have a problem."

I sent him the live feed, his curse letting me know he got it.

"Shit. This wasn't in our surveillance."

"What do we do?" I asked, keeping my gaze focused on Nicole.

"Unless the book is out in the open and one of you is a gymnast, I don't think you're prepared to disable that type of security."

I could hear the disappointment in his voice, and I wondered what it meant for The Order. But I couldn't think that way. This was real; I wouldn't leave my teammates in a bad situation. Switching back to Nicole, I knew what I needed to do.

"Okay, guys, I just need a few minutes to see if I can disable it. Are you okay with hanging there for a few minutes? Maybe see if you can spot the book?"

"Yeah, sure," Nicole said, and I minimized the camera screen. If Guzman was reliable, I'd have him monitor them, but since he was currently snoring, I didn't feel like putting my faith in him. I'd just have to be quick.

Pulling up the security system website, I cracked my knuckles as I logged in. Cohen had given me one of the most advanced encryption keys earlier, so I was eager to play with it. I just needed to get around the interface and firewall.

Quicker than I thought possible, I made it past the mainframe and began to scroll through the accounts. Earlier, we'd found one, and I disabled it, but this had to be separate since the lasers were still lighting up the room.

Everything had been in a woman's name so far, and I realized that was our mistake. For the legal stuff, it was all in her name. But I bet these lasers weren't on the business plan or budget proposal. No, these were paid with a different account and books, since that was what they protected.

Looking at the file, I found the man's name—Frankie Jacks.

Scrolling through with that name in mind, I smiled when I found what I was looking for a second later. Clicking on his account, I wasn't surprised that his password and two-factor authentication were more complex.

Maximizing the screen, I checked that the others were still okay and clicked on the comms. "I found the system. I just need a minute to deactivate it. You guys, okay?"

A loud rumble started far off, and I cursed, knowing that our time was running out.

"Um, you might want to hurry. I think that's them."

Minimizing the cameras, I focused on the security system,

knowing I couldn't be distracted at the moment, or we'd all be toast. My brow began to sweat as I punched in the code to reroute the two-factor so Frankie wouldn't get a notification. Once I had the code to decrypt everything set, I scanned it quickly, afraid I was missing something. The rumble grew louder, and I knew it was now or never.

Striking the key, I watched as the code flew across the screen, praying it would work. When it beeped green, granting me access, I stared at it for a second, convinced I was seeing things.

The rumble reminded me I was out of time, so I quickly clicked the cameras as I shouted into the feed.

"Go, you have maybe sixty seconds before the bikes are on you."

As I said that, I found them touching down into the bakery and running over to the drawer the book was supposed to be placed in. It felt a little too easy that there wasn't a giant safe, but I was guessing Frankie felt secure enough with his lasers to leave it unprotected. It made me wonder if the girlfriend was involved or if she was innocent in all of this. Lasers were easier to hide than a giant safe.

The noise outside grew louder, and I encouraged Nicole and Milo as they began to make their way back up. Quicker than I thought possible, they were up and climbing out of the hole. That was when I realized that Asa had climbed up there with them and had pulled them up quicker. Together, the three placed the vent back and removed their equipment just as the motorcycles made it to the parking lot.

Jolting, I reversed the sequence, setting the lasers and the alarm back on, praying I bought them enough time before the bikers realized we'd been there. Watching the front, I kept my eyes peeled on the three guys as they headed toward the door.

"Once they're in the building, you'll have a short window to get off the roof and book it," I whispered, too worried my voice would carry over their comms.

I watched as they nodded, affirming that they'd heard me. I glanced back down, glad that the bikers seemed to be here for a regular visit, their chatter and manner relaxed. Once the door was unlocked and they were all through the doors, I shouted the all-clear.

"Now!"

The three of them began to climb over the edge, Asa going first, then Nicole with Milo last. I couldn't help but feel pride that they'd put her in the middle, trying to give her some protection. Though I doubted she needed it with how badass she was, it made me love my guys' thoughtfulness. The door jingled open, and I sucked in a breath.

"Freeze."

Their movement stopped, and I could hear their breathing as they waited. One of the bikers looked to go to his bike, grabbing something out of his saddlebag before returning to the store. Once he was in, I hurried them down the rest of the way. Just as Milo's feet hit the pavement, sounds of disorder erupted from inside as things began to be turned over.

"Go! You don't have long." They quickly took off around the building, and I let out a breath as they ran out of view, finally safe from the men inside. I kept my eyes glued to the bakery, watching the bikers as I waited for my team to reconvene with me. I was parked a couple blocks over, so it would take them a few minutes.

Switching back to Cohen's channel, I was preparing to tell him we were safe when I heard a conversation. I instantly knew I shouldn't listen, but the fact that Ryker and Cohen were talking had me unable to switch off.

"Your team is looking good," Ryker said, and I could almost picture him crossing his arms, his smile smug as he made that statement like he was responsible.

"They are, but it's not because of you," Cohen said, echoing my thoughts.

Ryker sighed, the sound filled with an emotion I couldn't quite place. "If I need to say I'm sorry again, I will Cohen. I was an asshole with no clue how to deal with my own emotions. I panicked and punished you for them. That wasn't fair."

I wished I could see Cohen's face to know what he was feeling right then. The words felt true from Ryker, and I knew it would go a long way toward Cohen forgiving him, but I wasn't sure if it was enough.

"I appreciate that, but it's in the past now. I'd like to move forward in our working relationship and keep it civil."

"Is that all you want?" Ryker asked, his voice quiet, and I wondered if he was too scared to voice what he really wanted in life.

"Yes," Cohen said, but I didn't quite believe him. The door to the van started to open, jolting me out of my eavesdropping, and I clicked a button, trying to make it sound like I had just come on.

"The team has returned to the van and successfully completed our mission. Headed back to base," I said, keeping it brief since I knew Ryker was there.

Cohen cleared his throat. "Excellent. You've all shown great skills tonight and the ability to adapt to the circumstances. And if I'm not mistaken, you're the first team done. Looks like you four are Order material. See you back at base."

I smiled, not missing how he only said four of us. It felt nice that, for once, our group had been accredited the work we'd done, and the one member hoping to coast on our coattails wouldn't be able to.

I turned around, finding Asa and Milo beaming at me. Jumping up, I wrapped them both in hugs, needing to feel that they were safe more than I was willing to admit. They both briefly kissed me, their hands touching me, and I wondered if they'd been concerned even with me stuck on surveillance.

"That was some fast thinking with the security system. You saved our ass," Milo said, beaming at me.

"Yeah, I thought we were toast," Nicole added, pulling a sweat-shirt over her head. The rest of us also changed, making our appearance different in case we'd been picked up on a camera or were pulled over; we wouldn't look the same as whatever description they had. All of my disguises were coming in handy again.

Asa jumped out after he was dressed like a hippie surfer and took the magnet off the side of the van that had advertised tanning oil and put up one for floral arrangements. He got into the driver's side behind the wheel, and I felt my body relax entirely as we made it a few blocks without any trouble.

When he took a turn a little harder than necessary, I tried to contain my laugh when Guzman fell out of his chair and smacked his head. He jerked upright, confused for a second, and then pretended he hadn't been asleep. I didn't want to break it to him that he hadn't passed. I would let Ryker or Cohen be the ones to share that news.

Milo pulled me between his legs onto the floor, and I snuggled back into his arms, liking that he was becoming more comfortable with touching me. I guess seeing me get railed by two of my other boyfriends earlier opened the door more for physical touch. My cheeks heated at the memory, but I couldn't argue I wasn't a fan of how it had turned out.

Laying back against him, I closed my eyes, glad we'd made it through. I wasn't sure which I preferred now since, in the end, being in the van hadn't been as dull as I'd initially imagined. Though, part of me knew I'd always prefer to be on the front line, the need to control the outcome more in my grasp.

Yeah, yeah, I'd admit to being a control freak, and I was learning to be okay with that.

Cohen and Ryker were waiting for us when we returned. I couldn't make out Ryker's expression, but Cohen had a massive grin on his face, and it was all aimed at me. As soon as I stepped off the elevator, he swooped forward, picking me up into his arms.

"I'm so proud of you," he whispered. "You were amazing and the team leader they needed."

His words fell over me, taking me back. Leader? I hadn't been a leader. I was the non-valuable one on the sidelines.

Cohen watched my face, his eyes narrowing at whatever he saw play across it. "Yes, leader, sweetheart. It takes leadership to know your strengths and how to use them the best instead of just wanting to be the hero. But you were still that in the end with that fast code-breaking. I'm unsure if anyone else could've managed that in the time you did. The motorcyclists were another unforeseen hurdle, but you tackled it together."

He set me down on my feet, looking at the rest of the group. I caught Ryker's eye just before he turned his head, and I wondered if he'd been watching us.

"Great job, Team Campbell. You've all earned a night off from night watch. You can pick which one you'd like. Just let me know so I can alert the others to the schedule." He spun to leave, stopping in his tracks. He gaze flicked to Guzman. "Except you. You're out."

The big brute began to protest, but two guards headed toward him, one a little more aggressive than the other, and I wondered if that was his brother. He didn't look too happy with his younger bro if it was.

We all waited until he was escorted off the grounds and let out a cheer, laughter spilling out as the adrenaline continued to pump through us.

"You guys aren't bad. I'll catch you later," Nicole said, waving as she walked off and joined a group of people playing cards at one of the tables.

As one, we all headed toward our room. I didn't know if they were as eager as I to debrief together or just needed to not feel like we had eyes on us, but I was itching to change clothes and relax. And definitely keep ignoring the thing Cohen said.

Stepping into the suite, I headed for the bedroom, a change of clothes the first thing on my mind. An arm stopped me, and I turned, finding Asa watching me.

"Where are you going, babe?"

"I just want to change clothes. I'll be right out. Promise."

He looked down at his own attire, a grimace forming on his lips. "Yeah, okay, good call."

Laughing, I took his hand, dragging him with me. Pulling out a few things, I quickly realized I needed to do laundry again. I didn't want to admit I might be a bit high maintenance when it came to clothes, but only having about eight outfits was torture.

Asa and I changed and gathered all the dirty clothes scattered around the room from over the week, placing them in the basket. "Why do I feel like this is about to become my life? Always doing laundry?" I joked.

"We could all just walk around naked and eliminate the need

for clothes," Cohen offered, stepping into the room as he unbuttoned his shirt. I smirked, licking my lips, liking where this was headed.

"Um, there was a pizza at the door," Milo interrupted, holding the box like he wasn't sure what to make of it.

"Have you never seen a pizza before?" I asked, wondering just how rich he was. He'd been at the hotel when we ordered one for his graduation, so that couldn't be why he was looking at us strangely.

An uncharacteristic smirk grew on Milo's face, and I stopped, getting hot for a whole new reason. He peered at me from behind his glasses, and I felt like I should be saying, *"Yes, doctor, please check me there."*

"It's the note on top of it that I didn't know how to take, not the pizza itself," he sassed, his eyebrow lifting and making me wonder if he could suddenly read my mind and knew exactly what I'd been thinking.

My face heated, and I walked closer, wishing I had my glasses on so I could mess with them to take his stare off my face. Grabbing the envelope, I slid out the card and read it aloud.

"Thought I'd put the note on the outside this time so you wouldn't accuse me of tampering with it. I remembered how much you liked to eat pizza after a mission. Hope that's still the case. You did well tonight, little hacker. Ryker."

I looked up, taking in the expressions of the others. It seemed like they were waiting for me to respond. Even Cohen had a curious look on his face, and I had to guess the conversation I overheard had helped with the thaw between them.

"He's not wrong, and I'm suddenly starved."

"Ryker had to request that earlier since the kitchen closed two hours ago," Cohen said.

The importance of that statement wasn't lost on me. He knew we'd succeed and had thought ahead to get me a pizza.

Barnacles! He was breaking through my exterior and hitting me right in the mushy heart region.

"Who wants some pizza?" I placed the envelope on the dresser, picked up the laundry basket, and followed Milo. "Um, if you want to change, I'll throw some clothes in the wash."

"Oh, sure."

While I waited for him to return, I grabbed a slice, eating it as I thought. Never before had a piece of pizza felt like it held so much meaning.

"Want some help?" Cohen asked, the basket already in his hands.

"Yeah, that'd be nice." Wiping my hands and face, I walked out of the suite toward the laundry room with him. We were quiet as we made our way. I was lost in my thoughts, trying to put together the puzzle that my dating life was suddenly.

Separating colors and delicates, I went through the motions as I added the laundry detergent and softener. It wasn't until I hit the start button that Cohen even tried to talk.

"How are you feeling? You seem deep in your head."

When faced with a question you weren't prepared to answer, the best course of action was a deflection.

"I overheard your conversation with Ryker," I blurted instead.

Cohen smiled, moving forward to block and back me up against the washer. He braced his hands on the top, leaning over me as he stared down at me with his intense eyes.

"I know. I wanted you to hear. The comms beep when a new party enters the channel."

"Oh." I swallowed, licking my lips, trying to think of what to say. "I'm still sorry I didn't say anything."

"What did you think of what he had to say?"

"He sounded remorseful. I actually wanted to talk to you about that, but you're making it hard to think with you standing over me like this," I gasped, my eyes shuttering as his lips grazed my cheek.

"Is that so? I kind of like having you at my mercy." He moved back, placing his hands on my hips, and lifted me up to sit on the washer. "But this is important, and I think we need to have this conversation."

He stepped back, leaning against the other side, and I instantly missed him. So much so that a little whine left me, causing him to grin. Cohen stepped forward, and I wrapped my legs around his waist, liking the physical contact with him. My hands began to run through his hair and his eyes closed as he leaned against my arm.

"At first, seeing and learning who he was in my life was shocking. But after I had time to think about it, I realized that he hadn't been as awful as I made him out to be. Ryker hadn't promised me anything, but my young heart was in love, so it felt like a tragic betrayal. Knowing he's been watching over me shifts that a little. I wasn't always open with you about my feelings, so I can understand his actions a little more. I don't know if I want to be in a relationship with him anymore, but I think I can forgive him and find a way to be friends and colleagues where I don't want to punch him every five seconds."

Chuckling, I kept playing with his hair and massaging his scalp. It seemed to be the perfect balance of us being vulnerable without it being too scary.

"I know what you mean. I can recognize the fact that he wasn't the one to set me up now, and those feelings I had for him never really went away, but it's hard to trust when I've been jilted. When I was not so secretly listening, I had an epiphany that no matter what happens with Ryker, I think it's a decision we must make together. Because I don't want to lose you. You're my heart, Co-bear."

"Finley Amelia Reyes, don't you know how much I love you? A stupid amount." He grinned, his eyes so full of love that I practically melted.

"Stupid amount, huh? I could almost take that as an insult."

"I told you I love you for the second time, and you're worried about the fact I said stupid?" His brow creased as he tried to work it out.

"I love you a stupid amount, too," I said, my cheeks heating. Cohen stopped, the biggest smile ever crossing his face.

"Say it again, sweetheart. I wasn't prepared."

Swallowing, I braced my hands on his face, and he closed his eyes for half a second as my thumbs smoothed over his cheeks. "I love you, Cohen Campbell. A stupid amount."

"It's Michael. My middle name is Michael."

Smiling, I leaned forward, kissing him. My legs tightened around his waist, and I pulled him closer. His arousal met my core as our kiss became frenzied. We made out like teenagers and it was only the buzzer going off twenty minutes later reminding us that the clothes were done that stopped us from going further.

Laughing, I pulled back, leaving his hair a mess from my fingers. My face tingled from his stubble, and my panties felt damp, but I didn't care in the slightest. I felt full and happy, the feeling I'd been pretending to be for so long.

Jumping down, we both switched our loads into the dryer and then walked back to the room, hand in hand. The machines were connected to an app that would notify us when they were finished. Asa and Milo were spread out on the couches when we walked back into the suite, watching a movie. They smiled at me when we entered, and Asa stood to warm up some pizza.

In our conversation, I'd forgotten all about food. I guess there were some things more important than pizza, after all. Huh.

Sitting on the couch, I relaxed between Asa and Milo with a piece of pizza on my lap. "What are you watching?" I asked, lifting it up to my lips. Cohen chose to sit in front of the couch, pulling my legs over his shoulders so he could keep touching me.

"Just some movie on TV. Do you want to watch something different? We were too tired to choose."

I realized it was *Sweet Home Alabama*, so I shook my head, liking this one. The guys fell into a comfortable silence as we all relaxed, giving way to decompressing from the night. When the app buzzed a while later, Milo and Asa were both passed out on the couch.

"Looks like it's bedtime. I'll grab the clothes if you get them to move to the bed?" Cohen suggested. Sighing, I laughed, knowing it would be easier to get the laundry but letting Cohen have this one.

Gently, I woke both of them up, and surprisingly they got up without any issue, heading to the bedroom. I waited until Cohen returned and helped him fold the clothes and hang the ones that needed to be. As we finished, I smiled at the domesticated bliss we'd seemed to have found amongst ourselves, and I realized just how much I liked it. A girl could get used to this.

Eleven

FINLEY

The next week consisted of training sessions ranging from physical workouts or combat in the morning to learning a skill in the afternoon to evening. I'd perfected my lock-picking ability, worked on some new code, and gained muscle I never thought I'd have. I still hated running, but at least now I wasn't dying after a mile. In fact, I'd completed five miles today. It felt nice to achieve something, and like maybe I could defend myself at the end of this.

Ryker had been there through it all like an overprotective guardian. He was always watching, but out of reach. I didn't know if he was purposefully holding himself back or not wanting to cross lines while we were in training. The rest of us were growing closer in the meantime.

Nicole had been paired up with us on other missions, and thankfully none of them had been as stressful or down to the wire as the first one. I'd heard some rumblings that the only reason we were doing well was because of my relationship with Cohen. Still, I ignored them, knowing that, if anything, we were being held to a higher standard because of our relationship. Not the other way around. People would talk no matter what, especially whenever you did something well.

That was the thing I was learning about jealousy. Everybody was jealous over something, and some people would do whatever they could to take what you had. I'd worked hard to get to this point, fighting my demons and earning my retribution. There was only one obstacle left in my way of having the future I wanted. People who didn't even know me or my journey wouldn't be able to take that from me. Not now.

"Guess what?" Cohen asked, walking into the suite.

"What?" I looked up from my phone, finding him smiling at me. I'd been scrolling through photos of my brother and Sawyer's latest costumes, and I hated them. Unfortunately, there wasn't much I could do being this far away, so I was trying to think of a nice way to send my recommendations to the designer.

"Everything okay?" he asked, stopping what he'd been about to tell me. I guess I hadn't masked my frustration as well as I thought.

"It's nothing. What were you going to tell me?" I placed my phone down and looked at him with my big doe eyes. Cohen sat on the couch, taking my hand. He smiled at me, and I melted. Gah, he was too cute.

"I just secured you and one person a pass off the base."

I sat up straighter, intrigued by what this could mean. "Oh, and what would I get to do with this pass off the base?" I asked as excitement filled my voice. It wasn't that I didn't like it here. The Order had everything possible that you could want, from food to entertainment, exercise, and even a bar. But the one thing they didn't have was a clothing store. I was this close to making my childhood dream come true and finding some random fabric that wasn't being used, to make clothes. I felt that desperate.

Cohen lifted his eyebrows, giving me a look. "A trip to the mall, if one wanted," he said nonchalantly like it wasn't the best news ever.

Shrieking, I jumped up, waving my hands as I ran around the

couch. "Please tell me you're serious. This is not something to joke about, Co-bear."

Smirking, he stood and stopped my waving hands by placing his on my hips. He leaned forward and gave me a gentle kiss on the forehead.

"Oh, believe me, sweetheart. This is not something I would joke about when it comes to you. And as much as I would like to be the one to earn this. I think you should take Milo."

"Really?" I asked, surprised he would offer this chance to get off the base to someone else.

"Yeah, I'm learning that being in this relationship means that sometimes there are sacrifices, and I can admit that Asa and I have had more opportunities and time with you. And if Milo is going to feel more part of the bro club, then he needs alone time with you. And that's really hard to do while we're shoved underground at this base. So, use your pass wisely. Besides, I think he would probably enjoy shopping the most anyway. The guy seems like the type to enjoy that stuff." He shrugged like it wasn't a big deal, but I heard it for what it was.

"You just don't want to carry all my bags.," I teased, appreciating the sentiment of what he was giving up.

He snorted but pulled me a little closer, leaning down to whisper, "I'd carry all your bags at the snap of your little finger, but I know Milo needs time with you. Don't ever doubt I wouldn't spend every waking second with you, sweetheart."

He kissed my cheek, stepping back, leaving me all hot and bothered to go and tell Milo. Fanning myself, I squeezed his butt cheek as I skipped off to the other bedroom.

Milo was lying on the bed, flipping through a book. He looked up when I entered, and I smiled as I leaned against the frame, checking him out. Now that I could, I wanted to do it all the time. He watched me, a curious look on his face. He'd grown more comfortable with us over the week and a half here, and I loved that he was part of this.

"Hey, cutie," I said, smiling widely. "Would you like to go on a date with me?"

He pushed up his glasses as he sat up. "A date?" he asked. I couldn't tell from the distance, but it looked like his cheeks were reddening.

"Yep. Can you be ready in 10 minutes?"

"Yeah, sure. Where are we going?"

"Just to the mall. Cohen was able to get me a pass knowing how much I was dying without more clothes. And now that I don't have to hide from everybody, I can pay you back."

"You don't have to do that, Fin. I did it because I wanted to help you."

"I know. It's just—"

He cut me off, standing. "No, I have more money than I need. The fact I got to help a friend meant something to me. So please, it will hurt my heart if you were to deny me that gift by paying me back." He placed his hands in a begging motion, and I realized this was more than about money. "I understand you're not like other girls and just expect it of me. I know that. That's not what I think about you at all. This was more about me needing to feel like I was doing something different from my family and that I was making a difference. So please," he begged some more. Milo had walked closer with his speech, imploring me with his eyes.

I swallowed, gulping down the words I'd been about to say. "Okay," I agreed, realizing how much he needed this. I wasn't going to be a brat about it. "Thank you." I leaned up and kissed his lips.

"Now. Date time." I smiled widely, and his shoulders dropped when I didn't argue. "I'll see you in a few."

I walked into the other room to grab some clothes. While we all tended to sleep in here together, every now and then, one of the guys would go and sleep in the other bed. I understood it. It was a bit cramped and uncomfortable with four people in the bed. So, they'd rotate out every few days. They'd also moved all of their clothing to that room when they realized how stressed out it made me. I quickly dressed in some skinny jeans, a flowy top, a jean jacket, and my Chucks, since we'd be walking a lot. I instantly felt chipper getting out of my everyday yoga pants I'd been wearing for training with the knowledge of where we were headed at the forefront of my mind.

I wouldn't deny I was a girl who enjoyed shopping. I loved finding hidden gems along with the allure of getting something new. It instantly made me happier. The bonus was getting to spend alone time with Milo. I knew how precious time was here.

I walked out into the main area, finding Asa and Cohen standing together at the sink. Asa spotted me first and grabbed my hands as he checked me out from head to toe. He made a wolf whistle, causing my cheeks to heat.

"Fin, you look amazing. I'm kind of jealous now that I'm not going."

"What are you and Cohen going to do?" I asked.

"I think we're going to head down and play some pool. I'm going to see if Ryker is available, too. I think they could use some time to just hang out where they aren't working and maybe... without you as a distraction. "

I chuckled, but he wasn't wrong. He gave me a kiss, making my toes curl in my shoes. I reluctantly pulled away before things became too hot, and I didn't make it out of here. There were only a few things that would tempt me away from one of my lovers. And shopping was one of them. Chuckling, Asa smacked my butt and pushed me over to Cohen to say goodbye. It amazed me how comfortable we'd all grown with touching and kissing in front of each other.

Cohen gave me one of his saucy looks, quickly kissing me and telling me to be safe. When I finished my goodbyes, I found Milo standing, waiting for me. He wore a soft smile, making my heart race.

"You ready?" he asked.

I nodded, walking to take his hand. We headed out to the elevator, meeting our escort—a guard. While we were getting let off the base, we wouldn't be completely alone. It helped since I didn't know this area, and having to think about driving down that mountain again made me squeamish. Equally making me glad we had someone doing it for us.

When he drove underground a few minutes later instead of leaving the garage, I looked at Milo, confused. The guard driving chuckled, watching us in the mirror.

"Yeah, they make everybody who arrives the first time come up the mountain, but they built a tunnel underneath that will take you directly down it. You have to have special access to get to it. And until you're in The Order, you're not allowed to know it exists."

The thought of being in a car underground made me feel a little weird but as brilliant as these people were, along with their technology, I had to assume it was safe. Besides, wasn't there a really long tunnel under an ocean overseas? Surely then, a mountain was safer than being underwater. Being underground took us half the time to get down the mountain. Before I knew it, we were pulling out of the tunnel.

I blinked at the daylight, warming my face in the sun. I hadn't seen the actual sun in a week and a half. The Order did such a great job with the digital screens that I almost forgot that it was fake sometimes, but nothing could make you feel like the real sun. That wasn't something you could manufacture.

When we pulled up to the mall a little while later, I was practically bouncing in my seat. Milo laughed at me, but I didn't care. This was truly one of my happy places. The guard said he would follow but keep at a distance, making me like him even more. He'd told us his name was Leo, and he'd been with The Order for thirty years and only worked part-time. It was nice to see people respecting their organization enough to dedicate their lives to it.

Milo and I soon forgot about his presence as we began walking through the mall, and I pointed at everything. When I headed into a store, I became dizzy with all the new things and colors. I felt a little like Pretty Woman as I started trying on outfits, and Milo waited outside the fitting room for me. He would clap and give me a compliment for each outfit.

"Get them all," he said at one point, but I shook my head. It was fun to imagine them all, but I didn't need this many clothes. I might be a fashionista, but I was also practical.

I ended up getting quite a few, and it made him happy to give them to me. In turn, it made me doubly happy.

Oh wow, I was beginning to sound like such a sap.

I convinced him to buy some clothes for himself, and we picked a few things for Cohen and Asa. They didn't need too many things since most of our time was spent in loose-fitting athletic wear, but it never hurt to be prepared. Plus, I liked knowing that we had a choice. It didn't feel quite as prison-esque that way. For some reason, that was my unit of measure. Nobody could be fashionable in prison.

So, if we could wear different things, then it couldn't be all that bad. Loose association, but I never claimed to make sense.

"I'm starved. Want to grab something to eat?" I asked Milo, who was laden down with bags. He nodded his head in the affirmative, and I glanced over at the guard, who was also carrying bags. He shrugged. I guess I'd stolen their voices with all of my purchases.

"We still have a little bit of time left." My stomach grumbled, and I realized how hungry I was, so we headed to the Food Court as a group. They let me go first and then took turns grabbing food, so someone was always at the table with all of our stuff. I realized I might've gone a little overboard when it was all stacked together.

When we all had our food, we dug in, the already limited conversation going away. Maybe that was why we didn't notice what was happening at first, too consumed by our food and hunger.

When the first scream sounded, I thought it was people excited. But as chairs and tables began to be pushed aside, falling to the ground, I realized something more sinister was at play. The screams grew louder, and I could hear the fear as people ran in every direction. Leo jumped into action, turning and looking for the cause. I had a feeling he wouldn't find a person.

If this was MKG and Dex, then they would be smarter than being out in the open.

Just as I thought that a bullet whizzed past our table, hitting one of the bags. Shrieking, I dove for the floor, pulling Milo with me. My body trembled as I searched for my phone, wanting to call somebody. I hit the first name that I saw, praying the phone would ring. As it became quieter around me, I grew even more scared of what that meant. When the call dropped a moment later, I knew his next round of attack had been implemented.

He was taking out the cell phones, so no one could call for help, making us stuck.

I turned to Milo, my eyes wide with fear. He looked as lost and scared as me, as we gripped one another.

"What do we do now?" I asked just as a loud bang erupted close by. Milo froze as well, his answer dying on his lips.

Everything in our training fled me, and I squeezed my eyes shut as my heart began to race, my breathing becoming shallow. I didn't want to pass out, but my brain was overloaded, and I couldn't think. I didn't want to die. I was stupid to bring the guys into this. I should've just left it alone and lived out my life. I could've kept pretending.

But as my panic swirled, I knew that wasn't fair. This could've happened regardless, and I wouldn't want to give up the time I had with these guys for a chance I might avoid this. No. I needed to calm down and focus.

I'd been trained, so I just needed to use it.

Milo squeezed my fingers, reassuring me, and I looked up, nodding that we'd get through this together. I wasn't alone, and Milo was great at rescuing me. So, maybe it was time we helped these innocent people.

I took a deep breath when he placed a gun in my hand. Holding his eyes, so many emotions passed through them, and I shook my head, not wanting a goodbye.

I kissed him, not letting him say anything, just as a voice came out over the speaker system.

"Come out, come out, Oblivion. No one else has to get hurt."

Twelve

MILO

A shrill ringing sounded in my ears, and I blinked, trying to understand what was happening. Fin trembled next to me, the gun shaking in her hand. I needed to focus. The guys had trusted me to keep her safe, and I'd do that at whatever cost.

The PA system came on again, sending a shiver down my spine. "Now, now, Oblivion. It doesn't have to be this difficult. Maybe I should up the stakes?"

A gunshot sounded out, followed by a scream. I tensed, expecting it to hit us next. Sobbing was the only sound I could hear; everything else in the once loud mall was quiet. Too quiet.

I looked around for Leo, spotting his leg a few tables over. Things we'd purchased were scattered around the floor between us.

"Leo?" I whispered.

When he didn't move, I feared the worst. Swallowing, I nodded to Fin that I would check him out. I peered over the table, not seeing anyone standing. Staying crouched, I moved over to him, slumping down behind the table. I could see Finley from the angle as she bit her lip, watching me.

Taking a breath, I prepared myself to look at Leo. He was

sprawled out, blood seeping from a wound on his shoulder. My medical instincts kicked in, and I placed the gun down as I immediately began to address his injury. I found an exit wound, making it easier to manage. Ripping off part of his shirt, I applied pressure as I searched for something to use.

Grabbing one of the new tops Fin had just bought, I pressed it onto the spot and grabbed a thong that had fallen out; using the elastic, I tied it around the shirt, holding it in place. Taking Leo's pulse, I found it beating, if not a little slow. Slapping his face, I tried to stir him. I needed to know what the protocol in this type of situation was.

"Leo," I hissed, slapping him again. It seemed to work, and he opened his eyes, looking at me. "Is there an emergency protocol? Cell phones are down."

He blinked, coming to. "Wa-tch."

Understanding, I placed his gun in his hand and peeked over the table, still not spotting anyone. Moving back over, I slumped against the back of the table as I caught my breath. Fin squeezed my arm, her eyes boring into mine.

"He said there's something on the watch that should alert the others," I whispered. Or at least I hoped that was what he meant, and it wasn't an instant kill switch. Fin nodded, looking down at hers as she typed into it.

"Time's up, Oblivion. Another one bites the dust. I'll keep killing people until you show yourself."

The gunshot was closer this time, as was the scream. Fin tensed, her hands trembling as she began to shake her head. I knew what she was thinking, but there was no way I'd let her sacrifice herself.

"No. You can't give yourself up, Fin. It won't solve anything."

Her lip trembled as she stared at me, and I swiped away a tear, leaving a trail of blood behind. "What do you need?" I asked, deciding the best course was to focus on what we could do.

"If I had access to a computer, I could tap into the cameras and find him. But unless it's wired into the system, I doubt I'll have any luck since he's blocking the signal."

"Okay, so that makes it difficult, but not impossible," I said, thinking through possibilities.

"The security booth would have surveillance!" she said, some life coming back to her. "First, I need to tap into the code on these watches to send an alert." She fiddled with her watch as I looked around, spotting a few more people who seemed to be in need. Looking around at all the food places, I spotted a first aid kit on a shelf.

"I'll be right back," I whispered, crawling away before she could stop me. I stopped every few feet to hide and reached the last table before I'd be out in the open. Looking back, I peered around again, not spotting anyone. I wasn't sure where he was shooting from, but it didn't seem like he was close.

Taking a deep breath, I prayed I'd live long enough to see Finley naked again. It seemed dumb, but it was the one thing I thought about as I took off at a run, jumping over the counter as I rolled to the floor. I smiled, shocked that it had worked. A few workers were huddled together, looking at me in fear, and I couldn't understand why.

When I lifted my hand, I realized it was because of the gun. Placing it back into a holster, I raised my empty hands. "I'm not the bad guy. I'm a doctor. Is anyone hurt?"

They regarded me for a while before one of them nodded, moving to show me a man on the floor they'd been shielding. Reaching up for the first aid kit, I opened it and began to look through it.

"Shit, I'm going to need more. Can one of you go to the other food places and grab theirs?"

A young boy nodded as his mom began to cry, but she didn't stop him as he hurried off. I felt like an ass, but we'd need the supplies, and he might be the best option to get them. He was small and quick. I got to work, helping the man on the floor who looked to have hit his head.

"I think he has a concussion but should be okay for now." I cleaned his wound and sealed it for the moment. The woman patted my hand, thanking me.

Moving to the side, I was about to make a break for it when the boy returned, three more kits in his arms. Smiling, I took them from him. Taking a chance, I shoved them across the floor, not wanting to hinder my escape with them in my hands.

Once they were all against the table, I took a deep breath and ran for it. A shot rang out, and I cursed, feeling it graze me as I ducked down behind the table. Checking it over, I sighed with relief when I saw it was only a tiny cut. Taking more time than I had, I ducked and weaved my way from person to person, checking them over for injuries. Most of the crowd seemed to be okay, making me relieved that there weren't many dying people without medical attention here.

When I got to another section, I realized that wasn't the case here. Blood covered the floor, and I slid through it as I moved toward the woman holding a man. I knew before I got there that it wasn't good. There were bullet wounds in his chest and leg, both bleeding profusely. His eyes were closed, and when I checked his pulse, there wasn't one.

"I'm sorry," I said, tears brimming my eyes.

The woman sniffed, nodding. "He saved me. I don't even know his name, but I didn't want him to be alone." I squeezed her hand, feeling like she needed some comfort.

"Psst," a voice said behind me, and I turned to find Fin crouching. She swallowed when she saw the woman and man, her face dropping slightly. She nodded, and I looked back to the woman, but she had her eyes closed as she rocked the man back and forth, her lips moving over a silent prayer.

"I managed to send a message and found the security booth. But..." she trailed off, biting her lip again.

"What?" I asked, already knowing the answer.

"It's all the way over there," she nodded in a direction that was all open space. As I opened my mouth to tell her no, the PA system crackled on again.

"Times up, Oblivion. Another victim to add to your tally. It's beginning to get steep."

Fin squeezed her eyes, her body shaking as a gunshot rang out further away this time. "I have to go. I can't let him keep killing people."

Thoughts of what the others would say raced through my head. Everything in me wanted to protect her, to keep her from this, and I knew they'd want the same. But I couldn't cage, Finley. She was as strong and capable as I was of doing this. Maybe more so. Taking a long, stuttering breath, I opened my eyes and pulled her close to me, kissing her deeply.

"Be safe, Fin." I bit back everything else I wanted to say, hoping by not doing it, I'd have another chance, that the universe might owe me for once, for all the bad shit in my life before her.

"You too," she said, squeezing my hand as she took her own breath before she darted out, heading for the closest cover. A bullet whizzed past her, but she was able to dodge it. I looked in the direction it had come from, but nothing was making sense. Each shot came from a different angle. He either had multiple hidden shooters, or he could move and shoot from various locations without being seen. Neither seemed possible, but my eyes couldn't find a person to make sense of it.

When Fin took off for another section, I held my breath as she made it. She had only one more area before the security office, and then she'd have to open the door. I couldn't stop the shooter, but maybe I could draw their focus away. As she steeled herself for the last leg of her journey, I stood up, taking in the area. I wanted to paint a target on myself and get a lay of the food court, so I knew where to go.

A loud pop sounded next to me, and I ducked back down,

yelling as the thing I'd been hiding in front of was filled with bullets. Quickly, I moved over to a new section just as Fin made it into the office. Blood trailed on the ground, and I hoped it wasn't crucial. I couldn't let myself focus on it right now. She had her job to do, and I had mine. I'd seen three more people that needed medical attention when I stood, and I was all they had.

Crawling over, I made it to the first victim and began to clean and dress their wounds. I was down to two first aid kits, making it even more vital that help arrived soon. Over the next few minutes, I zeroed in on what I needed to do and tried to let everything else fade away. Fin would figure this out. I had faith in her.

The second person I came upon looked at me, shaking their head as they pointed to a small child.

"Help… her." I looked over and saw she had been shot, and I wondered if this person had tried to cover her with their body. MKG might've thought people would turn over Fin to save themselves, but if anything, I saw countless acts of heroism as mere strangers sacrificed themselves for others.

My hands started to shake, and I squeezed my eyes shut as I breathed. Taking out some tweezers, I motioned for the woman to hold the little girl down while I searched for the bullet fragments. The man who'd saved her closed his eyes, happy that she was safe, and I shed a tear for him. Focusing on the little girl, I concentrated, wanting to make his sacrifice worth it.

Finding a few shards, I pulled them out and then used the sewing kit to stitch her up for now. It wasn't ideal, but it would work for the time being. The woman thanked me, tears streaming down her face. Nodding, I wiped my bloodied hands on my jeans, trying to clean them as much as possible as I peeked around for the last person I'd seen.

When I got there, I didn't know where to start. This had to be one of the first victims, as multiple wounds were bleeding. None seemed fatal, but it wouldn't matter if she bled out. Focusing on the worst of the bunch, I cleaned and applied pressure, working through them as I used stitches and pads to hold off the worst of it.

"Thank you," the teenager said, and I prayed that help would be here soon. I didn't know how long these people had if it wasn't.

Slowly, I turned, looking at the door Fin had gone in. It was still closed, with no movement, and I had to believe that meant she was still safe. I debated where to go when the PA system came on again, this time, his voice a little frantic.

"Very well, Oblivion. We'll have to continue our *game* at a later date. I see you've gained some new skills. I'll keep that in mind. Enjoy this parting gift."

Just as he finished, I could make out sirens in the background, my body relaxing, knowing that help was coming. Fin opened the door, a smile on her face, peeking out and looking for danger. I smiled at her, so proud of her for managing to do it.

"You did—"

A loud explosion sounded behind me, throwing me forward, and everything went black.

Thirteen

FINLEY

The thrill of cracking Obsidian's position raced through me as I hit some keys. The tricky asshole wasn't even here, but he'd managed to place drones in various places and he was shooting remotely. The jerkwad was still hiding behind his computer somewhere. Tapping into the remote frequency, I used one of the new apps from The Order on my watch and located their positions. Shutting them down, I pumped my arms into the air in victory.

Exhilaration surged through me at having solved this and hopefully saved some more lives. I didn't want to think about the guilt I was sure to feel later.

Cohen: Sweetheart, you okay?
ME: I shut down the drones. We should be clear of danger now. ETA?
Cohen: Soon. Good job, sweetheart.

"Very well, Oblivion. We'll have to continue our game at a later date. I see you've gained some new skills. I'll keep that in mind. Enjoy this parting gift."

With Dex's retreat, I stepped out of the booth, the sound of sirens making my heart slow. We'd made it. We were safe.

Instantly, I spotted Milo, a massive smile on his face. He was covered in blood, and I hoped it wasn't his.

"You did—"

His words were cut off as a massive explosion rocked the space behind him. His body flew forward, and I stumbled from the after-shocks. My heart thumped in my ears as I ran ahead, slipping every few feet on debris and falling rumble. I focused on him, needing to get to Milo.

When I reached his body, I grabbed his wrist, remembering some of the first aid training we'd received. My eyes scanned him, looking for any signs of injury. He had a cut on his head, my free hand shook over it as I debated what to do.

Sound around me ceased to exist. I couldn't hear anything outside of my own heart. Looking up, I saw what I assumed were people moving, but they were blobs, indistinct in color and shape. My mind raced with what steps to take, but I couldn't grab any of it. All it seemed to focus on was that I was going to lose someone. That I was responsible.

Tears fell down my cheeks as I rocked back and forth. I smoothed the hair away from Milo's forehead, praying to whoever would listen to let him live.

"Darling?" a voice croaked, reaching my ears. A hand squeezed mine, and I realized it was Milo's who I was holding.

"Milo?" I asked.

"What… happened?" he whispered, trying to open his eyes.

"Ssh, don't. I'll get you help." I began to look around, my gaze landing on a familiar dark head of hair and dark eyes as they charged toward me. My body sagged in relief as I realized that help had arrived.

"It will be okay, now," I said to Milo to reassure myself as tears fell down my cheeks harder.

"Over here," Ryker shouted, directing an EMT to us. My body

shook, and I struggled to let go of Milo. It was only through Ryker's coaxing that they'd be able to give him medical attention, that I could release him.

As soon as he was on the stretcher, Ryker scooped me up and stormed out of the mall with me in his arms. I didn't fight him, not caring about our history any longer. It all seemed so trivial when people's lives were at stake. I buried my head in his arms, no longer feeling the high of defeating Dex at his own game. He might be a coward, but he covered his bases, and I hadn't anticipated that. Ryker carried me outside, and I clung to him, needing to feel safe.

"Ssh, little hacker. You did well. I'll take care of this. I promise. Dex will be held responsible."

I peered up into his eyes, finding them trained on me. They held the promise he spoke of and so much more. Ryker showed me at that moment I could trust him, that I wasn't foolish for doing it. Something in me shifted, and I nodded, my heart slowing as I accepted this.

I wasn't a scared little girl anymore. I'd become strong and wouldn't stop until he was brought to justice. Ryker was telling me I didn't have to do it alone, which felt like the greatest gift.

"Okay," I said. My heart began to settle, my nerves no longer trembling. I wouldn't give in to the fear. He might be a psychotic genius, but he was still a man, which meant he could be defeated.

"I need to go and check over some things. I will leave you with Cohen and meet you at the base. Milo will be taken there and given the best treatment."

Nodding, I watched as he hesitated before lightly pressing a kiss to my forehead, holding me to his chest. "I thought I'd lost you," he whispered so quietly that I almost wondered if I imagined it. Before responding, he set me on my feet, nodding to someone behind me.

"Fin?" Cohen asked, taking my hand. "Let's get you checked out, sweetheart."

I turned to him, my body exhaling at his nearness. Nodding, I wrapped my arms around him, needing to feel his comfort. "Asa?" I asked.

"Right here, babe."

I lifted my head, finding him near, and raised my hand to draw him closer. He came willingly, and the three of us stood in the parking lot in a three-person hug. They both petted my hair, reassuring themselves I was okay.

"Come on, we can get back to the base and check on Milo once you're clear."

They directed me to a paramedic who quickly cleaned and bandaged my cuts, stating I'd need to watch for a concussion, but otherwise, I was injury free. I had a slight sprain to my wrist, but it should heal in a few days. Considering the circumstances, I was lucky.

Asa and Cohen both seemed to exhale in relief at the news. As they began to lead me toward a car, I spotted a familiar face. I turned toward them despite my boyfriend's grumblings.

"Leo?"

He looked up, a faint smile on his face. "Hey, Fin. You okay?" he asked, assessing my injuries.

"Yeah, just a sprain and some minor cuts. How are you?" I nodded to the spot on his arm.

"Alive, thanks to Milo. I was shot, and he saved me. Where is he?" he asked, looking behind me. Tears welled in my eyes, and he caught them, his face falling.

"He was caught in the explosion. I'm not sure how he is. We're headed back now." My lip began to tremble, tears threatening to fall again, but I held them back. I couldn't fall apart here, or I'd never recover.

"He's strong. He'll pull through."

I nodded, hoping Leo was right. Patting his arm, I turned back to Asa and Cohen, taking their hands as they led me to the car. Once inside the vehicle, Asa pulled me into his arms, and I shut my eyes, hoping that things would be different when I woke.

The machine beeped next to me, the sound a steady rhythm to the background noise. It was quiet in the medical wing, only Milo requiring a room. Leo had been brought back here but was gone now. He'd needed stitches but hadn't required surgery for his bullet wound. The doctor credited Milo with saving him.

While we waited for Milo to return from surgery, Ryker called to tell us that all in all, Milo had saved ten people. The death toll was at four, with multiple injured. Two deaths were from the drones, and two from the bomb that had been set off in the shoe store on the corner of the food court. The Order had taken over the investigation, acting as FBI and Homeland security. There wasn't any information released yet to the press, but it was only a matter of time, and I was curious how they would spin it. It made me wonder how many things had been spun my whole life, like Mongoose's murder.

Now, I sat alone next to Milo's bed. He'd been back from surgery for a couple of hours. He'd woken once, but it had been brief. I debated if I should tell someone, but I didn't think outside of us that Milo had any family. None that he talked to anyway.

So, I sat in the quiet room, the heart rate machine my measure of how he was doing. Asa and Cohen had kept me company for a while, but I'd sent them to the room to sleep. Milo was in a stable condition, so there wasn't any need for them to stay here. I just didn't want him to wake up and be alone. My eyes scanned over his frame, taking in each new cut and mark.

He'd been grazed by a few bullets in multiple areas, but it was the burns and slight swelling on the brain they were most concerned with. Milo had come out of surgery well, and the doctor had high hopes for his recovery. Apparently, they had some advanced technology that cut rehab time in half. It was nice to know it wouldn't ruin his plans to start at Lux in the fall if he was able to recover from this. It would be one less thing for me to feel guilty over.

"Stop," a voice said, drawing my eyes to his. His glasses had been knocked off in the explosion, so I wondered how well he could see now without them. His eyes were clear, though, and I could see them without any intrusion.

"Hey," I said, moving closer to peer at him. "How are you doing?"

"Like I've had a whole building fall onto me. Oh, wait." He smiled, the motion looking more like a grimace. Laughing, I wiped a tear, unable to stop them.

"None of that, darling. I'm fine."

"No, you're not." I shook my head, my lip wobbling as I tried to find the words.

Milo lifted his hand, taking mine. With his other, he hit the button to lift the head of his bed up, allowing him to sit up.

"Bring me the chart, will you, darling?"

Sucking in a breath, I dropped his hand, padded over to the wall, and grabbed it. I waved at the nurse outside, and she smiled, returning to her computer. Carrying the folder to Milo, I tried to show a brave face. In reality, all I really wanted to do was curl up in his arms and sleep for a few days. I handed it to him, and he pulled the tray across the bed, surprising me with how well he knew how to operate a medical room.

"I just graduated, Fin. I've been doing clinical rounds for years in med school." He peered at me with a soft smile, easing my guilt.

"Right, doctor." I nodded as he winked. He flipped through it, taking in everything that looked like a foreign language to me.

"Okay, so it's not as bad as you're making it out to be. The way you're going on, I thought I was dying."

"Milo!" I gasped, shocked he'd be so carefree with his words.

"Yes, darling?" His eyes twinkled, and I couldn't reconcile them with him in the hospital bed.

"You could've died!"

"But I didn't. So, who do I need to see to get out of here? I'd prefer to sleep in a bed with you than this."

"But… your injuries! You just had surgery."

"Yes, it was minor, and I've been in recovery for hours. All of my wounds are superficial and have been bandaged. My burns are covered, and I'll need to have them checked out over the next few days, but nothing that requires me to be here. There will be tests to come, I know this, but again, there's nothing that requires me to be in a hospital bed right now."

"He's right," a voice said from the door. I turned to find Ryker standing there. He looked exhausted.

"You okay?" I asked. "Did you find anything?"

"It's been a long day. Can we debrief in the morning? I just came down to see how Milo was doing. The doctor on duty gave me a rundown, saying he'd be free to go once he woke up. He's awake and seems clear-headed to me."

His eyes held mine, emotion swirling in them, and I realized I had to trust them. I didn't know why I was so focused on Milo needing to stay anyway. It was better if he wasn't here. Dropping my shoulders, I walked over to the bag I'd put together and placed it on the bed.

"I brought you some clothes." I kissed his cheek, walking out of the room to give him some privacy. Ryker followed, taking me in.

"How are you doing with everything? I still can't believe Dex would go to this extreme."

"Whoever you thought your friend was, you were wrong. He's not that guy anymore if he ever was. I'm sorry, but you can't keep holding onto Obsidian as we knew him. For all we know, that wasn't even the real him. He's killed people. Innocent people. And I, for one, am tired of feeling guilty for his actions. So, how am I? I'm pissed, and I've never been more ready to take someone down. You said you'd hold him responsible. So, the question is, will you stand by me or just be in my way?"

Ryker watched me through my speech, my shoulders straightening with every word I said, a promise zipping through me to hold them. This had gone on too long, MKG and Dex needed to be stopped. And I hoped Ryker would be with me. But either way, I knew I had three men who would be.

His eyes held mine, and I saw the truth before he even said it.

"I'll stand by you, Fin. Always."

Fourteen

FINLEY

Ryker stood at the front of the conference table, a commanding look on his face as he debriefed everyone on what had occurred at the mall. The only thing keeping me from falling into a fit of hysterics from the ordeal was focusing on Dex and MKG. If they were this advanced, it would take the full force of The Order to deal with them, so I needed to focus.

"So, he was never there?" someone asked, drawing my attention as Ryker moved.

"No," he sighed, rubbing his hand over the top of his hair, the ends standing at all angles. "I don't know how far in advance he planned this or if he even had the capability of doing it so quickly, but there were five drones positioned around the mall, the majority of them in the food court area. The bomb was also placed in a shoe box display. He used a cell phone blocker to cut off communication. It was only our more advanced network with the watches that still worked."

Ryker placed his hands on the table, the weight of this visible as he glanced around the room at everyone. "There's something else."

I looked to Asa and Cohen, both shaking their heads that they didn't know. When I met Ryker's eyes, I knew it wouldn't be good.

"As I'd feared, Kristina has been killed by MKG. Her body was found at the mall. She's been dead for a few days. I've given her team a few days off, but I'm sure they'll want in on the takedown. Because there will be one. Dex won't get away with this."

Ryker's words were filled with truth, and I knew that even to his own detriment, he wouldn't rest until this had been dealt with. It had gone beyond duty at this point. It was personal, and Ryker didn't seem like the type of man to let something like that go. Dex had been his friend, and this was the ultimate betrayal.

"We have a team sweeping through the footage to see if they can find anything. I doubt there will be much, but no one is perfect. He's bound to have slipped up somewhere, and we'll be there to exploit it. Everyone else needs to train and work on their projects until we have more information. No one is to leave base unless it comes from me. As for now, only critical missions and agents already in the field will continue to operate until we have more of a handle on MKG. Dismissed."

Everyone began to gather their things to head off to do the tasks Ryker had set before them. I stayed sitting, wanting to talk to Ryker. I watched him, noticing how shaken up he was. The Order had been the thing whispered in the night for so long, restoring balance in the world one mission at a time, that now, to be the one being hunted was throwing them all off their game. I didn't think they knew how to act without their secrets and code names.

"Did you need something, little hacker?" he asked once the room was cleared, only I and my guys left.

"Yeah, I just wanted to make sure you were okay."

His brow furrowed, and I knew I'd taken him aback. He hadn't expected me to ask him how he was doing. I guess being the one in charge, he was used to always being asked for something. It made me want to check in with him more often.

"I'm…" he shook his head, dropping the act as the lie fell away.

He walked toward me, sitting on the table between Cohen and me. Despite the gruesome news, it felt normal for him to still flirt. At least, I thought this was Ryker flirting. "I'm trying to hold it together, but I feel like I'm failing at every corner," he said, his head dropping.

I swallowed, not knowing what exactly to say. "I don't think you're failing, Ryker. You're doing what you can to fix a problem. To stop a madman."

"But The Order is meant to stop these things before they happen. I can't help but feel responsible for the deaths in that mall, for the trauma you endured, for the scars Milo will have... it makes me wonder if someone else was in charge if they'd have caught it sooner. Did my friendship with Dex cloud my judgment of what he was involved with? How did I not see it coming?"

"Whoa, whoa, whoa. Okay, you can't go down that path, man. You're only going to drive yourself crazy," Cohen said, squeezing Ryker's leg. "And I think your history is what makes you the perfect person to be in charge because you know him the best. What did you always tell me? Hmm?"

Ryker turned his head, searing his eyes into Cohen's. If I ever questioned their chemistry, it was laid out right in front of me. It was magnetic, and I hoped they'd find a way back to whatever lay between them.

"Carrying the weight of the world around becomes burdensome and endless. There are plenty of things to genuinely feel guilt over in life, so you don't need to add to it by carrying someone else's. Instead, focus on what you can do to relieve the world of evil, redeeming your sins one mission at a time."

Cohen smiled at Ryker, and I let his words circle in my head. He wasn't wrong. I'd been carrying the sins of myself and others for years, and it hadn't brought me any closer to feeling redeemed. If anything, I'd felt guiltier each time I enjoyed something for myself. The lies I'd told myself had stained my soul like lipstick on a collar. I couldn't carry the weight of Dex's actions, killing those people to get to me, just as Ryker couldn't. I think I'd been focusing on everyone else to ignore the reality of the situation. But that wasn't going to help them or me.

I might not be responsible, but I could do something about it.

"Perhaps it was the hubris of The Order that blinded everyone to the threat brewing. It doesn't matter how he was able to amass power now; he already has it. What matters is what we do to stop him. Your friendship might have clouded your judgment, but I don't think it will any longer. You see him for who he is and what he's done. And I think that's what matters. We all have sins, Ryker. I ran from mine for so long that I thought the only way forward was revenge. I set out on a course with a plan to make you pay, and then I discovered that you weren't the monster I thought you were."

"Well, I might be a monster in other ways," he said, followed by a grimace. "Sorry, vulnerability is hard for me, and my go-to is either raucous sex jokes or guarded indifference. I'm trying to be present because you all matter. This matters. I don't want to lose you again."

Cautiously, I reached up and took his hand. His breath caught in a gasp at my touch, and I focused on looping my fingers with his. I felt Asa's hand on the small of my back, urging me on. Letting out a breath, I met his eyes.

"You won't lose me. Just be honest and no games. I can't take the lies anymore."

"I promise." Ryker turned his head, finding Cohen. "And you?"

Cohen looked over at me, and I nodded, letting him know I supported his decision. "I'm here too. We can discuss what that means after we handle MKG. Deal?"

"That's one conversation I look forward to having for once." Ryker's face broke out in a genuine smile, and I felt a part of my heart I'd thought long lost begin to thump again. "Well, I have a few more meetings I need to have. Can we all do dinner later? Karen's been asking about you in the canteen."

"That sounds like a plan. It might be good to leave our suite for once. See you in a few hours then?"

"It's a date." Ryker winked, jumping off the table and sauntering to the door. The three of us stood slowly, following, and I wondered just what we were in for. Ryker Jenson was a mystery I was eager to uncover.

WHEN WE WALKED BACK INTO THE SUITE, I FOUND IT FILLED WITH shopping bags. I stopped, blinked, and then blinked again when they didn't disappear.

"Okay, I'm not dreaming. So, why are there so many clothing bags in our suite?" I asked whoever knew the answer.

Milo limped out of the bedroom, startling a little when he saw us. "Oh, hey. I didn't hear you." He smiled sheepishly, and I knew, whatever the reason for all the bags, he was responsible.

"What's with all the bags?" I asked, walking closer to him. I instinctively placed my hand on his forehead, checking his temperature. He smiled down at me.

"I'm the doctor, remember?" He tugged me into his arms, and I carefully wrapped mine around him. "And I'm not broken. Still a little tired, which is why I didn't go to the meeting, but I promise, I'm good." He kissed my forehead, a soft smile spreading as he stepped back, his hands on my forearms. "As for the bags, well, I felt bad that all the things you'd picked out had gotten... misplaced. So, I took the opportunity to get replacements. I hope that was okay?"

I hadn't even thought about the clothes, which was a first for me. I guess I was worried they'd bring bad memories, but as I looked at the bags filled with untold treasures, the same feeling of euphoria began to crawl through my body at all the possibilities.

"More than okay. Oh, I can't wait to see what you got!" I

clapped my hands as joy escaped through my body from my head to my toes. This was precisely what I needed. A good distraction from everything else.

I began to open bags, oohing and aahing at tops, skirts, pants, socks, bras, panties, and even shoes. Milo had thought of everything, and not only had he gotten me new things, but the guys as well.

"That doctor memory of yours must come in handy, remembering everyone's sizes," I said as I looked in awe at the display.

"As much as I would love to take credit for that, I called and asked the guys." Milo blushed, the red creeping up his neck, and I found it adorable. Walking over, I was careful of his injuries as I hugged him, pulling his face down for a kiss.

"You're adorable, and I love it. Thank you. You're going to spoil me, though, if you keep doing this."

"Nothing would make me happier, darling."

Fluttering my eyelashes, I fought my own blush as I peered back at the guys. "Does this mean I can style everyone tonight?" I rubbed my hands together in excitement.

"Sure," Asa said, sitting on the couch and picking up a bra. "This is my color."

"Not really your size, though. I think you're more of a 38 C, bro," Cohen teased, picking up a shirt. Asa laughed, sitting the bra back into the bag.

"Now this I like," Cohen said, looking over the shirt. It was blue and went perfectly with his eyes.

"Good, because I want you to wear it with these." I handed him gray pants, and he nodded, taking the things and walking to the bedroom.

I began to put the clothes in piles so they could sort out their things, and I could get all of mine out of the living room. "Hope we have enough room in the closet," I groused, worried I'd have to pick and choose which to hang.

"Actually, we're being moved," Milo said, just as Cohen walked out, an odd look on his face.

"Is that why none of our stuff is in the bedroom?"

"Yes. I got the message after all this had been cleared through security. Ryker fears there's a mole in The Order. Someone had to tell Dex how to track our movements or where we'd be. So, he wants us in a more secure area. We're to get dressed and leave everything else, which will be moved while we're eating dinner."

"Wow, he could've mentioned it," I grumbled, feeling a little out of the loop. But knowing he had a million things on his mind, I wanted to give him the benefit of the doubt he would've at dinner. Packing up all the items, I left everything by the door that wasn't what I needed for us.

I handed a pile of clothes to Asa and Milo and then took my own into the bathroom. I jumped in the shower and rinsed off my body, managing to keep my hair out of the spray. Once I was done, I dressed in the new clothes, feeling all kinds of hot and badass in my sparkly shorts, slinky tank, blazer, and black high heels. Whoever said that clothes couldn't change the world clearly had never worn something this awesome.

When the guys took me in from head to toe, I could tell they also agreed with me.

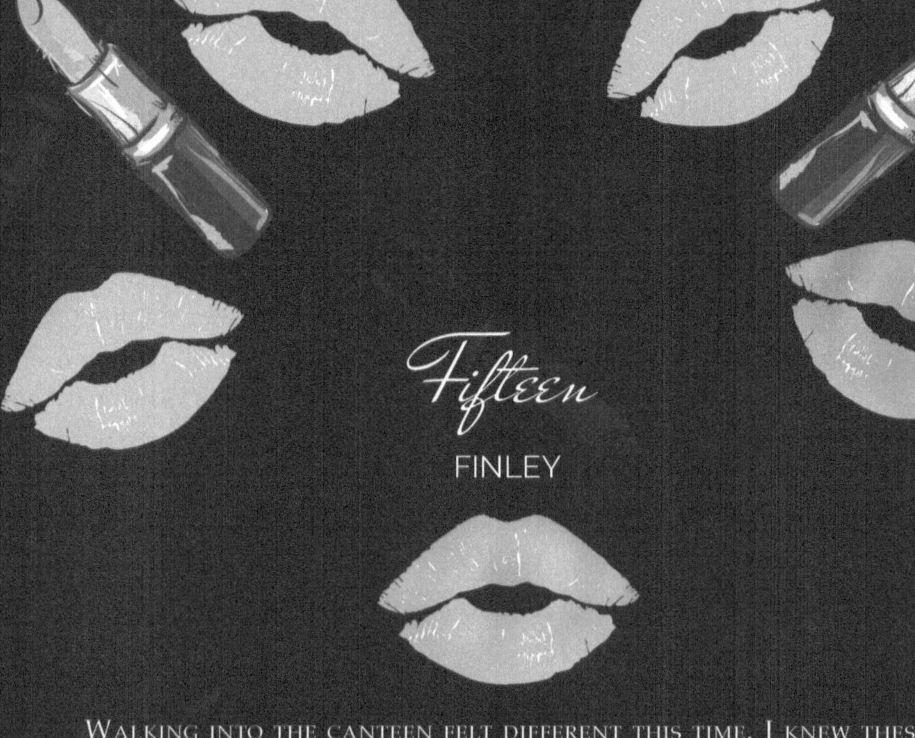

Walking into the canteen felt different this time. I knew these people and was one of them. That sense of belonging I'd always craved crashed down onto me, and my step faltered.

"Careful, little hacker," Ryker's dark and delicious voice cooed from my side, his palm resting on my elbow. "You look decadent."

As I looked at him, I tried to hide my blush, but it was a lost cause. Taking a few more steps into the place, I was yanked out of Ryker's arms as Karen pulled me into a hug. Her warmth and friendliness went a long way to cure some of the homesickness I'd been dealing with.

"It's so good to see you, Finley. I keep telling Cohen to bring you by more. I swear, he just wants to hog you for himself." She tutted at Cohen, who slung an arm around me, a broad grin on his face.

"Can you blame me, Karen? Fin's one of a kind." Karen stopped her huffing, smiling at Cohen with motherly love.

"Well, okay, I guess you're forgiven. I saved you the best spot in the place." She winked, walking us over to a large booth that was private but seemed to also have the perfect view of the whole canteen from the stage to the front door.

Asa and Milo sat on one end, and I scooted into the middle, wondering if Ryker or Cohen would be next to me. I didn't miss that they'd also be by one another. Asa squeezed my thigh, and I wondered if my boyfriend was up to some well-meaning matchmaking.

"I need to apologize about the room switch, Fin," Ryker said as he slid in next to me. "In the hustle of everything, it slipped my mind. It would ease my worries if all of you were better protected."

"Thank you. We appreciate your thoughtfulness," Asa said, speaking for the group. Before we could talk more about it, the server arrived and told us the specials for the evening.

"We have chicken Alfredo, broccoli Alfredo, or prime rib tonight. Who would like to start?"

Once our order was submitted, the server left, and silence fell around the table. Ryker cleared his throat, looking to Milo.

"How are you healing, Milo?"

"Pretty well. The technology and medical science you have here are outstanding."

Ryker smiled with pride, and I cataloged it away with the new information I was collecting about him. I liked that he was pleased with Milo's assessment, and I knew it meant Ryker worked hard to make The Order better under his command, even if no one knew it was directly him responsible.

Which, in and of itself, was a huge thing. Most people wouldn't be okay without taking the credit or being publicly recognized. I realized the brilliance of The Order for hiding people's identities. Not only did it provide a level of safety and keep the playing field equal among peers, but it kept away anyone who was only in it for the glory. It was hard to be power hungry when no one knew who was in control.

"So, Ryker," I started, then realized I'd blurted into a conversation. "Um, sorry. I was thinking and then thought of something I wanted to ask and didn't check to see if anyone was talking. Wow, self-absorbed should be my middle name."

The guys chuckled, and Ryker nudged me, gaining my attention. "You're the furthest thing from self-absorbed, little hacker. Maybe a little lost in your own thoughts at times, but I'd never think it was because you were only focused on yourself. So, what did you want to ask me?"

His eyes twinkled, and I decided I wanted to make them do that more. It was lovely and completely changed his whole face. In fact, I was a little lost in them as my brain seemed to lose all reasoning.

"Oh, right," I said when I realized I'd been staring. Licking my lips, I glanced around the table, finding all the guys watching me. It was a heady moment to find the four hottest guys I'd ever met all staring at me. "I honestly can't remember," I said after a minute, and nothing floated to the top. "I think I was going to ask you what your plans were after you retired. Yeah, let's go with that."

He chuckled, his face adoring as he gazed at me. "You know, until recently, I hadn't the slightest idea. I kept hoping for inspiration to strike me. But honestly, I figured I'd end up as one of those guys who couldn't stop working and stayed beyond his prime. A sad sack who everyone felt sorry for, but no one was willing to say anything to my face."

Ryker shrugged his shoulders, and something in me pinged in sympathy. I knew that feeling, where you didn't know which direction to go, but staying felt like you were only going through the motions, not really living. I didn't want that for anyone. Clearing my throat, I held his eyes and asked him the next part.

"And now? You said up until recently."

"That I did." He smiled, swiveling his gaze between Cohen and me. "I'm learning that there's more to life than work and that when you have the right people in it, you don't need to try so hard to push them away."

"Finley has a way of making you see that you're not the product of all your failures," Milo said. I peered over at him, seeing the earnest truth in his eyes. "I worked so hard to be the opposite of my family, but I wasn't really doing anything about it. When I met Fin, I saw what that indecisiveness was doing to me and the world around me. I wasn't making it better by being different if I was letting them continue their evil plans. You're in good company to be with while you determine the next steps if you want it."

I was surprised by Milo's offer to Ryker. Not by what he'd said, but that he was opening himself up to Ryker. Part of me hadn't wanted to think about this life working, but the guys kept proving it to me every day in big and little ways. They showed me how serious they were, so I needed to start accepting them.

"Thanks, man," Ryker said, nodding at Milo. "For what it's worth, I think you've done more good than you give yourself credit. And I'm all for figuring out what life has to offer outside these walls. First, we need to capture Dex and shut down MKG. Then, I'll gladly take you up on your offer to figure things out together. That means a lot."

Our food arrived not long after, and we ate our meal, talking about random things, no more big speeches or vulnerability shared. It felt nice to just talk, laugh at jokes, and catch up on things outside of The Order. And even trying to explain how our relationship worked.

"So you mentioned your twin sister is dating Fin's brother and six other guys, and you're cool with it?" Ryker asked.

"Yeah. It sounds weird, but I've played hockey with most of those guys for years. I know them. They're good guys. But also, she was already establishing a relationship with them before we knew we were siblings. So, it wasn't really my place to come into that and say anything. They've created a family, and I know they all love each other. It works." Asa shrugged his shoulder, the movement rocking me since one of his arms was draped around me.

"Is that how you got the idea to date three guys?" Ryker asked me.

"Actually, no. I fought it for almost a year. It wasn't until I ran to find you that these two teamed up and talked." I gestured to Asa and Cohen. "Milo I kind of pulled along for the ride. The three of them have been part of my life for this past year, and I was only fooling myself with the connections we had. I didn't think I deserved for multiple men to love me with all the things we'd done with MKG."

"I'm sorry you thought you were responsible for Mongoose. I never wanted you to carry that. I wish I'd tried to find you sooner. With everything that happened after, my hurt feelings got shoved to the bottom, and I didn't look at them, too afraid to see what you might have meant to me since I was under the impression you'd bailed. I was a coward, and for that, I'm sorry."

"Thank you, I appreciate it, but if I'm not responsible for Mongoose, you can't take responsibility for my guilt either. Let's just promise to talk through things instead of assuming and running off scared this time. Deal?"

"Deal. That goes for you too, Cohen. I don't want to lose you even if all we ever become is friends."

"No running." Cohen nodded, and I could tell something was swirling in his mind. "Well, we better head to our new room so we can get settled."

"Yes, I'll, um, show you where."

We slid out of the booth and waved goodbye to a few people as we made our way to our new suite. It wasn't in the same hall as before, and I tried to remember how to get to it as we took a few turns.

"Um, so, we kind of share a unit," Ryker said, and I could've sworn he blushed.

"Oh, um. Okay." I lifted my shoulders and eyes to the guys, not knowing what it meant or what to do in this situation. The perfect Fin in me wanted to say it was cool, but I couldn't tell if it really was or if that was my knee-jerk response. Sometimes, it really sucked being a people-pleaser when you couldn't determine whether your reactions were legitimate or from years of kowtowing.

"You have a separate sleeping area. These units are more for families, so the bedrooms are on one side, and the shared space is a kitchen and living room. So, if you don't want to see me that often, you don't have to. These are just more secure, and I wanted you to be closer. Sorry if that was presumptuous."

"I mean, it was a little, but I don't think you have anything to apologize for. Thank you for considering our safety, Ryker. Do we get into these the same way?" I asked.

Ryker seemed to exhale in relief, his whole body unraveling as he nodded, one corner of his mouth lifting in a smile. "Yeah. Just place your hand. Other than us, only my security detail has access to these."

I placed my hand on the scanner, the familiar tingle warming my palm as it scanned me. When it beeped, I opened the door and stepped in. Immediately I was hit with Ryker's smell. It was a combination of coffee, eucalyptus, and rain. Not that I smelled him often. Nope. Not this girl.

The area was modern and designed beautifully. It had a personality, and I could tell it was his home rather than a standard room we'd been staying in. There were paintings on the walls and little hints of him around the space. It gave me new insight into the man, and I liked it. To the right were an oversized sectional couch, two armchairs, and a coffee table facing a fireplace with a flatscreen over it. To the left was an immaculate kitchen that appeared to have all the latest gadgets. The whole space was nice and not what I'd expected. The guys looked as impressed as I, looking around our new space.

Ryker cleared his throat, rubbing the back of his head. "Your rooms are through here. There are three, though one of them has two beds in it. I didn't want to presume what your sleeping situation was. I put all of your belongings in the biggest bedroom, Fin. It had the largest closet and its own bathroom. There's another Jack-and-Jill bathroom between the other two rooms."

"And where's your room?" I asked, turning to look back at him. He pointed in the opposite direction.

"My suite and office are on this side. Both hallways have keypads, so you can lock your side of the suite off at night if you desire."

"I doubt that's necessary, but thank you for the option," Cohen said, taking charge of our group. "We should get ourselves settled. Tomorrow is a busy day. Thanks for dinner."

Ryker nodded, standing with his hands in his pockets as he watched us walk toward the other hallway.

"Help yourself to anything in the fridge, and if you find you're missing something, just let me know."

"Thanks, Ryker. Goodnight."

"Night, little hacker."

He smiled, relaxing some, and I waved as we headed toward our corner of the world, knowing that my life would be different from this point forward. I could feel it in the air. A turning point was just around the bend. And for once, it didn't scare me.

Sixteen

FINLEY

WALKING DOWN THE HALL, I PEERED INTO THE ROOMS. WHEN I spotted a mountain of bags, I knew I'd found mine. The room was gorgeous, decorated in grays and blues, with a massive bed in the center. There was even a little vanity table and mirror off to one side, and as I stepped into the master closet, I squealed. The guys chuckled, moving on to theirs.

"Now, this is a closet."

Sighing with happiness, I began sorting my new clothes, hanging them up with care like the treasured items they were. The closet had shelves and slots for shoes, and I realized it was almost my dream closet. Once I had everything in its rightful place, I checked out the bathroom, practically squealing again.

"Okay, this place is amazing. I might never want to leave."

"Talking to yourself," Asa said, coming up behind me.

"Yes, and I don't even care. This place is incredible." He wrapped his arms around me, kissing my head.

"Yeah, it is. You should see the other rooms." Taking my hand, he pulled me down the hallway to the room he'd claimed with Cohen. It was nice for a guest room with two queen beds and a decent closet. It was decorated in gray and hunter green, making it a soothing and relaxing environment. Walking through the bathroom, I was impressed with the shower and dual sinks they had as well. I softly knocked on the other door, finding Milo in a gray and red room. He smiled as I walked in, placing a shirt on a hanger.

"Hey, do you need help?" I asked but then realized there weren't any more clothes on the bed.

"Nope, that was the last one."

"How are you feeling?" I asked, taking a seat on the corner of his bed.

"I'm good, darling. I promise."

"Well, the reasons I ask, I was wondering if you'd like to take a bath and spend the night with me tonight?"

"Oh." His cheeks began to redden. "I'd love that. How about you get the tub ready, and I'll bring some clothes."

Nodding, I walked back through the bathroom, giving Cohen and Asa kisses goodnight before heading into my room. I stripped my clothes and walked into the bathroom. I'd spotted a bottle of bubble bath earlier and wanted to try out the jacuzzi tub. Turning on the water, I let it run as I squeezed some bubbles into it. Once it was halfway, I slid into the water, the warmth rolling over my skin in a caress. Pulling my knees up to my chest, I laid my head on them as I sat in the water, the sound of the tub filling lulling me into a place of relaxation.

"You look peaceful," Milo said. I turned my head, the smile I wore sliding off my face as I took him in. He was only in his boxers, and I licked my lips as I took him in. His muscles weren't as defined as the other guys, but I could see them in his arms and abs. Though it was the little patch of dark hair that trailed down into his boxers that had my attention.

"If you keep looking at me like that, I don't think the bath will last long," he purred.

Lifting my eyes to his, I winked. "Maybe that's my devious plan."

Chuckling, he slid off his boxers teasingly, pushing them down his legs, his cock falling forward once it was free. I blinked, not expecting it to be hooded. The longer I stared, the more it began to grow and peek out at me. It transfixed my eyes, and I kept staring as Milo walked toward the bath and stepped in. He slid behind me, and it was only when he was out of sight that I was able to blink again.

"I think you have a Medusa peen." I dipped my head back, catching his eyes.

"Oh? Because it's hypnotic, or you're afraid it will turn you into stone?"

"Definitely hypnotic. I hope it turns me into goo, not stone."

Milo laughed, the sound almost as hypnotic as his penis. I pulled his arms around me, his Medusa dick brushing against my back. I tried to ignore it and just enjoy being in his arms. We sat nestled together for a while, the warm water soothing my body as I ran my fingers up and down his arms, the bubbles leaving trails.

"I'm glad you feel like you belong with us," I said, tilting my head to look at him. "I ignored my heart for a while, but now that I'm letting it be open, I couldn't imagine my life without you. You give me comfort and peace, Milo. You make me feel needed and strong, but also like it's okay to not have it all together."

I turned, the water swishing as I straddled his lap, my arms going around his neck. My boobs were no longer concealed by the bubbles, and his eyes drifted down for a second, and I felt him swallow, his dick twitching beneath me.

"I was so scared when the explosion happened. It's hard to describe everything I felt during that attack. I'd been frightened when the gunshot went off, but then you reminded me I could do this. You took off, helping all those people, and I knew I wanted to be as brave as you. So, I pushed my fear aside and figured out a solution. You gave me the courage to do that. For a few moments, I felt so alive when I finally cracked the code, the feeling of adrenaline I chase pumped through me, and I couldn't wait to find you, to share in that victory," I said.

"You were brilliant, Fin. I was so proud of you."

I smoothed my hands over his face, partially because I could, but also because I still needed to reassure myself he was all in one piece.

"I thought this was the life I wanted. To be chasing that feeling and putting myself in danger. But watching you fly through the air was one of the worst moments of my life."

"I'm sorry, Fin. I…"

"Ssh, I'm making my big romantic monologue, and you're ruining it by being understanding."

Milo chuckled, his fingers sliding to my back. "Okay, carry on."

"I've learned so many things on this journey, but the biggest has been that once I stopped running from my past, I could see all the incredible things already in my life. Somewhere between fighting my feelings for you and you continuing to patiently rescue me, I fell in love with you. And when I thought MKG had taken you from me, I realized how stupid I'd been. I don't need to chase the high anymore because being with all of you is better than any puzzle I could solve."

"You love me?" he asked, his eyes soft and hopeful.

"More than words allow me to express."

Milo surged up, kissing me, taking over as he wrapped his arms around me and pulled me closer. Thoughts fled me as I gave in to the feeling of his tongue twirling with mine. The water moved around us, the sound competing with our pants and moans. His skin was slick, and I slid my hands over it, feeling all the curves and muscles his body held. I was careful of his wounds, making sure not to aggravate them. When my hands found their way back to his hair, he moaned, and I realized that Milo liked it when I tugged on it.

"Darling, if you keep doing that, I'm going to embarrass myself," he panted, breaking away from my mouth to peer down at me. "As much as I'm enjoying our bodies together in the water, I'd rather be able to cherish you from head to toe without the fear of drowning or falling on something. How about we end the bath and move to the bed?"

"You have the best ideas."

Laughing, I stood and stepped out of the tub as he pulled the plug, the water gurgling as it began to drain. Drying myself off, I kept my eyes peeled to his body as the water showed more of it to me. I was barely able to focus on the task at hand, so transfixed by him.

"You're going to make me blush if you keep looking at me like that," Milo said, standing as he took the other towel on the counter and began to dry himself. When his body was covered, it allowed me to blink and return to my task.

"Medusa dick," I muttered, shaking my head.

Milo laughed, and I tossed the towel onto the counter, standing naked before him. I did my power pose, placing my hands on my hips as I dared him to not become mesmerized by my naked body. He gulped, and I watched his throat bob with the action, a satisfied smirk spreading across my face.

"Come and get me," I teased. Spinning, I took off for the bedroom. I made it two feet out of the bathroom when arms wrapped around me, pulling me to their chest.

"Gotcha."

"No fair, long legs." I pretended to pout, but in reality, it felt nice to be held by him. He carried me to the bed, and I felt the hard flesh between his legs. I was becoming addicted to watching his twitching Medusa dick. I couldn't wait to feel him in me. The new experience was something I was eager to try.

Placing me gently on the bed, I wondered what kind of lover Milo would be. He seemed like the type to edge you all day and cherish your body until you wept for release.

"You're so beautiful, Finley," Milo breathed, taking my foot as he began to trail small kisses up my leg. "And I love all the little sounds you make, the way you smell and taste, and I love that you take things head-on, even if you don't believe you do. I see your strength, courage, and love for those around you. You might think that people only like you because of what you give them, but I see the truth, and the reality is that people want to be around you because of who you are. Not what you do for them. You're a beacon of light and love, bringing joy wherever you are, and it draws us all to you. I never imagined someone as beautiful as you are inside and out could ever see me. Now that you've said you love me, I'm never letting you go. I hope you realize what you've unleashed in me."

As Milo talked, he kissed his way up my body. I bucked and whimpered with each one, needing him to give me more.

"Good," I hissed. "Now I can call you my boyfriend."

Milo chuckled, taking my lips with his in another devouring kiss. Taking the opportunity, I wrapped my legs around his waist and drew him closer. I could feel the tip of his penis nudging at my center, and all I wanted was to pull him in.

"Milo, I need you," I whined, hopeful that he would take pity on me and give me what I wanted.

He pulled back, pushing my hair out of my face. "I had plans to bring you to three orgasms before I allowed myself entrance."

"While that sounds heavenly, can I get a raincheck? I want you in me more than anything else. Please, Milo. I'm begging."

"You should never have to beg, Fin. Do I need a condom?"

"No, I'm good."

"Me too."

"Then what are you waiting for?" I teased.

Milo pulled back, spreading my legs and peering down at my pussy. He licked his lips, and I worried he would go back on his decision. Thankfully, he stroked his cock before lining himself up to me. I felt him begin to push in, and I wanted to cry out in relief. I needed to be filled by him.

"More," I gasped, my hands clinging to the bedsheets as I arched my back.

Looping my legs into his arms, he drew closer and pressed further. It was hard to think about the other guys' dicks while he was in me, but it felt like Milo might be the thickest of them all. When he was finally all the way in, I moaned in relief. He panted, and I could tell he was holding himself back.

"Don't hold back. Wreck me."

Milo looked into my eyes for a second before pulling back and slamming into me. With my back arched off the bed, I felt every inch of him as he withdrew and plunged back in. The only thing I could grasp onto was the sheets, so I clenched them between my fingers so tight, I worried I'd ripped them. But I didn't care as I moaned, his cock hitting me in all the best ways.

His muscular thighs flexed beneath my butt cheeks, and I succumbed to the lust coursing through me as pleasure ran through my entire body. A tingle began to build in my stomach as he pushed in, and my limbs started to go numb as I tensed them so hard. Everything built around me, and all I could focus on was Milo as he thrust in and out, slamming into me over and over, wrecking me just like I'd wanted.

"Yes, Milo. So good. So so so so, good," I cooed, the words barely able to form on my tongue as I arched up into him.

"Fuck, darling, you feel better than I ever imagined. You're so tight and wet. I could do this all night."

"No, no, I need it deeper. Faster. I just need to let go," I cried, not knowing what words were.

"Yes, darling."

The feeling in my heart I got each time he said that about split me in two when he reared back and plunged so deep into me, I saw stars. The feeling I'd been chasing began to crest as he did it repeatedly, not letting up for a second as I mewed around him in nonsensical words.

When I couldn't take it any longer, I let go, the tightness in my gut erupting and flooding through my body as everything trembled before going lax. I felt Milo thrust into me a few more times before he stilled, falling to the bed beside me. I tapped him, my words slurring.

"That was… yeah…" Milo laughed as we lay there, both of us panting for breath.

"You said you loved me," I said once my heart rate appeared to be back to normal.

"I did. I love you, Fin."

"I love you, Milo."

Turning my head, I found his beautiful eyes peering at me, and I smiled. I never knew I could feel so much love for people, but these guys showed me I could beyond my wildest imagination.

After cleaning up, we curled into one another's arms, and I fell asleep feeling safe and secure, knowing that whatever tomorrow brought, I had love, which was the best feeling in the world.

Seventeen

RYKER

IT HAD OFFICIALLY BEEN ONE MONTH SINCE FINLEY AND HER TRIO OF boyfriends had arrived at The Order and into my heart. I'd thought I'd been living life, but in reality, I'd only been passing the time. It was sad to realize that the one thing you needed in your life had been right there, waiting for you to wake up and know it too.

A few days after the MKG attack, Finley, Milo, and Asa had graduated from The Order training program, along with twelve other initiates. It was one of our bigger groups to make it through, and I was proud that one of my last tasks before stepping down was to ensure the program's future. Despite all my failings and baggage, I believed in what we did here and was glad it would continue after I retired.

Now, to just capture Dex and I'd be able to sleep easier.

A tap at my office door had me looking up, and I forgot for a second where I was as I stared at the girl who'd turned my world upside down in the most splendid way.

"Hey," I said, the word getting half stuck in my throat. I kicked my legs off the desk as I scooted in. Fin smirked at me, watching my every move. "What can I do for you?" I asked when she didn't move.

Her smile grew wider as she stepped into the room, walking closer and swaying her hips. Her outfit was outrageous for The Order, but it worked for Fin, and it was something I was becoming to love about her style. I gathered my composure as she leaned on the desk.

"Whatcha doing?" she asked, a tease in her voice.

"Going through all the data again. I feel like I'm missing something."

"Well, I had an idea. I'm not sure if it's stupid or not, but I wanted to see if you'd come and look at it."

"Absolutely." I slid out from my desk, walking around to meet her. I placed my hand on the small of her back as we walked out together.

"How are you today? I didn't see you at breakfast or lunch," she asked, tilting her head to look at me.

"Sorry, I had a board meeting early this morning to update everyone on the MKG project, and my yearly physical was done." I peered down at her, watching her face.

"Did the board have anything to add?" she asked as we stepped into the main living area. It was empty since everyone was working. I stopped, not wanting to say anything out in the hall. She paused with me, turning to look at me.

"The board is worried that if we don't find him soon, his next attack will be even more devastating. They did a psych eval on his character to try to determine his motives. Based on everything we know, it's more than likely he's a sociopath with an antisocial personality disorder. This means he's prone to strike out in a fit of rage, taking out hundreds of casualties if he's not caught soon. We got lucky at the mall, but I don't know if we'll be as lucky next time unless he either gets what he wants or we find and stop him. Both of those options seem pretty hopeless at the moment."

By the time I was done, I was holding her arms, our bodies close to one another. I hadn't even realized I'd grabbed onto Fin, but she was becoming the life-vest I didn't know I needed. Laying my forehead against hers, I breathed her in, calming from her smell.

"You smell good, little hacker."

She chuckled, moving her head so she could look at me. "You do too. I always try to figure it out. There's coffee, but there's this fresh smell that reminds me of the rainforest."

"Ah, yes, my shampoo probably and aftershave."

"Hmm, whatever the combo, I like it."

Chuckling, I took a chance and pulled her into my arms, hugging her. Over the past week, we'd been growing closer, and I'd initiated a few small acts of touch. I always felt sick to my stomach before I did them, worried it would be the time she pushed me away. I wasn't used to feeling insecure about someone I liked, but I guess that was the difference. When I let myself think about it, Finley and Cohen were people I cared for. It was more than just getting her into bed. I wanted to be in her life.

"What was it you had to show me?" I finally asked, taking a step back. Her eyes lit up, and she took my hand, dragging me the rest of the way out the door.

"Like I said, I think it might be something, but I'm not sure." She bit her lip, a tell I was finding she did when she was nervous or unsure of herself.

"I'm sure it's something. You're way smarter than you give yourself credit for." I caught her cheeks blushing and felt pride bloom in my chest. I wanted to do more of that.

We quickly made it down the intersecting hallways to the workroom. When we neared, she dropped my hand, not wanting any of her peers to know. I knew it was necessary, but I hated losing her touch. Walking through the door, a few people looked up and nodded in greeting as we entered. I walked with her over to her workstation. Cohen and Asa peered up when we approached.

"Ryker," Cohen said, his eyes trailing over me. "How did the meeting go?"

"Some developments, but nothing we didn't assume. I'll fill you in more later."

He nodded in understanding, focusing on Finley. "You tell him what you found?"

She shook her head. "No, not yet." I looked at her, nudging her arm when she didn't say anything.

"What is it, little hacker?"

She began biting her lip again, and the number of things I wanted to do to her for the abuse, rammed into me. I quickly sat, needing to hide the erection growing in my pants.

"I began to think about Obsidian and how he operated. The fact that he did it out in the open for so long made me think. Did he want you to know? Was he trying to get your attention? If he's a scorned lover, that makes his thinking easier for me to follow. So, I put together all the information you have on MKG and Dex. Using an algorithm I created for Sariah, I tweaked it to look for any places it overlaps or connects to see if I could find a pattern. Once I have that, we could use the program to help us predict future behavior. I just need more information than I think is in the files."

"Wow, that's brilliant, Fin. What do you need?"

"Since you lived with him, what were his daily habits? Any brands of foods he liked? Did he take any medication? Routines? Things like that."

I placed my head in my hands, trying to think of any habits of Dex's that stood out. "He was obsessed with a certain energy drink. It wasn't name brand, so he'd buy it in bulk. The cans were always on the floor. It was… Bang Shock! Because I used to joke that it was the only way he got banged. Geez, I was an ass." I hung my head, scrubbing my hand over my stubble. I needed to shave.

"Anything else?" Fin asked, an excited look on her face as she typed in the new information.

"Hmm, he didn't get out much, but did like to go to raves at the local gay bar." I slapped the table when I realized something important. "He had an inhaler."

Cohen grinned widely, typing some information into the computer he was working on. "Jackpot. Prescription for Dex Callahan for Albuterol from five years ago."

"Perfect, let me add it and scan all the pharmacies in our search and see if any of his known aliases pop up."

I held my breath, feeling like it would be too easy to find him this quickly, but also glad to have it over with if it was. Dex was a noose hanging around my neck I was ready to shed.

"I... I... I think I found him," Finley said, raising her head to look around at us. She hit a button, and her feed went up on the big screen. I walked up to it, taking in all the parameters. It was a perfect match for a 25-year-old male who liked energy drinks, clubbing, had a prescription for an inhaler, high-speed internet, bought a smartwatch recently, and had been at the mall.

"Holy shit, little hacker. You're a genius."

I turned back to her, the whole room looking at the screen. She tried to duck her head, but it was no use; everyone was already looking at her with big smiles.

"What do we do next?" she asked, looking around at everyone.

Logistics and protocol ran through my head, and I knew I wanted to be on the team who scouted. "First, we send a small convoy to check out the intel. If it pans out, we'll look over everything and create a plan of attack."

"I'm going with you," Fin said, but I shook my head.

"No, little hacker." I hated seeing her upset, but she didn't need to be on this one. "It's just recon. I want you to keep searching and figure out his routine. Your algorithm has gotten us the closest we've ever been. We need to ensure that it wasn't his plan to leak that information to us."

"I'll go," Cohen said, standing and giving me a look that brokered no arguments.

"Fine," I sighed, pulling out my phone. "I need to handle some things; let's meet on the top floor in thirty."

He agreed, kissing Fin goodbye before striding toward the door.

I hesitated before I left the room, wanting to kiss Fin or say something, but when I saw all the eyes looking at me, I stopped and waved like a middle school dork before walking out the door. Cohen snickered at me, and I rolled my eyes, trying to hide my heating cheeks.

"You don't have to hide your feelings. I'm sure everyone in there knows you have the hots for Fin. You have a stupid look on your face whenever you're near her."

"I do not." I scowled at him, but I wasn't sure if I was trying to convince him or myself.

"Yeah, you do. And you know we're headed to the same room. We don't have to meet up on the first floor."

"Sorry, I'm so used to giving orders that I didn't think about it. Thank you for going with me, though."

"You nervous about seeing Dex?"

"No. He's hurt too many people, making me wonder if we were even friends. I think we might have been more in his eyes than my own. I feel stupid for not noticing his obsession or involvement, though. That's what really gets me. Especially when he tried to hurt Fin and Milo. I never would've forgiven myself if something had happened to them. Now, I have the chance to make sure he doesn't hurt anyone else. I'm worried I'll snap and just shoot him without going through the proper channels."

"I'll keep you in line."

"I know you will." I turned, taking in Cohen. He seemed more at ease around me and not as resistant, making me hope that there was a future between us.

"I need to grab some things from my office and change into something that doesn't scream security or tactical team, and let my team know."

Cohen looked at me, scanning me again, and I definitely felt more heat in his eyes as they caressed every inch of me. He eventually looked at himself, taking in his dark jeans and hoodie.

"I mean, I wear this all the time, but I guess I can change. What look are we going for?"

"Casual bystander. Don't want to stand out, just blend."

"Got it. I'll meet you here in a few." He raised one eyebrow, daring me to say the first floor.

"Fine. Here."

He smiled, and it cracked something in me. I felt a piece of my obstinate asshole attitude float away, and I wondered what these two were doing to me. Though, I had to admit it wasn't a horrible effect. In fact, I felt happier than I had in a long while. So, maybe I needed to shed some of my asshole ways and embrace this new softer side.

Changing into a dark pair of jeans, navy shirt, and shoes, I walked into my office and opened my gun cabinet. I selected a small Glock 43 for my ankle holster and a Walther PPS for my shoulder one. I slid a GPS tracker into my shoe and carefully placed fake fingerprints on the pads of my fingers. The nanotech dissolved into my skin once it made contact, making me shiver. Taking one last precaution, I swallowed a pill that wouldn't activate until after 24hrs, allowing it to pass any inspection if we were to be caught. It would give our team a chance to find us if everything else failed.

Taking a burner phone from the stack, I placed it in my pocket. The last time I'd used it had been when I thought I was playing a game with Fin. While that hadn't turned out the way I'd expected, at least she was here now and safe. In fact, with her passing The Order training, she could handle herself out in the field even better now.

And as much as that thought worried me, I knew she was more than capable of protecting herself and others. I couldn't cage Fin. She needed to fly, and I wouldn't be the one to hold her down. Even if I initially wanted to steal her away and make her mine, I saw and understood how her relationship worked now, and it was something I wanted for myself.

Sending a brief message to the board on the new updates, I

closed my computer and locked everything down. I headed back into the main area and found Cohen waiting for me. Together, we made our way up to the first floor. After a brief rundown to my detail of what was going on, I took the keys to one of the SUVs, and we began our journey down the mountain.

It was quiet most of the drive, the radio playing music softly in the background as I followed the GPS to the location. Fin's research showed that he'd purchased a building a few years back. It was the only property in his name, so we made a guess that he lived there. Considering he wasn't seen out in public too often, and there wasn't any traffic cam footage, he either wiped everything when he left or had everything brought to him.

Knowing Dex, it was probably both.

It only took a few hours to drive to the town the address was in. I hated the fact that he'd been so close this whole time. As we approached the address, Cohen turned off the radio as I came upon the road. I was hoping there would be other buildings nearby so we could watch from afar. But it seemed Dex had been more innovative than that. Much like The Order's base of operations, it was secluded with what looked like one road in and out. I passed it, turning off the GPS as she insisted I make a U-turn.

"What now?" Cohen asked, trying to look between the trees, but it was impossible. We'd need an aerial overview to get a good look, which wouldn't happen today.

"I guess we find a base of operations and hit up some of his frequent spots. See if there's a motel nearby."

I was berating myself for not planning more before we left, knowing my exuberance to catch Dex had led me to be a little reckless. Cohen pulled out his phone and began typing things in a search engine.

"There's one a few miles from here. I can call and see if they have a room?"

I nodded, but my eyes focused on the rearview mirror. We were still on a deserted road and hadn't passed any other vehicles in miles. So when the dark car pulled out behind us, I knew we'd been made.

"Shit. Hold on."

Cohen looked up as I took a sharp turn onto a dirt road, hoping the car wouldn't be able to follow. Speeding up, I pressed the accelerator to the floor, needing to gain some distance. Cohen held onto the door handle, casting me an anxious look.

"That him?"

"I think so. Hold on. I'm going to try to lose them."

Just as the words left my mouth, I crested over the top of a hill, catching some air with the speed I was traveling. Because of that, I realized too late that we'd fallen for the easiest ruse in the books. My obsession had led me to make careless mistakes, and now I was going to pay for it. The worst part was that Cohen, and subsequently Fin, would too.

The vehicle crashed down, and I barely had time to swerve the barricade as we careened off the dirt path, dodging trees as branches scraped the outside of the vehicle.

"Shit, shit," Cohen screamed, and inside I agreed with him, but none of my words seemed to want to come out, dying on my tongue.

As the SUV finally stopped, I knew it didn't matter. We would be surrounded within minutes. We'd willingly driven onto enemy territory and offered ourselves without a fight.

I'd laugh at how absurd it was if it hadn't been me.

The car clicked as the engine cooled, and I tried to think of a way out of this situation. But I knew it was pointless. I'd seen his compound as I crested that hill. Dex was prepared for everything, and there was no way out.

Turning my head, I took in Cohen's eyes, the storm brewing there had my heart skipping a beat, and I hated I had to be the one to say it to him.

"I'm sorry, Cohen. Fin was right. My own hubris has been my greatest downfall."

He didn't say anything. He didn't need to. I could see it written on his face. The car doors were yanked open a few seconds later as men surrounded us. With one last ditch of hope, I pressed the emergency button on my watch, praying it would get off a signal before everything was stripped from me.

Hands pulled me from the car, throwing me to the ground, their faces covered by black balaclavas. Holding my finger over the side, I kept it there until everything went black around me, glad that I'd made Fin stay back. At least now she'd be safe.

Eighteen

FINLEY

Something wasn't right. I could feel it in my bones. It was an hour past when Cohen and Ryker should've checked in. It had been quiet at the base, and I was trying to chalk my anxiety up to nerves, but I had a bad feeling, and it wasn't going away.

"Anything?" Asa asked, setting some food next to where I'd holed up. I had three computers opened, trying to find out as much information as possible on Dex and MKG.

"No," I finally answered, looking up to catch his green eyes. "I'm worried."

"Hmm, well, training states that if someone hasn't reported in six hours past their time, activate the tracker in the car and then the chip."

"Why do I feel like six hours might be too long? Am I being ridiculous? Is it just because it's Cohen and Ryker?"

"You're not being ridiculous. And yes, I think you're more worried because it's them, but it doesn't mean your fears are unfounded. Since both Ryker and Cohen are gone, both of our superiors are in the field, so I guess that makes you the de facto leader. So, team leader Finley, what do you want to do?"

His words shook me, but I realized I liked how they sounded. I kept thinking that I was the weaker of the group or lesser than when I had to stay back, but that wasn't the case. Before, I ran into danger without proper knowledge of what I was getting into. It was naive and completely what teenagers did. But it didn't mean I'd do that now.

In fact, I'd shown myself and the others I could be calm under pressure. I needed to quit putting myself in a box and kick those walls down and make my own way.

"You're right. I am the team leader." I sat up, my hands planted on the desk. "And that means trusting myself. I'm going to pull up the GPS on the vehicle. At least if I can get a visual, then I won't worry."

"Sounds like a plan, team leader. What do you need from me?" Asa asked, lifting his eyebrows when I looked up. Was it bad I found it sexy? Yes, I needed to focus. I could explore wanting to dominate Asa later.

"Can you get Milo and look through the blueprints I pulled up? We need to know what we're dealing with if they were taken."

"Absolutely. You know, you're sexy when you get all bossy. We can talk about whatever it was that flittered across your mind when everyone is back here safe and sound."

My cheeks heated, but I nodded, looking at the screen as I began to type in some credentials. When I didn't hit any walls, I was surprised to find that Ryker had given me full clearance. Well, hot donuts!

With ease, I located the vehicle they'd taken and picked up the bowl of noodles Asa had left me. I slurped them into my mouth as their route filled the screen. Based on the address, it all seemed standard until the end, when I noticed a sharp turn on an unnamed street. Clicking it, I maximized it as I began to study it more.

It was like this, with noodles half hanging out of my mouth, that Asa and Milo found me a few minutes later. They both laughed as I quickly slurped them down, wiping my chin as I zoomed in on the screen.

"I think I found something!" Their amusement shifted to concern as they crowded behind my computer screen.

"What is it?" Asa asked, not understanding what I'd stopped on.

"Ryker took a sharp turn here and then appears to stop based on the jagged line here. Then, the car is turned around and taken to a motel."

"Okay, so they're at the motel?" Milo asked, stepping back and crossing his arms. His glasses sat on his nose today, and I smiled at him.

"No, I think that's what MKG wants us to think. They had to know we'd check the GPS route and wouldn't be concerned if they ended there. They didn't take into consideration that the one checking it is a hypervigilant girlfriend who notices the smallest details."

"Oh, so you're Ryker's girlfriend now?" Asa teased, nudging Milo.

"What? Huh? I mean…" My face grew redder the longer I tried to find an answer for them. Waving them off, I focused back on the screen, clicking on a satellite to see actual footage.

"Ah, so she didn't deny it. I think we have a new brother-husband, Asa," Milo said, leaning into his counterpart. He'd gotten more comfortable with the guys since we'd proclaimed our love for one another.

"I'm ignoring you."

I kept clicking on folders, amazed at how much access to top secret things The Order had.

"Whoa, is that satellite legal?"

"I dunno. I didn't stop to ask. I could use it, so I did. I figured it wouldn't let me if I wasn't supposed to." I shrugged my shoulders, entering the coordinates I needed. "Besides, I doubt MKG would allow a satellite to be over their property, so I'm going to have to be fast at accessing this."

Using the information from the route, the coordinates of where they turned, and the time of day they appeared to be there to filter, I was shocked when an image began to load a few minutes later.

"Wow, I hadn't expected it to work that quickly. Technology really is amazing."

"Tone down the love affair with tech. Look, can you zoom in there? It's hard to see with the trees, but it looks like…"

"Bodies being pulled from the vehicle," I said, barely a whisper. "Monkey balls."

My mind began to race with what I needed to do. Hitting print, I gathered as many pictures as I could before they were lost to me. When I tried to follow the truck they were loaded into, the whole screen went blank, and I lost the connection.

My heart was racing, my hands shaking as I tried to focus on how to help them. Steps, steps, steps, I repeated, needing to remember them.

"Fin," Asa said, handing me a phone. "Call the security office."

"Right, okay, yes." I took the phone, typing in the number when I remembered we were supposed to keep this a secret in case of a mole. "Um, wait. Who was Ryker's guard today?"

Milo typed something into a laptop, pulling up a list of names. "Bishop, Anderson, and Sharpe."

"Nicole," I wheezed. "It couldn't be Nicole, right?" I knew it was a high probability that those three people were either the only people we could trust today or the three we couldn't. I just had to figure out where they fell on the line.

My head began to swim as dizziness took over. I didn't know if I could do this. Ryker and Cohen were in danger and depending on *me* to rescue them.

"I don't know what to do," I admitted, tears threatening to spill. "What if it's the wrong decision and I get them killed? I wouldn't be able to live with myself."

Hands gripped my face, and I stared into Asa's green eyes. "Fin. You're the best person for this. I believe in you. Milo believes in you. Ryker and Cohen believe in you so much that they left you in charge. Stop stressing about what could happen and focus on saving them. Don't let fear rule you. You're brilliant, Fin. Let your genius out to play. You said you wanted to trust yourself; this is your chance."

"You make me sound like a superhero." I smiled, sucking in a breath. "Okay, you're right." I was Finley Amelia Reyes, and I was a badass. Time to woman up and remember that.

Taking a few calming breaths, I quit worrying about not making it to them and focused on finding them instead. This was a puzzle I could solve.

"Okay, look into every communication and routine of the three on Ryker today so we can know if they're clear or our targets."

"On it," Milo said, taking over one of the laptops open on the table next to us. I looked to Asa, scanning through my head what we needed to do next.

"Contact Samson and see if there are any guys he trusts in the area. They might be able to get there before we can, and we know they won't be turned."

"That's smart. I'll make the call." Asa walked to the front of the room as he dialed his biological father, and I returned to the computer. I needed information about their headquarters. It was safe to say that if they were taken, we'd been right about their location.

My phone buzzed, and I jolted back in alarm at the name until I remembered this was Dex's MO.

Cohen: We're here. Ryker's being annoying as usual.
Nothing to report. Will probably head home tomorrow.
Miss you.

My hand hovered over the phone as I debated what to type back. Finally, I knew I needed to play along.

Me: Bummer. Hopefully, you can get some sleep. Miss
you too.

It was kind of lame sounding, but I didn't know what else to put without giving it away that I knew it was Dex. At least I could identify what was real and not, and that wasn't anywhere close to how Cohen talked. An idea began to build, and I ran over to Milo. He peered over at me as he scrolled through messages.

I reached over to him, selecting the three people's phones we were monitoring, and just as I expected, a message from Ryker came through.

Ryker: All clear. Will return tomorrow.

"Did all three receive that?" I asked.

Milo shook his head before clearing his throat. "No, Bishop didn't receive it."

"Bishop… so he must be our traitor—MKG's inside man."

A pit of despair wanted to swallow me whole at the implication. Bishop was Cohen's friend and had worked at The Order for years with Ryker. He was in his mid-thirties and, from what I gathered, was considered to be upper-management for The Order. It made sense how he had as much information as he did, but it also saddened me. Shaking off my melancholy, I focused on what I needed to do.

"Okay, we can use this. We need to gather a few people we can trust without alerting Bishop until we're ready for him to leak information."

"Got it. I'll work on it while you and Asa find us a way into the compound."

Kissing his forehead, I walked up front to the smart screen that had the blueprint on it. After a few seconds, I realized I didn't know what I was doing. It was all just a bunch of blue lines to me.

"Yeah, I can't read this. Who can we get to help with this?" I asked, looking at Asa. He hung up the phone, joining me.

"Samson has a few people he trusts he will send to scout out the location. I told them the information we knew so far, so they'll be discrete and see if they can get a drone to fly over to get the layout." He turned, taking in the blueprint. "As for this, Bishop is the best at deciphering them."

Grimacing, I shook my head. "Anyone else?"

"What did I miss?"

"I believe he's the mole. Texts were sent to me and to Sharpe and Anderson, but not Bishop, leaving me to believe he's the traitor. He wouldn't need a reassurance text because he knows they've been captured."

"Hmm, well then maybe Caleb or Asher. I can go and get them without causing a scene."

"Thanks. We must keep what we're doing quiet for as long as we can. It might be our only advantage."

Asa nodded before heading out the door, and I went back to my computer. I needed to develop the best tactical plan in the history of strategies and know what security measure I'd be up against. Knowing Dex, it would be a lot.

Cracking my knuckles, I zeroed in on my task, pushing the fear and insecurity away and zoning in on my boss bitch energy. It was time to rumble.

Nineteen

COHEN

Sharp pain radiated through me, and I grimaced as I tried to move. Everything hurt, and I struggled to remember why. We'd been driving and talking when we'd had to take a sharp curve... the chase, collision, and capture ran through my head at top speed, leaving me with a wince.

"Fuck, that hurts," I wheezed.

A grunt of pain sounded next to me, and I sucked in a breath as I turned my head. Something dripped down my face, obscuring my view. My hands were tied behind me, so I couldn't move to wipe it out. Blinking, I tried to keep it out of my eyes as I took in what I could. We were in a medical room. Which wasn't what I'd expected at all. White walls, stainless steel, and a white tiled floor surrounded me.

The sound was a little louder this time, and I recognized it. "Ryker, can you hear me? You awake?"

"Mmm, barely," he said, his voice pained.

"My memory is fuzzy, but I think we were captured?"

Ryker snorted, but even that sounded painful. "Yeah. Sorry, I got you into this mess."

"I'm pretty sure I volunteered," I said, my lungs beginning to hurt. "Any clue how long it's been?"

I didn't want to think about Finley, too scared I'd never get to see her again, which, of course, meant she was the only thing I seemed to be able to concentrate on. The part of my brain that was working also knew that she might be the one thing that kept me pushing through the pain to survive.

"What do we do now?" I asked Ryker, who wheezed a little laugh.

"Not sure," he said. "I haven't even seen Dex yet. It's just been goons giving us these blows."

"Is he mad, or is he wanting something?" I asked.

"With Dex, I never know."

Almost like he could hear us, which, knowing how tech savvy he was, he probably could, he walked through the door a moment later.

"Gentlemen," he said, spreading his arms in greeting with a smug smile.

The effort it took to lift my head to glare at him was excruciating. I wanted to sneer back, but the muscles on my face refused to obey. I blinked, trying to get the blood out of my vision to see him clearer. I tried to catalog all the features of the man in front of me. He was only moderately tall, probably around 5'10". He had mousy brown hair, a strong jawline, and wore a suit. Outside of his attire, nothing stood out about his features. Though, it was his eyes that scared me. They were hollow, no ounce of humanity in their depths.

"What do you want?" Ryker asked.

"To punish you, of course." I didn't miss the manic sound in his voice as he said it or the way his eyes shifted back and forth, always falling on Ryker. It was clear the dude was obsessed with him.

"Fine, take me. Let him go," Ryker said.

"But what's the fun in that?" Dex responded, clapping his

hands. "He needs to be punished. You care for him; therefore, he's valuable to me."

"I'll do whatever you want. Just let him go."

The psychopath walked forward, gripping Ryker's face between his hands. Blood poured over his fingertips, but he didn't seem to care. In fact, if I saw his eyes correctly, his pupils were dilated; he was enjoying it.

"Oh, baby. I have so much in store for you. Don't be giving in to me already. It takes out all the fun when you don't scream." Dex squeezed Ryker's cheeks before planting a kiss, and my whole body tightened as a feeling of possessiveness surged up.

I growled, pulling at my bindings, but they were too tight and my body too sore.

"Now, let's have some fun, shall we?" Dex asked as he grabbed a scalpel off the medical kit lying to the side. Faster than I could blink, he stabbed it into Ryker's leg, a shout leaving the man I knew I loved but had been too afraid to admit.

"No!" I screamed as Ryker bent over, his face pale. The chair moved only a millimeter, and I knew there was nothing I could do. This was beyond torture, having to watch someone you cared about be hurt while you sat back helplessly.

Tears I didn't know I was crying fell down my cheeks, mixing with the blood, blinding me even more. I'd never wished for something to turn back time as much as I was in this moment. I couldn't even decide where it had all gone wrong. Should we have not come back to The Order? Or was it just coming here to scout with Ryker, who had been too reckless and impulsive? I'd give anything to know what the right decision was.

Since I couldn't turn back time and wasn't a fortune teller, I focused on what I could do now in the situation. My options were pretty limited, considering I was tied to a chair. But I had training. I'd practiced; surely, I could find a way out of this. I focused on my wrist bindings, twisting them a little to see if there was any give.

They were tight, meaning I wouldn't be able to Hulk my way out of them.

Instead, I would need to do the most painful approach. Did I have time? Or was this my only moment?

Looking over at Dex, I wished I hadn't, considering I caught him with his hand down his pants as he stroked himself off looking at Ryker's bloody body. The leer on his face said it all.

"Just you wait, Ryker baby. I'm gonna make it really good for you." He started to unzip his pants, and I squeezed my eyes shut, not wanting that image in my head.

When a beeping sounded, he cursed, and the fiddling of pants stopped. I peeked open my eyes when it sounded like he was on his phone, assuming it was safe.

"What?" he screamed. "Take care of it," he said. "No, I'm busy."

It didn't seem like the person on the other end of the phone was agreeable. Dex let out some expletives, cursing them, before tossing his phone across the room.

He turned back to Ryker, continuing to ignore me as his cock peeked out of his unzipped pants. I squeezed my eyes shut, but the image was already there.

"I'll be back, baby. I have to go take care of something. I'm the boss, after all. No one knows how to do shit without me. I'll show these assholes how to do their job without their thumb up their asses. Maybe I'll give you some pain meds if you're good."

He stroked Ryker's bloody face, not at all bothered by the blood on his hands. I heard him zip up his pants before he strode out of the room without a backward glance. My shoulders sagged in relief before I tensed. This could all be a trap, and he was watching us, but I had to take it for what it was. A free moment.

Sucking in a deep breath, I braced myself for what I had to do next. Hopefully, I was in enough pain already that I wouldn't notice it. Pressing my thumb against the chair leg, I moved it back and forth until I heard the snap. My eyes watered and I grimaced. But I couldn't focus on it. With my thumb out of the way, my wrist could slip through the binding, and I pulled my arm forward.

My shoulder hurt from being yanked back, and it took a moment for me to get any feeling in my fingers. I cradled my hand against my chest, but I knew I had to move. Standing, I wobbled with the chair until I could grab something off the medical kit so I could cut my other binding. Once I was clear of the contraption, I picked up the phone to see if it still worked. I knew it was risky using his own technology. But knowing a few backdoors, I hoped to get around it so I could get a message sent out.

Logging into one, I made my way over to Ryker and cut his binds. Scanning his injuries, I grabbed a first aid kit and worked to bandage the most severe wounds.

He mumbled groans as I worked, but didn't resist. Once I had him patched up, I went back to the phone to see if I could get a hold of Finley.

ME: Sweetheart, use this IP to find us. I'm trying to break us out. Send help. I love you.

It wasn't the most romantic thing, but it was concise and all the time I had for. Erasing my footprint, I tossed the phone back where I'd found it and grabbed a few things from the room we could use for weapons. Who was I kidding? That I could use. Ryker was in no shape to fight.

Lifting him up, I placed one arm around my shoulder as we began the slow process to the door. He was already panting when we made it there, and I was sweating from the exertion myself.

"Just leave me. Get help and come back. If I don't make it, tell Finley I regret not kissing her just once," he whispered, most of his words barely coherent.

I wrestled in my brain with what to do. I didn't want to leave him, but I also knew he was right in that there was no way we'd make it any distance with his condition. But if I left him, I might never see him again. I might never have the opportunity to tell him…

"I…" the words died on my lips. Gulping, I wetted them as I stared into his eyes. "I'll come back for you. I promise."

I pressed a gentle kiss to his lips before very carefully setting him down on the ground by the door. I handed him a weapon so he might be able to catch whoever entered by surprise and save himself some pain. Ryker squeezed my hand and took a breath as I gripped the doorknob.

Turning it, I waited for an alarm, half expecting guards to swarm the area the second I stepped out. The hallway was oddly quiet and devoid of anyone, but I didn't take that to mean I was safe. Creeping along the wall, I tightened my hand around the knife I'd grabbed. The blood was no longer in my eyes, but the pain still throbbed through my body with each step. I didn't think I'd ever get the feel of their fists out of my head.

An elevator dinged ahead, so I quickly ducked into the first room that didn't have a keypad on the door. Shutting it quietly, I stayed hidden in the dark, praying the footsteps would keep moving.

"The boss has lost his marbles," a voice said, coming closer to the door. "First, he had us kidnap these two dudes and then beat the crap out of them. Now that we have an actual breach in our system, he doesn't even seem to care. I joined MKG because I wanted to show the world I was smarter than they thought."

"Pfft," another guy chuckled. "I joined to get rich."

"Yeah, okay," the first guy agreed. "There was some of that too. But this is beyond either of those. It feels more like a terrorist group than hackers quietly taking money out from under the rich's noses."

"For sure. That whole mall thing was insane. It still gives me nightmares thinking about that. I couldn't believe he had us plant those drones and then stay to watch. He's sick, man."

"Yeah, well, it's not like we can defect. You saw what he did to all those others who wanted to leave. We're down to half our numbers as it is."

The more I listened, the more hope bloomed that maybe we could make it out of here if MKG wasn't at total capacity. An idea began to form, and I knew it would be risky, but it might be the only way to make it out alive and back to Finley.

Taking a deep breath, I gripped the doorknob and opened the door. Both guys turned, guns lifted at the sound. I raised my hands, not even pretending to be a threat.

"Looks like we have a runner," one of them said, but I focused on the other, the one who'd been talking about the nightmares.

"I think we could help one another. The Order is onto MKG, and it's only a matter of time before they storm this facility and take over. Once that happens, your chances of not rotting in a prison cell are slim. I'd like to propose a trade."

The one guard scoffed, turning to look at his friend. He had a contemplative look, and I knew I had him.

"What's your trade?" he asked. His friend rolled his eyes, but the one who'd been haunted held mine.

Smiling, I laid out the deal, hoping to ensure our safety and give Finley and The Order enough time to arrive.

Twenty

FINLEY

Anxiety coursed through me, making my palms sweaty and my heart race, but I was here and confident about my plan, so I wasn't going to freak out now. Asa and Milo had helped me perfect it, and I trusted our judgment and plan to get our guys back. I believed in us… and me. It was a whole new feeling, and I wrapped it around me, helping to stop some of the trembling.

"You got this," Asa said through the comms, somehow knowing I'd be fretting. Smiling, I centered myself as I stepped out of the car and began my walk up to the building. I was decked out in leather pants, knee-high stiletto boots, and a red leather jacket. I'd taken my look six years ago and ramped it up, aligning it with who I was today. I'd never felt more like the femme fatale than I did right at this moment. Using that energy, I strode forward.

"I know this isn't the time, but damn, Fin, you look so hot right now. Go kick some ass, and try not to give Cohen and Ryker a heart attack when they see you," Asa said, making my nether regions heat.

A giggle escaped me at his insinuation, letting the rest of the nervous tension leave my body. Just because I was walking into a building that housed a psycho killer didn't mean I had to be scared.

Balderdash! Why did I have to think of it that way?

Before I could fret too much, the door opened, and a man I'd never met, yet who had caused me so much torment, stepped out.

"Can I help you? This is private property."

"Oh? Is it? I couldn't tell with all the signs and creepy boobie traps that you didn't want guests." It seemed my brat filter was activated when I was crapping my pants.

The man regarded me, barely holding a sneer back as he took me in from head to toe, playing dumb like he didn't know me, and I wondered how far he would take that. "If you don't leave in five seconds, I'm calling the police."

He crossed his arms, and I caught a streak of blood across his knuckles at the action. My heart raced faster, but I focused on his eyes. His dead, soulless eyes.

"Oh, yes, please do call the police. It will save me a phone call."

"Pardon?" he scoffed, clearly not amused with my witty banter. Too bad, I was hilarious.

"The cops. You said you would call them if I didn't leave in five seconds. Well, it's been fifteen seconds at least, so please, call them. I'll wait." I crossed my arms this time, pretending to be the one who was impatient and mocking him all in the same move.

Our plan was simple. I needed to keep Dex occupied and away from Cohen and Ryker long enough that the team could extract them with limited casualties. It was just the getting away part myself I was still unclear on. Hopefully, before that occurred, the actual government would be here with Samson's connections.

"I don't know who you think you are, but I'm done." He went to close the door, and I tutted, shaking my finger at him.

"Now, now, Dex. That's no way to greet an old friend. We were friends, weren't we at one time? Or was it all a play from the beginning?"

His face morphed from one of disinterest to calculating as his whole posture changed. "Well, Finley, I guess if you know who I am, then there's no need for us to beat around the bush. I was trying to be charitable since I already have who I want, but if you insist on annoying me, I can add you to my torture list. I do like to play with my things."

His face twisted, and a cold chill ran down my back. This wasn't a man that could be fooled or who'd go down easily. Dex was truly a psychopath who knew no bounds. He'd take what he wanted, not caring who or what he destroyed on his path to get there. My limbs became frozen as I held his eyes, not wanting to appear weak. But I was. I so was.

I was the prey here. There was no doubt about it.

"So, why don't you come in and tell me all the little stories you've concocted about me to make yourself feel better? I do find them so entertaining. I always loved manipulating you into believing Ryker liked you. You were so gullible, believing anything I told you." He paused, his eyes traveling up and down me. "It seems you still are naive. Your lipstick can't cover all the lies you tell yourself."

Dread filled me as my heart raced. I hadn't anticipated the mental battle he'd wage. He tilted his head, almost like he was listening to something, before a creepy smile spread across his face freezing me on the inside.

"Oh goody, it seems whatever backup you were expecting has been, how shall I say it, um, yes, *bombarded*." Dex threw his head back, cackling like he was the world's funniest comedian. He rubbed his hands together, that smile spreading across his face sending fear cascading through my body.

"Do not step into that building, Fin!" Milo shouted into my ear, and I winced, causing Dex to smile even wider.

"Your team telling you to retreat? How about we strike a deal? Want to play a game, little hacker?"

"Don't call me that," I said, anger burning the fear away. "You might have been able to pretend to be Ryker online, but you'd never pass in person, and you know it. You're not even a quarter of the man he is."

"Ah, it seems like someone's crush has come back full force. Too bad you won't get to have your happy ending. The only person who gets one here is me." He reached out, attempting to grab me, but I blocked it and knocked his hand away with one arm while holding the knife I'd slid into the hidden holster on the side of my pants. I palmed it, keeping it secret, ready to strike.

"Ooh, I guess the little hacker's gone through training now. That just makes this more fun."

He came at me from the opposite direction in a quick grab, but I ducked, sweeping out with my leg and making contact with his thigh, but I'd aimed too high and almost toppled over. I arched up with the knife, catching part of his arm as he grabbed my ponytail. I had a second to prepare for the sharp pain as he yanked me back. I tried to remember my training despite my thoughts screaming at me to get away.

A whimper left me as he began to drag me, and I kicked out, trying to catch the doorway with my feet. I swung back with the knife, making contact again, but it wasn't enough. My other hand went to his as I tried to pull it away. I didn't think in my panic, all my training and thoughts of escaping leaving me, only trying to disengage him from me. When I remembered I still had the knife in my other hand, I reared up, praying I wouldn't stab myself in the head.

When he screamed, I felt victory, pulling the knife free before he took my weapon. He didn't let go of my hair, so I swung up again, but he was prepared this time and blocked it, knocking the blade free of my hand. Tears stung the back of my eyes at the loss of my knife, and I scrambled, trying to pull free with both hands. I couldn't let him take me anywhere. I'd never see the light of day again if he succeeded.

Digging in with my nails, I threw down my weight and locked my hands around his forearm. Twisting, I pushed forward and got my knees under me, giving myself more leverage. My scalp cried out, but it was better than letting him get any further into the building with me as his captive. I wasn't sure if he was lying about the backup or not, so I didn't want to be stupid and go any further if I could help it.

"Stupid bitch," he screamed. I knew I only had a few seconds before he acted out in anger and just slit my throat. Dropping my hands from his forearm, I heard him chuckle, thinking he'd won. Falling back on my butt, I caught him off balance as I kicked my feet up and nailed him in the groin with my pointy heels.

Dex doubled over, finally letting go of my hair. Quickly, I climbed to my feet just as he sliced out at me with my knife. It caught the back of my leg, and I felt the sting of pain as I kept moving. I couldn't focus on it. I had to get to safety.

The question was... which way was that? He'd gotten me further into the building than I'd realized. My comm had fallen out at some point, so I tapped my watch, hoping the guys were still there. I kept moving, too afraid to go back toward psycho-douche.

"Asa? Milo?" I squeaked, my voice not wanting to work. My throat felt raw, and I wondered if I'd been screaming and not even realizing it.

"Fin!" someone shouted. It was too hard to hear on the tiny speaker on my wrist who it was. "Fuck, babe, you scared us. Are you okay?"

"Um, I don't know." I glanced back, sighing a little when I didn't see anyone following me. I'd taken too many turns to know where I was. "I got away, but now I'm lost in his building."

"Shit, okay. I'll use your watch's location and blueprints to see where you are."

I took another turn, hearing a door shut, so I ducked into a room, looking for a window or something. "Someone was coming, so I'm in a room," I whispered. There was one window, but there was no way of opening it that I could see. It was one solid pane of glass. "I need to hide or find another way out," I said, looking around the room in a panic.

There were boxes in a corner, but otherwise, it was mostly empty. There were no real places to hide. I looked for a closet or any vents in the ceiling, but it didn't seem like I was that lucky. Moving over to the boxes, I opened one, curious about what could be in them.

"No, freaking way," I breathed, staring at the cans of gas. The next box had a gas mask, so I pulled it out, hoping they weren't a hoax. But what were the odds that I'd end up in this room? No, these were to be used at some point by MKG, and I just happened to get to them first. Grabbing as many as possible, I secured the mask and walked to the door.

"I'm heading out. Let me know when you have an exit route. Any word on the others?" I asked.

"Silence on that end. Just get out, Fin. We can make a new plan together. But if you're taken too, there's nothing for them to hope for, and I don't know what Asa and I would do," Milo said.

"Okay. I promise. I won't be a hero."

Opening the door, I peeked out, checking for anyone, but it was once again vacant. This place freaked me out, and I was ready to get out of there.

"If you go to your left, there should be an exit door if he hasn't remodeled or blocked it."

Sucking in a breath, I blew it out, forgetting about the mask. It fogged up as I took a step, and I cursed myself. Keeping my breath even, I took a few more steps, using my ears to listen while I waited to see.

"Hey! You're not supposed to be here."

I froze, then remembered the cans in my arms. Pulling the ring from the top, I turned and rolled the can before sprinting in the opposite direction. I didn't know what this gas did, but I knew it couldn't be good. I couldn't think about the effects it might have, or I wouldn't be able to go through with it. It might be foolish, but for the moment, I had to see everyone here as the enemy, or I'd never get out of here alive.

"You're coming up to it," the voice said, barely audible above my heartbeat pounding in my ears.

My heels clicked against the floor, and I once again wished I'd chosen different footwear. No one who wore stilettos expected to be running for their life.

"Turn to your right."

Following the command, I felt the elation begin to course through me at being so close to freedom. So when I smacked into a chest, I wasn't expecting it. The cans dropped from my arms, and I stood, frozen. Arms circled around me, pulling me to a chest, and I deflated, knowing this was it. I'd lost. I only had one move left, the last can held tightly in my grasp. Looking up, I met the eyes of my captor just as I tugged the ring free.

Twenty-One

FINLEY

hand. He held it steady before meeting my eyes.

"How you doing, kiddo?" He smiled, and my whole body sagged with relief. I wanted to weep joyfully, but I knew this wasn't the time. I pulled the mask from my face, pushing it onto my head so I could speak to him.

"I'm so glad to see you. When he said the backup had been intercepted, I got worried," I whispered, moving toward the door I'd been running toward. Samson followed, shoving his hand out the door and throwing the canister before closing it quickly.

He braced against the door, and I grimaced, realizing he thought it was a bomb. "Um, sorry, I think it's just knock-out gas."

"Oh, yeah, I knew that." Samson straightened, and I wanted to giggle, the emotion feeling nice after fearing for my life. The realization sobered me, and I remembered I was still in danger.

"So, what's the plan?" I asked.

Samson looked down at me, and I could tell he wanted to yell at me to run to safety, and yeah, that had been my plan mere seconds ago, but now that there was backup, it felt foolish to run away. I was trained and ready for this. I steeled my spine, giving him my no-nonsense look. If he thought his daughter was sassy, wait until he realized where she learned it from.

The look seemed to work when he exhaled, resigning himself to including me. "Apologies, Fin, but when I look at you, I see the best friend to my daughter, the girlfriend to my son, the little girl who used to design costumes for every stuffed animal in her house. It's taking me some time to remember that you've been through The Order training and are capable of handling yourself."

He blew out a breath, looking upward for something. When he returned to me, he no longer looked at me like the little girl he knew from the shadows, but as a colleague. It bolstered my own confidence, and I puffed out my chest.

"All the entrances are covered by our men. The issue is that the team picked up explosives laced within the walls. If Dex feels like it, he could blow the building at any second. Most of the personnel and MKG guards have been apprehended. Some have been more than helpful in providing us with good intel on how to defuse the bombs, along with where Dex is more than likely hiding. The heat signatures only counted seven people before I entered, so we have to assume that there are at least three guards outside of Dex to contend with."

I nodded, cycling all the information through my brain. "He's going to fortify himself so that he can watch everything like he did at the mall. He's not one for confrontation, especially after I—who he considers the weaker sex—humiliated him by taking him down."

"That's what I'm thinking too. I studied the program you made. Stellar work. I'd like to talk to you about designing something for Alpha, but we can discuss that once we're out of here."

My face heated, and I nodded, pleased he'd liked my tech. "So, what are we doing?"

"I'm going to the control room to find the panel to defuse the bomb. You have to decide if you want to go after Dex or the guys."

I debated for half a second, but it was no contest for me in the end. I needed my guys back. I'd trust the rest of the team to take care of Dex. Even though it was tempting to kick his butt and slice off his penis so he couldn't use it again.

"The guys," I said when I remembered Samson couldn't read minds.

He nodded, handing me a gun and pointing toward a hallway. "They're on the bottom floor. There were two other body signatures with them, so assume they're guards. You won't be able to access the system without the right biometrics, so you'll have to climb down the elevator shaft."

Swallowing, I nodded, understanding the task. "Good luck, Samson. Thanks for coming."

"Always, honey. You're family." He gave me a quick kiss on the forehead before sprinting in the opposite direction he'd pointed for me. It took me a second to recalibrate myself to the fact that Agent Buttface had just kissed me on the forehead, but it seemed once he'd found his family and been reunited with the love of his life, he wasn't such a butthole anymore. Which was good for me since he'd be my father-in-law one day.

Shit. I wanted to marry Asa.

"Fin? You there?" I heard my watch say, and I wondered if Asa had heard me think that.

"Um, yeah. So, change of plans. I'm going after the guys, and your dad is going to defuse a bomb. How badass is he?" I asked, peering around the corner before I sprinted. There was still one guard unaccounted for, so I couldn't be too careless.

"Did you just say my dad was badass? I don't know if I should be jealous or impressed you actually cussed."

"Hey, I cuss. I just use it sparingly so that you know it's important when I do," I huffed, running toward the next hallway.

I could hear Milo and Asa laughing, and I knew they were helping me focus by giving me something else to concentrate on.

"You're clear. No other heat signatures on the first floor. Samson has moved into position on the third floor," Milo said, and I raced toward the elevator.

Stepping into it, I peered up at the ceiling and instantly knew I couldn't reach it. Running back onto the floor, I found a chair behind a desk and picked it up. Returning to the elevator with the chair in tow, I positioned it under the hatch. Looking at my boots, I knew there was no way I'd be able to make it with them on, so with a regretful sigh, I pulled them off and shoved the last can of gas into them before tossing them out of the elevator. Maybe I could pick them up later? They were designer, after all.

Balancing myself on the chair, I slid the hatch open and managed to lift myself up into it using the arms. It began to wobble, but thankfully, I'd worked on my core and arm strength the past few weeks with training. Otherwise, I'd be stuck down there trying to find a rope or something while everyone around me died. Morbid thoughts there, Fin. I could never let Asa know that I was thankful for sweating or he'd never let me live it down.

Taking a second to catch my breath, I stood up and peered around the shaft. I almost wept for joy when I saw the little ladder on the wall. Walking to it, I was happy to find it was clear of the elevator, so I wouldn't get smushed if it started. It would be terrifying to climb down it, but I'd be out of harm's way for the most part. At least, that was what I told myself as I descended down to the lower floor.

Landing on my feet, I stood in front of the elevator doors and hoped they were easier to pry open than I imagined them to be. Pushing them apart with my fingers, I cried out when my nail broke, the doors barely budging. Cheese on toast!

Glancing around, I needed to find something to give me leverage. When I spotted a toolbox and a crowbar sitting against the wall, I welled up with tears at the discovery. Grabbing them, I pried the crowbar between the two doors, and using all of my weight, I pushed against the bar, crying out in joy when they opened enough for me to wedge between them.

Climbing out, I laid on the floor for a few seconds while I caught my breath. Holy pajamas, this spy stuff was hard work. No wonder everyone was so buff.

When my breathing returned to normal, I sat up and glanced around. I could only see a hallway, but it gave me a creepy vibe, and I dreaded having to go down it. Rising up, I began to stalk down it on my padded feet, remembering there were two other people down here with my guys. When I was a few doors down, I could hear talking.

Pausing to listen, I stayed still as I tried to hear what they were saying.

"We should just go. Something isn't right. It's been too quiet," a voice said.

"Boss wouldn't leave us."

"You sure about that? Okay, new plan, you have the key; let's get out of here and see what's going on," Cohen said.

His voice bolted me around the corner, not thinking about the danger, as I stepped into the light with my gun raised.

"You're not going anywhere without me," I said, tears falling down my cheek.

The four guys stopped, and that's when I realized that while there might be two guards down here, they didn't seem to be against Ryker and Cohen if the four of them sitting together and talking was anything to go on.

My eyes raked over both Cohen and Ryker, taking in every cut and bruise. Ryker looked the worse for wear, and I wanted to run to him and tell him how I felt, but it didn't seem like the right time with the bomb still a possibility.

"Sweetheart," Cohen said, moving toward me. The guards relaxed when they saw I wasn't a threat. Cohen wrapped me in his arms, and I held onto him, too afraid to let go just yet, the gun still in my grip.

"You're okay," I said.

"That's debatable. If you're down here, what's going on? Where are your shoes, and what's on your head?" He held me at arm's length, then noticing the gun in my hand, he took it.

"Let's move and talk. Ryker?" I asked, peeking around Cohen.

He opened one eye, and it felt like he was happy to see me. "Hey, little hacker. Looks like you get to save the day."

Rushing toward him, my hands hovered over his body, unsure where to touch him. Everything looked like it hurt.

"Now I wish I'd gone to Dex so I could cut off his penis and shove it down his throat," I muttered.

Ryker snorted, then grimaced, and I looked to the two guards. "I'm assuming you're *not* on Dex's side?"

They shook their heads, though one appeared doubtful, but I'd let it go for now if they helped us get off this floor. There was no way we would make it up the elevator shaft otherwise. Taking my power pose, I pointed at them both as I started to give out orders.

"Okay, then prove it. Carry him. We need to go. This building is wired with explosives, and we need to get out."

That had the guys moving, and Cohen took my hand as we started down the hallway. He leaned down, whispering. "Bossy Fin is super hot. You need to use that voice in the bedroom."

My cheeks heated, but I kept moving. No time to give into temptation until we were clear of danger. If I wanted to use that voice, I needed to make sure we were out of this alive.

We made it to the elevator, and one of the guards scanned their cards to call it. When it arrived without any issue, I began to relax a little. The five of us climbed in and rode it up, quiet as it ascended. My toe tapped against the floor, worried we'd get stuck in here.

The doors opened, and my gut sank as we spotted Dex waiting for us. He had Samson on his knees in front of him, a gun held to his head. Fear ran up my throat, and I tried to think of a way out of this mess. Dex smiled maniacally, and I wondered how he could have gotten the advantage on Samson. When I met Samson's eyes, he nodded slightly toward the mask still perched on my head.

Remembering the can I'd thrown into my boot, I dropped my eyes to it, hoping Dex thought I was just scared.

"Well, well, well. Now that we're all here, who wants to die first?" Dex cackled like it was the world's funniest joke.

"How about you?" he asked and, a second later, shot the guard holding Ryker up. I screamed, not having expected the violence for some reason. The man fell, Ryker struggling to stay upright now that the man was bleeding from his chest. The other guard looked at Dex like he didn't even know the man.

Which let's be fair… he probably didn't. Not the real version.

My hands began to shake, my nerves overwhelming me. I couldn't think under this pressure. I needed to focus my attention, or I'd lose it, and we'd all die. I couldn't let us all die! I'd haunt myself in death, filled with guilt for taking all these people from the ones they loved—including myself.

Samson. I needed to focus on him. He seemed like the one with a plan. Glancing back at him, I noticed he'd been able to use the gunshot to his advantage, the canister now in his grip. He implored me with his eyes to pull the mask down. So, while Dex continued monologuing about how we were all such disappointments, I shoved the mask over my head just as Samson pulled the ring. The gas began to fill the space, and he lifted it up so Dex would get the majority.

I almost felt bad for Dex, the look of confusion on his face when his limbs began to grow weak. I just had to hope this was knock-out gas and not something lethal. Fudge, why did I have to go and put that in my brain?

The instant he dropped, I reacted, bolting toward him and taking his gun. I held it, my hands shaking, and I debated. He deserved to die, but could I be the one to do it? Would it be better to let him go to jail? Was that enough justice for the crimes he'd committed?

When a hand wrapped around mine, I saw Ryker standing there, his shirt over his mouth, keeping what was left of the gas out.

He implored me with his one good eye to give him the gun. Without hesitation, I let go, turning my back as I bent down to help Cohen lift Samson up. He'd passed out too, being so close. We'd only taken two steps when the gun's pop sounded. I tensed, my step faltering, but I didn't stop. I kept walking, wanting to leave that place and never look back. I already knew it would haunt me for the rest of my life.

Stepping out the door, I practically wept as Milo grabbed me, pulling me into his arms. Asa took over with Cohen to drag his father to a nearby medic. I peeked over Milo's shoulder as he carried me, needing to see Ryker emerge. When I spotted the uninjured guard carrying him out, my body relaxed, the tension easing out of my bones.

"We did it," I said, then realized I still had on the gas mask. Milo lifted it up, peering down at me with love.

"I've never been so scared, darling. But you were amazing."

The tears I'd been holding back spilled over, and I clung to Milo as he carried me to the medic. It was done. My revenge had been finalized. The man who'd stolen my innocence was dead. I didn't feel like I'd imagined I would, and I knew it was because it had been my own guilt that had weighed me down all those years. Now that I knew that Mongoose was alive and Dex had been the one behind it all, I could let go of it.

I might have started this journey off for the wrong reason, but I was ending it for the right ones. I'd learned so much about myself and opened my heart up to, I daresay, four men. Now, I had my whole life to live with them.

Twenty-Two

FINLEY

STEPPING INTO THE ROOM, THE FIRST THING I HEARD WAS THE STEADY rhythm of a heartbeat. The sounds of medical equipment beeping were becoming too familiar to me. Asa smiled at me when I approached, and I eagerly went to him, needing to feel his arms around me.

"Hey, kiddo," Samson said, drawing my attention to the bed. "You did good." He smiled at me, and I returned it, happy to have his respect.

"What happened after you left me?" I asked, taking in the cast and bandage. He gave a dark chuckle.

"I was able to incapacitate the other guard and make it into the control room. With the assistance of one of my hackers, I disabled the bombs and was looking for you on camera when I was attacked from behind. You were right, by the way. Dex had a hidden area in the control room that he'd been in. We scuffled for a little, but I was easier to subdue with a broken arm and stab wound than I'd like to admit."

I picked up his good hand, squeezing it. "You saved us. That's all that matters."

"Yeah, well, I wasn't sure what to do when I saw you all. Your mask gave me the idea when I saw the canister. I knew even if the others inhaled it, that at least you'd be able to get out. It was my last ditch effort to save everyone."

"Always got to be the hero," a familiar voice said as she entered the room.

"Sawyer!" Jumping up from Asa, I ran a few feet to my pint-sized best friend and wrapped my arms around her. She held me tight, and I didn't stop the tears that fell. There was nothing like a hug from your best friend to heal whatever you were suffering from.

"Wow, I can't believe she gets the greeting and not your own flesh and blood," my brother said from behind her. Rolling my eyes, I dropped Sawyer's arms and hugged my brother next.

"Hey, big Brother," I said as he wrapped me in his familiar Henry scent. His hug was longer and tighter than usual, and I wondered for the first time if I'd worried him.

"Hey, little Sis. I'm glad you're okay." Henry kissed my hair before stepping back, and I found Sawyer hugging Asa and her dad, griping at Samson for getting injured. Isla smiled over at me as she stood by her husband's side, holding his hand, smiling at their children.

When it was apparent we wouldn't get any more details from Samson, I excused myself from his room and went down the hall to check on Ryker and Cohen. They were being moved back to The Order once they were stable, but with the severity of Ryker's injuries, they'd opted to bring them here first since it was closer.

Knocking softly, I stood at the door and looked at the two of them. Cohen's smile immediately captured my heart, and he stood from the bed, already bandaged and dressed in some clean clothes. He tugged on my hand, pulling me into the room.

"Perfect timing, sweetheart. Please tell Ryker he's being a stubborn ass."

"You're being a stubborn ass," I said, not hesitating.

Ryker sputtered, looking at me in shock. Cohen cheesed, kissing me quickly before giving Ryker a smug smirk.

"What? You don't even know what about," Ryker argued, trying to shift but grimacing when something pulled at his injuries.

Jumping up on the bed Cohen had just vacated, I swung my feet as I stared at him. I shrugged one shoulder, looking at him.

"Don't need to. I know you, and you're always a stubborn ass. So, if Co-bear says you're one, then I believe him."

I heard Cohen groan behind me, but I kept my eyes locked on Ryker. His face stayed frozen for a second before he let out a laugh, then winced.

"Sorry, I'll try to keep my hilarity to a minimum." I jumped off the bed, tentatively sitting on the edge of his, and took his hand. "Ryker, what will it take for you to kiss me?" I dropped my head, the blush rushing up to cover my cheeks. But I figured we almost died. Why were we dancing around the issue?

He sputtered again, sounding like a drowning cat this time, so I braved it and peered up at him from under my eyelashes. His one eye stared at me, and I'd say I'd rendered the flirt speechless.

"You want me to kiss you? Even after everything that's happened? I thought—"

I lifted my fingers and pressed them to his lips. "Stop thinking. That's the problem." Leaning forward, I kept my eyes open, watching if he wanted me to stop. When I was only a hair away, I paused. "Too much crap has gone down to worry about niceties. I like you. Cohen likes you. I think you like us both. So, stop fighting it and sacrificing yourself for the greater good and just—"

This time it was Ryker who shut me up, pressing his lips to mine. My eyes stayed open, staring into his, and I saw the fear but also the relief and joy. Closing mine, I gently placed my hands on his jaw, cupping it as I pressed my lips harder into his. After a few seconds, I pulled back, giving him a lingering look.

"It was as perfect as I always imagined kissing you would be," Ryker whispered, lifting his one good hand to stroke my cheek and hair. "Even bruised, broken, and stitched up, I couldn't imagine a more perfect first kiss with you, little hacker."

"Now, will you agree to come back with us?" Cohen asked. He leaned into my back, and I suddenly realized how close he'd moved toward me. I dropped one of my hands and took his.

"That's what you're being stubborn over?" I rolled my eyes, giving Ryker a "see, I knew Cohen was right" look.

"Hey," Milo said, stepping into the room. "Everything is final with the real estate company. The house we wanted is ours." Milo grinned at me, looking at the other two men. "I'm glad you made it out, Ryker."

"Thanks, man. House?" he asked, looking at Cohen and me.

"Milo and Cohen are both stupid rich, so I decided to use that for my own personal gain for once. The rest of us will be returning to Utah, and you're coming with us. Lux has state-of-the-art physical therapy programs, and Milo will be the physician overseeing your care. We haven't gotten the opportunity to build our relationship the way I want…" Cohen cleared his throat, and I smiled. "Sorry, the way *we* want, and we both knew if, given the opportunity, you'd stay behind, siting something to do with recovery and overseeing the transferring of titles and blah, blah." I waved my hand, smiling. "So to circumvent all that, we made it impossible for you to say no. Besides, you deserve some happiness, and I want you around."

"Me too. Even though you annoy me at times, I can't deny the feelings I had for you are still there. The situation we're all in is unique, but I know if you stay back, you'll only grow further away from us, resigned to never be happy and just live for the job. I know you, Ryker. This is your chance to catch up, to get to know Fin and me, and see if this type of relationship works for you. You don't have to stay forever, just give us a few months and see where it takes you."

Ryker looked between the three of us, taking in our expressions. "You really mean all of that?"

"Yes, Ry." I smiled, squeezing his hand, and he softened.

"Okay, I'd like the chance to see how this type of relationship works. I already know what you all have is unique and special, and it would be a privilege to get a chance to find that for myself as well."

"Yes!" I jumped up, kissing his lips briefly before hugging both Milo and Cohen. "You know, despite almost dying… Nope." I shook my head, resetting my thoughts. "Actually, I don't want to qualify anything Dex did as fun. I'm glad it's over. I'm relieved we're all relatively unscathed, and I'm thrilled we've somehow all found each other through it. Yep, let's go with that."

The guys gave me soft smiles, and I knew that we'd all be okay despite our rocky beginning.

A week later, we'd officially packed up our suite, most of it consisting of clothes and Ryker's belongings since we'd all only come with a few suitcases. After a few days to recover, we spent the rest in meetings and debriefings, talking about the incident and how to make sure something similar didn't happen again. Bishop admitted to being blackmailed and was brought up on charges of assisting a terrorist. It sounded harsh, but people wouldn't have died if he hadn't given our location at the mall, not to mention Kristina.

What impressed me was how The Order used everything as a teaching moment. It was weird being discussed openly without people knowing it was you in the room. But it allowed the other agents to see what had been done well and what could've been done differently.

"I liked how Agent Oblivion thought to use an outside agency, but I also think there was a way to utilize more of The Order's agents without arousing the mole," someone said, and I tried my hardest to keep my face blank.

It was an odd experience to sit through hours of strategic planning on something you'd done. I was glad that we'd be inactive agents after this. Ryker had bargained for us all to remain as part of The Order, but where we could go back and live our lives, only taking on missions when it fit our skills. It seemed like the best of both worlds for me. I'd get to be back with my family and friends, living a life I loved, but also have opportunities to live a little dangerously every now and then. It made my adrenaline junkie heart happy.

"Well, that's all for today. Thank you all for your commitment to going over these files. There's a celebration in the canteen for our comrades who will be leaving the base to return to their homestead," the instructor said, dismissing everyone.

I looked at the guys, smiling as we gathered our stuff for the last time. Cohen slung his arm around my shoulder, and I grabbed Milo's hand as Asa walked behind us, talking with Ryker. Despite Ryker's claims of being on the outside, since the attack, he'd loosened up and let the guys into his life. It made me happy to see our family unit bonding.

"So, hot stuff," Cohen said, grinning down at me, "what do you have planned for the rest of your life?"

"Hmm," I said, tapping my lip with a finger. "Well, naturally I want to start my own fashion label for ice skating costumes. The ones Sawyer sent me for Nationals were atrocious. The kids desperately need my wisdom at Lux, or they'll majorly screw up their social media presence. But other than that, kicking some bad guy's butts every now and then doesn't sound half bad. Why? What do you have in mind?"

Cohen grinned, bending down to whisper in my ear. "Oh, I plan to have you every which way and then back again for the rest of my life. What do you say, sweetheart?"

I gulped, nodding enthusiastically. "Yep. I'm good with that plan."

Milo chuckled next to me, and I glanced over, squeezing his hand. "I'm good as long as you guys are there. I don't care how cheesy or loved up that makes me."

"You could never be too cheesy, Fin. It's one of my favorite things about you. Plus, I had your fantasy closet built, so I'm not going anywhere."

"You did what?" I asked, stopping and making Asa and Ryker almost collide with us.

"I didn't expect Milo to spill the beans first," Ryker said, nudging him. Milo's face was red, but he shrugged.

"I couldn't keep it to myself any longer."

"You're serious? You built me my dream closet? I think I might faint."

"Wait until after the party. We have a long night of traveling ahead of us. You can faint when we get to the house. Deal?"

Jumping up and down, I kissed each of the guys before tugging them into the canteen, even more eager now to leave. I'd come to The Order to settle a debt, and I was leaving with more than I could've imagined. Now, if I could only learn to not wear stilettos on missions, my life would be complete.

Who was I kidding? Fashion always trumped necessity.

Epilogue

FINLEY

ONE WEEK LATER

Unpacking the last box of things from my room on campus, I didn't hear my attacker when they jumped on me from behind. The person was small, barely moving me, but I took a step forward to balance. Her arms wrapped around me, her pomegranate scent washing over me.

"Oof, you didn't stick the landing. Gotta mark a point off for that," she teased before hopping down and flopping onto the nearest surface, which happened to be a humongous bed.

"Hey, Sawyer," I said, smiling at my best friend. "Did you guys just get back?"

She sat up, smiling at me as she pulled her feet up under her. Sawyer began to survey the room. "Yep. It was nice to meet Mateo's family, but I'm glad to be back here. Though, I wish school wasn't starting in a week. Madeline has us training practically every minute of the day to maximize our time before the ice is overcome with students. I'm starting to regret my dream of going to the Olympics."

"No, you're not." I tossed a pillow at her head, and she caught it, a massive smile on her face. "You love to train."

"Yeah, you're right. It just feels weird not to complain about it. So I put on a good show for you."

"Haha. I'll have you know that I can now run five miles without getting out of breath." And shoot a gun, but I decided to keep that tidbit to myself. Didn't need to freak out my bestie.

"Wow, I'm impressed. Does that mean you'll sign up to do the charity 5k with us? Is there a Team FinSin in your future? Gonna take on team Bosh?"

"Ha! No, I said I could run it, not that I liked to. And we don't have a cutesy name. There's only five of us, so I dunno." I shrugged my shoulder, my face turning bright red, so I moved over to a different box to hide it.

"Shrug your shoulder all you want, Fin. I know you. What's up?" A pillow hit me in the side of the head, and I gave up my pretense of hiding and went and joined her on the bed.

"When we first left the base, I couldn't wait to all be under one roof. To have time to develop my relationships and become a family like you have with your guys."

"But?" she asked, nudging me.

"Now that the guys are here, I worry they'll regret it. Especially Ryker. Asa is still coaching, and Milo is doing his residency, so it's easier for me to believe they have other reasons to be at Lux outside of me. Cohen is always moving around, so him working for Samson also doesn't seem as such a big stretch. But Ryker..." I trailed off, ducking my head as I began to play with the bedspread.

"I don't know him as well as the others, obviously, but I know you, Fin, and you're amazing. I get it, though. There's a certain level of doubt that starts to creep in when you have more than one boyfriend, but I can tell you from experience that it's a wasted emotion. Trust them to know what they want and don't devalue their actions. But most of all, know your worth, girl. You're a brilliant hacker who can sew, knows fashion, and looks killer in a pair of heels. You're one of a kind, Finley Amelia Reyes."

"God, I've missed you." I tackled my best friend to the bed as we hugged and giggled. Cuddling together, I thought about what she said. "Thank you. I needed to remind myself. Now," I said, sitting up, "tell me all about Mateo's family, Ollie going to culinary school, and the new hockey coach. I feel like I'm so out of the loop."

Sawyer chuckled but sat up and filled me in on how things had been on campus over the summer and how she'd finally convinced Ollie to stop taking classes on the weekend and to just go for it.

"Dimitri was happy for Ollie and asked his help in finding a replacement since the Senior level needed a head coach and new assistant with only Fletcher staying on. Ollie and Dimitri talked about promoting Jacob, but in the end, they decided some new blood was needed to get the program back to where it was before the whole Council debacle."

"Why didn't they promote Tyler?"

"Tyler wanted to stay on the Junior team so he could still have time to work with Samson and his dad."

"That was Asa's reasoning, too," I mused, remembering Asa debating what to do. "So, who did they pick? Anyone good?"

Sawyer rubbed her hands together in glee. "Well, I'd like to think my influence has made Ollie a better man because he picked Henley Henshaw to be the new head coach."

"Wait, but Henley's a girl..." I trailed off as a smile spread across my face.

"Exactly. What better way to make some waves than to shake everything up? I think it's brilliant, and I'm really proud of them for being open to the idea."

"I'm actually excited about attending some games now. Who's the other new coach?"

She shrugged her shoulder, bumping mine. "I can't remember his name, Reed something."

"Doesn't ring a bell. I'll get the scoop from Asa later."

A knock at the door had us breaking apart and glancing toward it. Ryker stood there, looking a little awkward with Sawyer here.

"Oh, hi. You must be Sawyer. I'm so glad Finley found you." He stepped into the room, his hand outstretched toward Sawyer.

She hopped off the bed and met him halfway. "It's nice to meet you, Ryker. Thanks for saving my girl's butt a few times. Speaking of butts... I should go and find my boyfriends and head home. Ollie and Tyler were hanging with my brother."

She skipped back over to me, giving me a hug and kiss on the cheek. "Be good and remember your worth." Sawyer lifted her eyebrows, wiggling them as she gave us finger guns as she left the room.

"She's a character," Ryker said, and I laughed.

"That she is. How are you feeling? How was your physio today with Dax?"

"It went well. Asa, and I think his name was Rhett, joined me. Big dude, scary eyebrows?"

"That sounds like Rhett." I chuckled, walking closer to him. When I reached him, I wrapped my arms around his waist, resting my head against his chest. Things had developed more between us in the week we'd been here, but I could sense how he always waited for me to make the first move. I wondered if he was still worried I blamed him for Dex's destruction. After a second, his hands fell to my back, and I let out a contented sigh.

"I still have to pinch myself sometimes when you come to me so easily. I was wondering if you'd like to go on a date with Cohen and me?"

"I'd love to," I said, pulling my head back to see his face. He smiled, and I was glad he was holding onto me, or I might've wobbled as my legs grew weak. Ryker Jenson smiling was a dangerous weapon. "When are we leaving, and what should I wear?"

"In about an hour, and dress however you want. I love your style."

He kissed me then, our tongues twisting together as we fell into an easy rhythm. Despite only being intimate with one another for about a week, it came naturally. It probably stemmed from years of knowing him. Ryker was part of me, even if I'd never wanted to admit it.

Pulling apart, we were both breathless as we stood, staring affectionately at one another. Ryker's mouth curled up on the side, and he stepped back.

"Right, I'll leave you to it. I'm afraid if I don't that things will progress more, and we'll never make it to the date."

"I'm starting to regret the date if it means no fun time." I pouted, sticking my lip out as my hands went to my hips.

"Never said there wouldn't be any fun time, little hacker." He backed out of the room with a wink, leaving me hot and bothered.

Remembering he said I could wear whatever I wanted, I quickly ran to my favorite room in the house, letting out a blissful sigh as I took in the closet. It was the size of my childhood bedroom, with more walls than I had clothes. Sadly, the same couldn't be said about shoes as they filled in the little slots designed for them. In the middle sat a colossal island with drawers on every side that held all my underthings, pajamas, and anything I didn't want to hang up.

The far back wall had a three-sided mirror in the middle, a vanity filled with makeup and hair care products to the left, and my own design studio on the right. My beloved sewing machine sat next to a mannequin and a wall that was fitted with rolls of fabric, buttons, and anything I could think of adding to an ensemble. From the plush carpet, the attached full bathroom, to all my favorite things in one place, it was a miracle I ever left this closet. The guys had done well spoiling me.

Taking my time getting ready, I pampered myself as I went full Finley. I hadn't gotten this dressed up in a while, and I missed it. For the most part, there weren't many places to go in Oak Crest, and I spent the majority of my time hanging out. So, if we were going on a date, I would make good use of the opportunity.

Dressed in a black fly-away skirt with a white blouse that hung to my mid-section, red lipstick, and red heels Ryker had gotten me, to replace the deceptive ones, I finally felt ready as I took myself in from all angles in the mirror. A wolf whistle broke my concentration, and I spotted Cohen leaning against the island.

"Fuck, sweetheart, you look amazing. I can't wait to show you off and let all these other dudes know you're mine."

"Hmm, is that so?" I walked toward him, taking in his dark jeans and button-down shirt. Running my hands up his front, I ran the tip of my nails over his neck, and he let out a soft moan. The tiny hairs tickled my palms as I flattened them against his head.

Cohen's eyes were hooded as he stared down at me. "On second thought, let's just stay in and break in this closet you seem to love so much."

I licked my lips, the thought suddenly sounding like the best plan ever, when a throat cleared. Peeking around his bicep, I found Ryker standing closer to the doorway. He was dressed in tight jeans and a fitted shirt, the sleeves rolled up, and my mouth was suddenly parched.

"As much fun as that sounds, let's have dinner first." Ryker held out his hand, and I walked toward him, linking Cohen's hand in mine. When I reached him, Ryker's fingers entwined with my other hand, and I was suddenly the Oreo filling to a very hot man cookie.

"So, where are we going?" I asked as we started to head toward the garage, my voice cracking a little from the lust running through my body.

"That's a surprise, little hacker. You're going to have to be patient."

"I'm afraid that's a quality Fin has a shortage of," Cohen said, snorting to himself.

Huffing, I kept my comments to myself, afraid they'd make it worse if I rebuked their claims. Because Cohen wasn't wrong. I hated waiting for things. But I could do it, if it was to prove a point. Deciding to do just that, I smiled, concocting a plan for myself.

"Uh oh. She's got that look. Shit. I've activated bratty Fin. Quick, give her something to eat or something shiny."

I stopped, blinking at Cohen as I dropped both their hands and crossed my arms. "Um, what? I'm not a dog or a dragon!" I scrunched my eyebrows, trying to figure out where he was going with his comment.

Both guys stood silent for a second as they stared at me before falling into a fit of hysterics. Rolling my eyes, I began to walk forward, debating going to get Asa and Milo and having this date with them instead. When I entered the kitchen, it was lit with candles, and Asa and Milo stood in mock waiter uniforms. They were both smiling, but the instant they saw me, their eyes grew hungry, and their mouths parted a little.

"Man, I think we got the raw end of the deal. You look amazing, babe."

"Yeah, I want to change my role on this date," Milo said, pushing his glasses up.

Feeling appeased by their responses, I walked over to them, giving them each a hug and kiss. Once I was done, I turned and looked at the two troublemakers. They were standing together, hands practically touching, and I could feel the chemistry between them like electrical currents. Despite their obvious connection, both were focused on me, eyes hungry, their smiles contrite.

"Sorry, sweetheart. Please let us make it up to you with this evening we'd planned."

Nodding, I let Ryker and Cohen lead me to a table covered in a fancy linen tablecloth, candles, and fine china.

"Where did you get all of this?" I asked. We'd been moving all of our belongings into the house over the course of the week, but we hadn't had time to go and get things the house needed. Mainly because I'd been focused on getting my closet haven ready before anything else, but I didn't take the guys for ones to have dinnerware and cloth tablecloths.

"Sawyer brought it over earlier. She borrowed some of it from

Aggie, and some are from my mom," Asa answered. "Now, for the rest of the meal, Milo and I will be your servers, not your boyfriends." Asa bowed and walked into the kitchen, bringing over trays of food that smelled delicious. "She also brought over some food that Ollie and Soren prepared."

"Remind me to thank her."

Ryker walked over and scooted my chair in behind me, and the three of us sat down and began to eat. It was quiet as we enjoyed the meal, and while it was nice, it felt awkward.

"Okay, I thought this would be a good idea, but I'm beginning to see my flaw in this," Ryker said, pushing his plate back and getting up. "Come on. Let's eat dessert from the containers while sitting on the counters. Being too formal is making it weird."

Giggling, I took his hand and walked with him into the kitchen. Before I could hop up myself, Ryker lifted me onto the counter and handed me a spoon. Cohen leaned against the other side of me, and I was once again in the middle. I dipped my fork into the desert, getting a big scoop of whipped cream.

"You have something…" Cohen moved to point at my face, leaving a glob of whipped cream in his wake. "Oops, I better clean that up."

His tongue flicked out, trailing over my cheek, and I sucked in a breath. His eyes dropped to my tongue, and a second later, his mouth was on me as he kissed me passionately. I lost all thought as Cohen ravaged my mouth, so when hands began to trail up my legs, I jumped, pulling back. Ryker stood between them, his eyes hooded at half-mast as he took me in. His hands were hot on my skin, and I moved forward, wanting more contact.

"You sure? I know we're—"

"Ryker, touch me." His pupils fully dilated, and he pushed his palms up my legs, under my skirt. His fingers gripped my thighs, and I moaned at the contact. Cohen began to nibble on my neck, leaving little bites and sucks as he moved.

When he got to my ear, he whispered seductively. "Tell him

what to do. It's sexy as fuck watching you take control, sweetheart. Tell him what you want, and I'll reward you."

My breath hitched, and I spread my legs open a little wider as my back arched. "Ryker, take off my panties."

Ryker's eyes jumped to mine, and I narrowed them at him. "Did I stutter?" He smiled, and I let out a little breath of relief I hadn't gone too far. Ryker was usually the dominant one, but it seemed like he wanted to submit to me. I'd never been in control this way before, but as Cohen urged me on, I found I liked it. If this was going to be the dynamic between the three of us, I was here for it.

Ryker's hand pushed my skirt the rest of the way up, my silk thong on display. I imagined the front displayed my wetness, my arousal leaking out onto my thighs already. Cohen began to move my top up, pulling it over my head as Ryker started to drag my panties down.

"Fuck, you're so sexy with your legs spread open for me," Ryker said, staring at the space between my legs.

"Then show me. Kiss me there."

Cohen began to massage my breasts, tweaking my nipples through the lace and driving me wild. When Ryker's mouth hit my clit, my head fell back, and I locked my legs around him. His hands gripped me, and I knew I'd have marks tomorrow from how tight he held me to him. When his fingers plunged into me, I almost wept.

"You didn't tell him to do that," Cohen whispered, and I whimpered, not liking what that meant. I wanted him to do it even if I hadn't said it yet. Cohen gave me a pointed look, removing his hands from my tits. Sighing, I straightened up, peering down at the devilish man between my legs.

"I didn't give you permission to use your fingers. Cohen, show him what that means."

Since I was still new to figuring out what this was myself, I decided to call in the master. He gave me a smirk as I returned one, waiting for him to join in the fun. Ryker pulled his fingers out and looked to Cohen, waiting for whatever he was going to do. He snatched Ryker's fingers that were covered in my wetness and stuck them into his mouth, sucking them dry. Ryker and I both moaned, and I didn't know what sort of punishment this was since it was hot. When he was done with them, he pulled Ryker to him by his shirt, slamming their mouths together in a rough kiss that had me panting.

Pushing my own fingers into my wet pussy, I began playing with myself as I watched them. They seemed to get lost in one another, making me wetter with their connection and love, even if they were too afraid to admit it. Massaging my clit, I circled it roughly as I began to grow closer to my climax. When they pulled apart and stared at me with hungry eyes, I came, shuttering as my pussy tightened around the emptiness.

"Fuck, that was hot. I think it's time we give her something more. Playtime is over, little hacker."

Before I could respond, I was yanked off the counter by my hips and spun around. My bra was unclasped, falling to the surface. I could hear shuffling behind me, and the sound of a condom wrapper before the head of a cock was pressed into me from behind.

"Shit, Ry. You got your dick pierced!" Cohen exclaimed, catching me off guard as said dick was thrust into me. Arms wrapped around me, pulling me flush to a chest as he bent down to kiss me. When he pulled away, more of the cocky, flirty guy I knew was there, and I was happy to see him relaxing into himself and this.

His hands dropped to my hips, and I braced myself against the counter as he began to push into me harder, and I felt something I'd never experienced before. My breaths were heavy as he pistoned in and out, the smell of sex filling the space as our skin slapped together. I turned my head to the left, finding Cohen was now naked, his own cock in his hand as he stroked it, watching us.

He winked when he caught my gaze, bending down to kiss me.

His free hand snaked down, rubbing my clit, and I detonated, unable to hold back the orgasm. White dots appeared in front of my eyes as I pulsed around Ryker, my body trembling.

"I'm coming," he roared, bracing himself against me as he pumped one last time. When he was done, he rested his head against my shoulder; our breathing synchronized as we tried to catch it.

"That... was... incredible..." I panted, making Ryker chuckle.

"It was. Now, round two." He kissed my shoulder before carefully pulling out, and I discovered what he meant. Cohen lifted me back to the counter, wrapping my legs around his waist as he plunged into me in one go. My body was sensitive from two orgasms already, so I held onto him, feeling every little move against my skin.

When a third orgasm began to creep up my spine, my whole body tingled from my toes to my eyelashes.

"You are amazing, sweetheart. Hold on," Cohen whispered, kissing me. It didn't take much longer, and I fell apart in his arms. When I came to, a few minutes later, I knew that my worries were unfounded and that, once again, Sawyer had been right.

We were meant to be together, and I wouldn't let any more doubt or fear diminish our future because it was going to be a happy one.

Turn the page for a bonus scene with Cohen and Ryker. If you prefer not to read MM scenes, then continue to the extended epilogue.

Bonus Scene

COHEN

ONE MONTH LATER

Finishing up my call, I pushed my chair back and walked out of my office. Today had been long, but I was looking forward to the evening. Ryker and I were going to celebrate his starting work today. Everyone else was busy, so it would be the first time it would just be the two of us. Our relationship had flourished over the last month, and now that he was done with his physical therapy, he was cleared for duty. It had taken both Asa and me to convince him to come and work with Samson.

At first, he'd maintained he wanted some time off. But once everyone had started working and he was sitting at home alone, he quickly grew bored. He'd started some new hobbies, but after a week of basketweaving and gardening, he'd finally succumbed to our suggestion.

"Hey," I said, stepping into the fitness room. The new security recruits were all panting on the ground, and I had no doubt he'd given them a run for their money. Ryker turned at my voice, a smile on his handsome face. It was nice to see it there, and it only confirmed my intuition that he needed this job. He was good at it, and this way, it didn't come with all the stress running The Order did.

"Hello, boss man." He smirked at me as he walked closer. I took in his athletic form, noticing how his shorts fit him just right, hanging off his hips. His shirt was stretched across his chest, with a few damp spots where he'd sweated. While I appreciated Ryker in his suit, it was seeing him in his element that really got me going.

"You like that, don't you?" I asked, leaning against the wall by the door. It was a new experience for us both, me being in charge of him. I couldn't say I hated it.

"You done for the day?" I asked.

"Yep. I was about to head to the shower. Want to join?" Ryker asked, lifting his eyebrows. I took in every detail on his face. His eyes were hooded, but there was some vulnerability there too. Ryker stepped up next to me, his body heat surrounding me, and his rainforest and coffee smell tickled my nose. I itched to reach out to him and kiss him right there, but we were trying to keep it PG, at least in front of people. So, I took his hand, and we walked out of the gym together. I nodded at a few people, but no one even batted an eye, going on about their business.

Stepping into the private bathroom, I wasted no time shoving him against the door as I locked it. I trapped him between my arms. Ryker didn't even try to fight me, his eyes hungry as he leaned against me. I could feel his hardness as he rocked himself a little against me.

When we first got together, Ryker had been the aggressor, the one in charge of our dynamic. But since then, a lot had changed, and now, it was a battle between us to see who would give in each time we were together. It looked like today I was going to win.

"You were in your element today, weren't you?" I gripped his chin between my hands, and he nodded, licking his lips. "Answer."

"Yes," he said, his hot breath cascading over me, sending chills down my spine.

"Say, 'You were right, Cohen. You're a God among men.'" I smirked at him, waiting to see if he'd answer. The corner of his lip curved up, but he didn't say anything. Reaching down, I rubbed my hand over his cock, and he whimpered at the touch. "Want to try that again?" I asked, lifting my eyebrow.

"You were right, Cohen," he said between gritted teeth. A hiss left him as I stroked him again.

"I believe there was one more thing," I said, but this time, Ryker had had enough and surged up, sealing his lips to mine.

"Enough chit-chat. If you're not going to take control. I will."

Biting his lip for the insolence, I thrust my hand down his athletic shorts before he could retort, grabbing hold of his erect cock. Ryker sucked in a breath, breaking my grip on his mouth as his head hit the door.

"Now, what were you muttering about taking control?" Ever so slowly, I slid my hand up his length, rubbing my thumb over the piercing at the end and sending shivers down Ryker. Dropping to my knees, I pulled my prize free of his shorts and shoved them all the way down. I didn't waste any time, and I wrapped my lips around him, sucking him down to the back of my throat. Ryker's hands threaded through my hair, urging me to keep going.

I could feel him twitching in my mouth as I sucked him, swirling my tongue over the pierced tip. Grabbing his balls with my free hand, I fondled them as I took him further. I felt him give into the release, his legs tensing as his balls drew up, and he exploded his salty cum down my throat. Licking my lips, I stood and began to undress while Ryker recovered.

Turning on the shower, I glanced back at him as he rested against the door, the blood returning to his brain. "I'm not done with you," I cooed, walking over and grabbing his throat as I slammed my lips to his. Ryker trembled beneath me, submitting completely to me as I took what I wanted.

Breaking the kiss, I walked over to the shower and beckoned him to follow. The shower was tiled and open, with a bench to one side and four shower heads. The water rained down from every direction, and I pointed for him to take the bench. Ryker didn't hesitate as I grabbed some lube, directing all the shower heads away from me.

When I looked back at him, his ass in the air, I stopped, not believing what I saw.

"Did you…?" I mumbled, lost for words.

Ryker glanced over his shoulder, a smirk on his face. "Wear this all day? Yep."

Peering at me from between his ass cheeks was a black butt plug. The sight made me harder if that was even possible. "Shit," I cursed, stroking myself.

I walked forward, reverently massaging his ass cheeks as I took in the sight. It said a lot for Ryker to do this, and I knew no matter what, our relationship would survive anything else. Taking hold of the plug, I gently pulled it out, his hole gaping as it waited to be filled. Ryker moaned at the movement, and I took some lube and dripped it around him.

Gripping his hips, I pushed in easier than I'd ever done before, sliding home. We both cursed when I bottomed out, and I stood there for a second as I breathed, trying not to erupt before I got to enjoy myself.

Slowly, I pulled back, feeling him tremble around me as I moved. "Fuck, Ry. You made me so hard doing that."

"Good," he wheezed out between pants, his hands braced on the bench.

We didn't say much else, both of us too lost to the pleasure coursing through us. My balls were tingling with the need to come, but I wasn't ready yet. It felt so good to just fuck him.

Ryker whimpered, the sound pained, and I knew I couldn't wait much longer. Pulling his torso up, I stopped and tilted his head back so I could kiss him.

"Ready?" I asked, and he nodded.

Tightening my grip, I pushed forward, loving how easily I slid back into him. Giving one more thrust, I roared as I came, my cum filling him.

When I could think again, I slowly pulled out, helping him to stand. Ryker turned to me, clasping my face in a tender hold, staring into my eyes.

"I love you, Cohen. I'm not afraid to admit it anymore, and I just wanted you to know that."

My throat felt dry as I tried to find the words. I blinked, the water hitting me now that I'd moved to the side. When I didn't say anything, he gave me an understanding look.

"I get it. I don't have the best track record—"

Shushing him with a kiss, I drew back, shaking my head. "No, that's not it. I'm just surprised you said it first. Finley totally won the bet. I love you too, Ryker."

He half laughed and frowned at my words. Shaking his head, he peered at me, his eyes lighter. "How about we finish up and go and have that date we'd planned? And maybe there will be time for round two?"

Smiling, we quickly rinsed, turning off the shower and dressing in record time. When we stepped outside, the sun was beginning to set. I leaned my head back, having missed the sun more than I realized when we'd been at The Order. Now, every chance I got, I soaked it in, even if only at the end of the day.

"Yeah, that's the good stuff. I'd gotten so used to being underground that I'd forgotten what the real sun was like. Those vitamin D lamps just aren't the same. Plus, you just can't mimic this view."

I peered over, nodding. "Yeah, I was thinking the same."

"You know, I think our subconscious tries to protect us by making us forget how perfect some things are. It's the only reason I can imagine for how I forgot how amazing you were. I tried to forget so I wouldn't be miserable each day."

My cheeks blushed as we started walking. "I'm not perfect. Far from it. But I'm glad we're here now."

Ryker squeezed my hand, and we headed back to the house, ready to live out our lives with the people we loved and the family we'd created.

Extended Epilogue

One

FINLEY

EIGHT YEARS LATER

I ducked and weaved to avoid the punch advancing toward my face, grinning as the young woman in front of me found her groove, pushing past her exhaustion. We'd been training for the past few hours, our typical Friday evening for the past few years. By now, our steps were synchronized like a dance as we moved around the mat, our feet familiar with what was next even as our muscles screamed in agony. Sweat clung to our bodies, our faces red and splotchy, but neither of us wanted to be the first to stop.

"Ready to tap out?" she taunted, her face smug as she clipped my rib.

"Are you?" I teased back, kicking her side in return.

"Nope."

We both grinned, continuing our battle across the ring, and loving every second. Most girls Rebecca's age wouldn't choose sparring on a Friday night, preferring to spend their free time shopping or hanging with friends. But Rebecca wasn't like other teenagers, having lived more life in her few years than most adults. Not that I could say much, considering at seventeen I'd been part of an illegal hacker club and arrested for breaking into the high school wearing stilettos.

Though they hadn't arrested me for wearing heels. That was just an unfortunate choice of footwear. I also hadn't known the hacker club was bad—yeah, I know, the words 'hacker club' should've been a clear sign, but I was in my rebellious phase—or that a jealous psychotic puppeteer had infiltrated my group.

But I digress...

"You think you're gonna be able to keep up with me once you're thirty?" Rebecca taunted, her breaths panting out in between the words, displaying her fatigue despite her bravado.

"Rude! Don't speak to your mother that way!"

She snorted, shaking her head as I advanced, kicking her side before punching her shoulder. She blocked the rib, but missed the jab, grunting as I clipped her.

Now, you might wonder how someone close to thirty had a seventeen-year-old daughter. Well, you see, when a man and a woman loved one another...

Record screech. Just kidding. It had nothing to do with the birds and the bees, but I totally had you there. Didn't I?

The answer was adoption, obviously.

I hadn't been able to kick the hacker bug, though my gigs were of the white-hacker variety these days and funneled through our security firm. Asa, Cohen, and Ryker had expanded A.S.S— Samson's firm—and opened their own branch—F.I.S.T.

No, that's not a typo. Apparently, when naming one's company, you didn't make it past third grade. Men. Smh.

Milo had accepted a position with a sport's clinic near Boston after finishing his residency at Lux. Working with top-tier athletes had given him a passion for sport's medicine, sending him in an all new direction. He now had his own clinic and volunteered his time at local schools.

Asa had learned a lot working with his dad, and with Cohen and Ryker's experience from the Order, they decided to start their own company—Foxtrot Innovative Security Training—on the east coast after we got married.

Foxtrot—as it was referred to over F.I.S.T (go figure!)—provided surveillance, technology, and training to Fortune 500 companies and major events like the Olympics, the Super Bowl, and even a Taylor Swift concert once. Asa, Cohen, and Ryker all performed various roles within Foxtrot, keeping them all busy. The best part about Foxtrot in my opinion was the off-book work we did, providing white-hacker jobs and training to those in need. I finally had a way to help others that actually made a difference.

We'd worked with women, men, and kids running from domestic violence to sextortion. It was these types of jobs that I loved, and where I'd met Rebecca five years ago. Ryker and I had gone out on a job, responding to an S.O.S message our servers had picked up. Majority of the time, the information ended up being useless, outdated, or in the worse cases, too late.

When my eyes met hers huddled in the corner with her arms wrapped around three other girls protecting them, I knew we needed each other. Strength and resiliency reflected back and spoke to my soul. Despite the horrific living conditions and trauma she'd been subjected to, she hadn't given up; protecting the others and fighting to find a way out. She was smart and resourceful, and snuck a cell phone to place the message, inevitably saving her and the other girls' lives.

The path to where we were now hadn't been easy, but looking at the strong young woman she'd become had been worth all the sleepless nights.

When I wasn't helping with Foxtrot, I worked on my athletic fashion label with HTC designing skating costumes. In the past year, I'd added hockey, skiing, and snowboarding to my brand. I worked a lot, but I loved my jobs and got to do them from home, giving me the flexibility and freedom I craved. Which was needed being a mom of toddlers *and* a teenager.

"You're both gonna be sore for the party tomorrow," Asa said from the side, leaning against the ropes.

"I already tried. They won't stop until one of them retreats, or a winner's called," Ryker added.

"So, basically they'll be here all night and miss the twin's party," Cohen chimed in.

"We're both right here and can hear you," I panted, wiping my brow with my wrist. Rebecca paused, her breathing just as labored as she looked from me to her dads.

"Is any of it wrong, darling?" Milo asked, joining the others, his glasses tilted as he stared at me sweetly. My body heated at his use of darling and the knowing glint in his eye told me he'd done it on purpose.

"Wait. If you're all here, who's with the twins?" I asked, panic climbing my throat. They might be turning four, but they were devious and not to be trusted on their own.

All four of my husbands smirked, and I glanced at Rebecca, who'd gone over to them. She took a water bottle from Asa and gulped the whole thing before accepting the offered towel from Milo. I smiled as I watched them, loving how much of a family we'd all become over the years.

The guys and I had been married for six years now, parents to 'soon-to-be' four-year-old twins, Campbell and Kennedy, and seventeen-year-old, Rebecca. We lived on the outskirts of Boston in a home the guys had renovated over the years, complete with a big backyard, tree fort, and a pond to skate on. We'd even gotten a dog named Daisy and a potbelly pig we called Lulu.

"Well?" I asked, standing akimbo when no one answered. The men I loved all stared at me with grins dripping in secrecy, instantly raising red flags. "What did you do?"

I turned to Rebecca, who grinned next to Asa, his arm around her shoulder. I lifted my brow. "Do you know? Were you part of this?" I demanded, waving my finger back and forth.

Rebecca shrugged her shoulders, miming that her lips were sealed. Climbing under the rope, I wiped the sweat from my forehead and pulled a shirt on over my head, not caring whose it was at this point. My Finley senses were tingling, and I couldn't tell if I would love whatever surprise they had for me, or hate it. And with my husbands, it usually erred on the hate side, unfortunately.

Over the years, my husbands often tried to surprise me, but it rarely went as well as they planned. Mostly because it was hard to get things past me when I could hack circles around most of them —Cohen and Ryker excluded, but I had different tricks up my sleeve for those two that involved a bottle of lube and a blindfold. Ah, good times.

The few times the four of them managed to actually surprise me had ended in disasters. There had only been two times in our eight years together that hadn't resulted in tears or ER visits—the night they proposed and the day the adoption was final.

So considering there was no big romantic gesture on the horizon, I wasn't holding my breath that I'd love *this* surprise, especially considering they'd managed to keep it a secret.

"Don't be so glum, Fin. I think we nailed this one," Asa said, his voice calm and soothing. He walked over, pulling me into his arms and rubbing my back. I placed my head against his chest, loving how strong he was. His heartbeat was steady, easing some of my anxiety.

"I want to believe you, babe. I do. But history hasn't been on our side and with the twin's birthday party tomorrow, I don't want to spend the night cleaning shaving cream off the ceiling, or glitter out of the dog's fur. No telling what they'd do to poor Lulu."

Cohen snorted, leaning his head on Ryker's shoulder as he wrapped his arms around him from behind. "There are far better ways to use—"

"Ew. Child still present!" Rebecca cut in, glaring at Cohen.

He stuck out his tongue. "I was going to say—"

She held up her hand, stopping him as she fervently shook her head. "Nope. I don't need that mental picture in my head. I'm still scarred from seeing you and Ry in kilts."

"Hey, I rocked that kilt!" Ryker protested, pouting.

"And you wonder why I don't bring friends over," she sighed, hanging her head. Her blonde strands fell around her face, covering her brown eyes. Freckles dotted her nose and cheeks, her ivory skin prone to burning in the sun. She was tall and fit, having worked out with all of us for years, giving her back her power.

"You have friends?" Cohen gasped.

"Yeah, but I know better than to tell you two or invite them over. Not that Mom's any better," she teased, glancing at me. "You'd have their entire history printed out with everything they'd ever googled. Nope. Don't need that embarrassment."

"Aw, do you hear that? We're embarrassing! Parenting skill unlocked." Cohen held his hand up for Ryker to slap.

"And this is why only Dad Milo is allowed to take me to school," Rebecca chided.

"Hey! I don't do anything embarrassing," Asa protested.

"Not intentionally," Rebecca cringed, wringing her hands. "But you called me pumpkin in front of half the school and they chanted 'pumpkin, pumpkin, eater' to me for months."

Asa's face blanched, his cheeks red as he grimaced. "Ah, sorry, pumpk—"

Rebecca shook her head, walking over and hugging him around the waist.

"It's okay. I like it when you call me pumpkin, Dad. Just not in front of my friends."

Asa's eyes filled as he pecked the top of her head. "Duly noted, pumpkin."

"So, Asa's the sweet one, Milo's the responsible one, and we're the embarrassing ones?" Ryker asked, tilting his head back to

Cohen. "Are we okay with that? Personally, I always thought we'd be the cool ones." Ryker stuck out his bottom lip, blinking his eyes at Rebecca. I chuckled into my hand, loving the fact Ryker's charm didn't work with teenagers.

Rebecca sighed, letting go of Asa and walking over to the pair. She wrapped her arms around both of them in a tight hug.

"You can be both, but I don't want you to change. I love you as you are, even the embarrassing bits. Just, teenagers are assholes."

"You're not wrong," Cohen said, snorting. They both stroked her hair, giving her cheek kisses.

"And because we're the cool but embarrassing dads, we won't even yell at you for language," Ryker said. "But I will need a list of these so-called friends. I'll only do a small background check. The tiniest kind there is."

"Mom!" Rebecca shouted.

"Guys, if you think I haven't done a thorough check on every kid at her school then I'm offended," I replied, making my husbands laugh and daughter groan.

"Argh! I can't wait to go to college."

"Lies! You love us too much to leave," Cohen said, tickling her.

I smiled as I watched my husbands be dads in action. Which reminded me…

"Ugh. You distracted me!" I stomped, spinning on my heels.

Before I made it, the door of the gym wrenched open and two tornadoes stumbled into the room right on top of one another.

"Mom!" Kennedy shouted, running with her twin hot on her tail. Her dark hair, so similar to Ryker's, swung around her, the curls bouncing as she skidded to a stop a few feet from me. Campbell didn't have the same luxury, barreling into her and knocking them both into me. I stumbled from their combined weight, my arms squeezing them to me to stay upright. Asa's hands landed on my hips, steadying me.

"Whoa! You guys okay?" I asked, pulling them apart and

checking them over. Their faces were pink, but otherwise they appeared okay.

Campbell gave me a sheepish smile as his cheeks pinked from his clumsiness. His golden hair fell into his brown eyes as he hid his face.

Despite being Cohen's son, he had Milo's sweet disposition and Asa's charm. Kennedy, on the other hand, was very much her father with her strong-will and assertiveness combined with Cohen's personality flair. I already dreaded the day she became a teenager. The girl was pure spitfire.

"Campy you're so clumsy," Kennedy whined, pushing out her bottom lip.

"I'm sorry, Kendy." Campbell rubbed his eyes as tears formed. Kennedy instantly dropped her pout, falling into big sister mode and wrapping her little arms around him.

"It's okay, Campy. We'll do it together next time. O'tay?" She asked, kissing his cheek.

"O'tay." He nodded, wrapping his arms around her.

While the twins weren't identical, or even shared the same father for that matter, they were very close.

How could they be twins if they didn't have the same father, you ask?

Well, after several years of unsuccessful pregnancies, we tried IVF. All four of my husbands provided sperm, and the doctor made a cocktail of sorts, and boom! Two eggs were fertilized by different sperm. I worried we'd be considered freaks, but apparently it's not an unheard of phenomenon. In fact, it even had a name—heteropaternal superfecundation.

Don't try saying that four times fast, though. Total tongue twister.

The guys had been over the moon, not caring who the biological fathers were, determined to love our babies as their own. It was only because Campbell and Kennedy looked so much like their fathers, and a health complication early on, that we even knew. But it hadn't changed their love for our children—Rebecca included.

I glanced around at the rest of the room, taking in the faces of my four husbands and teenage daughter. They watched the twins, love and adoration in their eyes, as they waited for whatever surprise they had for me to be revealed. Now that the twins were here and not running amok upstairs on their own, my anxiety settled and I opted to give everyone the benefit of the doubt.

See, I could grow and change too!

"What has you rushing in here so fast?" I asked, squatting down to their level. Their eyes swiveled to Asa behind me, their heads nodding at whatever he said, and they grinned, returning their gazes to me.

"Auntie Sawyer and Uncles are here!" Kennedy said, jumping up and down.

"Wait, what?" I asked, my mouth falling open. "For real?" I asked, twisting and looking at the guys. Because we lived further away from everyone, we didn't get to see them as often as I'd like, making visits rare and special.

"Yes, momma bear. They're here for the twins' birthday and then they're going to watch the kids while we take you away for our anniversary."

"Pop-pop and Gamma are here too!" Campbell added, using the words he had for my parents.

Tears gathered in my eyes at my husbands' sweet gesture. I was suddenly glad I hadn't known about this surprise. It was much better being kept out of the loop for once. I'd been so busy planning Kennedy and Campbell's fourth birthday that I'd forgotten about our anniversary. Well, more like figured that seven years wasn't all that special, and we'd go out to dinner and that would be it.

Knowing they hadn't been willing to sacrifice that, meant the world to me. Plus, a week away seemed sublime. I loved my kids and my job, but damn. Free time to myself and not answering a million questions every minute sounded exquisite.

And all the sex, of course.

But make no mistake, the quiet time had been my first thought. Ssh.

"Come on, turds, let's go show our cousins the new fort!" Rebecca said, stepping up to them and placing her hands on their shoulders. Both of the twins adored her, following her around as much as she would allow. But even when she pretended to hate them, she loved them, her protectiveness strong.

Campbell's mouth dropped open as he gripped Kennedy's hand, his eyes wide as he stared at me. "Do you think they will like it?"

"I think they'll love it!" I kissed his nose, and he curled into me, wrapping his little arms around my neck.

"Let's go, Campy! Race you, Becca!" Kennedy shouted, taking her brother's hand and dragging him out of the room. Campbell was the cuddler of the two, so it didn't surprise me when she ran without saying goodbye, too much excitement going on.

Rebecca rolled her eyes, but followed, stopping at the door. "By the way, I totally won, Mom. It counts on my record!" She grinned, tossing me a wave over her shoulder.

She'd been working toward a kickboxing instructor certification so she could work with Foxtrot to train victims of DV and trauma, something she was passionate about with her history.

"Fine," I groaned, blowing her a kiss. Once the kids were out of the room, I turned to my husbands, tears in my eyes. "I can't believe you got Sawyer and the gang here. It's been over a year since I've seen my best friend and brother."

"Which is why we were certain this surprise would be a good one for once," Milo said, kissing me.

"It was your sister's idea, wasn't it?" I said, when Asa wouldn't meet my eyes.

"I have no clue what you're talking about," Asa chirped, running away. I pounced on his back before he could get too far, the other three laughing.

"I think this is the perfect time to mention we also got you a present. Ones in the form of shoes and sparkles," Ryker whispered, his breath sending shivers through me as it fanned over my neck.

"Eep!" I jumped off Asa's back, sprinting out of the room.

My footwear might consist mostly of comfortable flats these days, but I could still rock a great pair of heels—even if I was an almost thirty-year-old mom of three.

Two

FINLEY

I stared at the small suitcase on the bed in horror. I loved my husbands, but they were out of their freaking minds.

"Why do you look like someone just told you Crocs were fashionable?" Sawyer asked, lifting her brow as she walked into my bedroom.

"Because apparently I'm only allowed to take this suitcase." I gestured to the suitcase, narrowing my eyes at it. "We've been together for eight years and they think I can pack a week's worth of clothes in this… in this baby bag!" I flopped back onto the bed, covering my eyes. I couldn't look at it anymore.

"Okay, Fin. I think you're being a little dramatic." Sawyer chuckled, crossing her arms. She stood at the end of the bed, eyeing me.

"No. I'm being the appropriate amount of dramatic. Thank you very much!" I sat up and we both giggled. Wrapping my arms around my best friend, I pulled her onto the bed, cuddling into her like old times.

"I've missed you." I sighed.

"I've missed you, too. Screw our husbands. Let's escape on this trip together and leave them with the kids."

"As tempting as that sounds, do you really want to deal with your brother's wrath? Because I know I don't want to deal with mine."

Sawyer grimaced, sighing. "Fine, you might have a point. But what I think I really hear you saying is that we need to plan a girls' trip."

"Now you're talking! We could check in with Henley and Chloe, too."

"Done. Okay, let me see if I can help you pack. Which drawer holds your underwear?" She jumped off the bed, her natural athleticism on display as she stalked to my closet. I pointed in the general vicinity, knowing her nosiness would lead her to the right drawer.

"Damn girl. Check you out!" Sawyer held up a black lacy negligee with garter straps.

I snorted. "Don't get too excited. It still has the tags on."

"Even more reason for you to take it. In fact, I think the only things you need are these." She dumped my entire underwear drawer into my suitcase, tossed in a few bikinis, and then zipped it shut.

"What about makeup and shampoo and shoes?" I asked, lifting a brow.

"Honey, if you have time to put on makeup, then you're not enjoying your vacation like you should." She sassed, smiling at me.

I rolled my eyes, too tired to contradict her after the whirlwind of a day. The twins' party had been a blast, but having a million houseguests was exhausting.

Climbing off the bed, I walked over to my closet, closed my eyes and picked out a few items and handed them to her.

"Here. This way I don't know what they are, but at least I have something other than bras and panties to wear."

"Fine," she groaned, huffing as she took them from me.

Next, I went into the bathroom and grabbed my travel kit and handed it to her, knowing that if I was out of anything, I could get it wherever we were going. I also grabbed a couple pairs of shoes that would go with anything, my chargers, and last, my passport.

"Alright, that about does it."

Sawyer pulled the suitcase off the bed and followed me out of the room. All the kids were asleep, and we'd said our goodbyes after the twins' party. My husbands figured it would be easier to ensure we actually left if we did it while they were asleep. They had a point. As much as I wanted this time away, it was hard to say bye.

Walking into the living room, everyone looked up, pure shock on their faces.

"What?" I asked, crossing my arms.

My brother stood, smiling as he walked over and pulled me into a hug. "They had a bet going on how many suitcases you'd try to smuggle and how long it would take you. The fact you didn't throw any fits or demand one suitcase for shoes alone means the majority of them lost money."

"Serves you all right! I can be reasonable." My parents and Sawyer's husbands laughed, so I rolled my eyes at them.

"It was good to see you, Sis. I wish it was longer, but I know you need this trip even if I don't want to think about what you're going to get up to on it."

I scrunched up my face. "Ew, Henry. Do what I do and pretend like you have Ken and Barbie doll parts." I shuddered.

Henry and Sawyer laughed, before Sawyer's face took on an evil glint and I knew I'd regret whatever she said next. Your best friend being married to your brother wasn't as fun as it sounded, though I couldn't say much since I'd married her twin.

"Except you walked in on us, so you know that's bull—"

"And that's my cue to leave."

"Don't walk into rooms without knocking then," Henry taunted.

It seemed no matter how old you got, your big brother still picked on you. After hugging my parents, Sawyer and my brother goodbye, I faced my husbands. Ryker gave me a soft smile as he walked over and took my suitcase.

"Come on, little hacker, they'll be fine. They'll have too much fun to miss us and you know I have a team on standby."

"We all need this, sweetheart," Cohen said, wrapping his arms around both of us.

I nodded, swiping away the tears. "It's just the first time we've all been away this long."

"Which is why you need to go," Sawyer reminded me. "Besides, if you don't, we haven't unpacked yet and will take your plane and leave *you* with the kids." She planted her hands on her hips, her face deadly serious.

Panic flooded me and I waved goodbye over my shoulder as I raced to the door.

"Bye!"

Laughter followed behind me, but I knew my best friend wasn't joking. She would leave me with her kids, and that was not the week I had in mind.

The guys were quiet as we drove to the airport, and I assumed it was because they were afraid of saying anything that would give away our destination. Now that they had pulled off a good surprise, they wanted to ride that wave until they crashed. Milo pulled me into his arms, kissing my forehead as I snuggled into him.

"You can close your eyes, darling. We still have a way to go and you're gonna need your rest."

Knowing he was right, I did as he suggested, the exhaustion of the past week catching up to me.

"FIN, IT'S TIME TO WAKE UP. WE'RE HERE, BABY," ASA MURMURED, HIS hand grazing my cheek.

Blinking, I rubbed the sleep for my eyes as I adjusted to the brightness of the sunlight coming through the windows.

"Where is here exactly?" I asked.

"Nice try," Cohen said, giving me a wink.

I didn't know if I was more in shock that I had slept for that long or that I still had no clue where we were. "I don't think I've gotten that many hours of uninterrupted sleep since the twins were born."

"If I have anything to say about it, it will be the only time this week," Ryker teased.

The heated looks in their eyes told me exactly what they had planned and I couldn't deny I was all for it. Between my two jobs, four husband's schedules, a teenager and the twin tornadoes, it was difficult to find alone time. The few crucial minutes we had, it was always a toss up between sleep or sex. And a lot of times, sleep won. There was never enough of it.

"But first," Cohen said, interrupting Ryker. "We will leave you with this."

He handed me a thick black envelope and pointed to the bedroom at the back of the plane. Walking toward it, adrenaline surged as I envisioned what it could be. When the guys had proposed, they did it with a spy game, much like the ones the four of us had solved to take down MKG.

Only our games had more of a sexual nature and ended with everyone having a happy ending.

The thought of a new game made my body shiver and my heart raced as I pushed through the bedroom door. Sitting on the edge of the bed, I realized how quiet it had gotten on the plane; not even the crew was left on board. I'd been so focused on the card, I hadn't heard anyone leave.

Taking a deep breath, I flipped the card over and pushed up the back. Thick card stock slid out, the same dark ebony as the envelope.

To our dearest wife,

This vacation isn't like your typical beach stay or amusement park visit. Far from it. For one, this island is secluded. Once you step off this plane, the only people here are your husbands, a driver, medic, and a cook. The three people you're not married to have strict instructions on when they can be out, what they're allowed to do, and where they can be. If you encounter them, you won't be able to use them for any help.

In order to reach the ultimate prize at the end of this game, you must make it past each stage to rescue one of your husbands. How well you do convincing someone to let you pass will earn you rewards, but take too long and you won't like the punishments. (Trust us on this one.)

All the tools you'll need are in the bag left for you. How you use them is up to you.

Feel free to be creative. It's encouraged, actually.

Once you step off this plane, you're no longer Finley Reyes-Jensen, you're Oblivion.

Happy Hunting.

Your husbands.

OPENING THE BLACK GARMENT BAG, I PULLED OUT A TRENCH COAT AND the black lacy negligee Sawyer had packed. I flipped it inside out, expecting something to be missing. Nope. Just these two. God I hoped we were somewhere warm.

Next to the garment bag was a shoe box, so I lifted the lid, and a red pair of stilettos glistened up at me. Unzipping the last bag, I snorted at the ribbon, handcuffs, and lipstick. I guess I knew which skills I'd be using today.

Arousal zipped through me as I changed into the outfit, feeling brazen and badass as I stepped off the plane in nothing but high heels, red lipstick, and a trench coat, the handcuffs and ribbon in my pocket.

Strutting to the black car parked ahead, I flipped my collar up and embodied my character for sexy spy.

"Alright, boys. It's time to play. You want Oblivion... you got her. Game on."

Three

FINLEY

The quiet wrapped around me as I walked to the car, the eeriness of it heightening my awareness. My heels click clacked against the pavement, echoing with each step, and reminding me why I quit wearing them on missions.

Stilettos might be sexy, but they were far from stealthy.

The hairs on the back of my neck stood up, the feeling of being watched present as I neared the idling car. The engine was practically silent, heightening the fact there wasn't anyone else around. At least no one I could see. There was no doubt in my mind that someone was watching.

Adrenaline shot up at the prospect of danger, excitement ramping as I opened the door and slid in. The partition was closed, not surprising me, and the car took off the second I clipped in my seatbelt. I cataloged all the information, not knowing what was important yet. It could be one of my husbands driving, or one of the few staff on site like they said. They hoped to rattle me by keeping me in the dark, breaking my concentration, and hindering my ability to sway someone to my side.

If I didn't know who the players were, I couldn't trust anyone.

The trick was, it took a lot more to shake me, something they'd soon discover. I smiled, leaning back in the seat as my heart thudded in my chest, reminding me how alive missions made me feel. It had been so long since I'd been out in the field—motherhood had a way of derailing those types of jobs. But with each brief glimpse of my past life, I gained a piece of my badassery back.

Crossing my legs, I spotted a small black box in the seat next to me. It practically blended in with the black leather, making it difficult to spot. Opening it up, I discovered another piece of cardstock. My fingers ran over the material, loving the attention to detail and thought that had gone into this operation.

Though, I didn't know if that meant I'd lost my skills at noticing things if they were able to keep this hidden for so long.

But that was something I could ponder later.

FINLEY,
"TRUE NORTH ALWAYS LEADS US BACK TO YOU."
LOVE,
ASA, MILO, RYKER, COHEN

A compass sat beneath the card, shiny and ornate. Picking it up, the weight surprised me, heavy in my hand. I turned it over, peering at all sides of it, and discovered a clasp, where I assumed the opening would be. There had to be a second piece to open it.

My mind sorted through all the information I'd gathered so far, putting it into columns. This might not be a proper mission where life and death were involved, but it didn't mean I'd take it any less seriously. I'd use everything at my disposal to make it through their tests.

With the way my body responded to everything so far, I'd needed this more than I'd known. Something my husbands had understood. They were reminding me I was more than a mom and wife. More than a sometimes hacker and designer.

I was strong and loyal.

I was smart and sexy.

I was a badass, and when I needed to be, deadly.

I was a woman.

When I was younger, I was a bit reckless, overly confident in my abilities, and stubborn to a fault. Maturing had a funny way of making you see things differently. Though, it seemed I'd forgotten you didn't have to be reckless to be a boss bitch. With maturity and patience on my side, there was no way I wouldn't ace this mission.

Sexy spy unleashed!

The car slowed a few minutes later, pulling up to an expansive building that spanned further than I could see. A fountain sat out front in the middle of the circle driveway. Tropical fauna kept the surrounding areas hidden, adding to the seclusion. My fingers itched to run a scan for security cameras and alarms, but without a phone or computer I had to rely on my other skills.

Climbing out of the car, the buzz of insects exploded in my ears with the faint sound of an ocean in the distance. Birds cawed, and the wind blew the leaves, creating a cacophony of island noises that erased all of my anxiety. Tilting my head up at the sun, I relished in the warmth as I inhaled the salty air. This was the best sort of medicine.

Giving the house a thorough glance, I opted to head straight through the front. With the lack of intel, I expected they had traps in the back for me, so I might as well go through the front. This felt more like a covert operation, playing a part to gather the intel versus one where I needed to break in and steal something.

With that in mind, I needed to play along and gather the clues as they presented them to me, then I could make my play.

Climbing the steps, I tried to be quiet as my heels announced my arrival, though it was unlikely it had gone unnoticed since the car had sped off. The flaps of my coat fluttered around my knees, the air hitting me in spots I wasn't used to. Lust pooled in my belly and I picked up my steps, eagerness fueling me as I approached the door. With a deep breath, I pushed it open and strode to the front desk.

Ryker stood up, crossing his arms as he watched me approach. He wore a black uniform and a fake mustache so hideous my steps faltered as I tried not to laugh. His eyes danced with mischief, daring me to say something as he reached up, petting it like an '80s porn star.

"You need a key to get past this level, Ma'am."

"Ma'am?" I lifted my brows, crossing my arms. "You can call me, Madame."

"Hmm, Madame is it." He rubbed his chin, his pupils dilating. "Well, the rule still applies, *Madame.*"

"That's the thing about rules, they're easy to break. I know a few ways to change your mind."

"Doubtful. I like to play by the book." He snickered, clearly enjoying this ruse as much as I did.

I walked around the white desk, crowding him between it. He dropped his eyes down to me, licking his lips as he took me in. The playful attitude was gone, the sensual lover I knew present.

"Let me introduce you to a new book," I whispered, grabbing his shirt in my fist. I trailed one hand up his chest, pushing him into the chair behind him. He went easily, not fighting me as I skimmed my palms up his thighs. I could feel his cock growing thick against his leg, rubbing my hand over it as I squeezed. He groaned, shifting so I'd grab more.

With my fingers on his zipper, I paused, meeting his eyes. "Are you sure we can't work something out?"

"I think I could make an exception just this once."

Smirking, I lowered his zipper and palmed the thick appendage. Ryker's head fell back, a deep moan leaving his mouth. Reaching into his boxers, I pulled him out, giving him a few strokes as I slid down to the ground. Licking the pierced tip, a drop of pre-cum hit my tongue as I stroked the base with my hand. Swirling my tongue around him, I sucked his cock before withdrawing, and licking up the underside. Saliva coated his hard dick and I hummed as I sucked, his whimpers urging me on.

Gripping his balls in my other hand, I tugged on them as I took him further down my throat, knowing exactly what Ryker liked at this point. He thrust his hips forward, my lips stretched around him as I watched him from below.

"Goddamn, little hacker. Your mouth is heaven." Ryker cupped my jaw, his thumb grazing me softly as he stared into my eyes, love and lust shining at me. "I'm already so close." He moaned as his head fell back, his grip on me tighter as he fucked my mouth. "Don't stop."

His tip hit the back of my throat, the piercing rubbing as I swallowed around him, making him groan harder. Sliding back off, I sucked him hard, running my tongue over the tip right as he erupted, twitching in my hand and filling my mouth with his cum. Once I had every drop cleaned off, I tucked him back in his pants, licking my lips as I stood. Ryker's face was blissed out, not even the mustache could hide how satisfied he looked.

"Good luck, little hacker." He kissed me hard, stealing my breath before he pulled away and handed me the keycard. "Top floor."

He pretended to walk the other way, whistling like he didn't see me. Chuckling, I took the opportunity and headed to the elevator bay.

My arousal was evident between my legs as I strutted, the slickness dripping onto my thighs with each step. I hoped whoever I encountered next would help me with that problem.

I slid into the elevator, using the card to gain access to the top floor. Once the doors closed, I leaned back against the elevator and looked around. There didn't seem to be a camera, but that didn't mean there wasn't one. They were so small these days, they could hide anywhere. When the elevator came to a stop midway up, I stood up, preparing myself for what was to come.

Hehe. Cum.

Milo strolling onto the elevator in an all black business suit was not what I expected. He didn't meet my eyes, but I caught the corner of his mouth as it tilted up on one side. He adjusted his glasses, hitting a button for a floor. The elevator resumed, the quiet now obvious as I waited to see if he would say anything or if I should.

Before I could, he reached out and pulled the stop button, halting the elevator. He turned, advancing before I could react, bracketing his arms on either side of me.

"You're not supposed to be in here," he purred.

"I have a key." I lifted it up, showing it as I smiled. Seeing Milo this way always gave me a thrill. His shyness was long gone and I loved seeing him as the confident man he was.

"And just what did you do to obtain it?" He trailed a finger down my cheek.

"I have ways of persuading people."

"Well, I won't be as easy. Turn around. I need to search you and see what other contraband you might have."

I did as he asked, pressing my hands against the wall. His body pressed into mine from behind and my heart thumped in my chest, as I waited to see what he'd do.

"Spread your legs. I need to ensure you're not carrying a weapon."

"I don't need to carry a weapon," I retorted as he dropped to the ground.

I am the weapon.

Milo's fingers skimmed up my legs, and I had to bite my cheek to stop from moaning. Goosebumps trailed after him, my breath catching as he went higher. When his fingers trailed under my coat, I pressed my forehead against the wall, my legs shaking.

Milo traced the garters, eliciting shivers through me as he hummed. His nose followed, his stubble brushing against my inner thigh as I panted. One finger trailed over my mound, his finger but a mere touch.

"You're dripping, darling." He didn't give me more as he stood, squeezing my ass in his hands before moving them to the belt and untying it. The trench coat fell open, his chest pressing into me again. His hands continued to fondle my front, his perfect fingers driving me wild as he touched me. But it wasn't enough.

"Are you satisfied?" I asked, my voice a raspy sound.

"Not yet. I have one more search." His breath fanned over my neck, his tongue licking up my throat. "If you move, I stop."

Before I could question, he pressed something at my entrance. He pushed in as the sound started, the vibrations sending pleasure through me as he pulled it in and out. When he hit another button, a new sound joined and my knees buckled as something flicked against my clit.

"Hot fudge sundae," I cursed, my eyes rolling back. I whimpered, the sound escaping against my will. Milo fucked me with the vibrator against the wall of the elevator, bringing me to orgasm so quickly, the world spun. My legs shook as it took over me, his arm around my waist the only thing keeping me standing.

"Good girl, but I think you can take more."

I whimpered, because while it had been amazing, I did need more.

"What do you want?" I asked, breathless.

"Wrong question. Keep fucking yourself with this while I prep your ass."

He took my hand, placing it on the handle of the vibrator. His body heat left me as he kneeled behind me, lifting my coat again. I pushed the vibrator in and out, my legs shaking in my heels as he pushed one finger inside my ass. Bracing my free hand on the wall, I spread my legs wider.

"Ah, yes," I moaned, my head a haze of lust as the vibrator flicked my clit and hit me deep as Milo pushed two fingers in, matching the pace of my thrusts.

"You're doing so good, darling. I'm going to be smelling your cum on me the rest of the day. You've drenched my hands."

"Holy cornflakes. I'm coming," I screamed as he plunged in another finger. My walls clamped around the vibrating dildo as everything else went dark and stars appeared in my vision as pleasure rushed through me like a tsunami.

Coming to, I realized I'd been turned around, cradled in Milo's arms. He kissed me softly, smoothing my hair back as I regained consciousness.

"I could watch you do that every day and never get bored. I love watching you take your own pleasure."

"Mm," I moaned, happiness floating through me. "I love how you show me new ways to find it."

He chuckled, kissing my nose. "Are you having fun?"

"The most."

"Good." He kissed me again, and I lost myself in the pleasure, floating in the afterglow. "I'm going to restart the elevator now. You're almost to the end."

I nodded, pulling away to stand on my own. Milo gave me a soft smile as he hit the button, the elevator resuming. I'd forgotten about us being stopped, so the sudden lurch had me gripping the railing.

When the elevator arrived on the top floor, I pulled out the handcuffs from my pocket and clasped one to Milo's wrist and the other to the bar.

"I thought you said you weren't carrying any weapons." He lifted his brow in a challenge, grinning.

"No, I said I didn't *need* to carry any weapons."

"What do you call this?" He lifted his wrist.

"A good time." I stepped off the elevator, turning as the doors closed and blew him a kiss, loving his laugh.

Now to find my prisoner and get my ultimate prize.

Four

FINLEY

I walked out onto a marble floor, the sun reflecting brightly off it as it shone through the floor to ceiling windows. The space was filled with luxurious furniture and had a fireplace. Not sure one was needed on an island, but it looked nice. I couldn't see much from my spot out the windows, and with the need to find my next test, I didn't stop to look.

Walking down the hallway, the plug Milo had inserted moved with each step and I felt tingles racing up my spine in anticipation. My clit pulsed with aftershocks as I moved deeper, scanning each door as I passed. They were all open and empty, so I kept moving, knowing my prize was close.

The last door was closed with a lock, so I used the keycard, excitement building as I stepped inside the dimly lit room. A tall man stood with his back to me, his profile in the shadows, making it difficult for me to identify who it was. That was the problem with marrying four men who were all tall and muscular, only Milo being trimmer than the other three.

So when they were clothed, it was difficult to tell them apart from just their backs. Four husband problems.

But if I had to guess, this was Cohen, more apt to play the villain than Asa. I surveyed the room as I neared, knowing whoever it was would say something first. It looked like a normal office with bookshelves and a desk, nothing interesting standing out.

"I've been waiting for you," the voice said, all dark and mysterious.

"Oh? That's nice. I can't say the same," I sassed, smiling.

He turned, and I held in my shock as I took in Asa. His hair was brushed back, his strong jaw on display as he stared at me. His navy suit was crisp and fit him perfectly, making my mouth water from the sight alone. He walked around the desk, leaning against it as he perched his delicious ass on the edge.

"You've put on quite a good show so far, using your skills to get what you want."

I glanced down at his crotch as I slipped the trench coat off. I walked forward slowly, letting him eye me as I neared.

"Oh? And have you liked what you've seen?" I asked, placing my hands on his thighs, bending so my breasts were perfectly eye level.

Asa swallowed, his eyes dropping down. "It's been good, but I wonder if you can do better."

"What do you have in mind?" I asked, trailing my finger over his groin. He groaned and I took his hand, leading it between my thighs. His fingers eagerly pressed into me, giving me a little of what I needed. He continued to fuck me with his fingers, my hand on his wrist, as our eyes held one another.

He growled, moving to whisper in my ear. "Put on a show for me and if it's good enough, I'll let you and the prisoner go."

"That it?" I asked, confused, riding his hand between my legs. It seemed to easy.

"It won't be as easy as you think."

Giving him a smug smile, I threw my head back as I came, covering his hand with my cum. He pulled his fingers out once my pussy released him, his eyes still holding mine as he sucked them clean.

"I don't know. I'm pretty good with my hands," I teased.

"Hmm, well, you won't get to start with them," he whispered, taking my hands and trapping them in his grip. He pulled a long ribbon out of his pocket similar to the one I had and wrapped it around my wrists, tying them together.

When he was satisfied, he stood, leading me to a secret door behind a bookcase. There on the bed was Cohen, naked, with his arms strapped to the frame.

"I've come to save you," I said, smiling at him.

"You have an interesting way of doing it," he teased, his eyes dropping to my tied hands.

"No, literally. I've come so many times already." I giggled, making Cohen snort.

"Make it good, Fin baby," Asa whispered, before pushing me onto the bed. He took a seat in the corner in a large chair, spreading his legs wide.

Asa had discovered he loved to watch and could do it for hours, edging himself before he caved. I guess now I could understand why he was playing the villain.

Crawling to Cohen on my knees, I placed his dick between my tied arms, stroking him. I moved closer to his face, capturing his lips with mine as he grew harder.

"Sit on my face, Fin. Give me your cream, sweetheart."

Doing as he said, I straddled his face and placed my own near his dick. Neither of us had the use of our hands, but thankfully we were both talented with our mouths. Swirling my tongue over his cock, I sucked the tip as I took him as far as I could. His tongue flicked my sensitive clit and I moaned, slurping on his dick as I chased it with my mouth.

We both fell into the rhythm as I rode his face, and he pushed up into my mouth, his tongue going deep. My legs shook next to his head, another orgasm impending as I drew back, flipping myself around and straddling him. His dick slid into me easily, and I braced myself on his chest.

"Fuck yeah," he groaned.

Flicking my hips forward, I stared at Cohen as we lost ourselves in one another. His eyes darted behind me, giving me a moment's notice as hands landed on my shoulder.

"You're doing such a good job, little hacker, so I'll either let your hands free or the prisoners."

"His," I said, not even having to consider it. I needed Cohen to touch me, to caress my skin and cherish me.

Ryker stepped up to the headboard, releasing Cohen's hands and giving me a saucy grin. He took Cohen's wrists, kissing them where the ribbon had held them, running his tongue over the skin to soothe it.

Ryker crawled onto the bed beside Cohen, kissing him and running his hands over Cohen's shoulders. I loved watching them together, but first I needed something from Ryker.

"I didn't say you could touch what's mine."

Ryker's head snapped up, his eyes flaring with lust as I challenged him.

"Sorry, *Madame*. What would you like for me to do?"

"I need you to stuff your big dick inside me and make me scream."

He glanced down to where Cohen and I were connected, clearly asking if I was sure.

"Is that going to be a problem?" I taunted. "Are you not brave enough to fuck me as your dick touches his?"

"Hot damn," Cohen breathed, pulling me closer to him, sucking my nipple through the lace. His hands gripped my ass, spreading them for Ryker.

"I want to feel you, Ry. Do it."

Ryker nodded, moving behind me and pressing me forward, watching our short thrusts. When he pressed the tip of his dick next to Cohen's, I debated whether I could do it, worried I'd bitten off more than I could chew.

"It will fit, sweetheart. Take a deep breath."

Doing as Cohen said, I relaxed and allowed Ryker in. When his thighs met the back of my ass, the three of us sighed in relief as pleasure pumped through us.

"Ready?" Ryker asked, pulling out before we could respond.

"Shit, fuck," Cohen cursed, pushing up as Ryker pulled out. They found a rhythm together, their cocks sliding against each other as they stretched my pussy, filling me up more than I thought was possible.

Grunts and moans pinged around the room, the smell of sex strong as the three of us fell into our own lust filled haze. Hands roamed and explored, gripping and flexing as our bodies moved together.

Cohen cried out first, his cum filling me as he came, his dick twitching and sending Ryker and me over the edge as we felt it. My body shook and I sighed as everything tingled and I momentarily forgot it was a game. We fell onto the bed, the three of us spooning as we recovered.

A throat clearing had me lifting my head, spotting a naked Milo with his cock standing at attention. Asa had also undressed, stroking himself as he watched me.

"Now you may have your hands untied before your big finale," Asa said, motioning for Milo to release the piece of material. He lifted me out of the pile of limbs, Ryker and Cohen moving closer together in my absence.

Milo kissed me gently, letting me cherish the afterglow as my body debated if it had anything left.

"You can do it," Milo whispered knowingly, kissing my neck.

I nodded, not wanting to disappoint them and the effort they'd gone to in order to give me this. Milo leaned against the pillows, cradling me in his arms, my back against his chest as he gave me time to recover. His hands roamed over my sensitive skin, sending tingles through me as the rough lace brushed against my nipples as they peeked out.

"You want to take this off?" he asked and I nodded, letting him unhook the top portion.

Now that my breast was free, he wrapped his mouth around it, sucking my nipple and making my toes curl. While he did that, his hands caressed my ass, gently removing the butt plug he'd inserted earlier.

I moaned at the loss, my ass twitching at its disappearance. Milo grabbed the bottle of lube, coating his dick and I clenched with anticipation. Leaning forward, I braced myself on my elbows and wiggled closer to him, holding my breath before he notched the tip of his dick to press in. Milo slid in easily, stretching me more since he was thicker than the plug. With slow thrusts, he worked me open, allowing me to adjust.

"Lay back on my chest, darling," he whispered and I did as he asked, moving slowly with his dick still impaled in me.

"More," I whimpered, as we adjusted, needing him to move. From this angle, he kept his thrusts short, and I opened my eyes to find my other three husbands watching. I'd forgotten they were there, so consumed by Milo.

Ryker and Cohen smirked, moving closer to us. When they were settled, Cohen gripped Ryker's chin and kissed him, owning him as Ryker became putty in his hands.

My body was spent, but I couldn't tear my eyes away from watching, whimpering as Milo filled me.

"Last test, sweetheart," Asa said, crawling onto the bed. "Can you satisfy me *and* Milo at the same time?"

I whimpered, but nodded. "Yes. I want that."

"Your pussy is dripping for me. I'm so close just from watching your show. It's gonna be hard and fast."

Asa kneeled between Milo's legs, lifting mine up and placing my knees on his shoulders as he centered himself at my pussy. He did exactly as he said, slamming into me in one thrust. Milo and I groaned together as Asa's cock pushed me back. Milo held my hips firm as Asa lost himself in his thrusts, pistoning in and out of me so fast, I was dizzy. His balls slapped against my ass, making Milo curse at the extra sensation.

After eight years together, they'd gotten used to accidental touching and just went with it. While they didn't actively engage in touching one another, they could accept it as long as I was involved, which worked for me.

"Fuck, fuck," Asa cursed, gripping my legs harder.

"Bet you can't come before she does again," Cohen teased, pushing into Ryker's ass.

"Game on," he said, meeting my eyes.

Asa smirked, pulling back to thrust in one more time before he came with a roar. Milo and I moaned, his body shaking beneath with the need to move, his own orgasm close now. Milo loved to edge, so he was typically the last to orgasm, only satisfied once I'd had several.

Asa pulled out, falling back onto the bed as he panted, taking my hand as Milo took over holding my legs, thrusting up into me quickly as he gained his rhythm.

Cohen fucked Ryker just as hard, tugging on his cock from the front as he held eyes with me, and giving me that sense of right-ness, the five of us united together.

"I'm coming," Milo groaned, stilling in me as he held me close to him, his cock twitching.

"Come, Fin," Cohen ordered smugly, groaning as he came in Ryker's ass. My eyes rolled back, and I heard Ryker's shout as I came, my body completely spent. I didn't know if he won, but I knew in the game of life I had.

At some point, everyone shifted and moved to a better position on the bed as someone cleaned me up, pressing soft kisses to my body. Every muscle in my body felt used and I loved how worn out I was. My pussy and ass throbbed in that decadent way that only great sex brought, and I smiled smugly, knowing this was only the start of our vacation.

"Did you have fun?" Asa asked into my shoulder, pulling me closer to his chest.

"So much. I like playing sexy spy."

"You're very good at it. Though, I'm glad you don't go out into the field anymore."

"Yeah, me too. I don't think I'd be as good in a real-life situation. I'll stick to hacking, designing, and the mom stuff."

"Mm, I like the sound of that. I think you're incredibly sexy as a mom."

"Definitely. Rebecca doesn't bring any boys over because they all think you're hot," Cohen said.

"What?" I asked, laughing.

"Yeah. It's not just us. All the kids at her school wonder how her parents are so young and hot."

"How do you know this?" I asked, lifting my head.

"Babe, come on," Ryker scoffed.

"Right. Just like I did the background checks, you probably have that school bugged."

"I would never! It's all perfectly legal."

I narrowed my eyes, not buying it. He laughed, relenting.

"We might've donated a new security system to the school and have to monitor it."

"Uh-huh, and why am I just now hearing about this?"

"I'm sure we told you," Asa said from behind. "Must've been when the twins were born and your brain was baby-fried."

"Dr. Milo, please explain how that's not true."

"Um, well…"

"That's it!" I rolled over, tackling them as I tried to put them in headlocks, but they were bigger and more of them, so they easily captured me, tickling me until I surrendered. My belly grumbled a few minutes later and the guys sat up, stretching.

"We should see if any food's been left out yet."

"Food? I'm in!"

We donned robes, and I followed them out another door, taking in the view of the ocean.

"Wow, this is beautiful."

"Oh, here," Asa said, handing me a smaller black box like the one from the car.

Taking it, I opened it, finding a small silver charm in the shape of a heart. "It's beautiful. Thank you."

"Press it to the compass," Milo suggested.

"Oh, it's in my coat."

Cohen handed it to me with a wink. Taking it, I pressed the heart to the compass, my eyes lighting up as it turned on. It showed eight hearts. Three of them together in one area, and five of them together in another.

"It's all of us and the kids. *'True north always leads us back to you.'* Now, you always have us close."

"And when you press this," Ryker said, pushing the side, "it sends a pulse to the recipient." He lifted his watch, a light blinking like the pulse of a heartbeat.

Tears filled my eyes as I took in the gift. They were my heart, and now, I'd always have them with me.

"I love it."

"And we love you."

Eight years ago, I never thought I'd fall in love, much less with four amazing guys. Our life had taken us so many places, bringing us joys and sorrows that we shared together, and three amazing kids.

My life might consist more of playdates than stilettos, of nap times than lingerie, and lullabies than lipstick, but I wouldn't change a thing.

Because they were right, true north always led us back together.

The End

Letter from the author

Hey, there reader! If you've made it this far, thanks so much for picking up this duet. I hope you've enjoyed Finley's story. It was one I knew I wanted to tell from the beginning. I think it's important for us all to find our own way; however, we choose to do that. Finley is strong in so many ways, but it takes her a while to see. Hopefully, through her story, you found some strength within yourself.

For all my Order duet fans, I hope the extended epilogue was everything you wanted for Team FinSin. If you noticed, I didn't give too much away about Sawyer, because I wanted the freedom to do more with her ending when the time comes. *Wink wink*

In the meantime, you should check out the other books in this shared world: The Council Series (Sawyer's story) and Lux Brumalis (Henley's story). Both are completed. I also will be releasing a Reese Standalone in 2024, so make sure to be on the lookout.

You can start here—> Council Series Lux Brumalis

As usual, this book was made possible because of my lovely PA and bestie, Emma's support. Thank you for everything, you greedy beaver.

Another huge thanks to my Drool MoFo, Megan. Your commentary and assistance help spur me on.

Thanks to Lindsay for being my awesome beta reader and tackling anything I throw at her.

To all my readers, thank you for sticking around for another one. If you loved it or hated it, I love seeing your reviews, edits, and TikToks. They make me remember why I write on the nights when I wonder if anyone cares. So, thank you for loving these characters.

To my husband, I love you. Thanks for the endless supply of Sunkist Zero to keep my going, and supporting my crazy dream of writing.

Also By Kris Butler

BEAUTY AND THE CLEATS

#baseball #standalone series #heartfelt

The Cleat Retreat (Blake's prequel)

The Pitch Slap (Blake's book, MMFMM)

No Balking Way (Bryce's book, MMF)

Whiff it Real Good (Ledger's book, MM)

LUX BRUMALIS (COMPLETED)

#hockey #girlboss #nonbinary sibling

3 guys, no MM

Penalty Box

Dead Lift

Breakaway

THE COUNCIL SERIES (COMPLETED)

#figure skating #secret past #dark elements

7 guys, lots of MM with bi-awakening

Damaged Dreams

Shattered Secrets

Fractured Futures

Bosh Bells & Epic Fails

The Council Boxset

THE ORDER DUET (COUNCIL SPINOFF)

#secret agency #spy + hacker games #fashionista

4 guys, light MM (in book 2 at the end, and bonus)

Stiletto Sins

Lipstick Lies

The Order Duet Omnibus

DRESSED TO KILL SHARED WORLD (STANDALONE)

#female assassin #quirky & curvy #twins

4 guys, no MM

Raven

F*CK STEAL KILL (STANDALONE)

#morally gray #bestie unalivers #sassy

3 guys, biawakening, (FF in Joy's chapter)

F*ck Steal Kill

DARK CONFESSIONS (COMPLETED)

#mafia #therapist #foster kids + dogs #tattoos

5 guys with MM

Dangerous Truths

Dangerous Lies

Dangerous Vows

Reckless (Cami's Novella)

Relentless (Nat's Novella)

Dangerous Love

Truth Lies Vows Love: The Complete Series

TATTOOED HEARTS DUET (COMPLETED)

#tattoos #penpals #music #curvy fmc

3 guys with MM

Riddled Deceit (Part 1)

Smudged Lines (Part 2)

Open Road (Road trip Novella)

Tattooed Hearts Completed Duet

MUSIC CITY DIARIES (TATTOOED HEARTS SPIN-OFF)

#motorcycle club #age gap #TW #cam girl

4 guys, no MM

Beautiful Agony

Beautiful Envy

Beautiful Unity

VACATION ROMCOM

#romcom #social media experiment #besties

3 guys, no MM

Vibing

SINNERS FAIRYTALES (STANDALONE)

#Rapunzel retelling #dance #TW

3 guys, no MM

Pride

About the Author

Kris Butler writes under a pen name to have some separation from her everyday life. Writing has become her second love, providing a safe place to normalize mental health through her characters. Kris enjoys writing emotional books with flawed characters, sassy heroines, and all the book boyfriends she loves to drool over. You can find her at home most nights reading with her husband and furbaby, trying to maintain her nerdy sock collection, or playing tabletop games with her friends. Kris loves to talk with readers about her books, even if it's just them yelling at her for that cliffhanger. If you enjoyed her book, please consider leaving a review. You can find her in her reader group or on social media.

Join my newsletter
Join my reader group
Check out my website